CREEPLES!

PATRICK D. PIDGEON

GREENLEAF
BOOK GROUP PRESS

Published by Greenleaf Book Group Press
Austin, Texas
www.gbgpress.com

Distributed by Greenleaf Book Group

For ordering information or special discounts for bulk purchases, please contact Greenleaf Book Group at PO Box 91869, Austin, TX 78709, 512.891.6100.

Cover and interior design by Patrick D. Pidgeon
Cover and interior illustrations by Marco Bucci
Cover, interior design and illustrations © 2020 by Patrick D. Pidgeon

Publisher's Cataloging-in-Publication data is available.

Print ISBN: 978-1-62634-775-5

eBook ISBN: 978-1-62634-776-2

Part of the Tree Neutral® program, which offsets the number of trees consumed in the production and printing of this book by taking proactive steps, such as planting trees in direct proportion to the number of trees used: www.treeneutral.com

Printed in the United States of America on acid-free paper

21 22 23 24 25 26 27   10 9 8 7 6 5 4 3 2 1

First Edition

In loving memory of my mother,
Sally Perkins Pidgeon, who always looked out for me…
in spite of my perpetual mischievousness, naughtiness,
foolishness, and many other complete lapses in judgment.

"Alone we can do so little.
Together we can do so much."

—Helen Keller

CONTENTS

PROLOGUE

CHESHIRE, ENGLAND: LINDOW MOSS BOG—1938

"DIG, infidels! DIG! Or you'll all bloody well end up as Bog People."
The British scientist's warm breath frosted in the cold air as he roared
over the fume-spewing diesel generator, his nose and cheeks blotchy
with rage. Oil-fueled spotlights belched smoke and dull orange light
over the massive, mossy bog pit and the workers within. In spite of
the chilly temperatures, the middle-aged scientist wiped his clammy
forehead and sponged spittle from his thick, distinctive handlebar
mustache. His finely cropped ginger hair stood out from his pristine
white lab smock as he leaned against a dingy utility truck with the
letters N.O.M.T., Ltd., stenciled on the door. It was the science expe-
dition's fourth straight night excavating heaps of black, mucky peat
from the Lindow Moss Bog, and they were all exhausted. The gold
coins the American had promised to the overworked and spooked
laborers made it worth their effort.

Creeples!

The expedition's intended artifact hadn't yet been located. They had, however, unintentionally recovered ancient archeological curiosities: the skeletal remains of a massive prehistoric pterodactyl, extinct for 150 million years; fifth-century Anglo-Saxon weaponry; and five gruesome Bog People that lay frozen in unnatural poses. The two-thousand-year-old human remains, remarkably preserved by the tannic acids within the peat bog, were lined up on the ground like a slumbering army patrol. The Bog People, terror frozen on their faces, had apparently died violently, as their limbs were kinked and broken into rectangular shapes, and many of their torsos shifted sideways on their hips.

"This has to be the place. The codex brought us here," the American insisted, nervously dabbing the sweat from his brow. In his mid-fifties and also dressed in a white lab smock, he wore round wire-rimmed spectacles that appeared too small for his doughy, goateed face. He glanced at the pinkie ring on his right hand. Its sizable oval magenta gemstone started to pulsate through the smoky haze. "It's here!" the American barked.

"We need more!" an elderly scientist with a Scottish accent ordered, and additional laborers raced over to help dig. The scientist's lips quivered as he gazed down into the bog pit with eyes alight.

The American's left hand anxiously tapped the bulky leather-bound manuscript clenched in his right. He nodded to his young assistant, whom he referred to as Keeper. The tall, painfully slender nineteen-year-old was the "Wisdomkeeper" of the opulent ruby-encrusted gold container. He gripped firmly a medieval reliquary tucked against his body. His other hand held a gleaming Colt Single Action Army revolver with a mother-of-pearl handle. He kept it pointed down at his side, yet his index finger remained on the trigger as he jittered with nervous energy.

"Hurry up! On with it," the irate Keeper groused in a clipped British accent. He raised his pistol in the air and squeezed off two shots . . . BANG! BANG!

The panicked laborers doubled their pace, digging through the soft dead-plant material with ease. THWACK! A shovel struck something solid.

"Watch it, you clumsy, stupid fools!" The eager American trudged through the quagmire and extracted a filthy, moss-covered spherical object the size of a rugby ball. "It's magnificent!" Delicately wiping off the peat, he exposed a marbled magenta surface. He raised the object over his head like a championship trophy and declared, "Gentlemen, the GREAT Draconem Beast has awakened!"

Standing at the edge of the pit, the two scientists and Keeper enthusiastically shook hands and slapped each other's backs in celebration of their success. The laborers whispered apprehensively among themselves. Suddenly, the magenta object glowed and throbbed as if it had a beating heart, causing the terrified workers to tumble backward, stumbling over one another. Luminous, flickering magenta beams discharged from the object's surface, ZAPPING straight into the American's eyes. The workers desperately tried to clamber up the sides of the slick, soggy pit, and the British scientist recoiled in shock. Magenta lightning beams of energy BLASTED from the American's mouth and fingertips. He stood rigid, arms spread wide and eyes blazing red. Then he lowered his head, entranced and expressionless. He gradually raised his right arm and fired lightning rays that seared through the Scottish scientist's body. Keeper and the British scientist dove behind the utility truck to safety.

Creeples!

A magenta energy force discharged from the object and enveloped the American's convulsing body. The six frightened laborers fainted, one after the other, stacked up like cords of wood. The supernatural turbulence dissipated, yet the American collapsed, clutching the treasured object with the hand bearing his pulsating gemstone ring. The oil-fueled spotlights exploded one by one into the bitterly cold night sky, plunging the excavation site into pitch black . . . except for the steady, pulsating radiance of the magenta gemstone ring.

CHAPTER 1

Aberdasher Academy of "Weird" Science

USA, PRESENT DAY

The grotesque, mucous-coated cephalopod sea creature used its eight arms and two sucking tentacles to encase Spigs's face, but the boy lay unresponsive. His legs were outstretched and his arms were crossed over his chest. A few moments lapsed; his limp body, garbed in a faded black T-shirt and slate jeans, began to sway from side to side; and then . . . *BOING!* . . . he bounced onto the hot, sticky floorboard.

Spigs thrashed about in his secured surroundings, flinging off the *Cryptozoology Quarterly News* magazine that featured the mythological kraken on the cover, which had been draped over his face to block out the sunlight. He opened his sleep-encrusted hazel eyes, startled and confused as he was wedged between two

Greyhound bus seats. He latched on to the front seat pocket to anchor himself for an upright shift.

"What the . . . huh?" He shook his head to clear his thoughts and reached down to retrieve his narrow-brimmed trilby hat, then scooted in his seat toward the window for a view of the road outside. "Dang, that was freaky. Thought for a second there a ginormous squid had snatched the bus and dragged us to the deepest depths of the ocean."

These were hypnotic days and nights full of nothing but asphalt roads and green mountainous terrain rushing by his window. The bus motored up another turn on the winding mountain road, but Aberdasher Academy was still blocked from view by a sheer rock cliff.

Spigs sighed and slouched as he pulled his cell phone from his pocket. *Almost there*, he texted Aunt Gussy. *Another five or ten minutes. Will have to rush to make orientation, so thought I should tell you now.*

He didn't expect a reply. However, some small part of him hoped for one. He knew her only interest in his safe arrival was it meant he wouldn't be bothering her for the next nine months. His entire life she'd branded him "that hapless misfit," "no-account," and "a downright pain in the arse." The only time she begrudgingly referred to him as her grandnephew was when she introduced him to new principals and teachers.

Spigs preferred to think of himself as a nonconformist, and he hoped he might find other scientifically curious minds like his at Aberdasher Academy of Science—preferably those with a penchant for mischief-making. It would be a fresh start for him . . .

at a mysterious institution known for studies in fringe science, but Spigs enthusiastically acknowledged it as "wonderfully weird" science. What had drawn him in was the academy's mystifying curriculum of unconventional phenomenology—alternative science. His bedroom was his sanctuary from spiteful ol' Aunt Gussy. And where he absorbed the fascinating world of the pseudoscience of crypto-creatures, from the infamous Sasquatch to the Jersey Devil, and every obscure cryptid in between. Spigs had applied to the enigmatic but elite academy, never dreaming he would get accepted.

When a thick envelope addressed to Mr. Johnny Spignola had been overnight delivered to his rural Tennessee town, Spigs had seen his chance to escape a bleak future. The school had also offered a full scholarship, so there was nothing to debate.

The academy was swaddled by sweet-smelling Ponderosa pine trees. Spigs viewed the school as a hidden jewel, isolated in the Adirondack Mountains near Letchworth Village in upstate New York. And he was truly engrossed in the morbid fact that Letchworth Village once housed an "insane" asylum in the 1930s, providing the perfect backdrop for him to delve into forbidden scientific mischief at the school.

It had taken Spigs two and a half days and four bus connections, but the school was now within reach. Flanked by dense, forest-blanketed mountains, the school's sleek, modern buildings appeared alien and imposing. Spigs checked his phone out of nervous habit. No big surprise Aunt Gussy hadn't replied. Eyes locked on the school, he sucked down the last bit of the soda he'd bought at the last stop, as if he needed more caffeine. He squirmed like a five-year-old on a sugar rush.

Creeples!

As the bus pulled into the school's outermost parking lot, Spigs eyed a blue pavilion stationed on the path into campus. A gleaming Mylar banner read *Orientation Registration* in blocky font, and a poster board sign outside the pavilion shouted, in handwritten letters, *New Students—Register Here.*

Spigs was never keen on protocols, but he figured he should probably play by the rules on day one. Just this once. Spigs rotated in his seat to keep the pavilion in his view, but his pale brown brows scrunched down at what he observed. A stout brute of a boy with a fiery red buzz cut had a smaller boy in a headlock and was rapping his head with his curled-up knuckle. The blond-haired kid grimaced in pain from the rapid noogies. Spigs could imagine what the brute was snarling in his victim's ear. He'd heard it all before: "Stay out of my way, pipsqueak" or "Hand it over, loser, or I'll send you home to Mommy with a shiner."

Spigs clenched his teeth and ripped off a chunk of his hamburger wrapper. He chewed it and rolled it into a ball between his tongue and the roof of his mouth. The slobbery wad went into his soda straw, and Spigs cracked open the window as the bus crossed in front of the pavilion. Steady. Aim. And with a deep gulp of air . . . FIRE! Spigs launched the spitwad right at the brute's forehead. He watched it fly with pride . . . and *SPLAAAT!*

"OOPS!" Spigs squealed. He cringed and drew his hat down over his eyes as a man in a classic blue blazer with leather patches on the elbows walked right into the projectile's path. The spitwad lodged in the man's ear. He whipped around and stared daggers into Spigs's soul. Spigs slid farther down in his seat and stifled a laugh with his hand.

The bus maneuvered carefully into a parking slot. Spigs planned to linger and disappear into the middle of the group of disembarking students. But he didn't get a chance to act out his escape plan because the goateed man in the blue blazer charged onto the bus and jabbed a forceful index finger in Spigs's chest.

"YOU! Jokester! Come with me," he boomed, shoving his tiny spectacles up his nose and squashing them against his doughy, red-cheeked face.

Spigs threw up his hands in surrender. "Sorry, Professor, uum, sir. I really am. Wasn't aimin' at you. I was—"

"Don't care who you were aiming at," bellowed the man. "Come with me." With a snarl, he lunged forward and grabbed Spigs by his jacket collar.

"Hey, hey, easy!" Spigs said as the man yanked him from his seat, his jacket digging into his armpits.

Forced to scramble after the man with his head down and his arms spread wide, Spigs stumbled on the bus steps. The man kept him from falling but nearly ripped Spigs's jacket.

"Stand up straight, boy," the man barked. "What's your name?"

Spigs had been in this situation many times before, so he put on his best apologetic face. "Freshman Johnny Spignola, Professor, uh . . . Mr. . . . uh."

"That's *Dean* Smathers." The dean crossed his arms and assessed Spigs up and down as if he were a cockroach ripe for the squishing.

Spigs gulped. Oh boy. He'd done it this time . . . and to the *dean*! He'd been kicked out of several schools, but expulsion on the first day would be a record.

A heavyset man in a uniform sped up on a Segway. "Dean Smathers, sir, may I be of assistance to you?"

"I can handle it, McTaggart. It's move-in day, so keep the traffic flowing."

"I'm sorry, Dean Smathers." Spigs removed his hat and held it in front of his belt like a good Southern boy entering a church. "But it's like this!"

He pointed over Smathers's shoulder, where the student had released his victim. Now he was grabbing at the boy's backpack as the boy held back tears and begged to be left alone. The dean spared the pair only a brief look over his shoulder and scowled back at Spigs.

"I am not concerned with what they're doing. This is all about *you*. Now take responsibility for your actions, Mr. Spignola."

The brute flung rocks at the kid and laughed with two brawny allies who'd appeared at his side. Spigs clenched his hands into fists at his sides and forced his eyes away from the tormentor. There was no use in arguing with the head honcho. If Spigs wanted to experience what this exclusive academy had to offer, he'd better play along.

"Yes, sir, uh, Mr. Dean," he mumbled, but refused to lower his gaze or hang his head. "I mean Dean Smathers. Sorry I caused you trouble on the first day. It won't happen again."

"Something tells me I'm going to have plenty of trouble with you." Smathers forced his glasses up his nose. "Got my eyes on you, Mr. Spignola. Now get in line and register."

The dean walked away without a backward glance, and Spigs begrudgingly did as he was told.

The start of every school year bustled with activities and disorientation. And it was no different at Aberdasher Academy, as throngs of backpack-toting students scurried about, not fully recognizing the campus topography, immersed in their electronic devices or grooving to their headsets. At the center of the sprawling, grass-covered grounds of this private co-ed boarding school rose the European classic–inspired ten-story Bell Tower. The tallest and oldest building at the academy stood out from the neo-Gothic architecture of the rest of the campus buildings. The tower's belfry displayed a clock face with elaborate carvings and round bejeweled stained-glass windows on all four sides. But the strange and perplexing reality was that nobody ever entered or exited Bell Tower, according to the information Spigs had gathered from online threads started by past and present students. There were spooky rumors it was built on a sacred burial ground so as not to wake the dead, and it seemed students weren't too eager to question the fact it had never been opened to the public. In fact, as Spigs tilted back his head, securing his hat on his mousy-brown hair with one hand, and drew close to the tower with mouth wide in amazement, he noticed he was the only one who walked within ten feet of the tower's front door.

Spigs strained to roll his worldly possessions—an oversized, overstuffed duffel bag on wheels—close to the ominous tower. To him, the spooky rumors made Bell Tower all the more intriguing and inviting, and he knew he'd manage to find a way to sneak inside. After all, if someone told Spigs not to do something, it made him even more eager to do it. He fancied himself an expert at bending the rules, even though he, unfortunately, was also an expert at getting caught. In these formative years, Spigs had gotten caught a lot. And after the first expulsion, Aunt Gussy had shipped him off to all-boys military academies. Even with nasty ol' Dean Smathers around, this place would be a picnic. Spigs sauntered up to the heavy oak door and stood on tiptoes to try and peek inside. He couldn't understand why the famous tower—used as the school's iconic logo in the brochure—was completely off-limits. So Spigs's reasoning was something weird or even apocalyptic *had* to be going on in there, and he *had* to get to the bottom of it.

"No can do, freshman," said a confident voice with a mature tenor.

Spigs whipped around and found himself face-to-face with a group of girls. As much as he wished he could maintain some semblance of composure, he emitted a low "Gaahhhhh"—the sound of brain freeze. Too many years at all-boys schools will do that. Spigs caught sight of the beautiful brunette in the group, and her baby-blue eyes. Spigs managed to smile at her, but though his brain screamed at him to ask her name, he couldn't form the words, not with her staring at him like he was nuts. She giggled and muttered, "Yep, a freshman." Then she patted down her bangs and walked off with her friends.

Spigs had been a baby when his parents died tragically in a car accident, and his great-aunt Gussy was unfortunately his only known living relative. She didn't have kids because she didn't want kids! She often droned, "Children are a life sentence!" Spigs had learned quickly not to disrupt her daily routine of playing Yahtzee and bingo and power-popping M&Ms. Aunt Gussy danced a jig when his rambunctiousness had given her the excuse to enroll him in military schools.

Military institutions were where Spigs learned to be self-reliant. But the instructors at his latest prep academy had been fatigued by Spigs's disruptive mischievousness and had highly "encouraged" Aunt Gussy to find another means of education. Spigs had been given three weeks to find another arrangement for his academic future, and Aberdasher had presented itself like magic. And to Spigs, it *was* pure magic—more than he would have ever realized.

Amid the hustle and bustle, excitement, and GIRLS, Spigs grinned as he neared his dorm room. With a beginning as auspicious as this, it was impossible for his new academic challenge to be anything but an amazing four years.

• • •

A bead of sweat trickled down T-Ray's face, caused by her struggle to balance a giant box of books as she turned sideways to squeeze through her dorm room door. She looked around the faded cobalt walls and saw an empty bed pressed against the left one. She dropped the box onto the bare mattress with a huff and turned with fists on hips to grin like Supergirl at her mother.

"Told you I could handle it," she said as she adjusted her horn-rimmed glasses up her nose and suppressed her heavy panting.

Her mother's smile was a little sad as she shook her head. "No roommate? Remember, you can't do everything alone, Theresa Ray.

That's a major part of the school experience—to make friends, work out difficult problems together."

"Yay! Teamwork!" T-Ray's little sister Kelsey enthusiastically added her youthful wisdom.

"Yes, I know . . . it makes the dream work, Kelsey," T-Ray recited, patting her sister on the head.

Kelsey had a genetic heart defect, and T-Ray had spent weeks in the hospital asking probing questions. She wanted to be a doctor one day and discover solutions to the problems adults hadn't yet figured out—and she'd discovered there were quite a lot. There were so many unresolved issues in the world, and T-Ray knew she'd have to get down to business right away if she wanted to solve them all. She simply had no time for the senseless questions of the younger, less gifted students she'd been roped into working with in the past. It wasn't conceit, she thought, just being true to herself. She hoped at Aberdasher Academy independence would be commended.

T-Ray had flown in from the West Coast with her mother and sister, and she would not see them again until the winter break. She tried her best to humor them. However, they had made these last moments nearly unbearable with all their "advice."

"The school experience is to learn and to find answers," T-Ray announced. "Some choose to do so in groups. The more serious of us choose to do it individually."

She'd been strong-willed since birth, which made for many awkward birthday parties. She was smart, proper, and attractive, but proudly reserved, burying it all under a schoolteacher veneer: long-sleeved cardigans and auburn hair in a bun, like her favorite scientist, Marie Curie. Marie Curie had won two Nobel Prizes; T-Ray planned to win three. She adjusted her tortoise-shell glasses as she glanced over her freshly printed list of a few of Aberdasher's uniquely alternative courses: Cryogenics, Quantum Kinesis, Genomic Medicine, Metaphysics, Molecular Transfusion, Cryptozoology, and Necrosis Physiology. She beamed. It was a candy store of academic opportunities.

"Everyone else wears contacts," Kelsey chirped out. She was wise for a ten-year-old, and especially verbal. If Kelsey thought it, odds were, Kelsey was saying it. "You wanna fit in, don't you? You know, be normal?"

"Normal is another word for ... AVERAGE, Kelsey. And who wants to be average? Please, sis, set your sights higher." With that, T-Ray kissed her mother and sister goodbye and opened a textbook so she'd be prepared for her first course: Genomic Medicine.

• • •

"*Ay, Dios mío, Pablo.* This dorm room is enormous," Peabo's mother exclaimed as she entered, followed by his father, grandmother, and three brothers.

"Mom, it's for two students. And parents don't actually come inside the dorm. It's uncool," Peabo insisted as he shoved his youngest brother off the bottom bunk bed.

"Can't believe my baby's going to this prestigious academy," she gushed, clasping her hands over her heart. She turned to

Creeples!

Peabo's grandmother and said in Spanish, "Mama, do you know how many people get accepted here?"

"One hundred," answered Peabo's father in English, chest puffed with pride. "And only five hundred students in the entire school. Guaranteed acceptance into many major universities after graduation." Peabo's father and older brother, Julio, were holding a crate filled with tech equipment. That morning, the entire Torres family had piled into the minivan with all of Peabo's gadgets and made the five-hour drive due east.

Peabo shoved another brother off the desk and made room for his computer, Snapchat Spectacles, GoPro camera, helmet, and drone device. "Once accepted, everyone is on full scholarship," Peabo had tried to explain. The school had rigorous entrance exams, and only the most scientifically minded got in.

"Love you guys, so don't take this the wrong way, but . . . GO! Please!" Peabo smiled as he endured bone-crushing embraces from his brothers, many kisses from his *abuela*, and a bear hug from his father. His grandmother pulled out a Saint Christopher chain from her purse and hung it around the bunk bed post. "This will keep you safe on your journey." She kissed him on the forehead.

"Study hard, *mijo*, but I want you to make friends. You skipped a grade, so it will be challenging. *Bueno?*" Peabo's mother looked at him earnestly and ruffled his hair. He'd been the smartest kid in his class in middle school and had always preferred technology to humans. Technology was straightforward, honest, and precise, whereas humans were unpredictable, confusing, and intimidating. Nevertheless, his mother held out hope that one day Peabo would make at least ONE loyal friend. "Promise me, okay? And promise me you'll be careful on that . . . motorized contraption. You know I don't like you having that at school."

"It's a Vespa electric scooter, Mom. Dad modified it, so don't worry. And I'll promise to make friends," Peabo reassured his mother as she combed his raven hair out of his hazel eyes.

As his mother turned away with tears shimmering in her eyes, Peabo's brother Julio elbowed him in the side. Julio held up two long, fat boxes wrapped haphazardly in tissue paper.

"Take these," Julio whispered. "Just in case you need to liven things up around this reformatory." Julio shoved the two boxes into Peabo's hands and snickered under his breath. "You'll thank me later."

Peabo waved his family goodbye as they trailed single-file from the room. No sooner had they retreated out of sight than a tall, thin kid with a mop of unruly brown hair escaping from beneath a creamy white hat stepped into the room.

"Johnny Spignola, at your service," said the gangly kid in a faded Led Zeppelin T-shirt. His hat tilted down over one eye as he thrust out a hand. "Ya can call me Spigs. I think we're roomies."

"Pablo Torres. Call me Peabo," he said, extending a fist bump.

• • •

"Now, between your lab assignments, homework, and scientific experiments, expect Genomic Medicine 101 to be your most time-intensive class," Professor Bodkins announced as she passed around the syllabus.

Creeples!

"That's what all the professors say. Don't worry. She's the best," a tall girl with a pink Mohawk whispered to Spigs and Peabo, who sat together in the center row. "Hey, love your specs."

"Thanks." Peabo adjusted his Snapchat glasses. "Plan to have the most popular YouTube science channel on campus: Peabo's Prodigious Projects."

"Stay in your lane, freshman, 'cause I have the most popular Twitter account on campus." The girl grinned. "Sadie Perkins, but known as Yapper on Twitter."

Professor Bodkins declared to her packed lecture hall, "I'm one year from tenure, stuck in my ways, and short on patience!" She winked. "But eager to teach, so, let's all have fun this year, shall we?"

Professor Sally Bodkins was an elegant and graceful woman in her mid-thirties yet always professionally reserved in her signature lab coat. She was on the cusp of being recognized not simply as a leading African American geneticist but also as a worldwide genomic pioneer with her soon-to-be-published research. All of the top universities courted her, but a decade ago, Dean Smathers promised her unlimited funding and full experimental autonomy, so she chose to teach at the quaint but renowned academy. Her reputation gave the unorthodox institution the legitimacy it was seeking.

After the professor rattled off her list of expectations for students this year, she gazed around the expansive room. "Okay, here's the moment you've all been waiting for. But first a quick summary for the incoming freshmen. Every year I choose three students to work with me on my genomic research. Fully accredited. I affectionately call them my Lab Rats. So, without

further ado, my new personal assistants this year will be ..."
She fingered through her cluttered pile of papers on the lectern. The class was peppered with a few upperclassmen who were still hoping for a chance to be the "chosen one."

The professor placed her reading glasses on the end of her nose and recited the first name on the list. "Pablo Torres."

"Call me Peabo. And at your service, Professor." Peabo stood and bowed, making Spigs throw a hand over his mouth to stifle a laugh.

Peabo turned to Spigs and whispered, "Whaaat?" He blushed and sat back down.

Without deviating from perusing the pages of his comic book, Spigs gave Peabo a friendly elbow to his arm. "Congrats, roomie."

Yapper was already tweeting the breaking news on her phone.

#LuckyLabRats! Major bulletin from Prof. Bodkins!
#PeaboTorres lands research gig with genetics expert!

Now that his new best bud's name had been called, Spigs lost interest and buried himself back in the comic book he'd concealed inside his textbook. The class waited anxiously as the professor read the second name: "Theresa Ray Rogers."

"ME?" T-Ray leaped up, practically knocking the student next to her out of his chair. "Of course it's me. Absolutely me. And you can call me T-Ray ... or Theresa, if you prefer. Seriously, it's up to you. I'm so excited, Professor Bodkins. Can I call you Professor Bodkins? Or do you prefer Ms. Bodkins. NO! That's stupid. I'm such a genius. I mean, *you're* such a genius. It's an honor. Sorry, I sort of babble when I'm excited. The reason I wanted to go here is because of you. You will *not* regret this. Okay, I'll shut up and sit down now!" T-Ray finally stopped, slinked down in her seat, and covered her own mouth with both hands, but not before a final elated SQUEAL slipped out.

"Sheesh! Boy, she is squirrelly, huh?" Spigs whispered to Peabo. He hadn't bothered to look up from his comic book during T-Ray's entire prattling rant.

"You think she looks like a squirrel?" Peabo looked confused.

"What? No. I mean she's like . . . squirmy and all," Spigs said through a laugh, then lost himself again in the colorful pages of his comic adventures.

"And the final Lab Rat is . . ." Professor Bodkins had garnered rapt attention as she looked out over the many bright, beaming young faces. "Johnny Spignola." No one responded. "Mr. Spignola?" Professor Bodkins's eyes scanned the lecture hall.

"Uh, dude?" Peabo poked Spigs as Professor Bodkins tilted her head curiously and casually strolled up the aisle of stairs to the seventh row.

"Huh?" Spigs grunted, again totally lost in his comic book.

Peabo sat up taller and stiffer in his seat as the professor drew nearer, and poked Spigs again, this time in the ribs.

The professor gestured to a girl in the aisle seat to move and sat down in her place, next to Spigs.

"Not now," Spigs muttered to Peabo, oblivious to the professor's presence on his other side until she whispered to him, "Looks pretty sick."

"Yeah, dude. The graphics are amazing." Spigs, clueless with his head still buried, pointed to an illustration panel. "So, ya see here,

Brutorus, the Creature from the Slimy Ooze, is this gargantuan gastropod that ate Philadelphia. Now, it's not so much a sea monster as it is a prehistoric megalith that was radiated by way of an accidental atomic infusion. One of my favorite crypto-creatures." Spigs turned the page to show her and glanced up. "AAAH!" He looked at her sheepishly. "Whoops!"

"Yes. 'Whoops.' I'll see you after class, Mr. Spignola."

"Uh, yes, ma'am." Spigs buttoned it, deciding not to even try one of his lame excuses on the professor.

She stood up, leaned down close to Spigs, and uttered, "Brutorus is actually a cephalopod, and it was gamma rays by way of nuclear *trans*fusion." Professor Bodkins winked at Spigs and strolled back to the front of the lecture hall. Spigs was embarrassed but felt an instant connection with his new teacher. However, he was in shock when Peabo explained he'd been selected as one of the Lab Rats.

When Spigs anxiously approached her desk after class, he lowered his head sans his hat, expecting the worst. "I'm real sorry, Professor, honest." He wanted to say more, but nothing came out.

"Mr. Spignola, I expect great accomplishments from my Lab Rats. I also expect focus, dedication, and teamwork. If you can't give me those things, let me know now, because there are many other students who would love this position."

Spigs looked up so fast he cricked his neck. "Yes, ma'am, I can do them things . . . er, those things. I *will* do those things. I promise not to let'cha down."

She nodded. "Excellent. I look forward to getting to know you, Johnny."

Creeples!

He exited her classroom with the thought that, all things considered, he was starting off on good terms and was determined to keep his promise. So few adults bothered to take a chance on him; he wasn't going to let down the one who had.

Spigs had lost Peabo after class, so he walked back to the dorm alone. As he passed the Metaphysics building, he heard a faint whimper and froze in his tracks with his hand cupped to his ear. There it was again! This time, he recognized it as a meow. He followed the weak, distressed wails around the side of the building and saw a tan kitten, with a golden streak down its back, tangled inside a discarded plastic grocery bag under a hedgerow. The poor stray was skin and bones. Spigs rushed to its side and scratched its head to calm it before he untangled the plastic bag. He picked it up and cradled it. "Little fella, with that brown streak down your back, you look like you came right out of the oven. Like a hot biscuit," he laughed, and positioned the scared feline inside his jacket and headed toward the cafeteria. "So, how 'bout it . . . Biscuit? Ya up for some tasty school grub?" Biscuit buried his head deep in Spigs's jacket. Spigs tipped his hat forward with a broad grin, zipped up the jacket to secure Biscuit, and jogged off.

CHAPTER 2

The Good, the Bad, and the Horrid

Spigs got a serious case of stomach butterflies as he and Peabo walked down the final stretch of hall in the Bio-Engineering building. He was sure those anxious butterflies had become vampire bats because the blood had rushed from his pale face.

He glanced over at Peabo with a tight grin. "Ya ready to mess around with some scientific ooze?"

Peabo let out a short laugh and avowed, "All in."

Spigs liked his roommate. However, he wasn't much for riveting conversation. But Spigs thought maybe he could eventually crack his shell and open him up. Peabo had shared his love for anime comics, and if you asked him about shiny gadgets, his mouth would spew out high-tech verbiage that would make many Silicon Valley executives jealous.

Peabo pushed open the lab door, and Spigs followed him inside. Spigs had never been asked to work one-on-one with a teacher before and had never been given this much responsibility before, so he was super nervous about screwing it all up. *Which there's a one hundred and ten percent chance I will*, he thought.

The first face the two boys saw was not Professor Bodkins but that squirrelly girl from class, T-Ray. She'd already decked herself out in a light blue lab coat.

Spigs searched for another lab coat until he noticed her name was embroidered above the chest pocket. The girl had brought her own lab coat. *Oh brother!*

"You two were supposed to be here at one o'clock." She tapped her watch with her finger.

Spigs glanced at his phone. "It's two minutes after, for cryin' out loud!"

T-Ray raised an eyebrow. "So, you *can* tell time."

"Where is the professor?" Spigs groaned.

"Gathering supplies," T-Ray said, gesturing with a head motion at the door on the back wall.

Peabo had gone mute and was staring at the floor.

"Ya okay, dude?" Spigs whispered.

Peabo nodded. He'd done the same thing in the cafeteria last night—clamming up around unfamiliar faces.

Professor Bodkins pushed open the supply closet door with her butt and shuffled out backward, holding a bulky file box. She smiled at the boys as she set it on a high-top metal table next to two plastic containers

"Oh good, you're all here. Come get your starter kits, Lab Rats," she said.

The teens examined the contents: lab coats, safety goggles,

plastic-wrapped beaker sets, and clear pencil cases full of twee-zers, slides, and petri dishes. Spigs and Peabo grabbed one of each, but T-Ray grabbed only the pencil case. She pulled her own set of beakers and customized purple goggles from her backpack and held them out to the professor for approval.

"Excellent, T-Ray, and super cute, I might add," the professor said with a wink.

Spigs did his best to suppress an eye roll.

"Thanks, Professor." T-Ray beamed as she pulled the goggles over her head like a necklace and propped them atop her auburn hair in front of her bun.

Professor Bodkins clapped her hands together. "Okay, let's start with some introductions."

"We've already met," T-Ray asserted. She pointed at each. "Johnny and Pablo."

"I prefer Spigs. And my main man here goes by Peabo." Spigs slapped his friend on the back.

Peabo nodded his approval, a thick hair curl bouncing down on his forehead.

"Whatever. Now I like to be called—"

"T-Ray! *We* remember," Spigs cried out. Peabo cracked a smile.

T-Ray crossed her arms and swiveled her head away from him with a huff.

"Well, excellent. Now that that's out of the way, let's talk about what you'll be doing for me. I'm assuming since you all applied, you know what my work entails?"

"In vitro DNA replication," T-Ray rattled off before Spigs could suck in a breath. "Gene splicing. A way to successfully copy DNA strands from blood samples. Just AMAZING!" She let out a giddy snicker and said, "I'm so honored to be helping you, Professor Bodkins. You have no idea. When I was eight, I read about you in *Scientific American* magazine and . . . well, I've devoured all your other papers since then. Seriously, I'm so happy you picked me. This is a dream come true." She inhaled a gulp of air and bit her lower lip.

"Oh brother!" Spigs retorted.

"Well, you're welcome, T-Ray. And yes, that's exactly right. After nearly a decade of research, I'm finalizing the process for the submission for a peer review. So a peer review is—"

T-Ray jumped in, again. "A board of scholarly assessors in the subject matter, reviewing material for quality of the research and adherence to editorial standards before the research can be accepted for publication." She grinned broadly.

Spigs and Peabo sneered at each other.

"Correct again, T-Ray. So I have to submit it to the foremost governing body of genomic science to examine my findings and my patented process. Everything has to be one hundred percent accurate. And you three will be working on the final analytics. Now, I've already developed a controlled testing method, but I need your help to speed up the process and finish the final round of testing to prove my experimental method works each and every time. We have to complete at least thirty more tests by December, so let's get down to business, shall we?"

She led them on a tour through the lab, teaching them the name and function of every piece of testing equipment. She demonstrated how to run the samples through the clinical centrifuge to examine and replicate the DNA strands. The wide-eyed teens were trying to hold back their excitement.

"That about sums it up, for now." She folded her arms. "Any questions?"

"It's *so* awesome to work on your groundbreakin' research, Professor. So let's dig in!" Spigs pressed.

"Love the enthusiasm, but unfortunately, I still have some equations to tweak and notes to finalize." As the teens' shoulders slumped, she said, "But tomorrow, I'll start letting you three take the wheel on certain steps, based on your strengths."

"Peabo here is the tech wizard," Spigs said with his hand on Peabo's shoulder. "Coding is his middle name."

Peabo blushed but smiled at Spigs. "Yes, well . . ."

"And I'M all about the blood plasma and goo." Spigs jabbed his thumb to his chest. "I can handle any genomic samples." He held up his hands and added, "Uh, if you want, I mean. Totally up to you, Professor."

"I'm good with calculus problems!" T-Ray piped up. "Most proficient with numbers, if I say so myself."

Bodkins laughed. "It seems I chose wisely this year. I love Lab Rats with spunk. Consider your chosen positions your official assigned responsibilities." Spigs cheered, T-Ray clapped, and even Peabo fist-pumped the air in victory. The professor added, "But today, I need you to handle some boring stuff. Sorry."

"Oh, nothing about this place is boring, Professor," T-Ray said.

Spigs rolled his eyes at her. "I'm on it . . . ah, we're on it, Professor. No problemo."

"That's what I like to hear. Sound all right with you, Peabo?"

The professor leaned down to catch his eye while he did his best to examine every scuffmark on the floor.

"On board, Professor. A team player here." He managed to nod at her.

"Precisely, Peabo. Developing a trusting partnership is the only way to become productive Lab Rats. You three would be wise to remember that. Now, I write all my notes by hand in notebooks. I'm old school. But I still need digital copies. So, I need you three to transcribe them for me. Every single word and equation. Use those." She pointed to three laptops on a table flush with the wall and handed them each a spiral-bound notebook full of her scribblings.

T-Ray rushed to the table first. As Spigs and Peabo strolled over to join her, Peabo whispered, "Thanks for the confidence. You know, for saying I'd be good with coding and all."

"Just speakin' nothin' but the truth, roomie." Spigs grinned to himself, thinking, *His shell is slowly cracking.*

"Okay, we need to create a shared data file system in the cloud so we can arrange the notes by topic and not just individual notebook contents," T-Ray affirmed as the boys sat beside her.

"Now just a chicken pickin' minute! The professor didn't say anything about cloud sharing," Spigs rebuked.

"That's right," Peabo said. "Let's just copy the notes, as instructed."

T-Ray sighed and slipped off her glasses to wipe them on her lab coat. "How old are you two?"

Spigs scrunched his brow at what he thought was an insult.

When she widened her eyes at him, as if waiting for an actual answer, he said, "You serious?"

"Yep!"

"I'm fourteen ... in SEVEN months," Spigs proclaimed proudly. "I jumped a grade. SO!"

"I've got ... uh ..." Peabo let it go. He knew he was the youngest of the Lab Rats.

"All three of us were smart enough to skip a grade. But I turn fourteen in THREE months, *so*, I'm the most mature. Which means I know the most. We have to go that extra mile on all assignments. Don't you want to make a good impression?"

The boys looked at each other, baffled, and finally Peabo shrugged. Spigs sighed. "Have it your way, then. Organized by notebook *and* topic."

Spigs pushed up his trilby hat and scratched the top of his head at the mere thought of all the extra work, but maybe this girl genius was right. He did want to start off with a good impression. They set to work, talking while they set up the shared file system.

After an hour had gone by, Spigs wiped his dry, aching eyes and glanced over his shoulder at the professor. She sat squished against a desk, peering at a computer screen through stylish, slender glasses placed halfway down her nose, a pen poised over yet another notebook on the desk. Two of the Analysis DNA Sequencing Detection machines were blinking and bleeping. Spigs felt like he might start bleeping if he had to listen to it for another fifteen minutes.

"Ya excited about all this heavy machinery, Peabo?" He poked him with his bony elbow.

"Yep, can't wait to get my hands on that centrifuge." Peabo gestured to the silver, boxy contraption in the corner. Spigs knew it had a mechanism like a superpowered washing machine to separate samples at different phases of DNA extraction.

"I'm DYING to get my hands on the school's new 3D bio-printer," T-Ray added. "The most technologically advanced system of its kind."

"Wait. Are you serious? A 3D bio-printer?" Spigs exclaimed.

"Just leased and announced on the school's website," T-Ray affirmed.

"Here, in *this* building?" Spigs rotated in his chair to scour the room. He'd played with 3D printers at the library, printing plastic models he'd designed of cryptids like Sasquatch and the Wampus cat on a computer. But bio-printing actual living tissue? Wowza!

"And I plan to be the first student to get my hands on it!" T-Ray poked herself in the chest.

"You really wanna play around with it that bad, huh?" Spigs said as he observed her determined frown.

"Play?" She scoffed. "I don't want to *play* with it. I want to master it so that I can . . ." She snapped her mouth shut.

"So that you can what?" Spigs queried.

She pressed her lips together and glanced at her screen. "We should get back to work."

"Come on, T-Ray. We can work while you tell us what your master plan is." Spigs beamed a wide sarcastic grin. "We're *very* intrigued. Right, Peabo?"

"Huh? Oh yeah, *very*." Peabo looked up from his screen and nodded.

"I want to work with bio-printing technology so I can help my little sister Kelsey get functioning heart valves. Hers are defective, and there are a lot of kids like her with similar conditions."

"Wow, sorry, didn't know. Cool master plan, T-Ray." Spigs was embarrassed by his initial cynical response.

"What happened to your lil' sister's heart?" Peabo voiced in a sympathetic tone.

"Genetic defect from birth—a gene mutation." T-Ray diverted her watery eyes from theirs. "She . . . she gets tired quickly and can't keep up with her friends. It's going to get worse as she gets older." T-Ray's face hardened with determination. "Unless somebody like me does something about it. Scientists have recently made advances in bio-printing. And I plan to enhance their work."

"I sure can respect a girl with a clear mission," Spigs said.

"That's 'young lady,'" T-Ray snapped, but then cracked her veneer with "But, well, thanks."

Spigs hoped he may have broken through, and maybe she now saw him as Lab Rat material.

"What's your grand plan, Peabo?" he asked. "Why'd you choose Aberdasher?"

Peabo brushed his thick black hair back from his forehead and chewed at the inside of his cheek. "I've got my eye on MIT. But it's, like, crazy expensive. Aberdasher's brochure implies I have an excellent chance. However, they don't promise you'll get a scholarship. And that's what I need if I want to go to MIT. Interning with the renowned Professor Bodkins is *huge* for me."

"Surely the professor will give ya a great recommendation," Spigs said.

"Only if you perform your job to the max," T-Ray added.

Spigs started to glare at her and saw there was no malice in her face. She wore a genuine smile.

"So, what's *your* story, Johnny Spignola?" T-Ray inquired. "Why'd you apply to be a Lab Rat?"

Spigs lowered the narrow brim of his hat to hide the shadow that crossed over his face at the thought of telling them all about Aunt Gussy and being an orphan. Instead, he opted for the sunnier side of the truth. "There's this awesome science curriculum that focuses exclusively on advanced cryptozoology. That's my thing. Giant, hairy, slimy crypto-creatures that lurk in the dark. Ultra-awesome cryptids like Mothman, the Fouke Monster, Yeti, and of course, the infamous El Chupacabra. And I figured workin' with DNA as a Lab Rat would give me a leg up since cryptid DNA is important to discovering their origins." He left out that the yearlong program would mean he wouldn't have to return to Aunt Gussy's house of horrors until next summer.

"Include me in that!" Peabo said emphatically.

T-Ray shook her head at their exuberance. She eyed the clock on the computer and squeaked. "Hurry, five minutes left for today. We should have gotten further. Oh, good grief, I shouldn't have let you two distract me."

Spigs leaned Peabo's way and whispered, "We're baaaad influences, dude."

Peabo stifled a laugh with his hand.

• • •

Spigs scratched Biscuit between the ears, and the tan tabby purred, arching his back to entice Spigs's hand all the way down to his tail.

"We hafta stop by the cafeteria on the way to Molecular Diagnostics lab and get him some more milk and tuna," Spigs said to Peabo, who was busy rummaging under their bunk bed with his hands in the crate full of drone parts, wires, USB and HDMI cables, nuts, and bolts.

"Someday I'll break you of puttin' milk on your tuna." Peabo snickered and crawled deeper under the bed. "Dude, Biscuit had, like, three cans and the anchovies off the pizza last night. That cat's going to explode." He resurfaced clutching a busted smart watch, a screwdriver, tweezers, and a GPS tracker.

"Nah, he's still kinda puny. A little worried about 'im." Biscuit brushed against Spigs's faded black T-shirt, meowing for more scratches. Spigs gestured at Peabo's tech goodies. "So, whattaya makin' now?"

"Thinking I can make my own mini tracking device."

"Nice! But who are ya plannin' to track?"

Peabo shrugged. "No one in particular. Just want to see if I can do it."

Spigs glanced at his hip-swaying Elvis Presley wall clock. "We've gotta scram; we're goin' to be late." He grabbed his security blanket—his hat.

The two took the elevator to the main floor of the dorm and headed past the sandy volleyball court.

Peabo set to work unscrewing the back of his GPS monitor as they walked.

"Aren't ya afraid you'll lose a screw or somethin'?" Spigs said. He took advantage of Peabo's distraction to lead them toward the cafeteria, a minor detour from class. It was a sleek sandstone building that was strangely smaller at the bottom than at the top. Spigs figured kooky architecture matched a school for kooky science. The kitchen and half the seating were inside, but more tables were outside. On balmy days, students and faculty usually took their food outside to eat on the picnic tables, shaded by a huge perched statue of the school's bizarre mascot: a pterodactyl with a vast twenty-five-foot wingspan that the students had affectionately named Percy. And rumor among the students was that Percy actually was the skeletal remains of a prehistoric pterodactyl now sheathed in green fiberglass.

Peabo gawked up at the imposing figure and yelped, "*Ay, Dios mío!*"

Spigs laughed and slapped Peabo on the back. "Relax. Percy won't bite. I'll be back before ya can say flux capacitor."

Peabo's laugh was cut short when a beefy hand slammed the GPS and the screwdriver out of his grip. The plastic device smacked the pavement hard enough to crack the screen, and without looking at the culprit, Peabo instinctively shouted, "Hey, watch it!"

Spigs turned back and instantly recognized the jerk from registration day by his stout size and red buzz cut. He sported a red polo shirt with the collar flipped up, partially concealed by a light bomber jacket. Spigs wasn't quick enough to shout a warning, and the brute grabbed Peabo in a headlock as he was bending down to retrieve the broken pieces.

"Watch what you say to me, *amigo*," the jerk whispered in Peabo's ear. "And stay out of my way or it'll be time for a knuckle nap."

Peabo looked to Spigs with terror in his wide eyes as the brute's bicep squeezed his windpipe. Spigs gnashed his teeth, and his hands formed fists at his sides.

The jerk smirked at Spigs's clenched fists. "You gonna fight me to save your girlfriend, dork?" He gave Peabo a rough noogie, digging his knuckles into his skull.

"Actually, he's my best friend," Spigs insisted, his cheeks bright pink. "And unless you want a dose of fire and fury, I suggest you let him go, like, NOW!"

The brute dropped Peabo on the ground and stomped toward Spigs, shouting, "What did you say?"

"Oh, so sorry, meathead. Thought I was speakin' your language." Spigs dodged one of the tyrant's groping hands. "Maybe I need to go further back in evolution?"

"I'm gonna knock *you* further back in evolution," the jerk snarled, throwing a wild punch that Spigs avoided by jumping back. Spigs raced behind the Percy statue as Peabo got to his feet and cried out in a shaky voice, "Hey, leave him alone, or we'll report you to the dean."

Spigs was pleasantly surprised that Peabo was backing him up.

The tough kid let out a loud guffaw and charged at Peabo. "Say what, *señorita*?" He cocked his head with a wild glint in his eye. "How about if I simply prune back that tongue of yours?"

"What's going on here?" a deep female voice boomed as Peabo quickly backpedaled.

All three of the boys froze as a broad woman who was at least six foot stalked toward them wearing a frown. Her long blonde braid bounced on her shoulder until she stopped with her hands on her hips. To Spigs's surprise and relief, she glared at the older student.

"Horace Horrigan," she said with a frown, sounding unimpressed. "Causing trouble, again?"

Spigs whispered to Peabo, "More like Horrid Horrigan."

"I wasn't doing anything," Horace countered with a defiant scowl.

"Uh-huh," she muttered. "I think you'd all better head to class now."

Spigs's relief turned to disappointment. This teacher wasn't gonna do anything. Although, she'd maybe saved them both from a black eye. He saw Peabo open and close his mouth, trying to build up the courage to snitch on what Horace had done, but Spigs grabbed his elbow. "It'll just be worse next time if we say somethin' now."

The downtrodden Peabo gathered up his busted GPS components and tucked them in his backpack. As they headed down the pathway that led to the Molecular Diagnostics lab, Peabo said, "Thanks, buddy."

"Right back at ya."

"Am I really your best friend?"

"Well, no, sorry I lied. Biscuit's my BFF. But you're a close second."

"I'll settle for that."

They dissolved into laughter together, and Peabo promised they'd grab extra tuna when they made it back to the cafeteria for lunch.

CHAPTER 3

Goon Patrol

One unique factor of Aberdasher's curriculum was students could choose their desired classes like at universities, so there was a collection of sophomores and freshmen in the Molecular Diagnostics class. Spigs and Peabo raced through the door before Professor Muckles closed it. Spigs saw T-Ray shaking her head disapprovingly at them across the room, but his heart jumped into his throat when he caught sight of a beautiful brunette, just as it did yesterday. He kept his eyes glued to her as he slid onto the stool beside her, nearly missing the seat. She had half her hair pulled back in a braid that rested atop the remainder of her thick locks, and when she felt him staring, she flicked her baby blues his way with a curious look. During roll call, Spigs learned her name was Rachell Hobbs. He gave himself a serious pep talk. No more brain freezes or uhs, ums, and ers. His plan was to talk to her like a normal human. No, wait, more like a mature upperclassman. Even better . . . like an X-Man! That's it. A suave, peace-lovin' superhero.

He hardly heard a word Professor Muckles said. But when the balding man announced the students should partner up for experiments and that it would be for the whole semester, Spigs blurted out with supreme confidence, "Rachell Hobbs, you and me, partners!"

With a manicured hand on one hip, she looked him up and down. "I couldn't pass on Justin Timberlake, now could I?" She smirked at his trilby hat, which Spigs decided to take as playful rather than mocking.

"Awesome sauce!" he blurted out, then cringed at how lame it sounded.

Peabo ended up with T-Ray at the lab counter across from Spigs and Rachell. The professor passed around instructions for the experiment to each pair, but Spigs was too focused on the golden freckles on Rachell's nose to do more than glance at the assignment.

Rachell ran her finger down the list of supplies and gathered each item from the cupboards.

"How 'bout a date? Uh, a study date?" Spigs leaned against the counter in his best attempt to look exceedingly confident. His heart raced so fast he felt if he didn't run a lap he might implode from the pent-up energy.

Rachell patted down her bangs and flicked her hair over her shoulder. She peered at him through her press-on lashes and made an amused "hmm" sound. "Are you some sort of a genius, I mean, working so closely with Professor Bodkins?"

"Huh?" Spigs was taken completely off guard. "Oh, yeah, *genius*. That's ME! Associates, we are. Me and Professor Bodkins, like two burrs in a mule's tail." He crossed his fingers. "Some of my work—"

Spigs stopped short as T-Ray's auburn bun appeared behind Rachell in his line of vision. She leaned over her counter to expose a disgusted expression and scoffed deep in her throat.

Rachell snubbed T-Ray's existence. Instead, she announced, "I'd like to hear more about the work you do with Bodkins."

"You're in luck. This X-Man . . . ah, I mean genius . . . is free Saturday."

"Hmm . . . maybe. Demonstrate something cool, something you learned from the professor." She winked and added, "Impress me."

Spigs couldn't believe his luck. She was ACTUALLY conversing with him! AND was considering a date! Holy schnikes!

His brain freeze had melted into boiled mush for a moment, but inspiration struck. He dug into his pocket and pulled out a bag of gummy bears. Sliding one of the beakers she'd placed on the counter toward himself, he said, "Easy peasy. Now this is gonna blow your mind."

Spigs crammed the gummy bears down the thin glass neck of the beaker. He reached for the white bottle of potassium chlorate powder.

"Um, if you're planning what I *think* you're planning, that's too many." T-Ray wiggled a finger in the air to get his attention.

Spigs frowned at her as he grabbed a small squirt bottle of brown liquid and filled all the crevices between the gummy bears. He peered at Rachell with confidence as he shook a final pinch of the white powder down the mouth of the beaker, saying, "And now, in goes the potassium chlorate and . . . TA-DAAAH!"

KA-BLOOEY! Greenish-brown gelatin exploded toward the ceiling in a geyser. It rained down sticky gunk on Rachell's head, soaked her bangs, and seeped between her long fake eyelashes. Spigs, who dove for cover under the desk, let out a humiliated half laugh. "Heh-heh. Sorry?" He could hear Peabo's and T-Ray's muffled snickers behind their cupped hands.

Rachell let out a high-pitched shrieking sound like an ensnared baby raptor from *Jurassic Park.*

"What ON earth?" Professor Muckles exclaimed. "Ms. Hobbs, what have you—?"

Rachell slapped her hands to her sides and glared down at Spigs—who was still crouched under the counter. "Thanks for the toxic shock . . . GENIUS!"

Drenched in murky brown goo, she stormed out of the lab, wringing out her hair.

"Uh . . . don't forget to write!" Spigs's grin faded as the professor's scowling face appeared over the top of the counter.

According to the fuming Professor Muckles, Spigs had just earned himself two Saturday detentions cleaning out beakers. Well, he'd done worse chores. But he was more concerned about messing up another chance with Rachell.

After class, Spigs booked out of there, with Peabo right beside him. He heard heavy breathing as T-Ray jogged after them.

"Hey, wait up, X-Man."

"Har-har." Spigs turned to face her in the hall.

"Okay, so alchemy is not your specialty," T-Ray said, grinning.

"But I'm being serious now. Peabo told me about what happened with that Horace kid. You should really report him to the dean. Bullying has no place at a school for young scientists, or *any* school for that matter."

"Maybe T-Ray's right. I mean, we should end it now before it gets worse. Remember, you kinda teed him off. We have to get an adult involved," Peabo said.

"Dean Smathers saw what happened and didn't do a darn thing. All he cried about was my world-class loogie I *inadvertently* nailed him with."

"*You* hit the dean with a spitball?" T-Ray was dumbfounded. "Do you go looking for trouble or does it just follow you?"

"A little of both. Anyway, I was aimin' for Horrid, but Smathers wouldn't hear my side."

"Could it be he was a little distracted by your disgusting saliva? Yuck!" T-Ray grimaced and crossed her arms. "Maybe Peabo should be the one to report it."

"NO!" Peabo whooped, his cinnamon skin paling a shade. "I need my wingman." He turned doe eyes on Spigs. "*Por favor?*"

Spigs sighed and drooped his shoulders. "I give. We'll go after class."

After Cryptozoology 101, they headed toward the administration building. Spigs felt on top of his game. Cryptozoology was his favorite class. His brain buzzed with thoughts of the Hodag monster: a four-hundred-and-fifty-pound crypto-creature the size of a Chevy van with coarse chestnut hair sprouting from the horned head of a bull. It had the back of a stegosaurus—an array of upright spikes, stout legs, extended clawed feet, and a spear tail. And to top it all off, the academy had life-size models of several of these fringe crypto-creatures in the classroom. As he and Peabo walked, Spigs mapped out the expedition he'd one day take into the forests of Wisconsin to find and capture the Hodag himself.

The faculty and administration building was an older structure with a more refined aesthetic, as opposed to the sterile, glossy vibe of the other campus structures. It smelled of leather and potpourri. They found the frosted-glass door labeled *Office of Dean Aleister Stan Smathers*, the words etched in gold-embossed Old English calligraphy. It opened into a reception area where a frumpy secretary with bushy brown curls cropped close to her head sat behind a plain desk. The faded plaque on the front edge read: *Ms. Wanda Wainwright*.

She smacked bright red lips at them as they approached, mumbling. "Yes? Speak up."

"Uuh . . . umm," Peabo stuttered.

"Don't have all day, youngins," Ms. Wainwright snapped.

Peabo stepped closer. "We want to report an incident of . . . harassment."

"Bullying!" Spigs interjected.

Ms. Wainwright narrowed her eyes and said with a sniff, "Bullying? That's it?"

"Intimidation, victimization, oppression, downright THUG-GERY!" Spigs barked at her lack of care.

"All right, simmer down, but make it quick. The dean's a very busy man."

"*Gracias*, Ms. Wanda." Peabo strained to hold a pleasant smile.

They entered the maple-grain double doors behind Ms. Wainwright's desk. Spigs's first impression was Smathers's office looked decidedly scholarly, immaculate with no item out of place. The built-in bookshelves, running the length of the back wall, were meticulously filled with volumes of periodicals, textbooks, and tomes. Oddly, though, manuscripts in one row were threadbare and tattered. Against another wall was an antique grandfather clock with splintered wooden panels throughout its shell, and on the opposite wall was an imposing executive oak desk. Behind it, Smathers leaned confidently in his leather chair as if it were a throne. Next to his desk was a two-foot-tall shrub sprinkled with blooming pink flowers that didn't quite fit in with the room's dark mahogany color scheme.

"Ah, Mr. Spignola," Smathers said as he adjusted his reading glasses on his doughy face, forcing them to stay put on his nose. His right pinkie finger bore a sizable oval magenta gemstone ring. "More trouble? AND with an accomplice?"

Spigs's neck burned hot with anger.

"No. He's . . . he's here to help *me*." Peabo's voice grew louder and bolder with every word. "He's *my* witness."

"Oh? Witness to what?" Smathers turned his beady eyes on Peabo. "What's your name, son?"

"Pablo Torres, Dean, sir." Peabo's gaze studied the floor, but every few seconds his eyes would flick up to the dean's face, focusing on his perfect coiffed hair rather than his eyes.

"So, what is Mr. Spignola a witness to?" Smathers asked, stroking his brown goatee.

"A junior named Horace Horrigan assaulted me today. He broke my GPS and put me in a headlock," Peabo explained.

"More like a full nelson death-hold," Spigs interrupted.

"Minding my own business, when Horrid, uh, Horace came out of nowhere and slammed it to the ground." Peabo removed the broken GPS pieces from his backpack.

"Mr. Torres, can you prove that your device wasn't already broken?" Smathers said.

Peabo's mouth gaped like a big sea bass on a hook.

"It was workin' fine. Period!" Spigs was frustrated all over again.

"YEAH!" Peabo cried out. "Uh, sir."

"Even if it wasn't workin', that's not the point." Spigs couldn't keep his anger out of his voice. "Horrid attacked Peabo for no reason. The *same* bully on registration day. I tried to tell you he was no darn good."

"You just watch your tone, Mr. Spignola." Smathers leaned back in his cushioned chair with his arms crossed at the chest. "Mr. Torres, a broken GPS is hardly proof that Mr. Horrigan attacked you. And no reliable witnesses." Smathers shot eye daggers at Spigs.

Spigs ground his teeth to keep from shouting something he'd regret.

"But it's the truth," Peabo said.

"You have not presented me with enough evidence to take action against Mr. Horrigan. Your *star* witness here has so far presented himself as an irresponsible, self-absorbed individual who's entirely unreliable. Mr. Torres, I would highly recommend you not associate yourself with a student who could be detrimental to your academic scholarship here at Aberdasher Academy." Smathers's mouth twitched in a tiny smile as he eyed Spigs.

Spigs felt like his head was a teakettle ready to boil; echoes of Aunt Gussy played in his head. *Stop all that back talking. You're nothin' but an irresponsible little troublemaker and won't ever amount to anything in your life.*

"So, THAT'S IT?" Spigs barked. "You're not goin' to help my friend because you have a grudge against me?"

"Do not raise your voice at me, Mr.—"

"What the hell kinda dean are ya?"

"Detention, Mr. Spignola! Tomorrow, at two. Room 202 in the Microbiology building. This discussion is now over. Dismissed."

Spigs stomped across the dense Persian area rug and threw open the door.

"Again, Mr. Torres, I'd advise you to rethink the company you keep. Your scholarship is on the line."

Peabo was tight lipped and trailed after Spigs, who'd rushed out onto the lawn in front of the faculty building. Spigs was panting as if he'd just run a marathon. Furious and frustrated, he tossed his backpack and plopped down on the large exposed roots of a lofty northern pine.

"Maybe it wasn't such a good idea to—" Peabo stopped short and scooted in next to him.

"It's not your fault that guy's a total JACKASS!"

"Well, his initials are *A. S. S.*" Peabo grinned, hoping to coax a matching smile from Spigs. "Come on. We've got Lab Rat duties this afternoon."

Spigs's stomach promptly knotted, realizing he'd have to tell Professor Bodkins he couldn't perform his lab obligations tomorrow due to detention.

Peabo studied Spigs's flustered demeanor. "What made you go off like that? You're usually Capt'n Cool."

"Ah, nothin'. Just don't like that guy." Spigs jumped up, dusted off his jeans, and headed toward their dorm.

"Got a feeling there's more to it. But if you don't want to tell me . . ." Peabo stayed close behind Spigs.

Spigs walked in silence for several steps, then heaved a great sigh. "It's just I . . . I've been called that stuff all my life, and I'm gettin' sick of it."

"What stuff?"

"Irresponsible! Menace! Troublemaker! Heard it all." Spigs held his gaze on the ground ahead of him, and adjusted his backpack.

Peabo stayed quiet, waiting for it all to spill out.

"Aunt Gussy often calls me those things." He voiced a tone of defeat. "Maybe . . . she's right. Sometimes I just don't feel like I belong in this world."

"Why do you even care what that mean ol' bat thinks?" Peabo said.

"Well, she is *my* guardian." Spigs looked away. "I . . . I have nobody else." His voice cracked.

Spigs peeked at Peabo and saw the usual pity and sympathy he often got whenever the subject came up. And usually, he detested it, but on Peabo's face, it looked genuine.

"Your parents are—?" Peabo began.

"Both dead." Spigs shoved his hands deep in his pockets. "In a car crash when I was five."

"Wow, sorry, dude."

Spigs got lost in the debilitating memory, his heart pounding as the old fear, the dreaded secret, bubbled to the surface. "I was in the back seat when it happened. Aunt Gussy said I was a wild child, actin' up, and that I . . . I caused . . . She claims my dad took his eyes off the road to deal with my 'misbehavior.'"

Peabo stayed silent for a long moment, seeing Spigs inhale a gulp of air to get his breathing under control.

"How would she know that? Was there a police report?" The passion in Peabo's voice surprised Spigs. "Your aunt is *loco en la cabeza*! Just outrageous to blame you. What a nasty woman."

Spigs rapidly blinked a few times. He'd never thought of it that way. Just accepted Aunt Gussy's words as fact.

"And the dean can choke on his lunch for all I care," Peabo grumbled.

"Maybe Smathers is right. Hangin' out with me could jeopardize your scholarship," Spigs said in a muted tone.

"Listen to me, Spignola! Smathers is a grade-A jerk—an ASS! His initials say it all. Now, I haven't known you long, but I can tell you're a true *amigo*. And I've got your back from now on."

"And I've got yours, roomie." Spigs finally had something to smile about, realizing he'd just cemented a one-of-a-kind friendship.

The two roommates kept their promise. Over the next few weeks, they were mindful as Horace zeroed in on them as his favorite targets. Horace always had two or three other juniors around him who followed his orders like minions. Spigs and Peabo aptly dubbed them Horace's hooligans.

The boys kept their eyes on Horace and his hooligans whenever possible, trying to learn their patterns. It soon became clear why Smathers turned a blind eye and deaf ear on their complaints about Horace. He frequently interrupted classes to deliver messages from the dean to the teachers. And on two occasions, Spigs saw him walk into the faculty building carrying a cup of coffee he never sipped. It became apparent Horace "Horrid" Horrigan was Smathers's number one butt kisser.

Spigs found out through small talk with sophomores—primarily to gain more insight into Rachell—that Horace should have been a senior, but he was held back his junior year under mysterious circumstances.

Spigs couldn't decide whether he despised Horace or Smathers more, but he refused to let them distract him from what had turned out to be a surprisingly promising semester so far. The best he'd ever experienced. Heck, even T-Ray was growing on him. She really was smart, and he started not to mind her constant reminders of it. Peabo was easily the best friend he'd ever had in his life. All in all, he predicted this would work out to be his most successful school year ever.

CHAPTER 4

All in for Monkey Ears

Peabo enjoyed the cool late-fall breeze whipping through his hair and turning his cheeks bright pink as he zipped over the manicured campus pathways on his scooter, complete with sidecar. His helmet, with GoPro attached, and windbreaker provided plenty of protection against the mountain gusts. He wore a wide smile as he adjusted the helmet camera for the perfect angle on the four African pygmy goats beside him. The tan and black goats were cruising along on . . . skateboards! Two goats on each, flanked by two roller-blading students. When the miniature goats lost momentum, the students gracefully circled around and gave the rear goats' butts a gentle shove. Peabo captured the flawless execution as the two students threw him thumbs-up. The goats bleated and tossed their heads, as if in agreement.

Peabo broadcast through his GoPro microphone, "Just off the hook, guys. Skateboardin' pygmy goats must be a scientific first. Check out my YouTube channel: Peabo's Prodigious Projects, episode fifteen. *Adiós!*" He turned toward the center of campus and goosed the scooter's throttle.

A chiming sound made Peabo glance at his iPhone mounted to his handlebars. A text from T-Ray. With his right hand on the throttle, he tapped the screen to open it. *CRISIS! Meeting at Professor Bodkins's lab!* He scrunched his brows. Crisis? He crouched low between the handlebars and twisted down the right grip for full throttle, then looked up, too late. "OOMMPH!" He clipped a curb and flew over the handlebars, face-planting into a rosebush. "OUCH!" The thorns ripped his jacket and scraped his bright pink cheeks.

"HEY! Ya okay?" came a voice with a familiar Southern twang.

Peabo clambered out of the thorny bush and plucked off pointy twigs with whimpers of "oof, oh, ouch." He grinned sheepishly at Spigs, who was shaking his head.

"Dude, hope it was worth it." Spigs gestured at the GoPro.

"Totally ... ouch ... worth it ... ouch!" Peabo raised his hand for a high five, which Spigs returned. Fresh pain shot through his pricked palm. "OUCH!" He wiped his bleeding hand on his jeans.

"Ya get an odd text from T-Ray?" Spigs held up his phone.

"Yeah, so we'd better get going."

"We surely don't want the wrath of Theresa Ray Rogers to crash down on us."

• • •

As Spigs rode in Peabo's sidecar toward the Bio-Engineering building, he tried not to think too much about why T-Ray called for an emergency meeting. Had he screwed up the professor's research analysis? Misplaced genomic samples? Overthinking was making him nervous. He'd been called into many school conferences over the years, and they were usually the result of his mischievousness.

Spigs spotted the perfect distraction to clear his mind. Bell Tower loomed ahead, and he fixed all his attention on its foreboding facade.

Peabo had slowed to five miles per hour on the central campus streets. Spigs hopped out of the sidecar to take another gander at the iconic tower. "I've just GOTTA get inside."

"To see what?" Peabo braked and idled his scooter.

"What they don't *want* me to see!" Spigs howled with a groan of despair as he strolled the Quad—the plush, grassy quadrangle that served as the campus's centerpiece and gathering place, branching out from Bell Tower. Peabo circled around Spigs on his scooter.

"Nobody ever goes in—" Peabo started.

"Or ever comes out," Spigs finished. "We've been in school for many months now, and have you *ever* heard any bells in Bell Tower actually ring? Just once? Now THAT'S strange."

"Y'know, you're right."

"And why is it off-limits to everyone? It's a giant monolith whose sole purpose is to MOCK ME by its very existence." Spigs craned his neck to eye the top of the tower's belfry, where the elaborate stained-glass window seemed to look like a pair of brooding eyes flecked in amber and crystal blue. He spotted the head maintenance man and his crew meticulously manicuring the dense, tangled hedgerows surrounding Bell Tower. He removed his backpack and rummaged through its contents. "Hey, Mr. D," Spigs called out, waving, and jogged over to him.

"Young Mr. Spignola. What can I do you for?" Mr. Dingle shook his hand assertively as if they were old friends. Moses Dingle had worked on campus for decades and knew everything there was to know about the historic tower. Even though the academy had been an accredited institution for only ten years, Bell Tower had been there for many more, and Mr. Dingle had always been its caretaker. He was a kind man whose long life was etched in the creases in his face.

Spigs had introduced himself on the third day of school and made it a habit to speak to him—often between classes. He'd inquired about the ominous rumors about the tower, but a pleasant byproduct of this relationship was Mr. Dingle and Spigs enjoyed each other's company and conversations, however brief.

"So, how's that noble caretaker to the Loyal Order of the Royal Keys doin' today?" Spigs tipped his hat and sarcastically bowed at the hips.

Mr. Dingle laughed. "You're relentless, ain't ya, son? Want another peek at 'em, huh?" He shook the massive key ring on his belt.

"Heck yeah! Especially the antique ones." Spigs trotted over. He clutched the keys with reverent respect. As Mr. Dingle barked out orders to his crew, Spigs riffled through the key ring but fiddled with a vintage two-notched brass skeleton key that clearly stuck out from the other standard flat keys and security keycards. Spigs glanced back over his shoulders, then slyly pressed the skeleton key's teeth against soft white material in his hand.

Spigs handed back the sizable key ring. "Most impressive, Mr. D. You're the best. See ya around." He fist-bumped Mr. Dingle and hopped in Peabo's sidecar and zoomed across campus to Professor Bodkins's lab. When they were one turn away from the Bio-Engineering building, Spigs saw an athletic brunette with thick bangs exit the Student Union cafeteria. He ordered for Peabo to hit the brakes but leaped from the sidecar before it stopped.

"Hiya, Rach," Spigs said.

"Hey, Johnny. What's up?" Rachell sounded bored and clutched her textbook to her chest. "Something else you want to drench me with?"

Spigs ignored her last question and hurried to catch up with her stride. "What's up, ya say? Just changin' the world. That's all."

"Really? So you still call yourself a genius after what you pulled off in the Molecular Diagnostics lab?"

"Real sorry about that, but my, um, my associate, Professor Bodkins, and I conduct extreme and radical experiments. And, well, things are bound to go wrong."

"*Your* associate?" Peabo murmured, coasting behind the two.

Spigs shrugged him off and focused on Rachell. "Yup, my associate, and you're in luck. This genius is free Saturday evening."

"And where exactly would we go on this . . . date?" she said with a small smile that set his senses on overdrive.

He'd hoped for a second chance. *Now don't blow it*, he thought. "Uuh . . . " He fidgeted, shoving his hands in his pockets to stop his nervous twitch. "How 'bout Bell Tower?"

Peabo groaned behind Spigs's back, but Rachell raised a curious brow. "Wait, you can get inside Bell Tower? But it's, like, totally off-limits."

Spigs nodded with an expansive smile.

Rachell tilted her head. "I'll think about it." She pinched Spigs on the cheek, flipped her chocolate hair, and sashayed off.

"She's WAY out of your league, Cool Breeze." Peabo chuckled as he rolled the throttle down.

"Whaddaya mean?" Spigs jogged alongside him.

"She's a sophomore, bro. The IT girl." He snickered as Spigs dove into the sidecar. Then, a familiar voice from behind made them both spin around. Rachell was waving them down. Peabo slammed the brakes, which nearly toppled Spigs out. He tried to recover as best he could. "Yeah, Rach?"

She bellowed, "Pick me up, the south side of the girls' dorm at seven Saturday. And don't keep me waiting, either."

"YES, MA'AM!" Spigs howled back.

Peabo stared at Spigs and stammered, "How did you? Did she just . . . ?" He pointed back and forth between Spigs and Rachell.

"I'm just *too* irresistible, my friend." Spigs locked his fingers behind his head and lounged back in the sidecar. "Now, onward, Jeeves! To the lab!"

Bell Tower's clock showed ten, but again, no bells rang as

Spigs and Peabo slipped into the lab. T-Ray was already dressed in her lab coat with a pocket protector holding various writing instruments.

"And where have you two been?" T-Ray demanded.

"Oh, just chattin' up the hottest girl in school." Spigs confidently tipped his hat forward.

T-Ray smirked.

Peabo added, "Guess who's got a date with Rachell Hobbs?"

T-Ray's expression changed to a dark scowl.

Spigs wiggled his thumb at himself. "This guy!"

"Whatever! Now listen up. We have a crisis!" T-Ray shoved her laptop's screen in their faces. It displayed an article from the school's newspaper: *After careful consideration, and due to lack of funds, Aberdasher Academy of Science's Board of Regents and Dean Aleister Stan Smathers have collectively decided to discontinue the Genomic department—effective immediately.*

"So, what does that . . . WAIT, WHAT?" Spigs cried out.

"Discontinue? Like, shut it down? They can't," Peabo said through a sigh.

"They can and they DID!" T-Ray was emphatic. "And Professor Bodkins runs the whole department."

"But what will happen to us . . . the Lab Rats?" Spigs paced between the workstations as he tried to process the devastating news. "Smathers can't do that to ME!"

"Does he have that kind of authority?" Peabo questioned.

"I've worked too many months . . ." Spigs stopped pacing. His arms began to gesture wildly as if it were Armageddon. "To get her research prepared for publication."

"Smathers probably wants to steal her research."

"Aren't you stretchin' it a little, T-Ray?" Peabo said.

"It only stands to reason. No Genomic department means no Lab Rats and no publication of her research, giving the school full ownership."

"Say, you're right. Everyone knows her research *is* ground-breaking. The school could generate tremendous positive press," Peabo said, agreeing with her reasoning.

"C'mon, Smathers wouldn't close an entire department just for publicity. Or would he?" Spigs wouldn't put it past Smathers but felt like there was something more to it. "The professor could fight it."

"She probably won't even try," T-Ray offered. "She's too close to tenure. She can't make any waves now."

"But I'm a mad scientist in training. I *need* those genomic courses. They're crucial for my shot at a college scholarship," Spigs drawled wearily.

"Ditto," Peabo bemoaned. "And what will happen to my Lab Rat credits? They look awesome on my resume."

T-Ray immediately took charge. "Will you just listen to yourselves? It's not about US; it's about the professor. Her whole world just came crashing down. And we have to put aside our academic goals and somehow come together to remedy the situation for her."

Spigs and Peabo looked sheepishly at each other and nodded in agreement.

"Okay, so we're all in for the professor. Now, let's think," T-Ray insisted. "We have to combine our talents and come up with a plan for immediate funding. I'm sure the professor will make a formal appeal, which will give us a few days."

"You wanna try and raise funds to reopen the *entire* Genomic department?" Spigs questioned. "Good luck with that."

"Spigs is right. Need another way that would trigger a possible reopening," Peabo said.

The three teens slouched on their respective workstations, deep in thought.

T-Ray shrieked, "GOT IT!"

The boys leaped a foot off their stools.

"Hear me out. We raise enough funds to just finish the peer review. The professor gets it published. The universal publicity she'll receive will bring major attention to her department, leading to a reopening."

"Well, okay, I'm in," Spigs stated. "Open for ideas on the funding part."

They both looked at Peabo, who sat mute. He was thinking. He scrunched his eyes, massaged his temples with his index fingers, and looked as if he might stop breathing. When he'd first assumed this position during a test one time, Spigs and T-Ray were so concerned they rushed the unsuspecting Peabo to the school infirmary.

"Bingo! I have the most amazing, brilliant, fantastical, stupendously awesome idea ever dreamed up." Peabo inhaled a deep breath. "I know what we should do." He closed his eyes and resumed thinking.

"WHAT?" T-Ray and Spigs wailed in unison.

"Huh? What? Oh, yeah." Peabo fluttered his eyes open. "One

word. Crowdfunding." T-Ray and Spigs stared, blank-faced. Peabo continued. "We set up a crowdfunding campaign to raise funds. It happens all the time."

"And that will help *how?*" T-Ray's nose wrinkled beneath the bridge of her glasses.

"If Professor Bodkins gets her dineros from another source, she can then fund the peer review analysis herself and get it published."

"And the worst case, the publication gives her complete ownership," Spigs added.

T-Ray beamed. "Peabo, crowdfunding IS brilliant. But, wait, we can't use the professor's actual research as the funding profile."

"Why not? Isn't she the most beloved professor at the academy?" Spigs asked. "People will wanna help."

"We just can't jeopardize her reputation. Not sure, but if she goes into private funding for any part of her research, it could void all her academic grants up to this point."

"So we set up our own crowdfunding profile and simply funnel the funds through us—the Lab Rats," Spigs said, recapping their scheme for clarity.

"Agreed, but the profile must be unique, outrageous. If not, I don't see an online audience coughing up money for it." Peabo closed his eyes tight again, fingers to his temples, back to thinking.

"HEY! I've got it! I've been studyin' the effects of hypnotizin' chickens. Extremely cost effective; no expansive real estate needed for them to free-range," Spigs offered.

Peabo opened his eyes. "Got that beat, roomie. I'm working on a new science video: 'How to Train a Dung Beetle to Fetch.'

A million potential viewers." Overly thrilled with his proposal, Peabo thrust his arm in the air. "*YAAASSS!*"

"Don't take this the wrong way, but are you two STUCK ON STUPID?" T-Ray waved her arms like a crazy person.

The boys' egos instantly deflated.

"Now I've got one word: *bio-fabrication.*" She stood tall with pride. The guys looked at her with blank gazes. "Helloo . . . remember the school's advanced 3D bio-printer? Specifically ordered by Smathers?" She tapped her chin.

"T-Ray, you've been dyin' to get your hands on that machine," Spigs said.

"For good reasons." Peabo gave T-Ray a nod.

"Thanks, Peabo. So, we all agree to start a crowdfunding campaign for the next generation of 3D bio-printing of tissue."

"I'll set up a crowdfunding account. You guys work on a campaign profile." Peabo pulled his laptop from his backpack.

T-Ray's thumbs typed feverishly on her phone. "Okay, listen to this. 'Brookhaven College successfully 3D bio-printed a monkey finger from primate DNA. Their success generated tremendous publicity and grants.' So, if an animal finger brought in money, what about an ear! It's only bone and cartilage." She gulped in a big breath to calm herself down. "But we stay away from human tissue or parts or this could go terribly wrong," she stressed.

"All in on a monkey ear. A freaky profile like that is sure to create online buzz." Peabo was jazzed at the thought.

He and Spigs high-fived, yet their enthusiasm quickly waned when public enemy number one entered the room.

"Well, well, if it ain't that popular boy band: Horrid and the

Hooligans." Spigs chuckled. "And performin' their greatest hit—
Sons of Anarchy!"

Horace, unfazed by Spigs's sarcastic dig, smirked and
approached their workstations with two upperclassmen behind
him. No doubt they were part of the lacrosse team Horace cap-
tained. "What a darn shame the entire Genomic department got
defunded," he bemoaned with sarcasm.

From the corner of his eye, Spigs observed that Peabo had
retreated farther around the table. Horace grabbed one of Peabo's
Spazzle soda drinks off the table and guzzled it down.

"Sure, help yourself." Spigs stood his ground, a foot from
Horace, hoping to keep his attention off Peabo. He knew a way
to disrupt blundering bullies was to counter with arrogant humor.

"What are you Bill Nye science rejects gonna do now?" Horace
jeered.

"Horrid, I bet you spend your downtime pullin' wings off flies."
Spigs eyed Horace's hooligans for any movements. "Actually, it's
good timing. We're looking for someone to help us with our study
of Moronsé."

"That's Horace to you! And what the hell's Moronsé?" Horace
snarled.

"Ya dunno what a Moronsé?"

Horace stepped closer, eye to eye with Spigs but fifteen pounds
beefier.

"Okay, what's a Moronsé?" Horace demanded.

Spigs snickered as the joke finally hit Horace. Horace clenched
his fists and reared back to swing, but one of his hooligans caught
his wrist. "Remember where we are."

The other hooligan finally got the joke. "Oh, what does a moron say? Now I get—"

"Shut up!" Horace squawked at him, and turned his attention back to Spigs. He yanked his arm free and pointed with a threatening finger. "You're lucky, freshman," Horace scowled.

"Horrid, go annoy someone else," T-Ray scoffed.

Horace scoffed at T-Ray. "Ah, forget it. You infidels will all be *enlightened* soon enough," Horace warned. "And good luck staying in school without your mentor—Bodkins." Horace waved his hand bye-bye at the three of them and stomped off in a huff.

"Hate to say it, but he's right," T-Ray said. "You two are already in the dean's doghouse."

"When am I *not* in the doghouse with adults?" Spigs moaned.

"Forget them, we have to get the crowdfunding going. NOW! T-Ray, do you know how to operate the 3D bio-printer?" Peabo asked.

"Uh, no. I . . . I figured since you're the techno whiz . . . ," T-Ray said sheepishly.

Peabo shrugged. "Never even seen one before."

"Listen, the more knowledge we all have goin' in, the less things we'll screw up," Spigs stated.

"Like how to sneak into this building at night," Peabo added.

"That's the least of our worries." Spigs looked at his friends and sighed. "We're gonna need the professor's help. At least to get us started."

"Agreed, but less is more. Can't let her get wise," Peabo said. "In case our crazy scheme—uh, master plan backfires."

"THAT'S what I'm afraid of." T-Ray voiced her concern.

The trio planned to meet up in Spigs and Peabo's room that night. On their way back to the dorm, Spigs gazed up at Bell Tower once again, and from his point of view, the tower's stained-glass window configurations appeared to stare down at him.

"So, ya want some of me, do ya?" Spigs shouted. "Then you're gonna get some of me, big fella!"

"Shhh, keep it to a low roar." Peabo shook his head at Spigs's obsession with Bell Tower and its mysterious history.

CHAPTER 5

The 3D Bio-Printer

Illuminated by sparsely placed oil lanterns, the crudely burrowed catacombs were dank and cold as Dean Smathers advanced along the winding underground passageway. The elaborate maze of tunnels snaking underneath the school was complex, but Smathers knew it well. He walked up a gentle incline, trailing his fingers along the narrow cave walls to keep his balance. Massive tree roots poked through the damp dirt walls, giving Smathers makeshift guardrails. He turned a corner and groaned as his posh Italian loafers slipped off the planked pathway into soft mud. Few issues irritated Smathers as much as messiness, and he would have to brush away his muddy footprints on the way back. His secretary, Wanda Wainwright, was a prying busybody and would most certainly notice any dirt trails in his pristine office. Smathers had so much to do and so little time to do it, and covering his tracks was an irritant to him and his sense of efficiency and drive.

Smathers ventured on with a grimace, down the smoky corridor until he reached a tarnished metal door partially concealed in the dirt wall. He drew a deep breath in the clear air and knocked twice, followed by three decisive raps. He waited a moment as the hefty door gradually opened with a moan.

A cloaked figure peered out. "You're late." The figure spoke softly in a phlegm-gurgled English accent.

"I also run an academy—remember?" Smathers groused, stomping the mud off the bottom of his shoes. "At least for the time being. So, are you ready?"

"Yes, master."

The slender, hunched figure led Smathers around the corner on frail, shaky legs. The hidden laboratory maintained the usual Bunsen burners, beakers, and test tubes. Murky, bubbling liquid spewed vapor from a series of interconnected beakers. However, despite the well-equipped laboratories on campus, this lab's paraphernalia was antiquated and primitive. Smathers had to blink several times to get his bearings. It had been years since he last visited this lab. Crudely carved on each of the four rock walls were inverted pentagrams—five-pointed stars. Each point of the etchings represented the elements of nature: Earth, Water, Fire, Air, and Spirit. Despite the narrow ventilation shafts to exhaust the fumes, Smathers's throat burned with each inhale of the smoky kerosene oil lingering in the air. He refocused his attention on each of the four walls.

Shelves lined the "Earth" wall, filled with jars of herbs and tinctures. Bones sat in trays, and small animals floated in jars of formaldehyde.

Ornamental red candles lined the "Fire" wall, casting ominous shadows.

A cast-iron cauldron the size of a serving bowl rested against the "Water and Air" wall. Smoke streamed from underneath, as the brewing elixir was in the preliminary stages of alchemy. Smathers swirled the milky liquid and allowed himself a slight grin.

The cloaked figure shuffled across the dirt floor to the "Spirit" wall. He struggled to bend down and unlock a timeworn, dented gray metal steamer trunk with the initials *N.O.M.T., Ltd.*, stenciled on the side in distressed black paint. With his quivering, bony hands, he carefully lifted an orb, the size of an ostrich egg, from the cushion-lined trunk. The object had the consistency of fluid, membrane, and tissue, all encased in a thin pliable shell. He dutifully shuffled over to a lab station. With a syringe, he painstakingly extracted the iridescent coppery fluid. A smidgen over five ounces was meticulously deposited in a glass beaker tube—a long, narrow tube. The cloaked figure corked it with a low grunt of satisfaction.

"This is it! The last of the Draconem Serum." He handed Smathers the tube. "Remember, there is *no* more." He bowed his head, taking a cautious step back.

Smathers lifted the glass tube up to a flame, letting the copper flecks in the iridescent liquid catch the flickering candlelight. "Ah, but I have a plan." He smirked, cautiously caressing the tube, and slid the precious cargo into his blue blazer's inside breast pocket, securing it with buttons. The oversize gemstone on his right pinkie ring began to pulsate with magenta radiance.

"I'll take it back so that it's properly stored, until—"

"Until it's OUR time," the cloaked figure eagerly interrupted.

Smathers looked into the small vanity mirror sitting on a granite shelf. Time had been favorable to the middle-aged dean. Though his spectacles still looked too small for his doughy face, his skin was smooth and youthful. The only hint of middle age was a few gray hairs weaved in his groomed Vandyke goatee—Three Musketeers style.

"Yes, my faithful friend. Soon, you, too, will be justly rewarded."

The cloaked figure nodded as Smathers turned on his heel and trekked his way back through the tunnel toward the sanctuary of his office.

• • •

A deflated Professor Bodkins placed a series of data storage disks in a wall safe behind a picture in her office. "Seven years of genomic research, and what does it get me?" She sighed and input a four-digit code on the lock pad before replacing the picture frame to conceal it. She glanced for a second at the picture of Albert Einstein and his quote: *The secret to creativity is knowing how to hide your sources.* "Very apropos, Albert!" she said with a sad smile.

The professor turned her attention to Spigs, T-Ray, and Peabo, who had entered her office. "Sorry, my mind got lost."

"We heard about the defunding and are real concerned about you," T-Ray voiced in a worried tone.

"Why would ol' nasty Smathers put the kibosh on my ... uh, your research?" Spigs complained.

"Those Lab Rat credits were a huge part of our academic future," Peabo whined.

"Anyway, no worries, Professor, we've gotcher back!" Spigs blurted out. T-Ray poked him in the side to say, "*Ixnay.*" Spigs groaned, massaging his ribs.

"You guys didn't deserve any of this." The professor scooted up to her computer station. She rubbed her puffy, rosy-tinged eyes. "Especially you, T-Ray. I know how much it meant to Kelsey. But I promise I will not stop trying to find ways to eliminate congenital heart defects."

"Your in vitro DNA replication was THE game changer." T-Ray hung her head, fighting back tears.

"IS the game changer," Peabo corrected.

"Thanks for that vote of confidence. So, what can I do for my pet prodigies?"

Spigs and Peabo nudged T-Ray, who took a deep breath. "We kind of . . . For this semester, we'd like to refocus our Lab Rat syllabus on bio-fabrication . . . that's 3D bio-printing genetic material."

"Why the sudden interest in that particular field?"

"Can't tell ya," Peabo uttered. T-Ray rammed her elbow into his side. "OOOF! Uh . . . just saying."

"The school just leased one. Sure hate to let it go to waste." Spigs tried to cover their slipups.

Professor Bodkins's brows creased together. Spigs and Peabo glanced at the ceiling, like toddlers caught in a lie.

T-Ray asked innocently, "But isn't that why you became a teacher? To shape young minds?"

"And we ARE the future," Spigs chirped.

"If you're the future, then Lord help us all." Professor Bodkins finally had something to laugh about. "Okay, Lab Rats, it just so happens I have extra time on my hands. So, let's get cracking."

The trio dashed to their seats. "*Ready!*" they squawked in unison and opened their laptops.

The professor commenced with the theory behind 3D bio-printing human organs and tissue. "It all begins with coding your desired component—"

"The specific organ."

"Correct, Johnny. Or tissue in some instances. And the component program is called the Computer-Aided Design."

"The CAD," T-Ray said.

"Yes. You've been doing your homework, Theresa. The CAD is the computer blueprint that instructs the 3D bio-printer's extruder arms."

"Where the bio-ink cartridges are attached." T-Ray smiled, shimmying her shoulders with pride.

Spigs rolled his eyes. "The bio-ink is a composition of the DNA." He leaned back with a confident smirk.

"Indeed," the professor said. "The extruder arms, with the bio-ink cartridges, deposit layers of a hydrogel solution made of DNA cells to create the desired component, or body part."

"Wait, the DNA or blood sample is injected into the bio-ink cartridges?" Peabo asked.

"Yes. The blood vessels will build the vascular network. And hopefully, one day, 3D bio-printing will become so advanced it could even treat brain imperfections."

Peabo tossed a paper wad at Spigs. "So there *is* hope for you after all."

Spigs shook his head and grinned, chucking the paper back.

"*And* heart imperfections," T-Ray added.

"Absolutely. But there's one crucial detail for scientists to remember. Use only one specific DNA specimen per bio-printed organ or tissue, or else . . ."

"Or else what?" Spigs sat on the edge of his seat.

"Or else, Mr. Spignola, you just might create something out of one of your comic books," Professor Bodkins uttered with a chuckle.

"I can see it now. Sons of Brutorus: The Slimy Ooze Offspring!" Spigs smiled broadly at the thought.

CHAPTER 6

Bell Tower

Crickets chirped and the wind rustled the towering balsam fir and jack pine trees as Spigs led Rachell through campus in the early Saturday evening.

"Why aren't you hanging out with your dorky friends?" Rachell asked, walking with hands in her pockets, much to Spigs's disappointment.

"Even geniuses need a break from their brutal schedules."

"What? And no hat either?" She smirked at him.

"Nah, may get in the way where we're goin'." He gave her a dismissive shrug, though the choice had been deliberate thanks to her teasing.

Spigs kept peering over his shoulder, wanting to stay clear

of the school's security force—two Segway roving campus cops: Chief Homer McTaggart and his overeager rookie, Deputy Elliot Whipsnade. The two bumbling guards spent most of their time hassling students for trivial issues—girls' skirts being too short, for example—but mainly guarding what they valued most: the food vending machines at the Student Union center. They were the entire Aberdasher Academy police department, if you could call it that, and a bane to Spigs's existence.

"So, what are you working on with Professor Bodkins?" Rachell inquired.

"You name it. Like super cool scientific thingies and such. Now, didja know that 3D bio-printers can print a functioning ear?"

"Nah, I'm more interested in the professor's genomic research."

"Thought you were a robotics coding major?"

"Well, uh . . . I am," Rachell stammered. "But I do have outside interests," she said with a cryptic grin before gazing up at the looming Bell Tower. "Why are we stopping here? Wait! You weren't kidding? But this place is off-limits to students and faculty. And how do you plan to get us in, bigshot?"

Spigs dangled a skeleton key from his index finger with a roguish grin and wiggling brows.

"Just where did you get that?" Rachell's voice jumped an octave as she shifted from foot to foot, hand on hip. "You stole it?"

"Why, bite your tongue, Ms. Hobbs. I simply made an impression of the key from Mr. D's key ring with a soap bar, then had a duplicate made in the arts and crafts shop."

"You're insane."

"Insanely curious."

"Idle curiosity can be a dangerous virtue."

"Let's call it probing curiosity. I'm dyin' to get in there."

"I hope not literally."

"Oh, so you *have* heard about the gruesome rumors? Like the tower is crawlin' with bloodthirsty demonic beings? No worries, I'll protect ya." Spigs delivered a sly wink and a half grin and cautiously high-stepped between flowerbeds and small manicured shrubs leading to the front entrance. He struggled to turn his crudely fabricated skeleton key in the rusty lock's tumbler. Finally, the hefty, ornately carved door creaked open. "Voilà!"

Spigs timidly peeked his head in, looking left and right. There were no signs of life, so he slipped inside with one last backward glance and pulled Rachell in behind him.

"I'm not so sure we should be in here." Rachell patted down her bangs as they entered. A nervous tic. "Nope, I'm positive we shouldn't be here."

"C'mon." Spigs beamed mischievously and grabbed her hand before she could shove it back in her jacket. "And keep it down. Don't wanna wake the dead. Remember those rumors."

The door latched behind them with a heavy clank. Vast archways loomed high above them, and cobblestones of all sizes made up the flooring. In the center of the musty room was the start of a cast-iron spiral staircase that wound its way up ten flights. Spigs led Rachell by the hand to the first step. Something scurried beneath their feet.

"What was THAT?" Rachell yelped.

"Shhh!" Spigs put his hand over her mouth. "Probably just a mouse. Doesn't seem like anyone's been in here in ages."

"Then maybe *we* shouldn't be here." Rachell planted her feet as Spigs tried to coax her up the staircase.

"You afraid of heights or somethin'?"

"No. It's just . . ." Rachell shivered.

"Don'tcha wanna see the best view on campus? Heard a traveling carnival set up on a campground outside Letchworth Village. Should be able to see it from the belfry." Spigs knew Rachell was apprehensive, but this was his moment to shine. "Ten minutes max. Now, c'mon."

Rachell squirmed out of Spigs's grasp. "Fine, but the second I get creeped out, I'm gone."

"Agreed." They began their ascent, and by the third floor, Spigs felt a bit lightheaded from the spiraling staircase. "I heard Bell Tower was the first building on campus. And built atop an infamous burial site."

Rachell shuddered. "Great."

"Yup. Smack-dab on top of rottin' bones from a secret society that was brutally massacred."

"Thought that was only a rumor." Rachell was trying to pick up the pace.

"Nope. Fact."

"Who was involved?" Rachell challenged.

Spigs was unprepared for her probing questioning. "Uuh, it was a group of people, and it happened a long time ago, and—"

"You have no idea, do you?" Rachell laughed.

"Well . . . I . . ." Spigs sputtered as they climbed higher through the dark, drafty tower. "I do know it was an inside job *and* happened nearly a hundred years ago."

"Can you please stop talking?" Rachell huffed and paused.

"We are the spawn of the great deceiver."

"Spigs, I said stop talking!" Rachell tried to gasp another breath, then continued to follow him up the spiral staircase.

"Vengeance is ours!"

Rachell grabbed the rail and stomped her foot on the metal step. "Spigs, STOP IT! You're really creepin' me out."

Spigs, four steps ahead, turned around. "Rachell, I haven't said a word."

"We thirst for vengeance!"

"Hear it NOW?"

"YIKES!" Spigs didn't hear the voices, but played it up. He reached back and grabbed Rachell's hand. "Let's scram!"

They both clambered up a dozen more steps.

"How many more?"

"That's strange. The steps are numbered." Spigs squinted at the numbers hammered into the side of the cast-iron steps. "This one is number thirty-three." He looked up. "I'd say we're about halfway."

"Well, tell me something to distract me. This is grueling," Rachell whined.

"They say the tortured, massacred souls will eventually resurrect and seek revenge by hauntin' the living."

"Again with the spooky stuff? Go back to not talking." Rachell glared at Spigs, who mimed locking his mouth and tossing the key.

They continued ascending in silence until they reached the belfry's bell chamber. Spigs's brain buzzed with anticipation. His excitement was at the thought they were probably the first students ever to see the inside of the tower in its infamous history. Dozens of polished bronze bells gleamed in the moonlight, backlit by the four stained-glass windows. It was impressive, but oddly well maintained for a structure that was completely restricted. Spigs had expected a thick layer of filth, yet the area looked swept and dusted.

"Sixty-six stairs." Spigs bent down and brushed his finger over the carved numbers on the top step. "I'm in better shape than I thought."

"I'm not." Rachell bent over to rub her toes through her boots.

"C'mere." Spigs stood on his tiptoes and peered through one of the stained-glass windows. Just beyond was a walkway that bordered the belfry. In the distance, Spigs could scarcely see the purple-and-yellow tents of the traveling carnival. His eyes canvassed the school campus through the tinted amber glass that made the panoramic scene look like a 1930s photograph. "You can see everything from up here."

As Rachell stood next to him, gazing out, Spigs cleared his voice and pronounced in a throaty whisper, "But as *you* just heard, there's extreme evil lurkin' beneath the cobblestones. And only *I* can protect you from the wickedness that's about to set upon us."

Spigs believed he had her ready to jump in his arms. Instead, Rachell punched him in the chest, knocking him into one of the bells. *BONG! BONG!* "You think that's all it takes? A scary story and I'll fall into your arms? Think again, buster."

Spigs lunged to smother the ringing bell. He gawked at it, baffled by how glossy the surface was. ALL the bells gleamed in the moonlight, due to a recent polishing. He squinted at an odd engraving—an eye inside an inverted pentagram circled by three nines. A quick scan revealed each bell had one. He swung the bronze bell up from its hinge and noticed the number *132* embossed prominently into the inner rim. Every bell Spigs examined had the same odd insignia and number. He snapped a photo of the bells' crests with his phone. Rachell came up behind him and spun him around.

"If you get ME into trouble—"

"Nah, I never get caught. Besides, it's just us and those poor tortured souls buried under the cobblestones, remember? You heard 'em."

Rachell finally chuckled. "You're surprisingly clever at breaking into places where you shouldn't be."

"Ah, curiosity runs deep in my blood."

"Let's try not to spill it."

"I'm with ya on that."

"Now, about Professor Bodkins's research, I'd love to see her groundbreaking data. I'm sure it's secured somewhere." Rachell paused. "And since you do have a knack for being in places you shouldn't be, maybe we could take a look?"

"Hmm, I don't—"

Suddenly, a robed figure wielding a flat wooden bat sprang out of the shadows. "YAHOW!" Spigs's yelp echoed inside the bells. Rachell shrieked as the figure charged with bat raised, ready to crack Spigs's head with a downward swing. Spigs sidestepped the blow and kicked the attacker in the knee, staggering him.

"Let's get . . . OUTTA HERE!" Spigs grabbed Rachell's hand, and they sprinted down the spiraling stairs two steps at a time.

The pursuing attacker's footsteps clanged on the metal steps. Spigs's disheveled hair fluttered in the gust of wind created by the swinging bat. He looked back in time to see another swing whiz inches from his face. The bat clanged against the iron railing.

Spigs and Rachell pulled ahead as the ground floor came into view, but as they landed on the cobblestones, a frail, hunched-over man appeared from the shadows and stuck out a similar flat bat, tripping Spigs. The attacker shoved Rachell aside and pounced on Spigs. He was husky, but wiry. Spigs was quicker. Spigs squirmed like a worm on a hook, kicking and flailing, and finally managed to slip out of the embrace. The attacker grabbed Spigs's leg in a wrestling hold. Spigs tried to plant a solid kick to the chest, but the attacker yanked him closer and wrapped an arm around his neck. Spigs grabbed at the choking arm and noticed a *TCB* tattoo on the underside of his left wrist. Spigs was now pinned to the floor, trapped underneath the attacker's heavy torso. The hunched man lurked in the shadows, silently watching the battle unfold. Spigs wriggled into a prime position and kicked the flat bat from his attacker's hand. It clattered across the cobblestone floor near Rachell.

"Whack 'im!" Spigs screamed at Rachell, but she remained motionless.

Spigs cocked his knee and landed a blow to the attacker's groin, allowing Spigs to roll free. He snatched a wooden bucket hanging from a wall hook and smashed his attacker over the head. Spigs grabbed Rachell and bolted toward the door.

"Never return, infidels!" crackled a scratchy voice from the shadows in a clipped British accent.

Spigs focused back to catch a glimpse of the raspy voice but could only make out a hideously gaunt mouth with discolored, rotting teeth.

Spigs gripped Rachell's hand like a vise, and they bolted out the doorway. They leaped over the flowerbed and shrubs and sprinted away until they were on the other side of the Quad.

"DANG!" Spigs tried to catch his breath. "That was friggin' extreme."

"Agreed. No need to go in there again," Rachell added, patting down her bangs.

"Roger that. Hey, how come ya didn't club that dude?"

"Just freaked, I guess." Rachell was still panting for air.

"Well—" Spigs looked at his phone's clock. "OOPS! I'm in big trouble. Gotta go. Sorry I can't walk ya back. Later, Rach." Spigs sprinted off.

"MUCH later. And thanks for such a delightful evening," Rachell howled sarcastically.

CHAPTER 7

Draconem Serum

A dozen empty Spazzle soda cans formed a pyramid on Spigs's desk. A NERF basketball net hung from a closet door. T-Ray took in the scene with a bemused face: dirty clothes sprawled on the floor and chairs, unmade bunkbeds, and overstuffed trashcans. She'd come to the conclusion a filthy dorm room was one of the perils of reluctantly forging a team—a team of boys!

"WHEW! Smells like a stale locker room." T-Ray waved her hand by her nose. She'd lodged many complaints about their living conditions, but to no avail.

"Just whaddaya know about the smell of a locker room? You wouldn't be caught dead in one," Spigs retorted.

"I think I see fungus crawling on that T-shirt." T-Ray pointed to the specimen in question. Spigs reclined on his cluttered bed and threw up his hands in defeat.

"Focus, Peabo. We've got work to do." Spigs teased his cat, Biscuit, by flashing the red dot from his laser pointer around the room in a figure-eight pattern. The gullible cat whirled in the air as he repeatedly jumped at the bouncing red light. Biscuit then went headfirst into the Spazzle-can pyramid, sending the hollow aluminum cans clanking across the floor.

If Biscuit could stay out of trouble, catnip was his treat. He was also an amazing bed warmer and purr machine. The boys had both slept much better since Biscuit had commandeered their dorm room.

"Done on my end," Peabo called out from the top bunk. He'd set up their crowdfunding account online, with a few donations trickling in—mostly from his immediate family. He called the campaign "The Awesomeness of 3D Bio-Science" and posted pictures of primate ears with the hashtag teaser **#TheFutureIsHere!**

Spigs slouched over his laptop, working on their CAD program—the Computer-Aided Design software. He guzzled down his cherry Spazzle and closed several websites dedicated to human organs. But one site featured an image of a monkey ear. Spigs took a deep breath and typed in the code for the primate ear.

His program flickered and zoomed through a series of images until the words *SOURCE CODE COMPILING* displayed on the screen. A positive sign . . . until an alarm blared from his laptop and flashed an alert.

"What's up over there?" Peabo asked anxiously.

"Did you screw it up?" T-Ray scolded.

Spigs typed so rapidly his fingers appeared to dance across the keys. "People, have a little faith. BAM! Done." Spigs cracked his knuckles and slapped closed his laptop's screen. "So, let's go. It's almost ten o'clock."

"Remember, we have ONE shot. And there's no turning back," T-Ray said ominously.

The trio, each clad in dark clothes and strapped with their backpacks, covertly trekked out the boys' dorm toward the contemporary Bio-Engineering building on the far side of campus. As they passed Bell Tower, Spigs shuddered with a chill to his body.

"So, was it as spooky in there as I imagined?" Peabo asked.

"I'm tellin' ya, the spookiest! It's been closed for decades, but all the bells were freshly polished. And I almost got whacked by the dude from *Assassin's Creed*."

"Just WHAT were you two doing up there, anyhow?" T-Ray asked with disdain.

Spigs ignored her insinuation. "AND a grizzled old man lives inside. Once was definitely enough to satisfy my curiosity."

"Can't believe you got in," Peabo said, impressed.

"I can get in anywhere," Spigs boasted.

"Okay, Houdini, so how're you gonna get us in there?" T-Ray pointed to the Bio-Engineering building as they approached it. They ducked behind a row of freshly cut boxwood shrubs. The black steel surrounding the entryway reflected the bright full moon. The double-door entrance and fire door on the backside were locked after ten o'clock. Only seniors and teachers had access to the campus's newest building after dark.

Spigs shrugged. He hadn't yet thought of a way to bypass the building's card-access security system.

"Time's not on our side." T-Ray's warning was in the heightened pitch of her voice.

Peabo swiped through his phone. "We may have to ramp up our profile for greater exposure. Apparently, bio-printing a monkey ear is not an attention grabber."

"We don't have time to change it." T-Ray shook her head, which jiggled her auburn hair bun. "Give it time. It's been less than two hours."

"Got a plan for how we slip in, easy peasy like." Spigs clicked on his phone clock as the other two gathered closer around him. "It's nine fifty-five, and the building closes at ten. Mr. Dingle mentioned that Jasper, the night janitor, comes on duty right after ten." Spigs looked toward the three trashcans set on a dolly in front of the building. "So, Peabo climbs in the trash can labeled *Molecular Diagnostics lab*. Ol' Jasper rolls the dolly inside. And once in, Peabo lets us in."

"You mean the can also marked *Hazard: Molecular Waste*?" Peabo asked incredulously.

"Yep."

"Why me?"

"You expect a girl to reek like you guys?" T-Ray smirked.

"What happened to the 'WE slip in' idea?" Peabo looked at Spigs for some backup.

"You're the smallest. Can't have Jasper haulin' us all in or he'll notice somethin' is up. They're supposed to be empty goin' back in. It's the only way. Now hand me your backpack."

"Ya know, I've been thinking. We only had *one* week to study about the bio-printing with the professor. Maybe—"

Spigs and T-Ray shoved Peabo out from the shrubs. He frowned, crouched down, tiptoed over to the trashcan, slid the plastic lid to the side, and slinked in. Several minutes later, a jovial Jasper came whistling around the corner, grabbed the dolly, and grunted as he fought to roll it into the building. "Darn that Philbert. He didn't empty all 'em cans. Well, ain't my job—union rules."

Spigs and T-Ray hid behind the boxwood shrubs while they waited for Peabo to emerge.

"So, Rachell, hmm?" T-Ray fished.

"Ah, she's cool. But seemed particularly interested in Professor Bodkins's research."

"That's odd. Why?"

Spigs remembered asking why a robotics coding major was interested in gene research, but he was too smitten to recall if she'd ever answered.

"Uh ... dunno. LOOK, Peabo's in." Peabo waved to them from inside the open double doors. They looked around for signs of other students or the campus cops, then raced to the entrance, where Peabo was wilting with a disconsolate expression, his jacket drenched in pea-green grunge.

"GROSS!" T-Ray and Spigs exclaimed.

"Ugh! I'm pickled in bio-scum." Peabo shook his sleeves, spraying tiny droplets.

"Watch it! Look on the bright side. Growin' a third eye does have its advantages," Spigs said, laughing.

Peabo reacted to Spigs's giddy grin with a blank stare.

The Molecular Diagnostics lab housed the very impressive 3D bio-printer, the size of a seven-passenger SUV. It took up a third of the room.

Spigs rushed over and flung open all the supply closets until he found what he was looking for. Bingo. He handed out lab smocks, hairnets, goggles, gloves, and blue booties to cover their shoes.

"What *are* you doing?" T-Ray demanded. "We're not conducting a CSI investigation."

"Gotta dress for success," Spigs announced, adjusting his white lab smock and flipping up the collar. He snapped on the hairnet and secured the goggles over his eyes. "Kinda look good, huh?"

"Kinda NOT!" T-Ray deflated Spigs's ego. "But maybe you're right. Can't contaminate the experiment, especially smelling like Peabo."

"I'm in." Peabo removed his drenched jacket and hurried to the sink to splash himself in water.

"First on our list is to locate the animal DNA specimen," T-Ray told Spigs as she slipped into the lab outfit.

"I got it covered." Spigs began his search inside the huge floor-to-ceiling refrigerator. He remembered from Professor Bodkins's lessons that blood could last for thirty minutes at room temperature before it broke down, so any samples would be in cold storage. He practically crawled inside to explore all the shelves and drawers. Several minutes later, he popped out sporting a scowl. "Dang it. Nothin'."

"Check the other lab rooms. We're sunk without a specimen," T-Ray instructed.

Peabo dried himself off and slipped into his lab clothes.

He removed his laptop from his backpack and flung open the screen. "Our campaign is showing ZERO activity. Gotta goose it somehow."

Spigs had disappeared down the hall, where he found two other refrigeration units on the floor. But he returned sweating and frustrated. "Comin' up empty. Not a drop of animal blood . . . or *any* blood. Let's try tomorrow. Another department?"

"NO!" T-Ray snapped. She thrust her hands deep in her lab coat's side pockets and hung her head. She paced the length of the lab, once, twice, three times, then eyed the boys and held up her palms. "Okay, hear me out. We need DNA, like, NOW! So, we have no choice but to use . . . our blood."

"Uh, I don't know about that." Peabo frowned. "And it's not animal DNA—for a monkey ear."

"This is life or death!" T-Ray cried out, and glared at Peabo with a huff. "We're in a jam, and time is not on our side. Everyone look around for any equipment for taking blood samples."

The three searched out shelves and threw open the cabinets and pulled out drawers.

T-Ray located a plastic packet of sterile scalpels and bandages. "This should do it. Now, to get enough DNA we'll all have to give a sample."

Peabo eyed the scalpels with trepidation. "Ugh, the sight of blood makes me woozy," Peabo whined. "Especially MINE!"

"Suck it up, buttercup." T-Ray looked at the boys and stuck out her right hand. "It's all of us or none of us. Remember, team-work makes the dream work."

Spigs slapped his hand on top of hers.

"Can't I just pee in a petri dish or somethin'?" Peabo begged.

"NO!" T-Ray and Spigs stated forcefully.

Peabo frowned and placed his hand atop theirs.

T-Ray located three glass vials and alcohol wipes. She tore open the scalpel packet and waved Spigs over.

Spigs stuck out his index finger. T-Ray squeezed and pricked it, draining a trivial amount of blood into a vial. She wrote Spigs's initials on the vial's tape label with a Sharpie pen.

"Peabo." T-Ray reached for his index finger.

"That's my thinking finger." He yanked it back. "Wait, give me a minute to gather my thoughts." T-Ray rolled her eyes. Peabo took a deep breath and extended his pinkie. "There, the smallest finger won't hurt as much."

Spigs shook his head at his roommate's illogical thinking.

Peabo squinted and bit down on a rolled-up towel as if he were being brutally tortured. "Gaah! Oooh . . . the PAIN!"

"That was the alcohol rub, you wuss. Hold still." T-Ray pricked and squeezed blood from his finger into a vial and labeled it. Again, a minuscule amount. She handed out Band-Aids.

"My turn." Without hesitation, T-Ray jabbed her own finger. A few drops of blood trickled out.

Spigs tried to swirl the insignificant amount of blood in the three vials. It barely coated the bottoms. "Not enough blood to feed a mosquito."

"It's enough out of me," Peabo insisted.

"Let's mix it together, then," Spigs suggested

"But the professor specifically said a single DNA specimen per component."

"T-Ray's right. There's too much at stake not to try somethin'."

T-Ray combined their blood samples. "It's still not enough." Her shoulders slumped with a huff of frustration. "I wanna fill all six bio-ink cartridges. We need room for error."

"Ah, there is *one* place I didn't check," Spigs offered reluctantly. "The Genomic Analytical lounge, the next room over. And no security key needed."

"That's strictly for faculty members," Peabo warned. "We can't . . . we *shouldn't* go in there."

"Really, you're gonna start worrying about breaking the rules now?" T-Ray said, and eyed Spigs. "Just locate any DNA."

"Gotcha!" Spigs hustled out. The Genomic Analytical lounge had a few couches, a TV, and a kitchenette, where several dirty plates and coffee cups were stacked in the sink. It looked more like a corporate lounge. He noticed a drawer half-open beneath the coffee machine. Not a place to store blood samples, but exploring places he shouldn't had always held a strong allure for Spigs. He pulled out the extensive drawer, and a Grinch-like grin spread from ear to ear as his finger looped through a ring that held a bundle of security keycards.

"These could come in handy," he whispered to himself and shoved the prize in his jeans pocket.

He hustled over to the refrigerator and poked in his head. It was loaded with Spazzle soda cans. "Whoa, don't mind if I do." He reached in deep to the back row to extract a cherry flavor, knocking over other cans in the process.

As Spigs straightened the cans, he noticed what looked like a four-by-four-inch metal flap to a compartment in the back wall of the fridge. Upon further examination, he discovered it was a safe. He thought it was sure odd, a safe in a refrigerator, so it must be important. And he relished the challenge of deciphering the password. The safe's combination lock was a coded three-letter dial. Spigs thought for a second before trying the most obvious letters: "AAS" for Aberdasher Academy of Science. The first and third letters clicked in; however, the middle letter was wrong. "A-something-S." Spigs did a quick inventory of all the possibilities, then grinned broadly—*Aleister Stan Smathers*. He turned the middle dial to an *S*, and the safe's panel sprang open. "Ta-dah!"

Spigs saw only a single item inside the safe: a corked glass tube filled with sparkling coppery liquid. He squinted to catch a glimpse of the word *serum* on the label. "Wait . . . serum? That's blood. Right?" He reached in and carefully gripped the tube to retrieve it. He also snatched that cherry Spazzle. Spigs hustled out of the lounge but stopped for a closer inspection of the peculiar inscription on the label: a symbol of an eye inside an inverted pentagram circled by three nines.

Now where have I seen that before? Spigs thought. *And what's Draconem Serum? Well, T-Ray did say "any" DNA.* He felt certain it would be enough to mix with their blood and load the machine's six extruders. "Desperate times call for desperate measures. And boy are we desperate!"

Spigs drew in a breath and raised his voice to call across the hall, "Guys! I found some serum—uh, blood!" As he entered the Molecular Diagnostics lab, he hastily removed the label and tucked it in his pocket so as not to have to answer annoying questions—like questions he couldn't answer.

T-Ray held the tube up to the ceiling lights to examine the luminescent coppery fluid. "What *is* this, Spigs?"

"Dunno exactly, but I think we should use it."

"Well." T-Ray examined the tube. "It kinda . . . glistens."

Peabo sighed with a shrug. "Hey, it's blood, right? DNA. And that's what we need."

T-Ray nodded and snapped on blue rubber gloves and proceeded to combine their blood samples with the coppery serum Spigs found. She capped the remnants left in their blood vials and tossed them in the medical waste bin.

"This DNA brew sorta oozes." Peabo was mesmerized by the dense liquid.

T-Ray attached the tube full of their concoction to a gyrating apparatus that meticulously mixed the substances.

"A gooey ooze," T-Ray agreed.

"Gooze!" Spigs proclaimed. "Lab Rats, I think we're on to somethin'."

"Team GOOZE!" Peabo announced. "I see a science reality show in the making." Spigs and Peabo fist-bumped.

"Before you two launch your TV careers, let's first see what our . . . Gooze . . . creates," T-Ray warned. "In case it creates some kind of medical mishap!"

"Ah, we just discard the evidence and start over," Spigs declared.

"Spigs, man your post." Peabo pointed to the workstation. "And since we're now basically using human blood, adjust the CAD for a human ear. Monkey ear was *sooo* yesterday." All three laughed.

"No problemo!" Spigs slid the bar stool up to the workstation. "Easy peasy to amend the CAD."

When the apparatus stopped spinning the tube, T-Ray and Peabo delicately poured the slow-flowing liquid into six bio-ink cartridges. Peabo and T-Ray had secured the safety goggles to cover their eyes. Peabo moseyed over to unlock the two substantial glass doors and climbed inside the sterile bio-printing machine. T-Ray followed. Despite its massive size, it was tight quarters inside among the robotic mechanisms. The two teens had to choreograph their movements to attach the Gooze-filled bio-ink cartridges to the machine's pendulous extruder arms. Several minutes later, both emerged and secured the heavy glass doors.

Spigs had set aside his laptop to search through the files on the school's desktop computer at the bio-printer's main workstation. He located several folders labeled *Human Ear*. He clicked through them and selected what he thought was the simplest CAD program for a human ear. But the computer was laboring through the huge amount of data, so Spigs inserted his USB and downloaded the human ear CAD so he could work from his laptop instead.

Spigs called out over his shoulder at T-Ray and Peabo, who were near the bio-printer. "Launchin' our revised CAD program. 'Ear ye, 'ear ye, the ears of the future!" And so to cheer the success of his new CAD, Spigs popped open the cherry Spazzle, which promptly fizzed and sprayed in his face and all over his keyboard, causing the laptop to momentarily spark.

"WHOA!" Spigs squealed.

"What's happening over there?" T-Ray asked in an anxious tone as she wiped fingerprints off the bio-printer's glass doors.

"AAAH, nothin'. We're good," Spigs fibbed. He turned

over his laptop to drain the liquid. But as he did, several files on his computer inexplicably opened. He wiped clean the moisture on the keyboard with the hem of his T-shirt. Inexplicably, *DOWNLOADING* flashed repeatedly on his screen. "Whoa! What the—! HUH!" He saw peculiar animated avatar figures, like little gremlins, scurrying across the screen.

"WHOA!" Spigs squawked again. Then he brought his voice down to a whisper. "Dang, got spammed by a gaming ad." He closed his eyes, mouthed a few words, held up his crossed fingers, and hoped the CAD program hadn't been infected by the ad. He opened his eyes and glanced warily over to see if T-Ray or Peabo had noticed.

"What?" T-Ray barked.

"We're good here," Spigs called back.

"Then stop saying 'whoa.' Are you ready?"

"Ninety-five percent." Spigs drummed on the table, waiting for the CAD program to fully load. "Bam! Okay, let's rock!"

"Count down," Peabo declared as he and T-Ray joined Spigs at the workstation. They all stared at the *RUN PROGRAM* button on the screen.

"There's no turning back, guys."

"Would you quit sayin' that?" Spigs said.

"In Gooze We Trust," Peabo stated humorously.

"We live by Gooze or die by Gooze." Spigs gave a cartoonish salute. "For there is no greater love than to lay down one's life for—"

"ENOUGH! We have less than seven hours until first period," T-Ray said. "Okay, now on three. Ready—"

"Wait." Peabo held up a finger. "Is it ON three, or is it three, two, one, then—"

T-Ray smacked Peabo on the back of his head.

Peabo moaned. "Someone here lacks a sense of humor."

"On one," T-Ray said. "ONE!"

Together they pressed the Enter key.

The imposing 3D bio-printer whirred to life. The six extruder arms descended and hovered over six hubcap-size disks. The arms started zigzagging back and forth, depositing layer after layer of bio-material from the cartridges onto the designated disks.

Spigs, T-Ray, and Peabo jumped around, trying to see what was being created, yet a magenta mist inside the 3D bio-printer made it impossible to see anything. Peabo rushed to the backside of the machine to see if he could spot anything from there. The trio were so focused on the machine they didn't hear Horace and his hooligans enter the room.

"And just what are you three deviants doing in here, and in the middle of the night?"

CHAPTER 8

Creeple Peeple

S pigs leaned against his workstation to block the computer screen from Horace's view. "Oh, hey, Horrid. Just tryin' to find a scientific explanation for your existence, but so far, no luck."

"Where's Pea Brain?" Horace demanded, scanning the room.

Peabo had hunched down on the other side of the bio-printer. Spigs glanced at T-Ray, who stared down Horace.

"Poor Peabo is extremely ill. He contracted a dreadfully contagious virus." T-Ray raised her voice so Peabo could hear her ruse.

Spigs caught on to her deception. "As his lab assistants, we've taken an antidote." He held up his index finger with the Band-Aid on it. "But you fellas probably should stay back, or else."

"Or else what? This place is off-limits to you freshmen freaks." Horace stepped closer, and his three hooligans mimicked his advance.

"Heed our warning, Horace. Peabo's got . . . Spazzilitis?" T-Ray blurted out, and eyed Spigs.

"Spazzilitis?" Horace crossed his arms to show his disbelief.

"Like she said, Horrid, a highly contagious virus, so ya don't wanna get near him or he'll—"

"He'll WHAT?" Horace demanded.

Peabo sprang out from behind the bio-printer, then plopped on the floor, convulsing and foaming at the mouth . . . from cherry Spazzle. His eyes vacillated, his fingers twitched, and he was wearing his pea-green, slime-drenched jacket, so he looked and smelled toxic.

Horace's eyes sprang wide, and his scream produced a high frequency known only to bottlenose dolphins. Peabo stepped it up. He started hacking and struggled to crawl across the floor, legs trailing uselessly behind him as one hand reached out to Horace for help.

"Let's get out of here!" Horace screeched to his hooligans, and they quickly raced for the door, slamming into each other as they all tried to cram through at once.

"OH NO! Peabo's virus is lookin' for a host!" Spigs bellowed as Horace and his goons scrambled around the corner.

T-Ray started to giggle. "Wow, that was like—"

"AMAZING! Yes, thank you all. And now for my next acting role, a scene from _Romeo and Juliet_." Peabo laughed. The three took a moment to celebrate their small victory. Peabo tried to peer into the opaque 3D machine once again. The bio-printer's extruder arms continued to rotate back and forth behind a dense magenta fog. "It's drivin' me crazy that I can't see in there."

"Wonder how long it's gonna take to produce our design." Spigs noticed the wall clock showed 2:48 a.m.

"IF it works, you mean." Peabo voiced his pessimism.

"Six extruder arms mean six prototypes. So, six chances to get it right, but we just need one to produce a result for our funding." T-Ray's voice didn't hold its usual confidence, and she fidgeted nervously with her hair bun.

The machine's soft humming mesmerized the teens, and one by one exhaustion caught up with them. Peabo fell asleep first, curled up in a corner. Spigs was next, head down at the workstation. T-Ray tried one more time to peek inside the cloudy machine before she, too, grabbed a nap before her morning classes. All three slumbered to the hums and whirs of the 3D bio-printer.

• • •

As T-Ray, Spigs, and Peabo snoozed, the magic of science commenced:

–DNA polymerase chain reaction, duplicating multiple strands from one double helix . . .

–Corpuscles traveling along a microtubule . . .

–Cells multiplying, dividing, and expanding rapidly during mitosis . . .

–Neurons firing . . .

The Lab Rats didn't stir when the ceiling lights flickered. Sparks spewed from all the electrical outlets. Finally, the bio-printer's extruder arms jerked to a stop. Complete silence.

Minutes passed before faint palpitating beats resonated from inside the bio-printer.

A pair of miniature ashen-gray hands with four fingers pushed open the 3D machine's thick glass doors, and vaporous mist escaped. One by one, six diminutive humanoids warily emerged. The bizarre creatures were twenty inches tall, with oscillating mustard-yellow eyes, prodigious ears, and lolling tongues protruding through crooked teeth. Their slender, elongated torsos attached to hairless, dumpy ashen-gray bodies featuring pronounced potbellies, all supported by two immense three-toed feet. Two of the humanoid creatures had peculiarly distinctive physical traits; one had six tentacles that sprouted up from its over-voluminous head, and the other featured two bolts protruding from the top of its sizable noggin. But the most obvious distinguishing trait among the creatures was the garish plume of neon hair sprouting from a small patch atop their bald heads.

Six little beings with six different hair colors: yellow, green, red, orange, purple, and blue. The creatures gazed at the napping teens with their eyes that vacillated independently of each other. They swayed with stoic curiosity. Finally, one leaped up on Spigs at his workstation.

"Stop it, Biscuit." Spigs sleepily swatted the creature over to Peabo.

"No reason to kick me," Peabo mumbled, his eyes still closed.

Peabo's voice woke T-Ray. She sat up, looked around, and adjusted her glasses to make sure she was seeing correctly. "Uuuh . . . guys?" she whispered, scared to speak too loudly as she and a creature stared each other down.

"Ah, just five more minutes, Aunt Gussy," Spigs uttered deliriously.

"GUYS! Wake up! Like, NOW!" T-Ray shouted with eagerness.

Creeples!

Peabo and Spigs rubbed their bleary eyes at the bewildering sight: six elfin creatures climbing and swinging about like kids on a playground jungle gym. Peabo gasped and Spigs's eyes widened to the size of cup saucers. The two scrambled over to cower next to T-Ray. The three were speechless for several minutes, at the astonishing and unfathomable scene.

"Widows and geeks first! I'm outta here!" Peabo leaped toward the door, but T-Ray jerked his shirttail.

"That's widows and *orphans*, and you're neither. Now get back here."

"YAWOW! What's happenin'?" Spigs whined as all-out chaos erupted. The red and yellow creatures pounced on him and proceeded to lick his face with their disgusting tongues. "Guys . . . HELP!"

"I just knew IT! We shouldn't have mixed in *our* DNA." Peabo howled when the blue creature leaped on his back. He tried to yank it off, but it was freakishly strong. Its tiny arms latched around his neck. "Can't tell if it wants to hug me or choke me to death!"

"Medical mishaps gone wild!" Spigs had the red and yellow creatures dangling from his shoulders. The two wedged their stubby fingers in his mouth. Spigs looked like a squirrel with cheeks full of nuts.

"They're kind of, uh . . . I mean, sort of cute . . . in a creepy way," T-Ray said as she cuddled the purple-haired creature, who looked into her eyes with a shared intelligence. "Look at their crazy eyes. Like geckos—moving opposite of each other." The creature flopped its lengthy tongue out like a panting dog.

Muffled mumbles came from Peabo. The blue creature had completely smothered his face like an octopus clutching its prey.

"I think it's safe to say . . . our lab experiment officially 'jumped the shark'!" Spigs watched the red and yellow creatures swing from the light fixtures. The blue creature hopped atop Spigs's head and grabbed a chunk of his brown hair like a cowboy riding a bucking bronco. "Ouch!"

"Don't think they're a he or a she. More like an IT. And I don't plan to investigate." Peabo wrestled with the orange creature, which smelled nearly as putrid as he did. "I told you guys we tried to bio-print too many samples."

"Too late. So what now?" T-Ray cuddled her purple creature.

The green creature, who hadn't stopped waddling about the lab room, finally made its way over to T-Ray and nestled into her lap. *CLICK-CLACKING* reverberated from its head.

Peabo had the orange creature in a tizzy, chasing the laser pointer's red dot.

T-Ray focused her indignation on Spigs, who was making faces with the red one. "So, Johnny Spignola, just what the HECK happened to our CAD? We didn't design these . . . these little beings!"

"Could've been a technical glitch?" Spigs cradled the red-haired creature with the unique six tentacles atop its head. He waved his index finger back and forth, and its six tentacles tracked every move.

"A glitch?" Peabo screeched as he tried to untangle the blue one from his hair. "THAT may be the world's biggest understatement. We've created an entirely new species!"

Creeples!

T-Ray stroked the purple one's hair, enthralled by its silky texture. "So what's up with their different hair colors? And why bright neon?"

Spigs tried to extricate the yellow one from his pants leg. "That's what concerns you? Their hair color?"

Peabo shrugged. "Must've used bio-cartridges that still had colored ink left from a previous bio-printing."

"You forgot to sterilize THE CARTRIDGES?" T-Ray's cheeks flushed. The purple and green creatures tilted their prodigious ears at her raised voice.

Peabo took a deep breath and roared, "SERIOUSLY? We mixed our blood with a mysterious serum for 3D bio-printing that we're hardly qualified to use, and you're on me about unsterilized cartridges? SERIOUSLY?" The outburst brought all three of them AND the six creatures to a grinding halt. They stared at each other for a few seconds.

Spigs snickered, then snorted out a laugh.

Peabo cracked up, doubled over.

T-Ray couldn't confine a giggle, and soon the three laughed uncontrollably at the ridiculousness of their predicament.

The creatures watched the teens with vacant expressions until they calmed back down from near hysteria.

"So, our original monkey ear campaign has evolved into SIX creepy monkeys." Peabo arm wrestled the blue creature—and lost.

"More like six creepy little people," Spigs said.

"Creeple Peeple!" Peabo announced.

Spigs looked at Peabo, on the same page, and proclaimed, "CREEPLES!" They fist-bumped to their stroke of cleverness.

"They don't seem *too* dangerous." T-Ray snuggled with the purple, green, and orange creatures.

"They are sorta affectionate." Spigs petted the red one on its head. "And this one has some gnarly tentacles. Gonna call this Creeple Naz."

"Wait, you *can't* name them," T-Ray scolded in a motherly tone.

"Why not?" Peabo tossed the yellow Creeple up in the air repeatedly. It seemed to enjoy the game, as flashes of electricity sparked between its two spikes. "And this one has two cool Frankenstein's monster bolts on its head. I dub thee . . . Tatz!"

"STOP NAMING THEM!" T-Ray commanded.

"Why?" the boys said.

"If you name them, you'll get attached to them, and we can't get attached to them. We'll get expelled if we're found with them. Or worse, ostracized from the scientific community," T-Ray proclaimed. "We have to think of something quick. Classes start in twenty-five minutes. So, what are we to do with the—?"

"Creeples!" Spigs and Peabo interrupted.

"Okay, Creeples. But we've got to hide them until we can figure out what to do with them."

"Easy peasy. We each carry two Creeples in our backpacks, show our faces in class, then scram and meet up in our dorm room." Spigs beamed at his solution. "And T-Ray, you start workin' on plan B."

"I've got Tatz." Peabo smiled.

"And I'll take Naz."

T-Ray sighed and collected the four cuddling Creeples, handing the orange one to Spigs. "And this one. It's all you."

"Why this one?" Spigs took the orange Creeple. "WHOA! Whew! Did it just—?"

"Yep." T-Ray scrunched her nose. "It's a little gaseous."

She handed the blue one to Peabo. "This one smells fine, but it's super strong."

"WE know," Spigs and Peabo said.

T-Ray gently positioned the green and purple Creeples inside her backpack. "Keep them hidden, and let's rendezvous after roll call."

Spigs and Peabo followed her example and gently snuggled the Creeples deep in their backpacks.

They exited through the Bio-Engineering building's rear door, but didn't notice Dean Smathers had entered from the front.

Smathers hurried through the halls as if he were on a mission. He made his way to the Genomic Analytical lounge and dashed straight for the hidden wall safe in the back of the refrigerator. A few clicks on the dial opened the metal panel. He reached inside for his priceless treasure and felt around. NOTHING! Panicked, he tossed all the soda cans and food containers on the floor. His desperate search came to the unimaginable conclusion that his precious Draconem Serum was—GONE!

CHAPTER 9

Skoota, Coco, Royal, Beezer, Naz, and Tatz

T-Ray usually looked forward to her first-period class, Necrosis Physiology. Students playfully referred to it as Zombification 101. But not T-Ray—she was strictly by the book. Nevertheless, her life had completely spun out of control in the last eight hours. She had an awful feeling her chances of remaining in class were slim to none, since her two Creeples hadn't stopped tussling in her backpack the entire walk from the Bio-Engineering building. She settled in her seat, but foolishly thought she could convince the Creeples to follow simple decorum.

She partially unzipped the backpack and leaned in. "Look, I really, really need you two to stay still. Do not move a muscle."

T-Ray glanced up to see a few students had trickled in. She studied the Creeples again, which confirmed her suspicion; they hadn't understood her instructions. T-Ray knew some Spanish and French, and even Latin. So just in case, she tried all three. The Creeples responded with *CLICK-CLACKING* noises.

"Do you know what I'm saying?" T-Ray sighed as the green and purple Creeples peeked out of the backpack, exposing their oscillating mustard-yellow eyes. Concerned they needed fresh air, she unzipped the bag wider, which revealed their mischievous grins and crooked teeth.

She opened her Necrosis Physiology textbook and whispered, "Class is about to start. Now hush, you two." The green Creeple ignored her, but the purple Creeple moved its head back and forth. T-Ray smiled. "You seem kind of regal. And purple *is* associated with royalty. Okay, Royal it is." She scrunched her eyes together. "Wait, no, I'm NOT naming you. But if I did—"

As if on cue, the green Creeple looked at her with a vacant expression.

"Okay, okay! I give in. Now let me see—" T-Ray scanned the room. Professor Twombly had motivational quotes placed around the room. Her favorite was a famous quote by designer Coco Chanel: "Don't spend time beating on a wall, hoping to transform it into a door." T-Ray spent a good deal of her life beating on walls, hoping to transform them into doors. She knew the moral of the lesson—do what you can with the situation presented to you, and try not to transform the impossible into something else.

She whispered to the green Creeple, "So, I'll call you Coco. Now, both of you . . . shhhhh."

T-Ray zipped up the backpack but left a small gap for air. She smiled nervously at the students who flooded into the room before the bell. Suddenly, the backpack bumped and bulged, as if two possums were fighting inside. T-Ray wedged the backpack between her feet on the floor.

"HUSH! Or else!" T-Ray poked the bag a few times, prompting several odd looks from students sitting around her.

"Ms. Rogers, is there something you'd like to share with the class?" Professor Twombly looked at her prized pupil.

"Um . . . nope, not at this time, Professor. Thanks for asking." T-Ray grimaced. As much as she enjoyed studying the biological functions of living matter from the regeneration of lifeless tissue, T-Ray had more immediate concerns. "Ah, may I . . . uh, be excused?"

"But class has started, Ms. Rogers."

"Yes. But, you know, I forgot to—" T-Ray's stumbling was cut short. She reached down to seize her quivering backpack, but it hurtled from her arms. Two stubby ashen-gray legs with three toes on each oversized foot popped out of the backpack. The Creeples' legs splayed out to the sides and scampered out of the classroom. Startled students dove out of the way from the astonishing scene.

T-Ray slapped a hand over her mouth in shock and let out a muffled yelp. She raced after the scurrying backpack, through the building's corridors, knocking approaching students to the side. She caught up and swooped down in time to gather up the Creeples before they slid down the stairs' handrails. Her phone beeped. Someone had tagged her in a retweet of Yapper's latest:

#FreshmanBrainiac has baffling backpack that scampers!

T-Ray bared her teeth in an anxious grimace. She'd forgotten the school's Twitter queen was in her Necrosis Physiology class.

On the way to Spigs and Peabo's dorm, T-Ray whipped through the school's lost and found kiosk and snagged a bundle of small T-shirts, then barreled across the Quad. Her mind was racing; this Creeples situation was just insane and out of control, and she hated feeling out of control. Other than her sister Kelsey's congenital heart defect, T-Ray's life had been perfectly coordinated and controlled. That was, until Spigs and Peabo were forced upon her. Both boys had a more cavalier outlook on life. Nevertheless, T-Ray reminded herself obstacles were intended to make one stronger, and only the weak avoided them. She continued her jaunt across campus to the boys' dorm and nearly made it when a booming baritone voice blared behind her.

"FREEZE, young missy."

T-Ray stopped in her tracks, then spun around only to square up to Aberdasher Academy's finest. Chief Homer McTaggart and his young deputy glared at her in their matching khaki shorts, long-sleeved dusty-blue collared shirts with the school's security logo emblazoned on them, and white tube socks extended to their knees. She snickered under her breath and wondered how ANYONE hoped to be taken seriously while in long shorts and knee socks. Chief McTaggart was in his mid-fifties, perpetually sun drenched, and quite plump and had the temperament of an irritated hippo. And the scuttlebutt among the students was for complete self-restraint when dealing with Deputy Whipsnade. Being a five-foot-five twenty-year-old and having flunked out of the local police academy, he carried a heavy chip on his scrawny shoulders.

"Where are ya running off to, little lady?" McTaggart asked.

Deputy Whipsnade unclipped his industrial measuring tape from his belt—ready for any offensive attire.

"Um. Nowhere." T-Ray muscled her squirming backpack over her shoulders and secured it tight, in hopes the campus cops wouldn't notice it. "Sorry I was running, Officer McTaggart. Just . . . ah, feeling kinda queasy."

"You don't look sick," Deputy Whipsnade snapped. What the deputy lacked in street smarts, he made up for in excessive by-the-book enthusiasm. "Let's run her in, Chief. On a four-twenty. Evading law enforcement personnel."

"Stand down, Deputy." Chief McTaggart gave T-Ray the once-over. "Shouldn't you be in class, Ms. . . . ?"

"Rogers. I should. But, like, I . . . I really feel super sick. I could blow my guts any minute." T-Ray glanced at the officers. But no response from them. She started *gagging* and *gurgling*, pressing her fingers to her mouth as if a gusher was coming. Again, no reaction, so she upped her game. "So last night I ordered this deep-dish pizza with tuna and eggs, layered with corned beef hash, cabbage, and mounds of mayo. And topped with anchovies, oysters, and liver pâté."

"Okay, okay, we get it," Deputy Whipsnade interrupted after an air gulp. They both stepped back from T-Ray.

Creeples!

"What's in the rucksack?" Chief McTaggart asked.

"Ah, just books and girly things."

"I'm sure I saw it wiggle, Chief. You transportin' exotic animals, fruits, or vegetables not indigenous to our great state?" Whipsnade spouted as he took another step back.

"What? No! Can I please go?" T-Ray's backpack jerked back and forth, so she shifted her feet to mask the Creeples' actions.

"Let's see what's in that bag," McTaggart ordered.

"Okay, Chief. I'll come clean, but it's . . . top secret." T-Ray wiped sweat from her forehead with her sleeve.

"Ah-ha! CONTRABAND! I knew it," Whipsnade blustered. "Want me to cuff her, Ace?"

"Not necessary, Deputy. Young lady, I think you're gonna need to open that backpack, or I'm gonna have to take you in to see Dean Smathers for questioning."

"Officer McTaggart, that's just it." T-Ray voiced a somber tone. "I'm a robotics lab assistant, and in *this* very bag are the most advanced scientific gizmos for a covert operation commissioned by our distinguished Dean Smathers for paramilitary use. I must get them back to the lab and make sure they don't fall into enemy hands." Playing up her top-secret role, T-Ray leaned forward and whispered, "And if they do, look out—because then *you've* got some explaining to do. To the . . . DEAN!"

"HUH? Well now, why didn't you say so in the first place? If it's for our illustrious dean and our military, then I'm behind it one hundred ten percent. Now run along, Ms. Rogers." Chief McTaggart saluted. "And I wouldn't mind if you mentioned our full cooperation to Dean Smathers."

. . .

Peabo strolled in a zigzag pattern across the Quad, straining to secure his squirming backpack.

Students hustling to class gawked at the *CLICK-CLACKING* sound echoing from his backpack. When two Latina girls approached, Peabo slung off the backpack and hugged it firmly to stop the Creeples from fidgeting.

"Quit trippin', you two. Juniors approaching at ten o'clock."

Peabo swaggered over to block the approaching girls. He cleared his throat for his next performance—a deep-voiced upperclassman. "*Hola*, ladies. What's poppin'?"

The taller girl scoffed, and the other inky-haired beauty wrinkled her nose. Peabo tried to salvage the moment. "Goin' my way?"

"Really? That's the best you've got?" the taller girl asked.

"And what's up with your voice? You sick or something?" the other said, running a hand down her thick braid.

The backpack THRASHED out of Peabo's grasp. Two ashen-gray arms and legs popped out and scurried toward the shocked girls. "Aghhhh!!" Peabo lunged for the backpack.

"What's IN there?" The tall girl staggered back and clutched her friend's arm.

"Oh, this?" Peabo jostled the elfin limbs back inside. "Uuh, an extraordinary science experiment. Can't go into specifics." Peabo flashed an insincere grin, back on his game. "So, how 'bout we chill over a Spazzle at the Student Union later?" The *CLICK-CLACKING* backpack jerked and wiggled, which forced Peabo to do a pirouette.

"Are you using . . . *puppies* in your experiment?" the tall girl asked.

"You some kind of animal abuser?" The girl with the braid put one hand on her hip and waved a finger with the other.

Peabo was caught off guard again. "Yes. What? NO! Just a couple of naughty gnomes. That's all. So, how 'bout it?"

"Forget it. Hashtag, Lame Freshman Loser."

"So long, weirdo."

The girls hurried off, giggling and shaking their heads. Tatz and Skoota popped out their yellow- and blue-plumed heads. Peabo lifted the backpack close to his face. "Remind me never to use you two as my wingmen. 'Easy peasy,' *my* butt! I'm now radioactive. Girls will never talk to me, like, EVER!"

• • •

Peabo and Spigs had hunkered down in their third-floor dorm room when T-Ray arrived. She released her restless Creeples and collapsed on the beanbag to catch her breath.

"Didn't you two go to class?" T-Ray asked.

Peabo was curled up on his bunkbed in a fetal position, one pillow between his legs and the other covering his head. "MY world is ruined," he whined, voice muffled by the pillow.

"What's with him?"

"*Puhleeze*, don't ask. Or you'll hear the heartbreakin' tale of the downfall of the once great Pablo Torres," Spigs grumbled.

"And what about you?"

"Nah, didn't even bother. Beezer was butt blastin' noxious

fumes, and I didn't want my classmates to think it was me. Could've cramped my social life, ya know. Man, those silent-but-deadly farts are the worst kind." The orange Creeple turned and smiled at Spigs, as if it understood its name.

"Are there *good* kinds?"

"I have NO social life to cramp." Peabo was still sulking, face buried in the pillow.

"Have you fed your Creeples?" T-Ray inquired, ignoring Peabo's cries.

"Haven't really thought what they eat. So, how were yours?"

"Oh, just *fine,*" T-Ray said, dripping with sarcasm. "They super embarrassed me in front of my Necrosis Physiology class." She scowled at the purple Creeple, who was leafing through Spigs's comic books.

"Don't be bitter, T-Ray. They're only a few hours old—still lil' brats." Spigs offered a little levity.

T-Ray cracked a grin at the green Creeple, who raced in circles like a dog chasing its tail. Eventually, it got so dizzy it zigzagged over to T-Ray and passed out in her lap. "Coco's fast, but not too smart. I'll work on it." She reached out and tickled the purple Creeple under the chin. "Now, Royal appears highly intelligent."

"Royal and Coco?" Spigs called out. "Thought we weren't supposed to name 'em. Hmm?"

"I mean, we can't keep calling them . . . IT," T-Ray said defensively. She held up a stuffed plastic bag. "And I figured they should probably have some clothes." She dumped out the clothes on Spigs's lower bunkbed. The Creeples rushed over and tossed and flung them in the air. In a matter of minutes, the dorm room was blanketed in children's T-shirts and pants. Peabo and Spigs started laughing. T-Ray finally beamed at the truly ridiculous sight.

"Good thinkin', T-Ray. Buck-naked Creeples are miserable Creeples," Spigs joked.

Skoota and Naz squeezed into kids' jeans. "No underwear? Goin' commando? Now THAT'S priceless." Peabo fist-bumped Spigs, while T-Ray shook her head.

"Royal, pick out a T-shirt and tell the others." T-Ray nudged the purple Creeple, who waddled over and grabbed a faded T-shirt. Royal *CLICK-CLACKED*, and the other five Creeples perked up. Their mustardy eyes oscillated wildly, enormous ears twitching back and forth, and they all stampeded for the discarded clothing.

Peabo officiated Skoota's and Tatz's tug-of-war with a T-shirt. Naturally, Skoota strong-armed Tatz. But Tatz was contented with a yellow sweatshirt that matched its hair. *No Mistakes—Just Happy Little Accidents!* was printed across the front. "Now *that's* definitely appropriate," Peabo laughed.

T-Ray unfolded her chosen T-shirt from the batch and dressed the green Creeple, who napped in her lap. She wrangled Coco's limp body into a bright red T-shirt that read *Short, Sassy, Cute, and Classy!*

Spigs's Creeples were uninterested in getting dressed. "Hey, fellas. Put 'em on?" Neither one heard him, so Spigs put his index fingers in the side of his mouth and blew. All the Creeples spun around and stared up at him. Naz's six tentacles bent in the direction of the whistling. Spigs traipsed over to the bed and picked through the remaining shirts. Naz slipped into a retro Donkey Kong tank top. Spigs handed Beezer a midriff top, but its belly flopped out beneath the tiny shirt. "*Not* a good look there, Beezer."

As if in response, the orange Creeple trumpeted from its bulbous wazoo a long, lingering fart.

"GAUHHHH!" T-Ray pinched her nose.

Spigs and Peabo couldn't stop snickering. They held their noses and talked in an exaggerated high-pitched tone.

"Did you notice all their reactions when Spigs whistled? They must have super-sensitive hearing," Peabo stated.

"So what are we going to do with them?" T-Ray queried. "I can see it now on Yapper's Twitter account: 'Private academy quarantined for mysterious medical blunder—**#3Banished4Life!**'"

"Could hide 'em at that travelin' carnival, right outside campus," Spigs offered.

"We can't hand them over to just anybody!" Peabo said. "Plus, those carnival owners aren't known for being nice to the animals they put in their shows."

Spigs flopped back on his bed and gazed at Peabo's bunk slates with brows scrunched. "Well, we could run a background check on that carny dude."

Peabo hopped off his bed and booted up his laptop at his desk.

Naz had plopped down on Spigs's chest. A staring contest ensued, which Spigs promptly lost. Naz's wonky, vacillating lizard-like eyes gave Spigs dizzy spells.

"Yep, just like I thought," Peabo said. "There are several reports on that carnival owner, Gideon Flitch. A total smarmy dude. Multiple instances of failed safety inspections and several allegations of animal neglect. And has a side business as an exterminator."

"Certainly explains why it's a *travelin'* carnival," Spigs uttered.

"We are NOT taking the Creeples there." T-Ray clutched Coco and Royal to her like a protective mama bear.

"This Flitch does handle exotic animals for a livin'. He may have an idea about what to do with 'em," Spigs insisted.

"Absolutely NOT!" T-Ray's scowl settled that argument.

"Our campaign is fading. Remember our original goal, guys—to fund Professor Bodkins's peer review?" Peabo logged off. "I'm just lost at our next move."

"Okay, listen up, Lab Rats. Got an idea for plan B that will cover our funding issues AND explain away the Creeples' sudden appearance," Spigs announced. "We rename our crowdfunding profile The Creeples Channel by rebranding Peabo's YouTube channel. So the Creeples are sorta like anthropomorphic beings—human qualities and all—so we pass 'em off as a top-secret research experiment based inside the Bio-Engineering department."

"Yeah! And we goad Yapper into running the story. It'd go viral in an hour." Peabo flashed his pearly whites.

"I . . . I just don't know." T-Ray shook her head. "That could be dangerous for the Creeples."

"The danger is the unknown repercussions by the adults if they're discovered," Spigs cautioned.

The trio sat silent, contemplating their predicament. Beezer, Coco, and Royal lined up for a swan dive off the top bunk and each plunked down on the soft beanbag chair. Tatz was wedged headfirst in the NERF basketball net attached to the door. Its potbelly prevented it from sliding through the net. Skoota and Beezer grabbed the ceiling fan blades, spinning them so fast their short legs flapped outward. Biscuit cowered under the bed, hiding from the bedlam.

"So hear *me* out, T-Ray." Peabo held out his hands to form a square that he peered through with one eye like a movie director looking through a camera lens. "The Creeples Channel could be a look behind the scenes of our amazing genetic discovery—Gooze and its astonishing anthropomorphic creations. It's sorta intelligent design brought to you by the Lab Rats at Aberdasher Academy of Science. The funding would explode with *that* hook."

"He's kinda makin' sense," Spigs said as he pulled Tatz through the basketball hoop. "Slam dunk!"

"NO! He's *not* making sense!" T-Ray flipped through Spigs's Cryptozoology textbook. "We have to know exactly what we've created. Control the narrative—for now. Got that?" She narrowed her eyes and pointed a finger like a dagger at the two, then gestured at the Creeples, who were frolicking about the room. "We may have to bring Professor Bodkins in on Team Gooze. But for now, it's imperative we keep them hidden, or people may try to take them from us." She lowered her voice to a solemn tone. "And use them for nefarious research."

Peabo's and Spigs's expressions turned glum.

"So, status quo, for now. We have to play this smart." T-Ray adjusted her glasses with an authoritative nod.

Creeples!

The boys agreed with nods of their own.

But it was apparent the teens knew it would be merely a matter of time before the Creeples were discovered.

CHAPTER 10

Mystical Mischief and Magical Mayhem

Spigs scurried around the dorm room like a stooped old man, trying to scoop up the Creeples, but they scattered like scared alley cats. "T-Ray, you mentioned feedin' 'em." Spigs secured Naz on one hip as he lunged for Tatz. "Ya think they're hungry?"

"OUCH, Skoota! More like *hangry*." Skoota was perched on Peabo's shoulder, wearing his Snapchat video glasses and twisting Peabo's ears back and forth. "THOSE don't detach! Skoota!"

Spigs finally corralled Tatz, but Naz wriggled free and scampered to the other side of the room, legs splayed outward. Spigs flopped on his bed with a huff, giving up on corralling the Creeples. He grabbed his laptop to do a quick search on their peculiar running style.

"Wonder what they eat." T-Ray popped her head up from the Cryptozoology textbook she'd been studying. "I'm having difficulty identifying a mammal connected to the Creeples." She pushed her horn-rimmed glasses farther up her nose. "Wonder if the Creeples are carnivorous."

"One way to find out." Peabo planted one foot on his desk and shoved, rolling his chair over to their mini fridge. The inquisitive Creeples perked up, *CLICK-CLACKED*, and wiggled their oversize ears. Royal waddled over for a peek inside the fridge. It gave a few *CLICK-CLACKS*, and the other five joined in, foraging through the mostly expired food products. The ravenous Creeples gobbled down their first taste of savory morsels: week-old pizza slices, stale ramen noodles, soggy chili fries, dried-out macaroni and cheese, mushy PB&J sandwiches, and Biscuit's half-eaten tuna. Skoota experienced a steep learning curve, as bursts from the Cheez 'Em can spewed inside its ears and not its mouth. Skoota turned the aerosol can of liquid cheese toward the arching, hissing Biscuit. The outcome wasn't going to be pretty for the cat.

Tatz strained mightily to figure out how to open the can of Spazzle. Its rotating eyes focused intently. It bent its head down, ignited its two energy bolts to torch an opening, and slurped down the effervescent liquid in one gulp. *BRRRUUUPPPP!* Out came a gut-busting SONIC BELCH!

"WHOA! That went nuclear!" Spigs laughed as he retrieved his emergency supply of Spazzle from under the bed and handed it out to all the Creeples. "Didja get that?"

"Yep! I'll save it for the pilot episode." Peabo smiled, his Snapchat glasses in place to capture the chaotic scene.

"Remember, we *can't* go public with this," T-Ray warned.

"Can't go public . . . yet!" Peabo corrected her. "But footage of their bizarre behavior will only help us study them."

T-Ray tapped her chin. "I guess having video data *is* a prudent plan."

The teens turned their full attention on the overstuffed Creeples, who had now guzzled all the Spazzle. With the combination of caffeine and sugar coursing through their tiny veins, they cranked up their boisterous shenanigans, such as barreling headlong at each other and slamming their oversized bellies together. Royal was the last one standing and did a gyrating dance in front of the others sprawled on the floor.

"Have you boys forgotten something?" T-Ray smirked as Skoota and Beezer lined up for another belly bump. "What goes in a Creeple *must* come out a Creeple."

"What'd ya say?" Spigs was engaged in a video on his laptop.

"Wait. You're right!" Peabo tore through the closet and pulled out bags of kitty litter.

"Look here." Spigs waved T-Ray over. "The Creeples sorta waddle like penguins, right? But their wacky running style is more like these Australian frill-necked lizards." He pointed to the video.

Peabo frantically poured cat litter in as many empty boxes as he could find.

"Let's test out your theory . . . Coco, RUN! Come on." T-Ray gently nudged her Creeple until it scampered around the room.

"They splay out their legs side to side, like those kooky Aussie lizards. An Aussie-splay run," Spigs stated.

Tatz had unscrewed the lightbulb from a lamp and stuck one of its fat fingers into the socket. *ZAAAAP!* Electricity discharged from Tatz's two head bolts. The teens ducked for cover by tucking their heads between their knees.

Peabo peered over at Spigs. "This is just WAY over the top. Are you holding out on us, bro?"

"Wh—whaddaya mean?"

"Come to think of it. Spill it. That serum!" T-Ray shot Spigs the same stinging glare Aunt Gussy would give him when she found out he'd eaten her bonbons—an unsettling combination of intense antagonism and decided disgust.

Spigs sheepishly dug out the remnants of the glass tube's label from his pants pocket. "Here's the thing. We desperately needed blood, right? So, I hacked into a hidden safe in the back of the Genomic Analytical lounge's refrigerator and found the serum."

"I can barely read the label. Drac ... Serum?" Peabo tried to decipher the faded, crumpled label.

"It's obviously the Creeples' mysterious DNA," T-Ray surmised.

"The fact is we hastily hatched a harebrained idea to save Professor Bodkins's department and OUR butts. And it sorta went wrong. Okay?" Spigs produced a cringing grin and shrugged in his own defense.

"Now *that's* the world's biggest understatement," Peabo laughed. "But he does have a point. We got involved in an experiment we weren't qualified to do."

Spigs picked up Royal and cuddled it. "Just look how creepy cute they are."

"Let's round them up and grab a selfie," Peabo said.

T-Ray stomped her foot and let out an exasperated growl. "Do you two realize that if this serum was locked in a secret safe in the lounge, it means it belongs to an administrator who's going to be furious when they discover it's missing?"

"I sorta have a feelin' which administrator it belongs to. Do the initials *A. S. S.* ring a bell?" Spigs said awkwardly.

"DEAN SMATHERS? How could you?" T-Ray collapsed onto the bed and put her hands over her face. "UGH, I can see it now." She groaned and made a phone gesture with her thumb and pinkie to her ear. "Hey, Mom, uh . . . well, I've been expelled from my dream school because me and my teammates stole something extremely valuable from the dean."

"I'm sorry! But what's done is done," Spigs expressed in a backhanded way. "So let's concentrate on the now. We hafta let Professor Bodkins in on everything. Let's get some pics of the Creeples to show her."

T-Ray groaned in agreement.

Peabo extended his selfie stick, trying to fit all nine of them in the shot. "Stop moving, Skoota, Tatz."

"Coco, quit squirming." T-Ray grabbed the green Creeple.

"Put it on wide-angle and take THE dang picture!" Spigs squawked, swatting away Skoota's blue and Royal's purple plumes of hair.

Peabo could snap only a few photos before the caffeine-fueled Creeples resumed their mischievousness. With its long, sloppy tongue, Coco snatched T-Ray's glasses off her face. Skoota dug out brown gunk from its ears, rolled it up, and flung it at Spigs. Spigs ducked, but the gross gunk ball bounced against the walls like Silly Putty.

Creeples!

Naz's six tentacles had a firm hold on Biscuit, licking the Cheez'Em off the gooey cat. Naz started to heave and coughed out a fur ball the size of a baseball. Beezer was wearing Spigs's CPAP facemask and had hijacked the Roomba robotic vacuum cleaner. It zoomed around the room detonating FARTS like the sound of a revved-up motorboat, gassing every square inch of the boys' room.

"EEEEWW!" T-Ray screeched.

"Beezer sure found a way to spread its talent." Spigs laughed and high-fived Peabo.

"That's SO disgusting," T-Ray whined. "Now c'mon, it's almost noon. We have to tell Professor Bodkins." As soon as T-Ray opened the door, Beezer zoomed between her legs into the hallway, riding the Roomba. T-Ray shrieked and lunged to shut the door but tripped over the other Creeples scrambling after Beezer. In a flash, the Creeples were all at the opposite end of the hallway, *CLICK-CLACKING* wildly.

"GET THEM!" T-Ray shouted. The teens gave chase down the hall and around the corner to a dead end. The Creeples stood motionless against the wall, like naughty kids caught in the act.

T-Ray edged toward them with arms outstretched, cooing, "Royal, we have to go back into the room."

Royal cocked its head, as if considering. Skoota had eyed a small metal flap on the opposing wall. With a *CLICK-CLACK* and ears wiggling, it waddled over and leaped through the flap, tumbling down a circular metal duct. The rest of the Creeples Aussie-splayed over and dove headfirst, sliding down on their potbellies.

118

T-Ray, Peabo, and Spigs WAILED!

"They're headin' for the laundry room! To the stairs!" Spigs yelped.

The teens raced down three flights of stairs to the basement, in time to witness the last Creeple, Naz, shoot out from the chute and ricochet high off a mound of dirty laundry bags. The toppling bags scattered the few students in the laundry room. Before Spigs could grab Naz's red plume of hair, it jumped up and Aussie-splay ran across the room to the other Creeples. Two girls in the far corner squealed and clung to each other at the bizarre sight. A boy studying a textbook atop a washing machine hopped on a countertop and squawked in a frightened tone, "What . . . What . . . ARE—?"

Beezer had climbed inside a front-load washer, and Tatz slammed closed the lid. A red flashing button lured Tatz to press the spin cycle button.

Peabo shrieked and rushed over to pull out a drenched, dizzy Beezer. The woozy and wet Creeple banged into an ironing board, causing the iron to slide off and thump Tatz's thick noggin. Now that's called karma!

Coco and Royal, hanging from the light fixtures, dumped laundry detergent over two unsuspecting students who had just ventured into the frenzy. The blue-powdered students, now resembling Smurfs, sprinted for the door but slipped in a puddle of liquid softener and bowled over Spigs and Peabo.

Beezer and Skoota grabbed pillows from a laundry basket and whacked Naz upside its head in a burst of feathers. Naz snatched a bag of dirty clothes and walloped them in return. In a matter of minutes, the laundry room was filled with feather-covered, detergent-shrouded students and Creeples.

Seventy-six-year-old Newt Frisby, the laundry attendant, emerged from the utility storeroom, still lethargic from his mid-morning nap. As per his daily routine, his hair net was secured around his thinning gray locks, his rubber gloves were snapped on, and a clothespin was clamped on his nose. Now, he was ready to tackle the students' usual filthiness. But as his eyes scanned the room for his push broom, his jaw dropped at the chaotic scene. Swirling feathers fluttered into his gaping mouth.

Mr. Frisby spat out a flurry of feathers, as if he'd consumed a whole chicken. "Jumpin' Jehoshaphat! Mad munchkins galore!" he SHRIEKED. Mr. Frisby raced for the exit but turned and careened headfirst into a row of lockers.

The quick-thinking teens had secured the disheveled Creeples in pillowcases and hauled them back up to the room before any more disaster struck. The trio had just made it to the third floor of the dorm when Peabo got a Twitter alert on his phone.

#MomentousMysteryOnCampus!

#MischiefMayhem Bizarre neon hair found in laundry room bedlam!

Peabo then received a direct text from Yapper. He read it aloud: "'P-Man, you and your Lab Rats were in the LR. Got a scoop about some crazy creatures there? Can U confirm?' What do I tell her?" Peabo grimaced.

"Okay, now we start to implement plan B—that a classified experiment got loose," T-Ray affirmed. "BUT don't go live yet,

Peabo. Tell Yapper they're animatronic robots from the Robotics department and not flesh and blood anthropomorphic beings. Insist they aren't dangerous, so no need to panic. Agreed?"

Peabo eyed Spigs for approval. Spigs flipped up his thumb. Peabo cautiously worded their plan B text to Yapper. Not two minutes after he'd pressed SEND, Yapper tweeted out:

#RumorsOverload Six Animatronic Robots skedaddle from school's experiment!

T-Ray held open the dorm room's door for Spigs, who strained with a heavy, wriggling pillowcase. But Spigs froze before stepping over the threshold. An envelope with Dean Smathers's office address had been slipped under their door. He handed off his squirming pillowcase to Peabo, who nearly collapsed under the weight of the Creeples.

Peabo unleashed them but was overcome by the heavy aroma of lavender from the soapy, soggy creatures.

Spigs studied the note that he pulled from the ripped envelope. He turned pale.

"So what is it?" T-Ray was chasing down a drenched Creeple with a towel. "A note from Rachell? Hmm!"

"We're being summoned to Dean Smathers's office, immediately." Spigs flopped on the beanbag chair.

"Why does Smathers—?" T-Ray glared at Spigs and then looked at the Creeples. "He KNOWS! But . . . how did he connect us?" Panic filled her voice.

"It's our moment of truth." Peabo was trying to wipe gunky feathers off Naz and Tatz.

Creeples!

"Truth? This is a moment for a big fat lie." Spigs struggled to remove the soapy T-shirts from Beezer and Skoota.

Peabo scanned the note. "It's official—on Smathers's stationary. This is NOT good, but we hafta see him."

"But . . . can we leave them alone?" T-Ray questioned with a trace of anxiety.

"We have no choice. Anyway, they finally look exhausted." Peabo pointed to them all curled up on Spigs's bed.

Spigs wandered over to the window, retrieved Biscuit's bushy catnip plant from the outside ledge, and placed the perennial herb plant near the makeshift sandboxes. He'd left the window cracked for fresh air in case Beezer's overactive bazooka butt discharged. "Biscuit," Spigs whispered as he dug deep in their clothes hamper, where the tabby was quite content. "We'll be right back. Be a gracious host and watch over our diminutive dwellers."

T-Ray, Spigs, and Peabo tiptoed out and locked the dorm door behind them so there was no way for the Creeples to escape . . . this time!

CHAPTER 11

The Catnip Crazies

With the click of the door lock, Biscuit crept out of the hamper, arched, and stretched his body for a few seconds. He pranced over to the catnip plant and peered back at the snoozing Creeples. Biscuit let out a mild hiss, as if to say, "Don't you dare come between me and my catnip!" The lethargic Creeples lazily opened their mustard-yellow eyes and watched Biscuit sniff and delicately chew on a leaf. He took his time, savoring every bite. Moments later, the catnip's nepetalactone compound kicked in. The herb's oils triggered the sensory neurons, making Biscuit equally dizzy and euphoric. He'd now entered the catnip craze; he rolled, flipped, drooled, and rubbed his butt across the rug. Shortly, the catnip's effect dissipated. The blissful cat unsteadily climbed back into the clothes hamper and zoned out.

Creeples!

The befuddled Creeples were now wide awake and had assembled, ears bent forward, a sign they intended to taste this delicacy. But they waited for Royal to give the sign. The purple Creeple *CLICK-CLACKED* and wiggled its ears in opposite directions, and they all leaped from Spigs's bed. In a flash, the Creeples bounded over and proceeded to devour the catnip plant. *CHOMP! CHOMP! CHOMP!* Potting soil and leaves swirled in a mini dust tornado. And once the debris settled, only scattered leaves, twigs, and roots remained. Minutes later, the Creeples descended into their catnip craze, but with a PROFOUND outcome.

The herb's chemical brought an extreme euphoric reaction to the Creeples. They drooled, rolled, and flipped about like acrobats. And they scooted their dumpy butts across the rug, as if they had a bad itch to scratch. Every muscle fiber in the Creeples' ashen-gray bodies constricted. Inexplicably, they became immobile and rigid. All six tipped over on their backs, with their arms and legs pointing skyward like the famous fainting goats.

For five minutes, the incapacitated Creeples quivered and twitched. But then came a dramatic METAMORPHOSIS. The creepy-cute Creeples totally transformed: their skin darkened, and menacing arching eyebrows and frightening piercing teeth appeared. Their mustardy eyes turned to black marbles. Biscuit cowered in his hamper as the creatures went BERSERK and demolished the entire room in sheer mayhem. Biscuit let out a blistering yowl and a long hiss as they tossed his hamper against the wall. It was as if the room had been hit by an F5 tornado. Food splattered against the walls. Clothes clung to the ceiling fan and light fixtures. The furniture that wasn't screwed down had been overturned.

BEEP! BEEP! BEEP! echoed outside of the cracked window. The Creeples stood motionless. They waddled over and plastered their morphed faces against the windowpane. Three stories below, a garbage truck had backed up to the dormitory's dumpster. Skoota pried open the window, and the six transformed Creeples leaped out, somersaulting into the truck's trash bed. At that same moment, the dorm room door gradually creaked open, a full key ring dangling from the lock.

• • •

"I have no record of any appointment with Dean Smathers," Wanda Wainwright, Smathers's surly secretary, informed the teens as she reapplied her bright red lipstick.

"But we received a note about a meeting," T-Ray insisted.

"Listen, youngins. I have *no* record," Ms. Wainwright responded with a curt smile that revealed a glob of lipstick on her left front tooth. "If it ain't in my book, you're off the hook. Besides, the dean isn't even here."

Spigs threw his arms up and turned to Peabo and T-Ray with a shrug.

"Now, if you'll excuse me." Ms. Wainwright stood. "It's precisely twelve thirty, and Wanda Wainwright always takes her much-deserved lunch now. And not one minute later!" She grabbed her thermos and a brown bag and excused herself.

"Must've been a prank," Peabo said.

"A prank? But why us?" T-Ray exclaimed.

"No one knows we created the Creeples. Do they?" Spigs lifted his hat to scratch his brain.

Peabo wandered over to the window at the sound of a commotion outside.

"Who would or could send us a note on the dean's letterhead?" T-Ray's eyes scanned the reception room in thought.

Peabo anxiously waved for Spigs to come to the window.

"Uuh, T-Ray," Spigs said as he rubbed his eyes, but the scene outside was still there.

T-Ray was lost in a line of reasoning. "Now, Horace has direct access to Dean Smathers. He's always delivering notes from the dean to teachers. So, Horace—"

"T-RAY!" Spigs cried out.

"Hush, I'm thinking." She snapped her fingers. "Horace must have told the dean we were in the Bio-Engineering building last night. And by now Dean Smathers probably knows that his serum is missing ... so maybe he sent Horace to search for it in the dorm room." She expressed a beaming at her deduction. "But ... if the dean had sent Horace, wouldn't he be here in his office to delay us while Horace searched?" T-Ray nervously bit the knuckle of her index finger. "We've got to get back to the room."

"T-RAY!" both boys shouted.

"What?" T-Ray reluctantly strolled over to the window, where she got her first glimpse of what Spigs and Peabo had been too stunned to articulate.

A garbage truck flashed its "Frequent Stops" warning lights

and cruised down the campus street. The Creeples swung from the back like sanitation workers, then LEAPED off and Aussie-splay ran toward the Student Union and cafeteria.

"LOOK! LOOK at 'em! They've . . changed!" Spigs howled. Peabo and T-Ray watched in shock with gaping mouths.

"Like some kind of . . . metamorphosis!" T-Ray squinted, as if that would change what she was seeing.

"Methinks a lot more folks are gonna get a big helpin' of Creeples soon." Spigs sucked in air through his teeth.

"But how did they get out?" Peabo asked.

"Forget that. Just LOOK at 'em. They've transformed." Spigs pointed as the Creeples vanished inside the Student Union.

T-Ray took charge. "Okay, plan of action—divide and conquer. You guys go after the Creeples. I'll locate Professor Bodkins."

• • •

T-Ray raced toward Professor Bodkins's office but cut a sharp corner, slamming into Rachell—knocking her textbooks to the ground. T-Ray forced a smile and helped retrieve her books. She did not like Rachell, for several reasons. She was an uppity snob. She was everything T-Ray was not: popular and fashion conscious. And Spigs was smitten by her.

"Where are you off to in such a hurry?" Rachell patted down her bangs and tucked her shoulder-length hair behind her ears.

T-Ray scrunched her brows, puzzled by the sudden attention. "I have a meeting with Professor Bodkins." She tried to sidestep Rachell, but the sophomore blocked her way.

"I hear the professor's genomic research is a medical break-through?"

"Um, yeah." T-Ray was confused by Rachell's odd inquiry. "But her funding is limited, so—"

"Ah, that's *too* bad." Rachell placed her hand on T-Ray's shoulder and gently squeezed. "Let me know if you ever want to talk about it. Later, girl."

"Yeah, sure." T-Ray shrugged off Rachell's condescension. She got to Professor Bodkins's office right as the professor had unwrapped a tuna sandwich.

"To what do I owe the honor, Theresa? More 3D bio-printer instructions?" Professor Bodkins took a bite of her sandwich.

T-Ray cleared her throat. "Professor, ah, there's been a bit of a . . . situation." She hung her head and shifted from foot to foot, her stomach knotted up with nerves.

"Should I be worried?"

"Uum, probably." T-Ray pulled her phone from her pocket. "Actually, most definitely." She sat beside the professor and scrolled through her pictures. "And you probably should finish your sandwich first. I don't look good with tuna and mayo sprayed on my face."

Professor Bodkins rewrapped her half-eaten sandwich and took a big swallow of iced tea. She looked at T-Ray with motherly concern. "Now, what's up?"

"These are . . . Creeples." T-Ray tilted her phone screen toward the professor, scrolling through the photos.

"Okay." The professor relaxed with an amused smile and took another sip of tea.

"Yes, well, uh. They are . . . the results of our . . . latest bio-fabrication experiment. And we sort of had a . . . slight medical mishap. Like, six, actually."

"Your *latest* bio-fabrication experiment?" Bodkins raised a brow and fixed T-Ray with a stern expression.

"Well, our one and only."

When T-Ray thumbed to the next picture—the selfie of the teens and their medical mishaps—Professor Bodkins rose halfway out of her chair, leaned closer, and readjusted her reading glasses. "Are these . . . Creeples living . . . breathing?" she stammered.

"Oh boy, are they ever! They're about twenty inches tall. The purple-haired one there is Royal, and it's the smartest and the ringleader. Beezer, here, has orange hair and is the smelliest. This green one is Coco, who's super quick. The blue-haired Creeple is Skoota, who's ridiculously strong. Naz has the red hair and six tentacles for super-sensitive hearing, and the yellow one is Tatz, who can shoot electricity from its head bolts."

T-Ray waited for the professor to say something. She was so flabbergasted that she snatched the phone out of T-Ray's hand without a word. The professor scrolled through the pictures of the Creeples playing in the boys' room. There was a photo of Coco bouncing off the bunk bed. Skoota lifting Peabo with one hand. Electricity sparking from Tatz's bolts. Naz with its tentacles stuck in the wall socket. And one showing Beezer cringing.

"And what's this one doing?"

"Again, it's the smelliest. So, it was about to release methane and carbon dioxide from its alimentary canal—"

"It was farting?"

"Um, yeah, but I *hate* that term," T-Ray stated with a prudish tone.

"Let me get this straight. MY Lab Rats created these . . . these little creatures?" Professor Bodkins's voice was as intense as her frown.

"Uh, yes, ma'am." T-Ray couldn't meet her eyes.

"Theresa, that is incredibly irresponsible. Not to mention dangerous! What were you three thinking? How could YOU let this happen, young lady?"

T-Ray bit her lower lip and fought back tears. "I . . . we just wanted to help you. We *had* to do something quick to save the Genomic department, your research!" she blurted out. "Sorry, Professor. I know we screwed up. We thought crowdfunding would cover the cost to finalize your peer review. And publication would bring attention to your department. But it kinda got out of hand."

Professor Bodkins made a gruff noise deep in her throat. "Just how did you Lab Rats manage to create these—?"

"Creeples. By way of the 3D bio-printer in the Molecular Diagnostics lab."

Professor Bodkins tried to digest the absurdity of the situation. "Okay . . ." She shook her head. "This is just absolutely mind-boggling! How?"

"It all went south when we came up short on DNA and used our own blood."

"All three of you? But I told you to—"

"Use only a single DNA specimen per bio-printed component. You did, but we didn't."

"And these Creeples are the end results?" The professor stared at the photos.

T-Ray was crushed by the disappointment in her mentor's tone, and she struggled to continue. "Uh . . . that's not the *whole* picture."

"I'm afraid to ask." Professor Bodkins crossed her arms and tapped an impatient finger on her elbow.

"We, uh . . . we combined our DNA with an unidentified serum—a mystery serum."

"Why on earth would you do that?" Professor Bodkins flew out of her chair and splayed out her arms in a mixture of anger, frustration, and fear. T-Ray couldn't quite tell which emotion was the strongest.

"Our blood samples weren't enough DNA to fill the six bio-ink cartridges, and Spigs found this serum. Anyway, we *just* wanted to help." T-Ray let out a tearful sigh threatening to turn into a sob.

The usually unflappable Professor Bodkins groaned and sank back into her chair, massaging her temple. "I don't know if I should be proud of the creativity or horrified by the results."

"I'm sorry. We're sorry." T-Ray tried to pour all her emotions into the words, to let the professor know she really meant it.

"T-Ray, I truly appreciate my Lab Rats' concern for me, but . . . Okay, so obviously something went horribly wrong during the process. So first thing is to get control of the situation. I want to analyze your DNA concoction."

"We call it *Gooze*. The bio-ink cartridges are still attached, but I tossed our vials of blood in the medical waste bin. Now it might not be wise for us to break into the Bio-Engineering building again."

"I'll take care of that. You locate the Creeples. And fast! I'll reverse engineer what's left of your Gooze. We need to know exactly what they're made of to know what we're up against." The professor's phone lit up. She looked at the text and frowned. "*This* can't be good. We've all been summoned to Dean Smathers's office."

"As in, all of us?"

"You, me, Johnny, and Peabo." Professor Bodkins sighed. "Two days ago, I was a dedicated professor, one year away from tenure and finalizing my genomic research project. Today . . ."

"You're still a brilliant professor, only now with a unique situation on her hands?"

"Unique is putting it mildly." Professor Bodkins wore a slight grin as she put her arm around T-Ray, gave her shoulders a gentle squeeze, and led her out of the office.

CHAPTER 12

Cafeteria Chaos

Spigs and Peabo sprinted toward the cafeteria. A student whizzed by on a skateboard in the opposite direction, screeching, "ALIEN INVASION!"

Another panicked student crashed into Spigs's elbow, shouting, "RUN! Rabid Ewoks!"

Spigs's arm jerked backward, and his hat launched like a Frisbee and was trampled by a mob of frantic students. "AAAH!" Spigs squealed, skidding to a halt to retrieve his hat.

"Hurry up!" Peabo glanced back.

"I'm comin'!" Spigs worked to secure his crumpled hat back on his head.

The cafeteria was in shambles when the boys arrived. Several picnic tables were splintered into pieces. They barged into the main eating area and found students cowering behind overturned dining tables.

Spigs and Peabo were stunned. The walls, ceiling, and floors were coated in half-eaten food and debris. And for the first time, they came face-to-face with the metamorphic Creeples.

"N-N-Naz?" Spigs's voice shuddered as he took a cautious step toward the foreboding red-haired Creeple. He held out his hand and motioned with his fingers. "Come on. Come to papa."

Naz's tentacles swayed forward as its black eyes focused on Spigs. It bared its now razor-sharp teeth and growled like a rabid possum. Spigs recoiled in fear, but Naz appeared bored and turned back to its menacing mates. The scowling Creeples formed a line in front of the soda and food vending machines that lined the wall.

ZAAAAP! The Creeples blasted magenta lightning rays from their black eyes, which enveloped the vending machines in a magical vortex. Peabo and Spigs SQUEALED when the vending machines started shapeshifting with loud clangs of reforming metal. The machines rose up on newly formed mechanical legs, having transfigured into eight-foot-tall robots. The Creeples' freakish magical powers had brought the inanimate objects to LIFE!

Spigs and Peabo stumbled backward on the slippery marble floor and covered their heads as the now Vending Machine Robots belched out soda cans, potato chip bags, and candy bars. The Creeples hopped atop the rampaging Vending Machine Robots, riding them like wild stallions.

A Spazzle Vending Machine Robot blasted cans at four skateboarders, who zoomed out of harm's way as the cans EXPLODED against the wall in a fizzy shower.

A sandwich Vending Machine Robot hurled hot hoagies at the screaming crowd, smacking the lunch monitor square across her face with ham, cheese, and mustard. One hungry student snatched a hot hoagie projectile in midflight with his mouth.

A yogurt Vending Machine Robot gushed out soft yogurt like a fireman's hose. Scrambling teens crashed into each other, blanketed in strawberry and French vanilla yogurt.

An ATM Kiosk Robot spewed out crisp twenty-dollar bills. Three jocks stood on the tables waving their lacrosse sticks in hopes of snaring the fluttering bills.

The Creeples' eyes blasted magenta rays at metal cafeteria chairs. They scurried about like roaches—with horrified students clinging on for dear life.

From their vantage point behind a dumpster, Spigs and Peabo noticed Yapper sprawled under a table. Spigs checked his phone for her tweets:

#MagicalMiniatureMutants blast vending machines to LIFE!

#HostileHobbits cause hysteria in food court!

"What do we do? It's TOTAL CHAOS!" Peabo exclaimed. "What *are* you doing?"

Spigs had stuffed hoagies in his backpack. "Waste not, want not. Lunch and dinner."

"We have to somehow round them up."

Creeples!

"Skoota!" Spigs called to the Creeple riding atop a rampaging robot. "Skoota, come here." But the blue-haired Creeple ignored him.

The morphed Creeples were beyond reasoning. Their menacing features and aggressive behavior made them appallingly different from the cuddly, creepy creatures the boys had left behind in their room.

"I think I've got—" Peabo leaped to yank Coco off the candy Vending Machine Robot, but the machine fired a candy bar, smacking Peabo in the forehead. "OUCH! Maybe I don't."

"Look!" Spigs pointed to Officers McTaggart and Whipsnade, who had ridden up on their Segways. "I can't be connected to all this, Peabo. They'll put me on double, secret probation." Spigs slid between two dumpsters. As he peered at the campus cops, he munched on the candy bar that had bounced off Peabo's forehead.

Peabo tugged on his arm. "We need better cover."

The boys hustled over to a bench, taking cover with several other students as McTaggart and Whipsnade tried in vain to stop the rioting robots.

"What ARE those?" McTaggart barked, securing a tighter grip on his baton.

"They're Megatrons!" Whipsnade howled.

The campus cops ducked and dodged hot hoagie missiles, completely dumbstruck by the Creeples AND the Vending Machine Robots.

"Deputy! Secure the perimeter and prepare for—" *THUD!* A Spazzle can slammed into the side of McTaggart's helmet.

"I'm declaring . . . martial law!" He shook his head to clear it and noticed his deputy sitting on the curb munching a hoagie.

"Deputy Whipsnade. What *are* you doing?"

"Sorry, boss. Didn't have lunch."

McTaggart smushed the rest of the hoagie into his deputy's mouth. "Now you have."

Whipsnade jumped to attention, yellow mustard smeared across his uniform. "Ace, look out!" he muffled through a mouth stuffed with the hoagie. Another Spazzle can banged into his superior's helmet. Whipsnade, not one to miss an opportunity, popped the dented raspberry soda and washed down his lunch.

The delirious McTaggart lay flat on his back. "AAARRHHH! Backup! Where's my backup? Someone call in the marines! Call Rambo! Call Triple A!"

Whipsnade helped his chief onto his Segway. From their perches, the Creeples had zeroed in on their Segways. With *CLICK-CLACKING* from Royal, all six vaulted off their roving Vending Machine Robots and waddled over to the officers.

"What do we do, boss?" Whipsnade slouched down to shield himself behind his Segway's handlebars. "They look rabid."

"We come in peace!" McTaggart told the Creeples, holding up both hands. Deputy Whipsnade followed suit but with one hand sporting the Star Trek Vulcan salute—*live long and prosper.* But the brooding Creeples ignored them and gathered up scattered Spazzle cans. They shredded the aluminum tops with their razor-sharp teeth and guzzled the soda in one gulp. The results were mammoth *BURPS*—directly in the campus cops' faces.

Creeples!

"HEEEY!" McTaggart looked down as Beezer clung to his leg and burped and farted simultaneously. "WATCH OUT! Toxic fumes! We're being gassed to death."

Whipsnade held his nose and squealed in a high-pitched voice, "OVER THERE, OUR BACKUP!" Paramedics and firefighters had arrived on the scene.

The firefighters charged the building, beating back the riotous Vending Machine Robots by way of poles with a hook and ax at one end.

"The Aberdasher police force will *not* go down without a fight!" McTaggart declared, bolstered by the firefighters' presence.

"Chief, where'd them lil' varmints go?" Whipsnade asked. It was impossible to discern the chaotic scene: a melee of flying food products, Vending Machine Robots, and bruised bodies.

"Yeah! Where *did* they go?" Spigs echoed as four firefighters cornered a Vending Machine Robot and lanced it with their pike poles.

The boys emerged from hiding and scoped out their surroundings. Down near the Quad, they caught glimpses of fading plumes of flowing neon hair. Beezer, Skoota, and Coco were stacked high on one Segway, Tatz, Naz, and Royal on the other.

"We need transportation, Peabo," Spigs said. "No way to catch 'em on foot."

"To the Batmobile!" Peabo fist-bumped Spigs. They raced toward the motor pool.

Massive hands clamped down on the two teens' shoulders. "You two geeks aren't going anywhere." Horace flashed a despicable smirk. "Except to see Dean Smathers."

"Sorry, Horrid, we're a little busy now." Spigs twisted hard and freed himself from the vise grip. "So go pound sand!" he snarled.

"The honorable Dean Smathers doesn't take no for an answer," Horace groused. "And neither do I. Now get moving." His two hooligans shoved Peabo and Spigs in the direction of the administration building.

• • •

Professor Bodkins and T-Ray were waiting in Dean Smathers's outer office when Spigs and Peabo arrived. Peabo smirked at Ms. Wanda Wainwright. "Told ya we had an appointment."

"Sit, Mr. Torres," she ordered him, irritation at missing her midafternoon break written all over her face.

"Ms. Wainwright!" Dean Smathers boomed from within his office.

"Dean Smathers will see you now," Ms. Wainwright called out with a simpering grin that clearly wished them all ill fortune with the dean.

Spigs stepped forward first, determined not to let the dean think he was intimidated by him. He again observed how Smathers's office looked immaculate, every item precisely in place.

The antique grandfather clock ticked off noisy seconds as the others gathered on each side of Spigs. Smathers sat perched behind his elevated executive oak desk, leaning sideways to delicately caress a leaf from his pink-blossomed shrub.

He reclined back in his leather swivel chair and began flipping through a file. Smathers didn't acknowledge their presence for five minutes. Professor Bodkins, T-Ray, Peabo, and Spigs stood at attention before him, growing antsier by the second. Spigs started an imaginary game of tic-tac-toe with his foot. T-Ray elbowed him in the ribs.

"OOF!" Spigs muttered. "Ya know, you should break that habit."

Smathers glanced up from his reading material, breathed two puffs of air on his wire-rimmed reading glasses, wiped the lenses, and replaced them on his nose. His thin lips curled into an ugly grimace as he glared at Spigs. "You will NOT get away with this."

"Get away with what, Dean?" Spigs answered with a tinge of sarcasm, hoping the dean hadn't heard the news about the Creeples. Spigs tried to maintain eye contact with Smathers but noticed the peculiar gold pendent around his neck depicting an eye inside an inverted pentagram circled by three nines. The same insignia he'd seen on the bells in Bell Tower *and* on the label for the Draconem Serum. Spigs furrowed his brow in thought.

"What were you three doing in the Molecular Diagnostics lab last night?" the dean snarled at the teens.

"Well, Dean." Peabo surprisingly spoke first. "As freshmen, we aren't even—"

Professor Bodkins blurted out, "Blame me, Dean Smathers. We're studying bio-fabrication and the medical use of 3D bio-printing."

"Oh, there's plenty of blame to go around. From this moment forward, all of you . . . *infidels* . . . are on academic probation. As for you, Professor Bodkins, your tenure is now under review."

"Infidels?" Spigs whispered to Peabo. "That's an odd term."

"Consider the source," Peabo whispered back.

"But I've heard it used recently."

"Quiet!" Smathers barked.

Dean Smathers got up from his desk, stepped down from his perch, and stood in front of the professor and the teens.

"Which one of you *misfits* knows about a chemistry vial that's missing from the Genomic Analytical lounge?" Smathers searched their faces for any hint of deception.

"Vial?" Spigs snapped, and nudged T-Ray.

"But why would we go in there?" T-Ray grinned innocently. "It's off-limits to freshmen."

"Something's missing—something IRREPLACEABLE!" Smathers fumed and slammed his fist on his desk.

"Irreplaceable, sir?" T-Ray's voice cracked.

Dean Smathers glared at them all. "It's imperative this stolen item be returned to me." He inhaled deeply and cleared his raspy throat. "What I mean is, it is immensely vital to this institution," Smathers voiced in a calmer delivery.

"Best of luck in findin' it, Dean," Spigs said mockingly, but with a nervous shake in his voice.

"Oh, I WILL find it. And I promise you, the consequences will be extreme." After giving them all an extended death stare, Smathers sat down. "Dismissed."

"Your *Nerium oleander* needs watering, Dean." The professor's tone was uncharacteristically cold as she gently stroked a leaf on the pink-blossomed shrub.

"You may go."

Creeples!

"Try a sprig in your tea. It's quite soothing," the professor said sardonically.

"DISMISSED!"

Professor Bodkins whispered to Spigs on their way out, "Those leaves are poisonous. He can choke on that, the arrogant twit." Spigs muffled his laughter.

Spigs looked back at the dean, who had answered his cell phone.

"Flitch, affirmative . . . dead or alive!" Smathers ordered, and leaned back in his chair.

The blood rushed from Spigs's face as he closed the door behind him. *Dead or alive! Who? Us? The Creeples?*

CHAPTER 13

Campus Curfew

Spigs and Peabo sneered back at Ms. Wainwright on the way out of her office.

T-Ray whispered to Professor Bodkins, "What now?"

"We have to get to the bottom of your . . . Creeples?" The professor led the teens out of the administration building.

"Yeah! Our cute Creeples have gone to the dark side," Spigs worried.

"They're on a rampage that'd make the Incredible Hulk green with envy."

"The Hulk is already green." Spigs thumped Peabo on his arm.

"There you go."

T-Ray rolled her eyes. "Something must have triggered their drastic transformation. But what? Contaminated bio-ink cartridges, maybe? Hazardous waste?" She scowled at the boys.

"Now wait a second!" Spigs crossed his arms in protest.

"There's no time to argue." Professor Bodkins now knew her role. "Get back to the boys' dorm and see if you can find any clues about your Creeples' mysterious transformation. I'll head to the Molecular Diagnostics lab." The professor tapped her chest. "And try to retrieve one of the Creeples' spent 3D bio-printer cartridges. I may be able to analyze your Gooze. I just need a small amount of the bio-ink to determine the exact breakdown of the DNA."

"And how long will that take, Professor?" T-Ray bounced nervously on the balls of her feet.

"A few hours. Then we should learn what makes your Creeples tick."

"Well, if *you* can't get to the bottom of it, then no one can." T-Ray flashed her big fangirl grin.

"Oh brother." Spigs winced at T-Ray.

"Thanks for the vote of confidence." The professor winked at T-Ray. "Good luck, Lab Rats. And be careful!"

With this daunting task looming over them, the teens headed back to the boys' dorm room. On the stroll back, Peabo's eyes were glued to his iPad as he frantically tracked the Creeples' whereabouts from Yapper's string of live tweets.

#EvilGrayGoblins steal Segways!

#VendingMachineRobots demolish food court!

Peabo showed Spigs and T-Ray photos of the Creeples driving Segways through the cafeteria.

#MightyMischiefMayhem!

"We *have* to find the Creeples before Smathers does!" T-Ray cried out.

"Or Horrid and his hooligans," Spigs added.

Peabo refreshed Yapper's tweets:

#NefariouslyNastyNymphs deliver
atomic wedgies to unsuspecting sophomores!

#WeeOnes devour doughnuts from food truck!

Peabo tapped on an uploaded video clip from Yapper. "HUH?" He slapped his forehead and dissolved into laughter. "This is just TOO awesome."

The video showed Skoota's and Coco's eyes blasting magenta lightning rays at volumes of ornithology textbooks in the campus bookstore. The books on bird species came ALIVE and flapped off the bookshelves. They soared high, circling the student lounge like a flock of crows, SQUAWKING and POOPING droppings all over screeching students.

#AliveFowlBooks assault students!

"They're still on campus. *That's* a positive sign," T-Ray said as they raced across the nearly empty Quad.

McTaggart and Whipsnade zipped by the teens on their backup Segways. McTaggart blared an announcement through a bullhorn, in full hysterics. "On the authority of our distinguished Dean Aleister Stan Smathers, curfew will be enforced at eighteen hundred hours."

T-Ray and Spigs attempted to conceal their faces from the cops. Peabo stopped in his tracks to read more of Yapper's tweets:

#CampusCurfew @ 6:00!

#TinyTerrors run free!

Creeples!

#Armageddon! Is this Judgement Day?!

#ViciousVendingMachineRobots raging!

#HotHoagie missiles!

The teens' phones simultaneously blared a campus alert text: *Campus Curfew @ 6:00 p.m. No students or faculty members allowed on campus grounds until these deplorable beings are secured or permanently eliminated.*

"Permanently eliminated? What's that mean?" The alarmed T-Ray gazed at the campus carnage. Screaming, running students dashed toward the Quad from the Student Union. There was widespread destruction in the form of toppled benches, scattered confections, and sidewalks shattered from marching Vending Machine Robots. T-Ray wrapped her arms over her head as those soaring bird textbooks dive-bombed her and the boys. "Let's get inside and regroup."

"Guys, I've been thinkin'." Spigs reached the steps to the dorm. "I got a sinkin' feeling that Smathers has an ulterior motive for defundin' the Genomic department."

"Gee, ya think?" T-Ray mocked. "Clearly he's up to something, and it probably has to do with that serum you stole. And he won't stop until he gets it back."

"But we used every drop for our Gooze," Peabo said.

"He's a desperate man. No telling what he's capable of," T-Ray warned as they climbed to the third floor of the dorm, passing only a handful of anxious students.

Spigs unlocked their door but had to shove it open with his shoulder—something was blocking it. He peeked in, with T-Ray and Peabo peering over his shoulders. They were speechless as they surveyed the destruction. The bureau drawers were ransacked, the bunkbed wrecked, the desks in shambles, the chairs splintered, the books flung to every corner of the room, and every item of clothing shredded and strewn about like colorful rags.

The trio's shocked silence was broken by Biscuit's hissing. They looked up to the cat's roost, where the cabinet was surprisingly undisturbed—a lone island in the sea of mayhem. Spigs retrieved the nervous cat, who was a gooey orange mess.

"Looks like you lost out to a can of Cheez 'Em." Spigs comforted the hissing cat by scratching its chin.

"It's just . . ." T-Ray rarely had trouble coming up with words.

"Thank goodness my drone's not damaged. Those things aren't cheap!" Peabo trudged through the wreckage and bent down to examine his trunk of electronics—amazingly one of the few objects in the room that hadn't been pillaged or upended.

"What could have happened?" T-Ray asked.

"Shhh, Biscuit." Spigs scraped off the dried processed cheese and set the fretful feline down. The cat pranced over to what was left of the catnip plant.

"That's strange. It's been stripped clean. Biscuit's never done *that* before." Spigs examined the remaining twigs on the obliterated plant. "But who would . . . ? The CREEPLES! That's it! The catnip must've turned them psycho. Morphin' them into maniacal monsters."

"Like in a . . . Beastly Mode." Peabo nodded.

"A mean streak that would humble a Gremlin," Spigs offered.

"Six uncontrollable humanoids with fantastical powers." T-Ray bit on a nail at the thought. "We may have unleashed powers that humanity has never experienced before." She sighed ominously as she read another tweet:

#CrazedCreatures cause campus calamity!

#SupernaturalShenanigans galore!

"The catnip HAS to be their 'crazy switch.'" Spigs collected the few remaining dried catnip leaves strewn about and tucked them into his pants pockets.

"Catnip? To *this* extreme?" T-Ray questioned.

Spigs scoured the room for his laptop and spotted it under the bunk. "What I wanna know is . . . will the Creeples ever change back?"

An anxious Peabo typed furiously on his keyboard. "Hey! Somebody tried to log in to my computer at nine twenty-seven this morning. Around the time we were first called into Smathers's office."

"That confirms it. Someone deliberately punk'd us to get access to your computer," T-Ray concluded.

"My bet is it's that slimeball Horace and his hooligans!" Peabo added.

"Under direct orders from Smathers." Spigs logged in to his computer. "He's stepped up his game by sendin' in his goons to steal our data."

"Or the professor's data," T-Ray asserted.

Peabo had a horrible thought. "And if it was Horace, you think he tried to kidnap the Creeples?"

The teens froze for a second at the idea.

Spigs pointed to the open window. "Their escape route."

T-Ray turned her attention back to her phone. "Twitter's on fire. The Creeples just passed Bell Tower."

Spigs and Peabo rushed over to view T-Ray's phone for Yapper's never-ending tweets:

#RambunctiousRugRats cause raucous near Bell Tower!

"Bell Tower! *That's* where I heard that word before," Spigs recalled.

"What word?" T-Ray asked.

"'Infidels.' That ol' geezer inside Bell Tower called Rachell and me 'infidels,' *and* Smathers did too."

"Again with Rachell," T-Ray muttered.

"And Horrid! Remember? So what does that word actually mean?" Peabo asked.

"A term used in certain religions for those accused of unbelief in the central tenets of their own religion, or for members of another sect." T-Ray showed off her vast vocabulary.

"A nonbeliever." Spigs smirked. "That can't be a coincidence. I mean, it's not exactly a word you hear often."

"But it doesn't make any sense because Aberdasher Academy is not associated with any particular religion," T-Ray stated.

Spigs thought for a moment. "Okay, I said I'd never *ever* go back, but it's for the team, and we now have new responsibilities—the Creeples." Spigs walked to the closet, placed his distressed trilby hat on the door's interior hook, and retrieved his hoodie. He flipped the hood over his head and tied the drawstrings tight.

"What are you up to?" T-Ray probed.

"Gonna pay that ol' geezer another visit."

"Who's this old geezer you keep referring to?" Peabo asked.

"Dead man walkin'."

"And what are we supposed to do?" Peabo said.

"We are NOT going to sit here while you're off investigating your own . . . uh, investigation." T-Ray stood up, hands on hips. "They're *our* Creeples too! Remember, we're the other part of the team."

"You two go and scout out that travelin' carnival that just set up near Letchworth Village."

"What? NO!" T-Ray stomped her foot like a scolding teacher. "We're coming with you!"

"Listen, as we were leavin' Smathers's office, I overheard him on the phone. He was talkin' to Gideon Flitch, the carny who owns that travelin' carnival, and Smathers sounded desperate. Flitch must be involved somehow. Remember, he captures and cages exotic animals for a living."

T-Ray relented with a sad frown and a nod. "I couldn't bear that happening to the Creeples," she said softly.

Spigs headed out the door. "Keep trackin' Yapper's tweets. Somehow, she's always in the middle of everything. And let's meet back here in an hour."

CHAPTER 14

Gideon Flitch's Famous Traveling Carnival

"**H**urry, Peabo, faster!" T-Ray shouted from the sidecar of his Vespa. "And stay between the lines."

"There aren't any lines. And this thing only goes fifteen miles an hour—with one person." Peabo gunned the throttle, but the unpaved road was full of potholes and loose gravel. His shoulders ached as he strained to keep the scooter straight.

"Still, hurry up." T-Ray hoped no one had seen them as they headed out the campus's back access. At least curfew was still several hours away. T-Ray refreshed her Twitter feed.

#VendingMachineRobots fizzle out!

"It seems those Vending Machine Robots are only transformed for a few hours. Good to know." T-Ray made a mental note in case the Creeples decided to animate any other objects.

She noticed a paint-chipped road sign ahead that read *Gideon Flitch's Famous Traveling Carnival—One Mile* in black paint. "Have you ever been to a traveling carnival?"

"Nah. I've wanted to, but *mi madre* told me those shows are kinda shady."

"What do you mean?" T-Ray's stomach lurched, nervous about their perilous mission.

"A lot of times the carnival animals aren't treated well. They're constantly traveling and, like Spigs said, caged up all the time. Like, they're mean to elephants. And I love elephants."

"Pachyderms. Me too. You think they'll have them?"

"Dunno. But from what I've seen online, it looks like a real cruddy outfit. They'll definitely have some exotic animals. Great for publicity. Just hope they don't mistreat them."

"We can't let this Gideon Flitch get his filthy hands on our Creeples," T-Ray insisted.

"We won't. At least, we'll try our best. Remember, we've got a demented dean and his hooligans on our tails. A scheming carnival barker just may be too much for us. We'll have to be clever if we want to keep him from catching the Creeples."

"Clever is my middle name." T-Ray puffed out her chest. Then she scowled and muttered, "Unlike Ms. Rachell Hobbs. *Her* middle name is . . . Snob Ball!"

"Huh? You're thinking about Rachell at a time like this?"

"She's always lurking around Spigs, keeping him from his Lab Rat duties. It's strange, though, she kept asking me about Professor Bodkins's research." T-Ray crossed her arms with a harrumph sound. "Just don't like her one bit. So there!"

"Could it be because you sorta, kinda like Spigs?" Peabo quickly jerked the steering wheel to dodge a pothole.

"What?" T-Ray whipped her head around. She was ready to deny everything, but instead, Peabo glanced at her with kind eyes and a soft, understanding smile.

"I figured it out."

T-Ray opened and closed her mouth twice without saying a word. She heaved a great sigh. "Ugh," she groaned. She wasn't about to come clean, especially not to Spigs's roommate.

But it was Peabo's great perception and deduction that convinced him. "Number one: Spigs super annoys you, but you never stay mad. Two: whenever he brings up Rachell, you contort your face like you just sniffed Beezer's farts, *and* you always say something that sounds jealous like."

"I do NOT sound jealous!"

"If you say so. But it's not a crime to like Spigs, ya know."

"You think he knows? What I mean is—" T-Ray cringed.

"Totally oblivious." Peabo laughed, which helped T-Ray to finally grin. "Maybe an obvious hint, one day, in some clever way."

T-Ray shrugged, trying not to think too much about it. It made her feel like a silly school girl, and she hated it.

"Remember, clever *is* your middle name." Peabo laughed. He winked at T-Ray. "Your secret's safe with me."

T-Ray nodded. With another soft sigh, she said, "Thanks. Thanks for listening and not telling."

"We Lab Rats stick together . . . for richer, for poorer, in sickness, and in health."

"Those are wedding vows!" T-Ray smacked Peabo on the

back of his helmet. "Stop up here!" T-Ray shouted. Peabo pulled up to a placard: *Welcome one and all to Gideon Flitch's Famous Traveling Carnival.* It was another crude sign cut from rusted metal with faded lettering. "Let's hide the scooter here and see what we can find out."

Peabo cut the motor and rolled the scooter in between a row of red-berry-laden hobblebushes on the side of the road. The pair secured their backpacks and sneaked down the derelict road, sticking close to the shrubbery in case they needed to dive for cover. A quarter of a mile down, they strayed close to the perimeter of the carnival campgrounds.

"I can't see anything," T-Ray said.

"I can fix that." Peabo beamed. He knelt and pulled his drone out of his backpack. "This baby is gonna be our eyes and ears. Okay, Double Trouble, do your thing." He flicked the on switch and took out the controller, complete with an HD monitor at the center.

"You *named* your drone?"

"Sure. People name their cars and boats and . . . Creeples!" That got a smile out of T-Ray. "Only fitting, since I customized it myself." He turned on the twelve-inch circular drone and handed T-Ray a set of headphones.

Peabo hovered the drone ten feet above them, and in a split second, it shot out of sight. It carefully circled the center of the carnival above the tattered tents and yurts.

"Still can't see anything." She frowned at the monitor.

"Patience is a virtue." Peabo steered the drone closer in.

The teens were glued to the monitor for any signs of activity.

No elephants, but there were several peculiar animals roaming the campgrounds.

An eight-foot-long, seven-hundred-and-fifty-pound Vietnamese boar rooted in a garden patch. A sign next to the mammoth swine read, *Hogzilla: Monster Hog of the World.*

Several peculiar hoofed animals called "Zonkeys"—a zebra and donkey hybrid—grazed underneath a thicket of trees.

A two-humped Bactrian camel drank from a brass watering tub. A lanky sheep munched listlessly on a patch of thick grass. And rangy exotic roosters and lop-eared rabbits pecked at scattered feed.

"They all look miserable," T-Ray said glumly.

"They don't seem to be fed regularly." Peabo worked the drone controls. "Hang on, going into 'hush-mode' for a closer look at the main attractions."

The drone flew deeper into the campgrounds, past several rickety "thrill" rides: a rust bucket of a Ferris wheel with safety bars missing, a collection of dented bumper cars, and a timeworn arachnid-shaped ride called Black Widow. It had six carriage arms that resembled spider's legs attached to seat tubs. The amusement rides were clearly not up to code and appeared dangerous. Next to the decrepit rides were three dilapidated vehicles: a 1960s semitruck and trailer, a cargo van, and a vintage Ford station wagon with fake wood side panels.

A middle-aged man with rolled-up sleeves was sitting outside the larger camper and did not seem to notice the drone humming fifteen feet above. The man was focused intently on his laptop computer. T-Ray recognized him from Peabo's online search as

Gideon Flitch. He was lanky and sported a pair of front teeth with a gap that could hold a credit card. He looked every bit the classic carny in his striped pants and plaid shirt. What little hair he had he combed over in strings that migrated down to the lower half of his face and collected into a thick, unruly beard. Thanks to Peabo's impressive custom improvements of the drone's telephoto capabilities, they were able to observe Flitch scroll through Instagram pictures of the Creeples wreaking havoc.

Flitch set aside the laptop and guzzled a big swig of green liquid from a jar labeled *Sour Gherkins.*

"Sour pickles? How appropriate," Peabo said.

Flitch's beard couldn't conceal his nasty scowl as he called out to his two carnival cronies, who lounged on nearby aluminum folding chairs playing the card game Old Maid.

"Suit up, chuckleheads, and grab your chem-tanks. Got a temp job to exterminate six mangy varmints. The ten-twenty is Aberdasher Academy," Flitch barked.

His two cronies ignored him, bent over their cards and locked in a staring contest, completely engrossed in the children's game.

"I got a pair of lumberjacks," the chubby one announced as he laid down the cards. His belly was so vast it shaded his toes. "Beat that, Lil' Lyle."

"Back at ya, Big Lyle! A pair of magicians." The second young man slapped the pair on the table with glee. He was far shorter in stature, but by the way he spoke and the roguish glint in his eye, T-Ray assumed he was the craftiest of the two—which wasn't saying much. Their facial resemblance gave them away as brothers, apparently with the same first name.

"Pair of ballerinas."

"Pair of roosters." Big Lyle licked his lips. "That reminds me; I sure could go for a bucket of fried chicken."

"A pair of Angus cows!" Lil' Lyle cried out with confidence.

"Mmm, spareribs sound mighty tasty," Big Lyle grumbled. "Pair of clowns."

Flitch stormed over and kicked the chairs out from beneath them. "Precisely why this ramshackle sideshow's losing money and I hafta chase exterminating gigs. Now get tanked up, ya flunkies!"

As Flitch and the Lyle brothers scrambled to suit up, Peabo skillfully guided the drone back to their hiding spot. "We have to get back to campus. It's official; Smathers knows about the Creeples *and* their location. And Flitch is definitely the hitman. You heard. He's talkin' about exterminating them."

"They CAN'T! I won't let them harm the Creeples." T-Ray balled her fists.

The pair sprinted back to uncover Peabo's scooter from the shrubbery. Peabo goosed the throttle full speed—fifteen miles per hour—and they headed back to campus. T-Ray searched through her phone. Yapper's updates suggested the Creeples were still in their Beastly Mode.

"Step on it, Peabo!" T-Ray glanced behind them and saw Flitch's van had pulled out of the campgrounds, heading toward campus. "And let's hope Spigs is getting more information than we got."

CHAPTER 15

The Grim Keeper

With his hoodie tied tight to conceal his face, Spigs crept stealthily from bush to bush to avoid being seen by the campus cops. He soon arrived at his intended destination, Bell Tower, but couldn't enter the front as he and Rachell had done. "Now what?" A row of thick, twisted hedgerows covered the backside. Spigs pulled back his hood to get a clearer picture at the unusual placement of the foliage. Why were there manicured evergreen bushes planted on the sides and front of the tower, yet a dense hedgerow covered the backside? Spigs's curiosity was deeply ingrained, and he intended to see what was behind this natural barrier. He struggled to peek through the dense, tangled hedgerow as sharp twigs poked his head and branches scraped his arms. And—BINGO!

Spigs discovered a weathered door with faint etching in the worn wood. With his makeshift skeleton key, he scraped away the packed dirt that filled the grooves. He recognized it, an eye with an arched line at the top for the brow and a vertical line down from the eye to resemble a streaming tear. A sweeping line extended left from the tear to form a spiral. It was the same eye inside the bizarre symbol worn by Smathers and embossed on the polished bells.

Spigs inserted the skeleton key in the rusty padlock and fought to turn it. A closer inspection revealed a completely different locking mechanism than the front door. "Great! End of the road." Spigs stood for a few moments in thought. "Well, whatta I have to lose?" He simply . . . knocked. A round porthole window, like on cruise ships, flung open and scarcely revealed the gaunt visage of a grim man, hidden partly in the shadows. He croaked with a British accent, "Go AWAY! No one's home."

"Yes, but, uum . . . I have a pressin' question, and—"

The shadowy man shut the porthole window.

Spigs, undeterred, knocked again, but with more conviction. And again, the round window flew open, but this time a quivering hand waved a rusty muzzle of a Colt Single Action Army revolver with a mother-of-pearl handle.

"Now, *I* have a pressing question: Is anyone home?" the shaky voice said dryly.

Spigs trembled at the sight of the gun barrel. "Uuh, n-n-no, s-sir. But I—"

The porthole window slammed closed, leaving the shaken Spigs frustrated. He gritted his teeth and tightened his jaw at the thought of the Creeples' plight and Dean Smathers's role in all this. "Smathers? That's it!" He pounded rapidly on the door with the palm of his hand until it throbbed. And as soon as the window flung open, Spigs started his dialogue.

"I'm here per the directive of our eminently supreme leader, Dean Aleister Stan Smathers." Spigs stood erect, arms back and chest out.

The window closed once again, and Spigs's shoulders sagged in defeat. But a second later, the stout door creaked open. He entered apprehensively. The inside was exactly how Spigs remembered it—only the wooden water bucket he'd smashed on his attacker's head was back in the corner, as if it hadn't been disturbed. The hunched-over man didn't lead Spigs to the spiraling staircase. Instead, he opened a door to reveal a set of stone steps. Spigs followed him down into a dusty room that felt claustrophobic and was festooned with cobwebs. Spigs nervously swiped the cobwebs away from his face and sneezed three times in rapid succession. He resisted a fourth and tried not to freak out at the thought of spider eggs hatching in his hair. He took a deep breath and looked around. But the old man had disappeared.

"Hey, where'd ya go?" A rat scurried under Spigs's feet. "YAAWOW! Great! Filthy rats and swarming spiders. I'm beginnin' to realize why no one ever wanted to visit this creep show." He leaped out of the way of another rapid rodent and noticed footprints in the dusty cobblestones that led around a corner to yet another stairway.

"Uum, hello down there?" Spigs tracked the footsteps down three flights of steep stone steps into an even darker part of the tower. The only light came from flickering candle sconces in the walls, which were placed way too far apart for Spigs's comfort. At the bottom of the stairs, the footsteps made a sharp left into an undersized dwelling.

"Nice décor . . . for Dracula's man cave!" Spigs tried to humor himself to keep from soiling his pants. He entered the gloomy quarters, a tight space dimly lit by several ceremonial red candles that smelled of burned honey from melting beeswax. There were crudely carved, cryptic inscriptions strategically covering the four walls. A series of shelves were affixed to the stone walls. Spigs glided his fingers over the many dusty leather-bound books and their faded gold-leaf titles. He beamed at the titles referencing the science of alchemy—the medieval practice of chemistry. "Awesome stuff! Just the kinda freaky science I wanna take next year."

The motion of the cloaked man now in his peripheral vision startled Spigs. He squinted for a clearer picture of him in a hooded, monk-like cape as he seized something from a cabinet. The elderly man busily arranged moldy gray cheese and dry wafers on a tray and poured a cloudy brown liquid from a dented canteen into two dirty glasses. He tugged back the hood to reveal a pasty white individual who looked a hundred years old and probably weighed about ninety pounds—soaking wet. His pale skin seemed as though it was simply stretched over bone. It was as if he'd never ventured above ground in a century. And it was apparent he'd once been a tall man, but he was now hunched over, with sparse hair and one milky blind eye. Spigs could not stop staring. That is until the man opened his mouth to reveal a mangled row of horribly discolored teeth. Spigs was confident he was peering into the same repulsive mouth as the one belonging to that cloaked figure who had tripped him the other evening.

"Why would our dean send the likes of you?" the man said peevishly. He looked straight at Spigs with his one good eye. "No Disciple has ever set foot in here."

"Disciple? Uh, yes, well, you see . . . Dean Smathers dispatched me on a critical errand."

The old man cocked his head. His gaunt face had a mass of deep-etched wrinkles. "Have I seen you before?"

"My association with our superior leader is confidential," Spigs said with feigned confidence. He noticed a battered military foot-locker with the faded letters *N.O.M.T., Ltd.,* on the side, and was about to sit down when—

"DO NOT TOUCH THAT!" the old man woofed, and Spigs hopped up. The gaunt man shuffled his way across the sandy dirt floor right up to Spigs's face. His gnarly teeth, bloody gums, and diseased eye were even more menacing when they reflected the red light from the candles. Spigs shuffled back a step.

"Continue."

"As the dean's assistant—I mean, Disciple—"

"Speak up," groused the old man.

Spigs raised his tone. "I'm here to learn of your progress. I trust that you've *made* progress."

"Yes, yes. Proceeding as planned." He held out the tray to Spigs. "My provisions are meager, but we must discipline ourselves in preparation for the Golden Dawn." With his trembling hands, he pushed the tray closer to Spigs. "Go on. Eat. Drink."

"Oh, that's okay." Spigs took another step backward. "Uuuh!" He looked at the moldy cheese and tried not to gag. "I'm actually lactose intolerant, ya know, cheese and all—"

"EAT! DRINK!" the old man repeated, now suspicious. It was less of a request than it was a direct order.

Spigs gingerly picked up the wafer with moldy globules of cheese and struggled to choke it down with the brown liquid. *GULP! COUGH! COUGH!* He grabbed his gurgling stomach and struggled to breathe through his mouth, using every fiber of will-power he had NOT to toss up his hoagie. Between the nasty cheese and the urgent need to pee, Spigs was desperate to get out of there.

"And would you have a name?" The old man bit into a wafer with his awful rotting teeth.

Biding his time and searching for any clues, Spigs pushed aside a lit candle on the table and perused several brittle brown parchment papers unfurled in a precise way. "Name?" Panicked, Spigs hastily surveyed the room. He saw a distressed wall calendar sponsored by Cadbury chocolates featuring an English cricket team. He noticed the players held the exact same flat-fronted bat his attacker had used to attack him and Rachell. Spigs inexplicably mumbled, "Barry."

"Speak up. Your first name or last?" the old man demanded.

"First name is, uum . . . Cad." Spigs's nerves got to him.

"Well, Mr. Cad Barry, I'm the Wisdomkeeper. But you can address me as Keeper." With his thumb and index finger, he reached into the back of his mouth and casually extracted a blackened tooth, bloody at the roots.

"More like the Grim Keeper," Spigs muttered. "Wonder what he'd charge to haunt houses?"

Keeper offered Spigs an unsteady, arthritic hand. His bones were visible through the wax-papery skin.

Spigs reluctantly clasped Keeper's ice-cold hand. "What are you the keeper of?"

"Well, you would certainly know if you were a ranked Disciple."

Spigs tried to cover his error. "Yes, I'm the newest Disciple. That's why Dean Smathers had me come here. So you could, uh, enlighten me."

"Of course." Keeper grinned and flashed his repulsive teeth. "I *am* the eminent guardian of the Draconem Expedition codex. I have waited many, many years for the—"

"Golden Dawn?" Spigs got distracted trying to decipher the writings on the parchment papers. "I mean, yes, the Golden Dawn."

"Our glorious enlightenment is finally upon . . . Wait, what's your rank, Mr. Cad Barry?"

Flustered, Spigs tried to sidestep the question. "Rank? I'm here on Dean Smathers's behalf. That's all you need to know."

"That's NOT the answer I'm looking for. So, I believe *your* glorious enlightenment starts . . . NOW!" Keeper gripped the Colt revolver in his waistband.

Spigs delivered a fake smile and steadily shuffled backward toward the door. "Well, it's been super fun, Mr. Keeper, and many thanks for the salmonella and crackers."

The hunched-over Keeper darted around the table, surprisingly agile. "Leaving so soon?"

Spigs stared down the shaky barrel of the pistol and continued to inch away toward the staircase. "Whoa now, easy there, Jesse James." Not knowing what else to do, Spigs slapped the lit candle onto the pile of brown parchment papers, starting a fire. Keeper

WAILED and frantically rushed to put it out. Spigs scrambled and stumbled up the staircase, through the back room, and out through the back door of Bell Tower.

Spigs waved his arms wildly to hack through the thicket of hedgerows, and once out in the clearing, he doubled over in agony from the putrid cheese and noxious liquid gurgling in his belly and hurried across campus.

S.H.A.D.O.W.

High Energy Laser Defense System

Exotic Technology Department
Washington, DC
Codename: PROJECT GOOZE

Name: Coco

Aliases: Green Creeple

Identity: Twenty-inch-tall humanoid. Neon-green hair. Prodigious ears. Oscillating mustard-yellow eyes. Click-clacking noise emanates from the skull region—a form of communication.

Creators: Three Aberdasher Academy of Science students.

Personal Abilities: Extreme quickness.

Magical Powers: Draconic Kinetic Energy blasts from their eyes that super-charge inanimate objects into living, breathing entities.

Mystical Limitations: The metamorphosis can last up to twelve hours.

Potential Application: Particle-beam weaponry.

Comments: Cheez 'Em connoisseur. Impatient. Energetic. Proclivity for sugary products.

CHAPTER 16

Rambunctious Rampage

"**U**urrghh!" Spigs managed to put two buildings between himself and Bell Tower before his protesting stomach forced him to hug a trashcan. The rancid liquid, moldy cheese, and crackers tasted even worse on the way out. He strained to lift his head out of the can. "Remind me not to invite the Grim Keeper to a potluck. AAAH! So long, cruel world." His head dipped back in the trashcan. It took several minutes before he regained his wits. He checked his phone, hoping for an update from T-Ray and Peabo on their mission. Instead, his screen was filled with Twitter notifications:

#GrayGoblins jam the gym!

#KneeHighNixies pack awesome powers!

One tweet had a video of the Creeples rushing into the gym. A *Pogopalooza Tournament* banner stretched across the entrance. This was the X Games of pogo stick jumping.

Two pogo jumpers on high-tech air-powered sticks launched

themselves six feet into the air. They synchronized perfect free-style backflips, causing the students to go wild. The mystifyingly morphed Creeples *CLICK-CLACKED*, wiggled their enormous ears, and tore through the crowd.

Beezer and Coco bumped the pogo participants off their sticks and snatched them. Their tubby lower bodies gave them the leverage to spring fifteen feet in the air for a double back flip. The students hooted and hollered.

"Whoa! They've got mad skills," said one of the contestants.

Off a wall and off the backboard, Beezer and Coco bounced high and locked hands midair. The next great Cirque du Soleil act?

BRRUUMP! A deafening boom echoed throughout the gym. The student recording the event choked and wheezed. "YO! Did someone just shave a skunk's butt or what?"

"EEEWWW!" the crowd squealed in unison as Beezer detonated a series of RUMP ROARS in every direction, which scattered the nose-pinching students. Yapper tweeted out:

#OdorousOrangeCreature spews toxic fumes!

#RampagingRascals!

Spigs sprinted toward the gym, hoping to head off the Creeples before they brought other inanimate objects to life. But his phone dinged more tweets:

#PercyInPeril!

#CrazyLegsGoblins waddle toward food court!

Spigs texted T-Ray and Peabo to meet him at the cafeteria. He veered one street over and headed for the food court. He arrived in time to see the Creeples gathering below Percy—the pterodactyl statue and school mascot. A silly oversized baseball cap sat atop Percy's oblong head.

This time all the menacing Creeples locked their magical black eyes on Percy and simultaneously MEGA-BLASTED it with their magenta lightning rays, enveloping the mascot, bringing it to LIFE! With an earsplitting screech, Percy broke out of its green fiberglass casing and detached from its base. So the rumors WERE true! The prehistoric pterodactyl fluttered its massive skeletal wings and rose high into the air. Spigs skidded to a halt by a picnic bench and covered his head as the pterodactyl soared above him. Its blazing red eyes and pointed teeth, attached to a six-foot-long head, made it even more terrifying as it dove at the crowd, pecking and slashing with its talons.

Spigs crawled under the table and held out a hand to the Creeples. "Come on. Cheez 'Em for all!"

Naz and Beezer tilted their batty ears at him, mouths open in either grins or snarls, Spigs couldn't tell.

"That's right. Come on, ya crazed critters. You're not safe here. *I'm* not safe here." Percy screeched and dive-bombed students to prove Spigs's point.

Royal let out a strange gruff *CLICK-CLACK* warning and wiggled its ears at an approaching white van—a rusty old bucket heap. *Flitch's Varmint Extermination* was crudely written in black paint on the side doors. The speeding van arrived with a squeal of metal as the worn-out brakes brought the heap to a stop. Two dudes emerged in matching beige jumpsuits with

EXTERMINATOR stitched across their jumpsuits and patchwork nametags that both read *Lyle*. The Lyle brothers looked like a poor man's Ghostbusters—they carried corroded chemical tanks connected to spray nozzles and a slip noose fastened to a pole. The bumbling buffoons raced after the scattering Creeples.

Spigs rushed out of his hiding place. "Hey, bozos, leave them alone!" he shouted.

The yellow Creeple shot magenta lightning rays at the carnival flunkies' metal tanks, which gave their hands a nasty shock.

The Lyle brothers recovered and advanced after Tatz with their spray wands. As their fingers were about to squeeze the triggers, the *SCREECHING* pterodactyl swooped down and plucked the two brothers up by their tanks with its massive talons. It carried them high into the air before dumping them in the nearby fountain. Spigs grabbed for Tatz, but in a flash, it Aussie-splay ran between Spigs's legs.

"Spigs, over here!" Peabo screamed as he and T-Ray dismounted the scooter across a grassy berm in front of the cafeteria.

Spigs dashed over. "Ya see that? Percy is a real pterodactyl. It's been, like, millions of years since the last pterodactyl flew. And OUR Creeples did it!" He gave Peabo an enthusiastic fist bump. T-Ray didn't raise a hand to participate.

"Never waste killer footage." Peabo adjusted his GoPro helmet.

"What the heck happened in Bell Tower?" T-Ray asked. "You've got scratches on your neck, and stems and leaves in your hair."

"Where do I begin? That gnarly ol' geezer—I now call him the Grim Keeper—made me eat disgusting cheese and drink toxic brown gunk. And I almost took a dirt nap from his six-shooter, AND nearly wet my britches." Spigs tried to comb the leaves out of his thick hair with his fingers.

"And *that's* why you went back in there?" T-Ray said with contempt.

"It's a good thing I did! 'Cause somethin' major's goin' down real soon. But I can't figure out what."

Peabo motioned over Spigs's shoulder. The three caught the Creeples climbing back on Segways and zipping off. Flitch's van spit loose gravel and sped off after them. Spigs hopped in the scooter's sidecar and barked, "Let's GO! We hafta get 'em before that carny does." T-Ray swung her leg over and grabbed Peabo's jacket as handholds.

Flitch's van screeched to a stop behind the fountain.

"Get in!" Flitch called to his drenched flunkies.

Big Lyle tossed Lil' Lyle in with one heave. "Dem varmints are vicious, boss."

"Did ya see them jowls?" Lil' Lyle complained.

"Quit ya cryin'," Flitch demanded. "We got unfinished business."

The teens' scooter sped past Flitch and went after the Creeples. Spigs tapped Peabo on the shoulders, pointing to the rapidly gaining van. Peabo tried to cut Flitch off, but Flitch swerved out of the way. Once in the clear, Flitch gunned it, ready to mow down the Creeples on the Segways.

Peabo, T-Ray, and Spigs screamed, "LOOK OUT, CREEPLES!"

The Creeples swung their heads back to the familiar voices

and saw the danger. They leaped off the Segways and onto the approaching van's hood. The Creeples climbed atop the roof. Flitch frantically whipped the van in a mad circle and smoked the old bald tires on the asphalt. One by one, the Creeples slid off the roof and down onto the windshield. With their dark, menacing faces pressed against the glass, their hypnotic black eyes locked on the Lyle brothers, stunning them. Flitch turned on his windshield wipers to knock them off, but only annoyed them. Skoota and Royal scrambled to the roof and gnawed through the metal with their razor-sharp teeth.

Tatz, Coco, and Beezer were in the mood for some old-fashioned naughtiness. They squashed their bare ashen-gray butts against the windshield—like pressed ham from a butcher shop. Of course, Beezer let out a HUGE fart that fogged the van's entire windshield. Naz and Royal sprang inside the cab and swarmed over Flitch and his two flunkies, who flailed, kicked, and screamed hysterically. In the ruckus, Big Lyle reached in the back for the chem-tank but triggered on the spray wand, spewing brown gas. Flitch and the Lyle brothers passed out. Naz, a little woozily, latched its tentacles onto Lil' Lyle's face for support. Skoota dropped through the van's new "sun roof" and planted itself on the steering wheel.

The uncontrolled van skidded around a bend and swerved down a side street, wiping out a Click It or Ticket street sign. It smashed into the shrubs surrounding the ivy-draped Cryptozoology building. Flitch woke as the Creeples sprang from the van. He turned to the Lyle brothers and smacked them across their chests. "Wake up, puddin' heads! And follow them virulent varmints."

The scooter rolled up as Big Lyle lifted Lil' Lyle onto his shoulders to try to seize the Creeples—who had scampered up the building's gutter.

"Stop shaking. Can't reach 'em," Lil' Lyle complained.

"That's my face, not a step," Big Lyle complained.

"Stairs! Use the stairs, NITWITS!" Flitch yelled at his flailing flunkies.

Peabo, T-Ray, and Spigs watched the Creeples shimmy up the building's drainpipe with ease to reach two thirteenth-century gargoyle statues squatting on the second-floor windowsill of the Cryptozoology auditorium. Royal *CLICK-CLACKED,* and its black marble eyes zapped the grotesque granite gargoyles, enshrouding them in a mystical maelstrom. The Creeples shot through the open window and into a full classroom of students.

"THAT'S how they do it, with their magical eyes," T-Ray squawked.

"Like supercharging objects to LIFE!" Spigs asserted.

Everything was eerily quiet for a moment. The alive gargoyles' eyes suddenly turned blood red. They aggressively flapped their wings and dove straight down the side of the building, slamming into the two Lyle brothers, who crashed down onto Flitch.

Spigs, Peabo, and T-Ray raced inside the Cryptozoology building. They bounded up two steps at a time.

"We have to figure out how to contain their magical powers!" T-Ray let out an exasperated groan.

They reached the second floor, and Spigs cracked open the classroom door, seconds behind the Creeples.

Professor Schmidlapp's senior Cryptozoology class was assembling in the auditorium. The curriculum covered the science of obscure and undocumented animals of folklore and mythology. Spigs's freshman introductory class only studied the iconic cryptids, such as the Loch Ness Monster, the Yeti in the Himalayas, and the Dover Demon.

The teens surveyed the packed auditorium. Many of the students were on their phones, but several began to point at the roaming Creeples.

For show-and-tell, the auditorium was peppered with life-size plaster-cast models of classic cryptid creatures, as well as several obscure mythological monsters. The excitable Creeples started trembling, *CLICK-CLACKING*, and wiggling their huge ears.

"Uh-oh," Spigs whispered. "We're in for some trouble now."

"Like, BIG trouble!" Peabo declared.

Nothing coherent came out of T-Ray's mouth. She was too stunned to find the right words.

The Creeples approached the cryptid models. Their ears wiggled, they *CLICK-CLACKED*, but their oscillating eyes were now fixed on their intended targets.

"ROYAL . . . NOOOO!" T-Ray yelled.

The undeterred Creeples blasted their lightning rays and animated the models of the array of terrifying crypto-creatures. *ZAP!* Skoota animated the Mongolian Death Worm—twelve feet in length with a five-foot tubular girth. The gelatinous parasite was wrapped in exoskeleton skin. The Gobi Desert invertebrate had the nasty ability to spit acid venom that burned straight to the bones. YIKES!

ZAP! ZAP! ZAP! ZAP! ZAP! Coco, Naz, and Beezer animated the five well-preserved mummified Bog People that had been excavated from the English Lindow Moss Bog in 1938.

ZAP! Royal animated the Ayia Napa sea monster model towering fifteen feet tall. It was a bizarre monstrous form of a maiden in torso, with a serpent for its lower body, having six snarling dog heads protruding out from its midriff, including their twelve forelimbs.

ZAP! Tatz animated the Hodag model, a two-thousand-pound crypto-creature the size of a Chevy Suburban SUV, with coarse chestnut hair. This horrible behemoth block of muscle extended clawed feet and thrashed about its spear tail.

The Creeples *CLICK-CLACKED* intensely, prancing around in delight as the crypto-creatures lumbered up the aisles of the auditorium. The noxious Mongolian Death Worm slithered over rows of seats. Dozens of students were too petrified to move, while others leaped out of their seats and screamed for their lives.

The two-thousand-year-old slimy, moss-soaked Bog People lumbered laboriously toward the students in the front row, blocking the emergency exit. A valiant girl grabbed her heavy textbook and slapped one of the Bog People's heads. Cheers roared throughout the auditorium. The Bog Person's head spun around a half-dozen times on its partially decomposed neck, and when it stopped, it was facing backward. It simply lumbered forward while keeping a lookout on its rear.

Throughout the pandemonium, the absentminded Professor Schmidlapp had been meticulously shuffling through a sheaf of notes at the lectern. He adjusted his thick coke-bottle glasses, squinting out at the melee. "Ms. Perkins, please return to your seat. Well, good afternoon, class. Before we start our daily lessons, has anything exciting happened since we last met?"

The fearsome Hodag raised its horned head and snorted through its booming nostrils, releasing a stench like a rancid chum bucket of fish guts. The disgusting whiff flustered Professor Schmidlapp's stringy white coiffure. He patted his hair back in place and blew his nose in a handkerchief. "Ah, would someone like a breath mint?"

The Hodag stomped and crushed two chairs at the front of the auditorium with its clawed feet. It charged after four students, who backpedaled into a corner, shrieking. The beast reared on its hind legs, snorting a slurry of snot from its bull nose, splattering students in slippery mucus.

The winged gargoyles dive-bombed through the window, snapping at frightened students. Total pandemonium ensued as students banged into each other trying to escape the auditorium. In the front of the class, Tatz and Skoota appeared on either side of Professor Schmidlapp's lectern and blasted him with magenta lightning rays from their eyes. But it did nothing to energize the dreary professor. "Hmm . . . got kinda warm in here. Now, as soon as the Bog People take their seats, we'll begin. So where were we last? Oh yes. Pukwudgies! Myth, monsters, or misunderstood?"

Spigs, T-Ray, and Peabo battled to stay out of the spitting range of the slithering Mongolian Death Worm. It spewed acid globs on the exit door, melting it down to a sizzling metallic puddle. The Ayia Napa sea monster roamed up the aisle, and its six snarling dog heads lunged for students who got in its way. The sea monster's enormous torso blocked the exit as the six dog heads growled and snapped at the Hodag. The Hodag scuffed its front right foot over the carpet and lowered its horns. A snort from the Hodag blew its shaggy mane out of its eyes, and then it charged like in a Spanish bullfight. The Ayia Napa sea monster's dog heads chomped down on the Hodag's horns and tossed it onto its scaly back. The Hodag regained its footing and charged again.

"Hit the deck!" T-Ray shrieked as the Hodag sent the sea monster flying toward them.

Students dove for the back row seats and crouched between them. With one exit clear, desperate students made a mad dash into the hall.

As Spigs, T-Ray, and Peabo crawled out from under the seats, Naz appeared in front of them, its tentacles shifted to the left.

"Naz hears something." Spigs grabbed for its leg, but the Creeple jumped back with a *CLICK-CLACK.*

"I hear it, musical instruments." T-Ray peered over the seat and cupped her ears. "Look at Naz." Music emanated from Naz's six vibrating tentacles, transmitting the sound. All the Creeples' huge ears perked up, intrigued by the music. They dashed to the window. "AFTER THEM!" T-Ray leaped up and chased after them, Spigs and Peabo close behind. The Creeples bounded out and darted up the drainpipe to the next floor.

The moss-sheathed Bog People shuffled after the Creeples by way of the stairs. The Hodag and Ayia Napa sea monster continued their battle royale through the hallway, tumbling down to the first floor.

Creeples!

When the auditorium was cleared of cryptid monsters, the exasperated teens gazed at one another.

"This is NOT how I envisioned my freshman year playing out." T-Ray wiped the lenses of her dusty glasses.

"Didja see THAT? A livin', breathin' HODAG! A Mongolian Death Worm! An Ayia Napa sea monster! Just KILLER cryptos!" Spigs was euphoric. "It must be Christmas!" Growing up, Spigs's sanctuary from Aunt Gussy's meanness was his bedroom and his cryptozoology journals. "Now, all I need to see is a Woolly Booger monster and I can die a happy man."

"I'm now convinced. THAT boy needs help." Peabo shook his head at Spigs's enthusiasm.

"Listen, you two. It's going to get worse before it gets better," T-Ray proclaimed. "So c'mon, follow those Bog People!"

As they reached the exit door, the teens ran straight into a furious and battered Chief McTaggart and Deputy Whipsnade.

CHAPTER 17

The Prevention of Cruelty to Animals . . . and Creeples!

"**E**xactly what do you three degenerates know about them Segway-stealin' varmints?" McTaggart crossed his arms and blocked the door with his rotund body.

"First, infidels. Now, degenerates. Sure miss those days when I was just called a misfit," Spigs groaned in an undertone to his friends before he looked McTaggart in the eyes. "Why would we know anything? We're only kids. Freshmen. Bottom of the food chain."

"That's right. Freshmen science students, studying, uh, science."

Peabo tried to help but made it awkward. He sneaked a peek at T-Ray to save them.

T-Ray spoke softly and in an authoritative tone. "Chief McTaggart, Deputy Whipsnade, remember I informed you I was on a *deep* covert assignment for Dean Smathers?"

McTaggart and Whipsnade nodded.

"And remember I told you our work was top military secret?"

They nodded again.

"And remember when I told you that I intensely had to puke?"

They gave an emphatic nod.

"So, how in the world would we have time to get mixed up in all this? We're at a loss, just like you."

Whipsnade thought long and hard about this. "She does have a point, Ace. Tossin' your cookies does take a considerable amount of time to recover from, and believe me, I—"

"DEPUTY!" McTaggart hissed, then turned to the teens. "Something's still amiss here."

"Right, Chief. But since those lawless Lilliputians aren't here, what's our next move?" Whipsnade replied.

"'Lawless Lilliputians'? Now *that's* a new one for the Creeples," Peabo whispered to Spigs.

"Sounds like a grunge band," Spigs whispered back.

"Let's run 'em in, Ace. Been itchin' to try these bad boys." Whipsnade eagerly whipped out his shiny handcuffs.

"Cool your jets, Deputy," McTaggart barked. "We're just gathering intel, for now."

"Now that you've collected your *intel*, can we go?" Spigs asked.

The teens' attention now turned to the auditorium windows.

Skoota and Royal appeared agitated, hopping from one window ledge to the next. The translucent Mongolian Death Worm slithered like a giant gummy worm along the side of the building. Its thick body busted windows as it contracted and squirmed. The mummified Bog People were surprisingly active as they slogged up and down the fire escape in pursuit of Beezer, Naz, and Tatz. The Ayia Napa sea monster and Hodag were nowhere to be seen.

Spigs cleared his throat and pleaded, "Can we go now, officers? Please?"

"Uugh! I feel—" T-Ray slapped her hands over her mouth and clutched her stomach.

McTaggart scratched his belly in thought and blustered, "You're clear . . . for now. BUT we've got you misfits on our radar."

The trio bolted out of the auditorium, dodged the collateral damage in the hallway, and hurried down the stairs and out the Cryptozoology building's double doors.

"I caught a glimpse of the Creeples in a faceoff with the Bog People by the Cybernetics building," Peabo said as the teens stood out front, undecided on their next move.

"Grab 'em while in their Beastly Mode and get to Professor Bodkins." T-Ray eyed the chaos over at the Cybernetics building.

"And just how do ya propose we do THAT," Spigs groused.

"I've got cans of Cheez 'Em in my bag," Peabo said. "They love the stuff."

"You always carry cans of Cheez 'Em around, do you?" T-Ray sighed.

"No need to get snarky, T-Ray."

"Well, I'm certainly out of ideas—" Spigs began.

Creeples!

"LOOK!" T-Ray shouted in alarm. Spigs and Peabo followed her pointing finger.

Two Creeples launched themselves from the side of the building into nets held out by Horace and three of his hooligans. The Creeples seemed to think it was a game. Skoota and Coco had been netted. Royal was in midflight. Tatz and Naz clung to the second-story window. And Beezer was at the top of the fire escape playing tug-of-war with the Mongolian Death Worm's tail.

"STOP! DON'T DO IT!" T-Ray yelled as Royal safely landed in Horace's net.

"STOP!" Peabo echoed to Tatz. But it ignored the warning and somersaulted into a hooligan's net.

"NO, BEEZER. NO!" Spigs called up to the orange Creeple. Beezer ignored him, curled up in a ball, and plopped down perfectly in another net.

The teens rushed up to Horace.

"Tell your gorillas to let 'em go, Horrid!" Spigs shouted.

"No can do. Dean Smathers wants these fiends of nature."

The Creeples *CLICK-CLACKED* loudly, trapped in the tight netting. Horace's hooligans fought to control them, biceps flexing as they struggled to keep from being dragged along the ground. The Creeples let out a strange collective grumble. They didn't try to blast their way free with their magical eyes or chew through with their sharp teeth.

"We mean it, Horace." Peabo was fuming. "Let them go or—" He made a fist and an aggressive stance.

"Or what, Peeboy?" Horace's grin melded into a malicious

sneer as he glared at the three. "Your Lab Rat days are numbered. Wait until the—OOF!" A student in a bright blue ASPCA T-shirt tackled Horace to the ground. The fit boy wasn't alone, and a dozen blue-clad students pounced on Horace's hooligans.

"Pick on mutants your own size," they chanted as they seized the nets. "Mutants are people! Mutants are people!"

"They're NOT MUTANTS," T-Ray cried out, frowning at the ugly term.

"CREEPLES! They're called Creeples!" Spigs ordered.

"Creeples are people! Creeples are people!" the ASPCA warriors continued to chant as they held down Horace and his hooligans. The agitated Creeples CLICK-CLACKED and squirmed out of the nets. They waddled over to a bike path, with Peabo close behind them waving cans of Cheez 'Em.

The Creeples wrestled six motorized skateboards away from a group of students and zipped off. Weaving out of control, they flailed recklessly as they zoomed away from their captors—and the teens.

Peabo hurried back to Spigs and T-Ray, shoulders slouched in defeat. "They got away."

"What DID you do?" The struggling Horace bared his teeth as he strained to look up at his attacker. "You idiots! You've ruined everything. The Golden Dawn is—!"

"Put a sock in it," said the fit boy, who had Horace in a headlock. The ASPCA leader flexed his bicep, choking off Horace's words.

"What's he talking about?" Peabo asked Spigs.

"Beats me, but this Golden Dawn thingy sure seems to be an open secret around here."

Horace grunted, thrashed, and tugged at the ASPCA leader's arm, but he was unable to free himself.

"Horrigan, you are *not* to harm those little creatures," the ASPCA leader decreed.

"Thanks for your help. Oh, I'm . . . Theresa Ray." She smiled at the handsome teenager.

Spigs and Peabo looked at each other and mouthed, "Theresa Ray?"

"But call me T-Ray."

"I'm Onslow." He flashed T-Ray a superhero smile, his dimples melting into his cheeks.

"Let me go, you animal-lovin' freaks!" Horace yelled.

"Should I?" Onslow asked.

T-Ray nervously brushed stray strands of her auburn hair away from her glasses and let out a giggle Spigs had never imagined her capable of.

"He's basically harmless. More bark than bite," T-Ray said.

Onslow and the others released Horace and his hooligans from their clutches.

Horace hopped to his feet and brushed himself off, trying to maintain some dignity. He glanced at his watch and motioned to his hooligans. They stormed off.

"You geeks will be sorry!" Horace screamed. He jabbed a finger their way. "Especially you, Onslow!"

"Is it me, or did this situation take a super weird turn?" Peabo asked Spigs.

"Helloooo, earth to T-Ray, we hafta save a certain species and a teacher . . . ANY of that ring a bell?" Spigs spread his elbows and shoved his way between T-Ray and Onslow.

"Hey, we're on your side," Onslow assured Spigs. "Right, gang?"

The ASPCA members clapped in unison. "Rights for animals! Rights for people! Rights for *Creeples!*"

"They sure like to chant a lot," Peabo grumbled.

"Don't know how we can thank you and your team," T-Ray said.

"Anytime." Onslow flashed her his glistening pearly whites.

"Yapper's tweeting about some kind of commotion at the girls' dorm." Peabo looked up from his phone.

Onslow had T-Ray mesmerized.

"We've gotta go." Spigs yanked T-Ray along with him and Peabo. "And what the heck was that about?" Spigs demanded as he climbed into Peabo's scooter's sidecar.

T-Ray hopped on the back of the scooter. "Just being friendly." She glared at him. "Maybe *I'll* take Onslow to Bell Tower to see the view."

"Are you kiddin' me? Is *that* what that was all about? Gettin' back at me for . . . ?" Spigs dissolved into a fuming sputter and threw up his hands in frustration.

"Onslow did just SAVE the Creeples!" T-Ray snapped.

"Guys, enough! We have a bigger problem than your lovers' quarrel." Peabo coasted up and parked the scooter near the girls' dorm.

As they hurried in, Spigs muttered, "And it's NOT a lovers' quarrel."

"DEFINITELY not," T-Ray declared.

"And who in their right mind names their kid Onslow! SHEESH!" Spigs scowled as he followed them inside the girls' dorm. He tried to tamp down his exasperation, worried he may have just exposed his jealousy card.

CLASSIFIED

S.H.A.D.O.W.

High Energy Laser Defense System

Exotic Technology Department
Washington, DC
Codename: PROJECT GOOZE

Name: Skoota

Aliases: Blue Creeple

Identity: Twenty-inch-tall humanoid. Neon-blue hair. Prodigious ears. Oscillating mustard-yellow eyes. Click-clacking noise emanates from the skull region—a form of communication.

Creators: Three Aberdasher Academy of Science students.

Personal Abilities: Super strong.

Magical Powers: Draconic Kinetic Energy blasts from their eyes that super-charge inanimate objects into living, breathing entities.

Mystical Limitations: The metamorphosis can last up to twelve hours.

Potential Application: Particle-beam weaponry.

Comments: Cheez 'Em connoisseur. Quick-tempered.

CHAPTER 18

The Ritual

Horace hustled across campus alone, repeatedly glancing over his shoulders and avoiding eye contact with fellow students. He stopped in front of Bell Tower and again scanned back over his shoulders. He circled behind the tower and effortlessly wiggled his body through the dense hedgerows as he approached the back entrance. It was obvious he'd done this routine many times before. However, his hands were shaking uncontrollably as he inserted his key in the padlock to the wooden door with the porthole window.

Deep beneath Bell Tower, and one level below Keeper's dingy dwelling, Dean Smathers, in a ceremonial black hooded robe embroidered with a silver inverted pentagram and a red dragon's head, stood on a three-foot podium in front of a select group of teenagers. The walls of the chamber were covered in deteriorating ornate stonework. Floor-to-ceiling oxblood-colored drapes hung sporadically throughout. Smathers held an opulent ruby-encrusted gold box in his hands. It was a medieval reliquary, used to store holy relics, and it looked like it was a thousand years old.

Smathers scowled as Horace slipped in the back and received a robe from one of his bulky friends. Smathers fixed cold eyes on Horace and growled, "Bring forth our ranked Seekers and present them with our divine resurrection." Smathers carefully placed the reliquary on a stone pedestal as Horace ushered a line of five quivering students toward the gilded container. The students locked hands and walked with a deliberate but apprehensive pace toward the partially opened reliquary. Two students pivoted their heads, taking in their surroundings. Several linked hands tremored, and Smathers scowled at their weakness with lip curled in disgust. His voice boomed and echoed in the subterranean chamber. "Show your loyalty to me and to our most righteous cause."

He pointed to the reliquary, which radiated a pulsating magenta glow from within. The first student, a skinny sophomore with too many freckles to count, was terrified.

"I'm not sure that I—"

"Quiet. Proceed," Smathers ordered.

Still holding hands with the second person in line, the freckle-faced boy nervously stuck his free hand into the reliquary's opening. Without warning, he was yanked inside the container up to his elbow. The other students gasped, and all five of them started writhing and twitching as a magenta glow surged through their bodies, shooting from their feet and hair. They collapsed on the floor, convulsing. Dean Smathers watched with bored indifference as the eyes of the trembling students turned bright blood red. Seconds later, the glowing surge stopped as quickly as it had started, returning their eyes to their natural colors. Yet now there was something odd, something apathetic, about the students. Their docile eyes were vacant. Willing and obedient. Completely compliant.

Dean Smathers nodded to Horace, who helped the students up and brought the dutiful flock back into line. They kneeled, heads bowed, and waited.

"You may rise."

The group raised their eyes, and any semblance of fight or spirit had been removed. Smathers spoke softly, a kind tinge in his usually brusque voice. "My newest Disciples, you have now achieved the truest conversion. You are purified, ready for the final transition. Now go. Prepare yourselves for this last step, and we will reconvene at eleven tonight."

The newly ordained Disciples filed out in an orderly fashion. But Horace remained. His head and eyes dropped to the cobblestone floor, expecting harsh words. When the room had nearly emptied, Smathers turned and glared at his incompetent high-ranking Disciple.

"I've been deceived." His voice was full of furious vitriol. "Get me those vile ogres. They possess my insurmountable powers. DO NOT FAIL ME!"

"Yes, sir." Horace nodded and hurried out, with an expression of mild relief.

Smathers turned to a lone robed Disciple seated in the corner of the room. "You may stand and approach."

The robed figure rose and removed her hood.

Smathers allowed himself a tiny grin as he turned to the eager young woman. "My most devoted Disciple. It is now time for you to spread our virtuous word. The Golden Dawn is upon us. Let them know that they may stand with us or suffer the cruelest of consequences. You know your mission. Proceed undaunted. You may go."

Rachell Hobbs nodded once and left the chamber.

CHAPTER 19

Creeples' Got Talent

Spigs, Peabo, and T-Ray reached the recreational room on the third floor of the girls' dorm. They caught a fleeting glimpse of flowing neon-red hair turning the corner at the end of the hall.

"This is our rec floor," T-Ray boomed. The sound of music blared from the end of the hall. The three dashed around the corner but skidded to a halt at the outrageous scene. Royal led a parade of dancing Creeples in a conga line—flinging themselves from side to side to the rhythm. The music seemed to have captivated them and calmed their inclination for menacing, magical mischievousness. Their large ears appeared sensitive to the loud sound but twitched to the beat. Their enthusiastic dance route and the lure of the music drew the Creeples to the last room at the end of the hall.

Spigs raced into the room two steps behind Naz, but he froze as an awkward blush filled his cheeks. The spacious lounge was full of girls in athletic tops bouncing to hip-hop moves led by instructors in a video on the TV screen. Spigs breathed a sigh of relief when none of them acknowledged his existence.

The excitable Creeples started mimicking the workout routine—or mocking it. Tatz, Naz, and Beezer did a crude version of the Carlton dance. As T-Ray and Peabo caught up, Spigs put a finger to his lips and tiptoed toward the Creeples. Of course, Beezer's wild rump gyrations resulted in the silent release of a lethal fart!

"GRRROSS! Are there *boys* in here?" a girl whined, but didn't stop her aerobic routine.

The grooving girls giggled, and one said, "*My* money's on Jordan."

"Now wait a minute!" Jordan's dark braids bobbed in rhythm to the song. "The one who smelt it, dealt it."

The girls dissolved into breathless giggles, not noticing the lurking, diminutive humanoids during their workout.

As the hip-hop song's bass increased, Skoota, Coco, and Royal *CLICK-CLACKED* and scurried to grab up the girls' discarded colorful gym towels. T-Ray took a step toward the distracted Creeples, but Peabo held her back. He readjusted his Snapchat glasses for a better angle. The three Creeples straddled the towels between their legs, clutching each end.

"Now what are they up to?" T-Ray wondered.

Spigs was beside himself. He knew what was coming. "Wait for it. Wait for it . . ."

The Creeples vacillated the towels back and forth between their short, stubby legs. The girls all screamed in unison.

T-Ray cringed at the sight. "What ARE they doing?"

Creeples!

Peabo and Spigs cracked up, doubling over and clutching their stomachs, and high-fived each other. Once again, T-Ray didn't participate in their celebratory reaction.

"Oh, c'mon. They're doing the Dental Floss dance!" Peabo beamed with pride. He leaned in for a better video shot.

"They're flossin' their butts!" Spigs bounced up on his toes to take in the whole scene. "You gettin' all this?"

"THAT'S going viral," Peabo vowed.

"Nothing's going viral," T-Ray snarled, and pointed a scolding finger at Peabo and Spigs.

"Come on, T-Ray! The secret's out. If I upload that"—Peabo pointed at the Creeples popping each other on their dumpy rumps with the rolled-up gym towels—"then people will learn they're not like . . . killer creatures."

"I don't . . . You may have a point." T-Ray nervously chewed a fingernail.

"*Now* it's time to implement plan B—change Peabo's channel to the Creeples Channel," Spigs asserted. "It'll be the attention we've been missing. A subscription channel for exclusive Creeples footage. And it just may get us the funding we need . . . deserve."

"T-Ray?" Spigs delivered a mammoth grin. "Social media gold!"

"Well . . ." T-Ray forced a tight smile.

"Gracious ME!" shouted the elderly, pugnacious, and vision-challenged dorm mother Ms. McGillicuddy as she barged into the room. She squinted at the Creeples. "Nakedness? In *my* house! OUT! OUT!" She seized a broom and swung it with deadly aim. The bristles swatted Skoota and Beezer into a weight rack. Tatz sprang on Ms. McGillicuddy's back, slathered two of its short, fat fingers with gooey saliva, and stuck them in both her ears. Tatz twirled its fingers back and forth in her ear canals. *SQUISH! SQUISH! SQUISH!* The mortified Ms. McGillicuddy stood petrified for a second and then snapped out of it with a deafening shriek. She shook Tatz off and defended her girls with gusto. Choking up on the broomstick like Babe Ruth, she swung for the fences. The Creeples bobbed, ducked, and weaved for their lives.

"*Now* I know where the Creeples learned their disgusting behavior!" T-Ray looked at Spigs and Peabo. The boys looked away, sneaking a fist bump. "Enough, you two. This is our chance to nab them!"

"I'm on it." Peabo removed a can of Cheez 'Em from his backpack. "Skoota. Got your fav." Peabo sprayed some of the rubbery cheese in his palm. Skoota moved in, wiggled its ears, *CLICK-CLACKED*, and licked up the cheese, then snatched the Cheez 'Em can from Peabo and rejoined the dance party.

"Oh, THAT went well," T-Ray remarked. "We need a better plan, and fast. Look!" She pointed to Whipsnade and McTaggart standing in the doorway with their batons drawn.

Royal unleashed its magical lightning rays at Whipsnade's and McTaggart's shoes, enveloping their tactical boots in a mystical maelstrom. With the boots now possessing minds of their own, the two officers began a poor rendition of the Stanky Leg dance.

"What's happenin'?" Chief McTaggart yelped.

"Dunno, but I'm dang good at this!" Deputy Whipsnade grooved his head side to side.

T-Ray grabbed Royal and snuggled it like a newborn. Royal *CLICK-CLACKED*, and Coco leaped to swing from T-Ray's elbow.

"Grab those pesky pipsqueaks!" McTaggart ordered Whipsnade, but he was doing a 1940s boogie-woogie jazz routine.

"No worries, Chief," Spigs said. "It'll wear off soon, and you'll be back hasslin' students in no time."

T-Ray nabbed the last of the Creeples and raced back into the hall with them all clinging to her like a family of baby monkeys.

"Hey, WhipSNERD, you available for Cinco de Mayo?" Peabo laughed and turned his head to make sure his Snapchat glasses caught the dirty-dancing cops on video as he and Spigs followed T-Ray out. "You dudes are goin' viral."

"How'd you do that?" Spigs pointed to the Creeples clutching T-Ray's neck, waist, and legs.

"Apparently they still like to cuddle. Even in their Beastly Mode." She nuzzled Royal's head with her cheeks.

"Music hath charm to soothe the savage beasts," Spigs chuckled.

"Well, that's not quite right, but I guess it's appropriate in this instance." T-Ray looked down at the Creeples. "Now, let's introduce you guys to someone who can help us."

Royal *CLICK-CLACKED* to the rest of the gang.

Spigs held open the dorm's door for T-Ray and the Creeples to exit. The three hustled to the scooter.

Spigs hung back to let T-Ray get in the sidecar. Beezer swung from her arm and kicked Tatz in the stomach with a playful

CLICK-CLACK. Tatz hiccupped, and electricity blasted from its two head bolts and zapped the scooter.

"Beezer, shame on—" Spigs's words choked off at the sight of Gideon Flitch's unoccupied van parked in the shadows.

"T-Ray, LOOK OUT!" Peabo shouted, but it was too late.

Big Lyle and Lil' Lyle seized T-Ray with all of the Creeples attached to her, throwing a large gunnysack over them all. T-Ray fought with all her strength, and the Lyle brothers struggled mightily to get the writhing gunnysack into the van.

"T-RAY!" Spigs pounded on the van as it pulled away. Spigs and Peabo bolted to the scooter. Peabo pressed the ignition switch. Nothing; no juice! Its electric power was drained. The boys could only watch in horror as the van sped out of sight.

CHAPTER 20

The Million-Dollar Attraction

T-Ray watched Flitch smirk from his director's chair as he swigged his pickle juice and observed the Creeples hung in cages from the beams of a tattered yurt.

"Lower them down and put on horse blinders." Flitch struck his gloved palm with a riding crop.

"Boss, if I do that, I won't be able to see," Big Lyle whimpered.

"Ya know, Big Lyle, with a little effort, one day you might make a full-fledged halfwit. I MEAN ON THEM CRITTERS!" Flitch lashed the whip against his pant leg.

"But what'll that do, boss?" Lil' Lyle retorted as he lowered one of the cages.

"It'll contain their extraordinary magical powers," he grunted, with another thrash of the whip to his pant leg. "So don't stand in front of them. Their eyes are lethal."

"You'll wish you hadn't done that," T-Ray shouted from behind

Big Lyle. Furious, she kicked up dust, struggling against the ropes that tied her to a chair.

"Want me to put horse blinders on this one?" Big Lyle asked, pointing to T-Ray. She walloped him in the shin. "Ouch!"

"NO, numbnuts. We'll hold on to her until I figure out what to do with her."

"We gonna give these critters to the dean?" Big Lyle rubbed his aching shin.

"And collect our reward, huh?" Lil' Lyle asked.

"No, men. I've decided to terminate my employment contract with Dean Smathers."

"Uum, how do we get paid, boss?" Lil' Lyle cautiously opened Naz's cage, with blinders in hand.

"Yeah, boss. Tired of eating the zonkey's leftovers." Big Lyle's stomach grumbled to prove his point. He struggled to place the blinders around Coco's head.

"REE-lax, my feckless flunkies. And behold!" Flitch stood, arms spread wide. "Our NEW, million-dollar attraction!"

The Lyle brothers waited for him to say more, but he stood there guzzling pickle juice and grinning dementedly while pointing at the Creeples with his whip.

"Boss. All I see are them six critters." Lil' Lyle struggled to slip blinders over Royal's head while avoiding eye contact. Royal shook its head in protest, but the blinders stayed put.

"Because you knotheads don't have the mind of a carny!" Flitch strolled over to Tatz's cage and poked it with the whip. Lightning energy sparked from the yellow-haired Creeple's bolts. "It's in my blood. I can sniff out golden opportunities."

"Just like 'em zonkeys, huh, boss?" Big Lyle said.

"Forget those zonkeys. As P. T. Barnum once proclaimed, 'There's a sucker born every minute.'" Flitch lowered his voice and added, "Unfortunately, two of them work for me."

"Ah, thanks, boss." Lil' Lyle scratched the top of his head.

"These magical little marvels will thrill audiences worldwide." Flitch poked Tatz again.

"STOP IT, you dirtbag! You're hurting Tatz." T-Ray jiggled her chair so vigorously she started to tip over, but Big Lyle reached out a lazy hand and caught her with ease.

"Tatz? Terrific, they have names. Now just visualize six mini-mutants on unicycles, jugglin', jumpin' through hoops," Flitch expressed with glee as he tried to pet Naz's tentacles. The red Creeple moved to the far side of the cage, trying to get away from the nasty man.

"You'll be in SO much trouble when I get out of here. And don't call them mutants!" T-Ray warned.

Flitch ignored her and proceeded to the next cage. "Maybe a trapeze act where this purple fella catches the green one in the air." He flashed Royal his gap-toothed grin. "Picture this strong one balancing all five while walking on a tightrope." Flitch stroked Skoota's blue plume of hair.

"It'll never happen!" T-Ray screamed.

Flitch stuck his deep-set, hollow eyes and pointy nose up to Beezer's cage. He poked through the bars and lifted Beezer's chin with the whip.

"So, gentlemen, see them as six diminutive clowns enter-taining sold-out crowds with feats of magical—" Flitch was interrupted by one of Beezer's infamous sonic farts, which sent Flitch sailing over chairs.

T-Ray couldn't help but laugh. "That'll definitely bring down the house."

Flitch gagged from the whiff of boiled cabbage but was undaunted.

"But, boss, what about that Globster and Fangtooth Fish we stole from the school's cryo ... cryo ... frozen room," Big Lyle said.

"Yeah, thought 'em were the new attractions?" Lil' Lyle added.

"That's cryogenics!" Flitch growled in exasperation. "I swear I don't know how you two even generate enough brainpower to breathe!"

"But they're for our freak show," Big Lyle added.

"A frozen sea slug and a snaggletooth guppy ain't puttin' butts in our seats. Now these mutants—*pure* gold! And they're gonna make ME world famous!" Flitch crowed. He walked over to the yurt's exit. "Okay, knuckleheads, it's that time again. Now, decamp. It's movin' day."

· · ·

"Sure could use my CPAP machine now." Spigs panted and wheezed.

Peabo stopped and placed his hands on his hips. "No chance I ever make the school's track team."

Flitch's van had sped away fifteen minutes earlier, and they

Creeples!

had barely covered a mile and a half on foot. The road leading to Flitch's carnival wasn't even in sight.

"Come on, Peabo! Can't stop."

"I'm a thinker, not a runner. Besides, my backpack is full of electronics." Peabo huffed and continued his lethargic pace.

"We have to find T-Ray." Spigs looked around for another option, but the only vehicle in sight was a white truck with the blue ASPCA logo on the door. The driver's chiseled jawline was noticeable even through the tinted windows.

"It's that Onslow dude." Peabo had followed Spigs's gaze to Onslow's truck.

"NO!" Spigs snapped.

"What's up with you? He helped us stop Horace's goons."

"It's just . . . Did you see the way T-Ray looked at 'im?" Spigs couldn't quite come to terms with what his issue was with Onslow. "Plus, he has an obnoxious name."

"But he *has* a running truck. So, work out your personal problems later." Peabo waved both hands to get Onslow's attention and rushed over. Spigs hurried behind.

"T-Ray's in trouble. Can you give us a lift?" Peabo asked.

"Hop in."

Peabo slid into the middle front bench seat next to Onslow.

"You coming too?" the junior called out to Spigs.

"Yeah, yeah. I'm comin'." Spigs swallowed his pride and got in next to Peabo.

"Can you drop us off at that carnival a few miles outside campus?" Peabo asked. "It's an emergency!"

"I'm on it." Onslow smashed down the gas pedal. Gravel and rocks spewed off his rear fenders.

Peabo pulled out his phone and bumped Spigs with his elbow. "It's time to go all out with plan B. And we need it to go viral."

"Yapper?"

"Who else? I'll give her the scoop on our Creeples Channel and their abduction."

"Roger that. Plan B's a GO!"

Peabo's thumbs typed frantically on his phone. Spigs listened to the dings of Yapper's text responses as Onslow sped down the narrow gravel road to the carnival. A loud ringtone filled the truck. Spigs pulled an iPad out of Peabo's backpack. Professor Bodkins was calling by way of FaceTime.

"Hey, Professor, give me one sec." Peabo turned to Onslow. "How long till we get there?"

"Three minutes, max."

"Boys?" Professor Bodkins appeared in full view on the iPad. "I'm in the Molecular Diagnostics lab and managed to get enough samples of your Gooze to analyze."

"Gotcha, Professor, but we've got an update for ya," Spigs said. He and Peabo chattered over each other, trying to explain to the professor the lunacy of the last few hours.

"Complete outrageousness!" Peabo squawked.

"Yeah, and the Creeples are just whacked," Spigs added.

"Guys, hold on," Professor Bodkins sighed.

"Their tiny bodies are packed with total awesomeness. Peabo just sent you some pics, Professor."

Creeples!

"Guys," Professor Bodkins said patiently. "I don't understand . . . you're talking over each other."

"Professor, the Creeples have completed a metamorphosis—into dark, menacing beings. Passive one minute, volatile the next." Peabo couldn't contain his anxiety.

"Their black eyes blast out magical lightning rays, like supercharged energy particles," Spigs added.

"It seems to be basic molecular manipulation, but with ridiculous results," Peabo finished with a deep breath.

"Okay, got the pictures. Hmm, well, from their looks and what you're telling me of their extraordinary powers, I'd have to conclude it's a form of . . . transmogrification," Professor Bodkins stated.

"Transmog . . . huh?" Spigs caressed the back of his neck.

"It means to transform in a surprising or magical manner."

"Yeah, I'd say supercharging inanimate objects to life classifies as 'surprising and magical,'" Peabo sputtered.

"We think—or hope—all the animated objects only last a few hours. At least, that's what T-Ray figured out," Spigs said.

"Where's T-Ray?"

"Well . . . er—" Spigs began, until Peabo elbowed him in his ribs.

Professor Bodkins held up a test tube with a small amount of the iridescent Gooze. "It's rather amazing. I've never seen anything like it before. I'm going to sequence the genetic code. The important thing is that since the Creeples have shape-shifted into their—"

"Beastly Mode!" Spigs and Peabo blurted together.

"Fortunately, their magical mayhem hasn't cost any lives, but that could change . . . at any moment! It's the great unknown. So, it's imperative once you capture them, you bring them to me."

"We're on it, Professor. They're . . . ah, with T-Ray. We should have them shortly," Peabo assured her.

Professor Bodkins started to ask another question, but Spigs cut her off. "Talk soon, Professor, bye." He switched off the iPad and turned to Onslow. "Are we there yet?"

"Three—two—" Onslow screeched to a sliding stop on the gravel road next to the rusted bumper-car ride. "One!"

Spigs eyed Horace's Jeep parked ahead of them. "Looks like we could be in for another rumble."

S.H.A.D.O.W.

High Energy Laser Defense System

Exotic Technology Department
Washington, DC
Codename: PROJECT GOOZE

Name: Naz

Aliases: Red Creeple

Identity: Twenty-inch-tall humanoid. Neon-red hair. Prodigious ears. Oscillating mustard-yellow eyes. Click-clacking noise emanates from the skull region—a form of communication.

Creators: Three Aberdasher Academy of Science students.

Personal Abilities: Superior hearing from six cranial tentacles.

Magical Powers: Draconic Kinetic Energy blasts from their eyes that super-charge inanimate objects into living, breathing entities.

Mystical Limitations: The metamorphosis can last up to twelve hours.

Potential Application: Particle-beam weaponry.

Comments: Cheez 'Em connoisseur. Extremely skittish.

CHAPTER 21

Boisterous Bedlam at the Carnival

O nslow grasped the door handle, ready to jump out, but Spigs hissed through his teeth and threw an arm over Peabo to tap Onslow on the shoulder.

"Not yet." He pointed to where Horace and three of his hooligans crept toward a nearby tent, oddly decked out in matching clothes: white pants and gray shirts. "We're outnumbered. Let's see what they're up to first."

Spigs's phone bleeped. He noticed that Yapper took the bait:

#RoboticExperimentExposed!

Creeples!

#CreeplesGoWild!
#Creeptropolis Creeples Channel goes live!

Through the truck's open window, the teens heard Horace order, "Let's bag 'em and tag 'em."

"Are they carrying . . . guns?" Peabo swallowed hard.

"What the . . . ?" Spigs observed two of the hooligans as they pulled out bolt-action rifles with scopes from two rucksacks.

"Why that little . . . I mean, I don't believe it." Onslow leaned over the wheel for a better look.

"*Now* what do we do?" Spigs leaned into Peabo. "These dudes aren't playin' around. There are four of 'em and just two of us."

"Three of us," Onslow declared.

"Yeah, sure," Spigs muttered.

"Look, if you want my advice—" Onslow started.

"Which we don't," Spigs interrupted.

Onslow continued, looking annoyed. "Horace is after those . . . Creeples. So, he'll be distracted, which gives us a better chance to save T-Ray."

"Again, not interested in your—"

"Guys!" chirped a voice.

The three boys nearly fell out of their seats. T-Ray pressed against the passenger-side window.

"What're you doin' here?" Spigs scrambled to get out of the truck.

She puffed out her chest. "Seriously? My IQ is ten times that of any carnival barker's, and I was a Girl Scout Gold Award winner. They left me alone for two minutes, and I was out in thirty seconds." She smiled at Onslow. "Did you come here to help *me*?"

"Of course." Onslow grinned back.

Spigs cleared his throat. "Uh! We're ALSO HERE."

"Oh, yeah." T-Ray embraced Peabo and Spigs. "Let's go rescue the Creeples. Flitch is packing up the carnival. He plans to cross the border into Canada."

"But Horace is one step ahead of us," Peabo said.

"Perfect. He'll distract Flitch and his goons, and we can nab the Creeples," T-Ray surmised.

"Now, wasn't I *just* saying that very same thing?" Onslow stated.

"NO!" Spigs crossed his arms.

"Great minds think alike." T-Ray motioned toward the main tent. "C'mon, I'll show you where they are."

She gestured to the boys to be quiet as she led them up to the yurt, where Horace and his three hooligans had entered to confront Flitch. The four teens crouched down next to the holding pen of potbellied pigs. They pinched their noses against the stinky swine odor and huddled up to listen to the conversation inside.

"Sir, we've learned that you're dealing with highly unusual mammals that are possibly illegal." Horace had modulated his voice to sound more bureaucratic and much older.

"You from Exotic Animal Control?"

T-Ray whispered to the boys, "That's Flitch."

"We represent the Animal Welfare Department . . . of Animals," Horace stumbled.

"Now, look." Flitch's voice became more defensive. "Our zonkeys are perfectly legit. And that Bactrian camel is, well—"

"No, sir," Horace interrupted. "I'm referring to a rare species . . . ash-colored skin, diminutive mammals."

"Can't help ya there, pally." Flitch's voice hardened. He figured out they were after the Creeples. "And like our name says, we're a travelin' carnival, so . . . we're travelin'. Now take a powder, punks."

Outside the tent, T-Ray signaled for the boys to follow her. Onslow and Spigs vied for who would follow directly behind her, tugging on each other's shirts and arms until Peabo wedged himself in between the two rivals. Once inside, Peabo and Spigs groaned at the sight of the caged Creeples.

"Still in their Beastly Mode, so watch out for their awesomeness," Spigs said. "'Cause I'd look silly dancin' the Nae Nae right now."

"Skoota! Tatz!" Peabo cried out and ran to his Creeples. He popped open the door and struggled to remove their constricting horse blinders.

"C'mere, Naz. Hey, Beezer." Spigs helped unlock his Creeples with one hand and held his nose with the other, knowing what was coming. The overly excited Beezer unloaded a booty bomb that sounded like a long yank on a distressed tugboat's foghorn—*BARROOOMMPH!*

"Does it always sound like that?" Onslow asked T-Ray as he helped her remove the blinders from Coco and Royal.

"Who, Beezer or Spigs?" T-Ray smiled when Onslow laughed, and explained, "It's the way it expresses itself . . . Beezer, that is." She stroked Coco and looked at Royal. "I'm sorry that dreadful man did that to you." Royal *CLICK-CLACKED*, wiggled its ears, and hugged T-Ray. They were still physically in their metamorphosis stage but seemed unusually docile.

The Creeples gathered together and *CLICK-CLACKED* maniacally, like a dysfunctional family gossiping at the dinner table, until Naz's six tentacles bent toward the tent's doorway, seconds before a shrill voice sounded.

"Well, well . . . what DO we have here? Sneakin' in for a free performance?" Flitch uttered through his spacious gapped teeth. He shielded the exit with his tall, gangly frame. He began to roll up his plaid sleeves to reveal hairy, skinny forearms.

The Creeples became agitated by the sound of Flitch's whiny voice. Royal led the charge as the Creeples Aussie-splay rushed at Flitch, who caught one look at Royal's demented black eyes and threw himself down on the dusty ground, arms covering his head. Each Creeple tramped across Flitch's back as they waddled out of the yurt.

Once outside, the crazed Creeples bolted in six different directions, with the vengeful goal of causing cataclysmic calamities.

The four teens scrambled after them out of the yurt.

"Where'd they go?" Peabo scanned left and right.

T-Ray raced after Royal, but it was too late. Royal focused its magical eyes on the rickety Black Widow ride and blasted magenta lightning rays, animating it to LIFE. T-Ray backpedaled as the six carriage arms holding the seat tubs lurched at her like a colossal spider straight out of a 1950s sci-fi movie. Spigs rushed to help her, but Onslow got there first. He grabbed her hand and yanked her out of harm's way as the Black Widow smashed Horace's pickup truck, flipped Flitch's semitruck trailer, and shredded the tents and yurts.

The Lyle brothers crawled out from under the flattened tent

and tried to catch Royal, but two driverless bumper cars knocked them both into the seats and sped off.

"Get back here, you chowderheads!" Flitch shouted.

Big Lyle yelled back, "But we can't control 'em."

As Flitch continued to curse the Lyle brothers, he didn't see Skoota behind him. Skoota lifted Flitch off the ground with its stubby four-fingered hand and flung him. Flitch shrieked and flew onto the flimsy Ferris wheel. He clutched the side of a swinging rust-bucket seat to keep from plunging back down. Peabo charged after Skoota, but Skoota sprang atop a trailer and blasted lightning rays out of its black eyes. The energy blasts disintegrated the Ferris wheel's main axle.

"HELP!" Flitch cried out as he swung his legs back and forth, finally hoisting himself inside the wobbly seat. "HELP!" With no axle support, the Ferris wheel dislodged from its base.

Skoota *CLICK-CLACKED* and Aussie-splay ran over to the zonkeys' pen, with Peabo trailing close behind.

"Look at it this way, Flitch. You're now the newest freak show," T-Ray called up to him as the Ferris wheel bowled throughout the campground. Flitch's complexion turned pale, and his knuckles turned white from his death grip on the seat's handlebars. T-Ray turned to laugh with Onslow, who hadn't left her side.

Spigs pursued Tatz into a yurt with a sign on it that read *Nature's Oddities.* Inside, Tatz stopped short in front of two bulky glass aquariums that held the cryogenically frozen sea creatures. One was the pea-green Globster—a sea slug the size of a basset hound. Spigs recognized the other as the rare Fangtooth Fish, a frightful deep-sea anomaly with a massive head, ferocious fangs, and a scaly, prickly dirty-brown body. It had the longest teeth on any fish in proportion to its body size.

"NO, TATZ. DON'T!" Spigs shouted, but it was too late.

The Creeple's lightning rays enveloped both ocean oddities in a magical maelstrom. Not only did the frozen creatures come to life, but they GREW and GREW and GREW into behemoths, shattering their aquariums. The now massive Globster slug, the size of a school bus, slinked toward one of Flitch's carnival trucks, leaving behind a pea-green trail of wet, rancid sea ooze. Its slime reeked of decaying whale blubber. The Globster reached the truck and slothfully encased it with its slippery body. Muffled screams were heard as two pea-green hooligans slinked out of the truck's bed.

"Now THAT'S the creature from the slimy ooze." Spigs wiped his brow and looked down at Tatz with a grin. Before he could deliver another wisecrack, the ten-foot-long Fangtooth freak smacked him in the face with its wet front fin. Spigs soared back four feet, crashing on his butt as the Fangtooth flopped and flailed on the grass, angling itself for a deadlier shot at Spigs. *CHOMP! CHOMP! CHOMP!* Its munching jaws brought its razor-sharp teeth closer and closer to him. "T-Ray? Peabo? Anyone? HELP!" With one eye trained on the amphibious oddity, Spigs shifted backward but couldn't gain separation.

Tatz appeared between Spigs and the Fangtooth creature. It focused its bolts and fired electric sparks that stunned the fish. Spigs managed to regain his feet, snagged Tatz by the arm, and sprinted away from the freaky fish's gnashing jaw, only to see Royal and Naz leap atop the two-humped Bactrian camel. Peabo

Creeples!

recorded the chaotic scene with his Snapchat glasses from behind a zonkey and streamed it live on the Creeples Channel.

Peabo narrated a play-by-play of the action. "Attention, faithful followers, you're now witnessing the mother lode of all monstrous mosh pits: a possessed Black Widow amusement ride, berserk bumper cars, and an errant Ferris wheel. Top it all off with the ginormous Globster sea slug and the ferocious Fangtooth Fish. And all sponsored by the Creeples Channel."

Within seconds, Spigs's phone dinged.

#FuriousFlitch Carnival honcho rides roving Ferris wheel!

**#Catawampous Creeples bareback
Bactrian camel like cowpokes!**

Spigs was frantic as he saw T-Ray chase after Hogzilla. Naz, Coco, Skoota, and Beezer had mounted atop its bristly hide and were waving their right arms in circles like cowboys with lassos. Spigs charged after them all but let out a howl when he saw Horace and his hooligans positioned in a sniper stance behind turned-over card tables. The monstrous porker hurtled right toward them, squealing in fright. Horace and his hooligans cocked and aimed their rifles, not at Hogzilla but at the Creeples.

"NOOO! Horace, don't!" Spigs screamed, pumping his legs as fast as they would go.

T-Ray saw the danger as Horace ordered, "Ready, aim—"

T-Ray bounded in front of the line of fire. "STOP!"

"Them are our mutants!" Lil' Lyle screamed as he caught up to Spigs. He had suited up in his exterminating outfit and sprayed a puff of brown chemical gas at Horace, but he was holding the nozzle toward his own face and sent himself crashing face-first into the dusty earth.

T-Ray shook her head at Lil' Lyle's incompetence and refocused her attention on Horace and his hooligans, whose rifles were still drawn. Spigs stopped in his tracks and glanced back at T-Ray. He turned and made a beeline to the confection cart, but as he did, Tatz jumped off his back and ran to its siblings.

T-Ray told Horace, "You'll have to shoot me first."

"With pleasure, Ms. Rogers." With that, Horace squeezed the trigger, but Spigs hurled a caramel apple at Horace's head with deadly precision and knocked him off his aim.

Big Lyle, also with his chem-tank strapped on, started gassing the area in a cloud, which gave the Creeples cover. Tatz, Coco, Skoota, and Beezer joined Royal and Naz atop the Bactrian camel. The six Creeples gripped the thick ridge of beige mane as the camel bounced and galloped away from the campground, leaving everyone in their dust.

"After them!" T-Ray cried. Spigs shrugged and looked around for transportation. Peabo dashed over to the zonkey, grabbed a hunk of mane, and hopped on its back. The zonkey trumpeted a raspy bray—*HEE-HAW!* T-Ray and Spigs cautiously followed suit and mounted a zonkey.

"Giddyap! Yee-haw!" Spigs hollered, and gave his zonkey a slight kick to pick up the pace.

The Creeples bounced between the stampeding camel's two humps. T-Ray galloped past the boys. She closed in fast and reached beyond her zonkey's neck with a hand extended, ready to snag Coco, who bounced about near the camel's backside. But the skittish camel kicked out its hind legs, which made T-Ray's nervous zonkey veer off course. Then suddenly . . .

POW! Royal plopped to the ground. The camel let out a frightened, throaty bleat and darted farther ahead.

Spigs's, T-Ray's, and Peabo's hearts skipped a beat as five more shots rang out.

POW! Skoota went down.

POW! Tatz down.

The camel stopped and turned in small, frantic circles to search for the source of the loud noises.

POW! Beezer down.

POW! Naz down.

POW! Coco down.

Six lifeless little figures lay slumped on the dirt road, each with a small metallic barb protruding from their ashen-gray bodies.

"NO!" T-Ray shrieked. She jumped off her zonkey and raced toward the Creeples with Spigs and Peabo directly behind her. But Horace and his hooligans got to them first in Flitch's smashed van. They screeched to a stop next to the motionless Royal and stuffed it in a burlap bag. With a wicked smirk, Horace pointed his rifle at the trio to keep them from approaching as his accomplices raced to the other dormant Creeples and gathered them up too. They flung them all into the back of the van like dead animals and sped away. T-Ray, Spigs, and Peabo stood helplessly in the middle of the dirt road.

CHAPTER 22

Dead or Alive

"**T**-Ray, they're alive, I just know it." Spigs was trying to stay positive as they entered the boys' destroyed dorm room. He reached out to touch her arm, but pulled back. Something had changed between them. He didn't know exactly what. But he felt differently around her now. More anxious and awkward.

"We've looked everywhere, and they're nowhere." T-Ray paced the room. Tears filled her eyes.

The teens had scoured the campus for the Creeples on Peabo's scooter, which they'd recharged with Onslow's truck battery.

Restless, T-Ray meticulously cleaned the destroyed room, gathering up frayed T-shirts and tossing them into the trashcan. "You were the one who told me Smathers said 'dead or alive.' You saw them, Spigs. Horace shot them."

"But not with bullets. I'm sure of it." Spigs opened the closet door to retrieve his trilby hat. "It looked more like darts or somethin'—probably tranquilizers."

"But what if those tranquilizers were for large mammals

like bears or lions? The dose could put our little Creeples in a coma. Or worse!" T-Ray's voice was raspy as she wiped her runny nose.

Spigs was overcome with a need to hug her but worried it might freak her out.

"Okay, let's step back and think this through." Peabo placed his forefingers to his temple. "Why would Horace want or need the Creeples?"

"For Smathers!" Spigs proclaimed.

"Of course! It's the one thing that makes sense. He's been working for Smathers since we stepped foot on campus," T-Ray declared.

"So," Peabo continued calmly, "Smathers wants them alive. If not, why didn't they use real bullets? I didn't see blood. Did you two?" Peabo shot T-Ray a small smile and bent over his laptop.

"You may be on to somethin'," Spigs agreed.

"Right! Uh . . . what is it I'm on to, again?"

"Remember what we learned in Molecular Transfusion class?" Spigs paced in a circle. "Living blood is more adaptable than dead blood cells. Whatever Smathers needs, he's gonna get it from a viable living source."

"Do you even know what you're saying?" T-Ray spun around and glared at Spigs with hands on her hips.

"Well, why not?" Spigs stopped his pacing. "I'm just tryin' to stay rational about the situation."

"So you're saying that I'M being irrational?" T-Ray shot back.

Spigs clamped his mouth shut. Everything he did seemed to irritate her, and he couldn't find the appropriate words when he needed them. Spigs resolved to stare out the window at Bell Tower in the distance. Something else tugged at his mind, and he couldn't let it go. "Guys, did you notice Horrid and his hooligans were dressed the same way?"

"I try not to focus on the despicable," Peabo responded. He tapped the Enter key on his keyboard. "Aha! Uploaded and posted! Have to keep the Creeples visible to the public."

"*And* they each were wearing a peculiar insignia pin." T-Ray tapped her chin with one finger. "A pentagram circled by three nines." T-Ray noticed everything. She'd placed all of the drawers back, and Spigs worked on reassembling the partially damaged bunk bed.

Peabo looked up from the screen. "The pentagram was an early Christian symbol, representing the five wounds Jesus received during his crucifixion."

The stifled ringtone startled them. Peabo snatched his iPad out of his backpack and held it up so the other two could see the screen. "FaceTime from PB."

Spigs circled around behind Peabo for a better look, but his mind was preoccupied with the mysterious pentagram symbol. "Smathers had the same symbol around his neck, *and* it was etched on all the bells in the tower." Spigs shook his head. "Too weird to be a coincidence."

"So?" Peabo said.

"That symbol was also on the label of that serum we used in the Gooze." Spigs knew there had to be a connection.

"Hello? Lab Rats?" Professor Bodkins's face appeared on the iPad screen. The room was dimly lit, but based on the reflecting metal file cabinets in the background, she appeared to have set her iPad on her desk in her office.

"Professor, we're tryin' to solve a cryptic clue that may be of major significance," Spigs jumped in.

"What I have to tell you may help solve a much bigger mystery." The professor shuffled through sheaves of printouts.

"Smathers has the Creeples, Professor." T-Ray wiped a dried tear from her jawline. "We don't know if . . . they're dead or—"

"OH, they're most definitely alive, T-Ray," the professor said emphatically.

"How can you be sure?"

"We know that DNA is the main component of our genetic material." She tapped a key on her computer. "I did an autosomal DNA test on your Gooze."

"Good idea. An auto . . . autoso . . . huh?" Spigs stuttered.

"I can identify the autosome chromosomes of DNA inherited from specific ancestors. Which reminds me, Johnny. I have some particularly interesting results from your DNA strain. I ran it through a genealogy database."

"Oh yeah?" Spigs leaned in closer. He knew nothing about his biological family. His spiteful Aunt Gussy would never share any information, as if there was a dreadful family secret. But Spigs had always dreamed he came from greatness. Maybe an uncle discovered the legendary Squonk creature in the hemlock forests of Pennsylvania! A great-grandparent discovered penicillin! His parents were international spies, and their car accident was no accident! The possibilities were endless. He cleared his throat. "So what'd ya learn? I'm the descendant of a genius? A mastermind?

A virtuoso? DARTH VADER! Break the news to me gently, Professor. I'm modest but a little sensitive."

"Your ancestry DNA shouldn't define you, Spigs," T-Ray stated in a calming voice of reason.

"*Que cada palo aguante su vela,*" Peabo said. "It's an old Spanish proverb that means 'May every mast hold its own sail.'"

"Very poignant, Peabo. And T-Ray's right," the professor said.

"Guys, that's nice and all." T-Ray was antsy. "But it's serious crunch time around here!"

"You're right. We'll discuss it later, Johnny. Now, as far as the Creeples go, my autosomal DNA test identified four genomic traits. Three human . . ." Professor Bodkins paused and gave them a long, stern look. "However, it's the fourth trait that is extraordinarily baffling—an anonymous reptilian genome with no match in any animal DNA database. This mysterious genetic trait has to be the catalyst to the Creeples' astonishing magical powers. Now, who located that serum?"

Spigs looked at the other two and sheepishly raised his hand.

"Tell me about that label, Johnny."

"Aah, ya see, the label had somethin' written like . . . Draco, Dracon. I didn't think it was a big deal, because we were so desperate for blood."

"Dracon . . . Draconem," the professor pondered. Her eyes expanded to the size of coffee cups. "Draconem Serum?"

"Uh, maybe. Hold on." Spigs fished in his pocket and pulled out the faded label. "Yup, that's probably it."

"OH NO!" Professor Bodkins hung her head and clasped her hands on the back of her neck. She looked up with a deep sigh.

Creeples!

"It's an *extremely* big deal. Yes, and this particular serum was blood. *Draconem* is Latin for ... *dragon!*"

"DRAGON BLOOD?" T-Ray squealed.

"YEE-OW!" Peabo exclaimed. "Total awesomeness!"

"No, it's not *total awesomeness.*" T-Ray punched Peabo's shoulder. "It's dangerous."

Spigs tried to weasel out of the blame. "But it was all in the name of science. For the team!" He shrank back as T-Ray turned narrowed eyes on him.

"In the name of ... WEIRD SCIENCE!" Peabo added.

"But aren't dragons mythological beasts, Professor?" T-Ray asked.

Professor Bodkins started to pace the room. The trio watched her as she came in and out of the iPad screen. "Historically, many cultures around the world—completely isolated from each other—have a tradition of giant mystical winged serpents."

"Wait!" Spigs's mind was racing. "The Grim Keeper in Bell Tower mentioned somethin' called the Draconem Expedition."

"So our Creeples are part dragon?" Peabo interjected.

"It's the only conclusion I can come up with. The 3D bio-printer must have activated the transmutation of your Gooze concoction."

"What does that mean?" T-Ray asked.

"The amalgamation of each of your DNA with the dragon blood, and by way of the 3D bio-fabrication machine, transmutated all the chromosomes—meaning they divided and grew rapidly. The transmutation created live beings infused with extraordinary powers from the dragon DNA!" The professor's voice was tinged with a combination of fear and awe.

"That's why Royal's smart, like me." T-Ray raised her hand.

"And why Beezer is, well—" Spigs stopped himself.

"But the most baffling aspect for me is why the Creeples look the way they do," the professor said. "I double-checked the CAD software, and you guys definitely didn't design those little buggers, so why do they look like that?"

The teens turned to each other with blank expressions and shrugged.

"But there's another issue, Professor," Peabo piped up. "The Creeples had a bizarre transformative reaction to catnip."

"A beastly reaction," Spigs jumped in. "Dark and menacing."

"I can only deduce that the nepetalactone chemical in catnip triggered their Draconic Kinetic Energy—the amazing magical abilities inherited from the dragon DNA."

"Okay, so *why* does Smathers want them? I mean, Flitch's actions make sense, as a carny," Peabo queried. "But Smathers?"

"Dunno, but his intentions seem more sinister, and way more desperate." Spigs couldn't stop thinking about the triple-nine symbol coincidences. Some sort of hidden meaning.

The professor continued. "So here's what we know. The Draconem Serum that Johnny found must be Smathers's precious item that he so desperately wants back. And Smathers has connected the sudden appearance of your magical Creeples on campus around the time the serum was stolen."

"Right. And Horace caught us in the bio-printing lab and must have told Smathers," T-Ray added.

"My hunch is Smathers wants the Creeples for some specific reason and will keep them alive. But for what and for how long?" Professor Bodkins let the question trail off into tense quiet. "Anyway, once—" A creaking door behind the professor made her glance back over her shoulder. She was startled. "Just *what* are you doing here?"

"Professor Bodkins, you're going on a little trip," a deep voice whispered. "Not far, so no need to bring anything."

"Who is it, Professor?" T-Ray asked. She gripped Spigs's shoulder. "What's going on?"

The shadowy male intruder stayed on the periphery of the iPad screen as he circled around and stood behind her desk, completely out of the teens' sight. The professor frowned, eyes narrowed in suspicion.

"My office was locked. How did you get in?" Several unidentified teenagers stepped out of the shadows and stood at attention—like mindless soldiers with chilling, blank stares. "Leave at once, or I'll call security."

"Professor, who's there?" Spigs said in a concerned tweaked voice.

"This is NOT a request," the deep voice asserted. A hand came into the frame and clicked off her iPad, but not before Spigs noticed the faint *TCB* tattoo on the underside of the wrist.

CHAPTER 23

The Secret Society

Fear for the professor's safety squeezed Spigs's guts like a vise grip. "Did that really happen?" His voice trembled. "Did someone just kidnap the professor?"

T-Ray grabbed both boys by their arms. "COME ON!"

"The curfew starts soon," Peabo declared as T-Ray pulled them out of the dorm room.

"Too bad. OUR professor may be in danger!" T-Ray snapped. She shoved the boys ahead of her. "Take the stairs."

"But Peabo has a point, T-Ray." Spigs tried to be the voice of reason. "We're just kids." As they dashed down to the second-floor platform, Spigs stopped and yanked Peabo and T-Ray back. "We may be in over our heads here. Remember? Someone tried to whack me with a bat, our room was ransacked, I had a six-shooter pointed at me, Horrid and his hooligans shot the Creeples, and now a gang of students kidnapped the professor."

T-Ray jostled Peabo and Spigs down the last flight of steps. They slipped out of the dorm and into the waning afternoon sunlight but stayed close against the outer wall.

"*We* have to get to the bottom of this," T-Ray said. "We're the only ones who understand the magnitude of the situation. It's all on us."

"We need backup," Peabo said. "Let's call the Letchworth Village police."

"Are you crazy? Letchworth Village is where they locked up the crazies. Sorry. *But* if somethin's in the water, those cops might go psycho on us," Spigs said, ever the conspiracy theorist.

"Adults won't listen to us, anyway." T-Ray signaled for the boys to follow her behind the dorm, where they'd have more refuge as they snuck through the quiet campus. A group of older students laughed together as they headed inside the dorm.

"We CANNOT let outsiders learn what the Creeples are really capable of with their . . . . Draconic Kinetic Energy," T-Ray instructed.

Spigs rolled his eyes. "You mean . . . magical dragon powers. But that's just it. Why is there no interest outside the academy? I mean, videos of the Creeples' antics are all over the internet."

"Three hundred hours of video are uploaded to YouTube every minute," Peabo said. "So, my guess is it hasn't gone viral beyond our campus."

"AND this campus is now basically under martial law," T-Ray added.

"So McTaggart and WhipSNERD are our only line of defense?" Spigs's nose crinkled. "Okay, agreed, it's all on us."

"Keep it down," hissed T-Ray. "And pick up the pace."

With the curfew about to be fully enforced, the teens kept to the shadows, roving through the manicured lawns and around the backs of buildings instead of using the sidewalks. They heard loud chatter inside the neighboring dormitory and crouched below the windowsill. Judging by all the whoops and cheers, Spigs knew something cool was going down inside.

He couldn't resist, so he peeked over the window ledge into a student lounge where kids had congregated to ride out curfew, with piles of candy wrappers and sub sandwiches spread across the tables. A row of iconic arcade-style games were staged against the back wall.

Sebastian "Seb" Mackenzie, a freshman exchange student and a genius at computer coding, stood with an intense focus at the seventy-inch screen attached to the wall. He was competing in a multiplayer eSports game titled *Mighty Minikins*.

T-Ray tugged on Spigs's shirt for him to get down, but he brushed her off, far too intrigued by what he'd spotted on the large video screen. Short, creepy Minikin avatars waddled across the screen swinging feudal clubs and swords. Small tuffs of flowing hair sprouted from their round heads. An epiphany lit up Spigs's brain. He wedged his fist in his mouth and bit down to stifle a gasp. Those Minikins looked exactly like the ... CREEPLES! "RUH-ROH!"

"What? Get down from there." Peabo yanked on Spigs's shirttail.

Spigs had a sickening thought. Could it be? Was this *Mighty Minikins* game the malware that had infected their CAD software when he downloaded it to the 3D bio-printer? T-Ray and Peabo jerked on his shirt together, and down tumbled Spigs. His butt met the ground with a thud. "UMPH!"

"Let's make our move!" T-Ray shuffled along the building in a crouch. Spigs and Peabo stooped low and followed her to the bushes next to the Necrosis Physiology building.

Spigs sidled up next to T-Ray and Peabo to tell them what he'd seen, but T-Ray glared at him.

Spigs stayed silent, reconsidering if now was a good time to reveal what he'd just seen. If he told them the CAD was hacked before their experiment and he didn't say anything, they might kill him, or worse . . . excommunicate him as a Lab Rat. He'd bring it up later. Maybe.

They scurried through campus as stealthily as they could, but all the ducking and dodging lengthened their journey to Professor Bodkins's office in the administration building.

They dashed through the hallway to her office. Her door was ajar, yet no sound came from inside. T-Ray peeked in and clicked on the ceiling lights, which highlighted a distressing, shambolic scene.

"She's GONE!" Peabo said.

"Of course, but who took her?" Spigs rushed to check the safe behind the Einstein picture—it was intact, no jimmy marks. Her research data was still secure, for now. But a desperate search had ensued. Chairs were overturned. Papers and documents from file cabinets were scattered everywhere. Textbooks were scattered about, with various pages ripped out.

"Those *slimeballs* were looking for her research." T-Ray was seething. "And left as quickly as they came."

Peabo and Spigs eyed each other in disbelief at T-Ray's sudden salty language.

"I know one thing. One of her kidnappers is that *Assassin's Creed* dude who tried to whack me and Rachell in Bell Tower," Spigs said, pondering the *TCB*-tattooed attacker.

"Again with Rachell," T-Ray muttered.

"The professor's computer has been hacked." Peabo looked up from her desk. "I think I can find out what they were after."

"Hop to it. And we'll try to find out where they might've taken the professor." Spigs led T-Ray out of the office, tiptoeing down the empty hall. T-Ray tugged on Spigs. "What's the plan?"

"All these despicable acts seem to start and end with Smathers," Spigs explained. "So, we break into his office and find out what the scumbag's up to."

T-Ray grinned at the insult. "Okay, but how are we going to do that?" She sighed.

"It's after hours, and we know Ms. Wanda's home feedin' her thirty-five cats." Spigs winked and pulled from his backpack the ring of security keycards that he'd swiped from the teachers' lounge in the Bio-Engineering building.

"I am impressed. Now, I don't advocate stealing. But in this case . . ."

"Wow, so I've *finally* impressed a girl."

"I'm pretty sure it won't become a habit." T-Ray ventured over to the janitorial closet. "Got an idea. Follow me."

Several minutes later, T-Ray and Spigs emerged dressed in janitorial overalls and pushed cleaning carts down the winding hallways. They stopped at the locked door with Smathers's name etched in glass. Spigs pulled out the keycards.

Swiped one . . . Red light. No entry.

Swiped two . . . Red light. No entry.

Swiped three . . . Red light. No entry.

"Seriously?" T-Ray growled.

"Oh, like you know which card it is?" Spigs handed her the key ring.

"Watch. And learn." T-Ray stared at the ring of cards, found one to her liking, and inserted it in the door.

Swiped . . . Green light. Entry.

"How'd ya do that?" Spigs asked as they entered Wanda Wainwright's outer office.

"Face it, I'm smarter than you." T-Ray beamed. "Besides, the cards have everyone's initials on the bottom." S. A. S. was stenciled in tiny letters at the bottom of the security card she used.

"But Smathers's initials are A. S. S."

"You think that arrogant lowlife would allow those initials to be on his security card?"

"Gotta hand it to ya. Great deduction."

The pair crept through the secretary's office and opened the door to Dean Smathers's inner sanctum for the second time that day.

Spigs was about to flick on the lights when T-Ray grabbed his arm. "They'll see the lights from outside the building. Here . . ." She opened her phone's flashlight. "Now, look for hidden places, but put every item you move back in the exact same spot."

Their amateur detective work commenced. Spigs hurriedly slid out desk drawers, and T-Ray swiftly browsed a bookshelf. She ran the tips of her fingers over the books' spines; they were meticulously lined up—tallest to the smallest. She knelt down on the thick Persian rug, carefully examining specific books of interest to her.

Five minutes later, a dejected Spigs looked up from Smathers's desk. "Nothin' here. Maybe this was a bad idea."

T-Ray continued to methodically retrieve books. "Keep at it. It's our only lead."

Spigs groaned. Patience was not one of his strong suits, but he settled down and started thumbing through the papers in Smathers's filing cabinet. "Look for somethin' out of place," he whispered. "The smallest details. Smathers has, like, OCD."

"Wait, you're right." T-Ray hustled back for another look at the row of tattered books on the shelf behind Smathers's desk. She took a big step back and scanned up and down all five bookshelves.

Spigs, who'd been watching her out of the corner of his eye, shuddered when T-Ray yelped.

"Quick, c'mere! See, this book in the middle is a quarter of an inch taller than the one before it. It's out of place." She removed the book and again sat down on the carpet. Spigs joined her. She carefully opened the manuscript to find a hollow center. From the secret compartment, she lifted a loose, tattered document made of faded yellow parchment paper.

"Whaddaya got?"

T-Ray handled a document with the familiar pentagram insignia. "You know that peculiar symbol you've been seeing? Well, it's referenced in here as . . . the 'Magister Templi.'"

"Keep goin'."

"Hang on." T-Ray searched for the term on her phone. "Whoa!" She blew out a long breath.

"What? Cough it up." Spigs glanced over her shoulder.

T-Ray spoke deliberately, giving weight to each word. "The Magister Templi was a secret medieval sect."

"Like a secret *society?*" Spigs's voice rose in pitch. This was getting spookier than he had imagined. "What else?"

"Members of the Magister Templi were infamously massacred exactly one hundred years ago . . . TOMORROW!"

"Shhh," he hissed, finger to his lips. "Sounds like a cult. But so?"

"So, *our* Bell Tower sits on the exact site of the massacre."

"WHOA!" Spigs cupped his mouth. He scratched beneath his hat brim with one finger. "So all of those wild Bell Tower rumors to scare students away *are* true."

"But why would the tower be built on top of the site of some massacred secret society? That's downright morbid—and gross," T-Ray said.

They stared at each other with grave confusion. Spigs lifted the mysterious book from T-Ray's lap and carefully flipped through more parchment pages. "Listen to this." He squinted at the faded calligraphy and read it aloud. "'At the precise time and place, the great Draconem Beast shall bestow omnipotent powers on a spellcaster, granting invincibility and eternal life.'"

"Eternal life?" T-Ray looked at Spigs.

"Like immortality?"

She nodded, her thumbs typing furiously on her phone. "Get this—so a spellcaster that acquires omnipotent powers will become a 'Master Sorcerer.'"

"Here's somethin'—" Spigs scanned the document with his

forefinger. "'Only those who possess the Dragon Stone of Magic can acquire its profound powers.'" He tapped the page. "It's described as an oval-shaped magenta gemstone." Spigs looked intently at T-Ray. "Smathers has a large pinkish gemstone ring."

"There are just *way* too many coincidences here," T-Ray expressed in a panicked tone.

"Ya think somethings goin' down tomorrow, on the hundredth anniversary?"

"Well, it does . . . Ah, I don't know."

Spigs glanced down at another loose document. "Hey, whadd-aya make of this?" He handed it to her.

"'And the great dragon was cast out, that old serpent, called the devil, which deceiveth the whole world. He was cast out into the earth, and his angels were cast out with him,'" T-Ray read. "Some kind of biblical passage, perhaps?"

"Another dragon reference." Spigs shuffled frantically through the remaining parchment documents, and all were headlined with the embossed symbol. He cocked his head and slightly tilted the document.

"YEE-IKES! Why didn't I see it before? This symbol is *not* a circle of three number nines. But three SIXES! Mark of the Beast!"

"Another cult angle?"

"Certainly pointin' to some kinda satanic cult. This is just way *too* freaky. I don't have a good feeling, T-Ray." He gazed at her as the gravity of the situation sank in.

"I agree, but we need confirmation, and I think I know where to look." T-Ray carefully replaced the fragile documents back in the hollow compartment of the book. "I volunteer at the library's Rare Books Collection room. I index bulky old manuscripts all the time. If Magister Templi is cited anywhere in the library, it's there. Let's go—maybe we'll find the thread that ties all these mysterious clues together."

"You know how you're never supposed to ask a question that you're afraid to know the answer to?" Spigs asked.

"Yeah."

"Well, I'm worried we're not gonna like the answers we find," he cautioned as he stood up and held out his hand. She grasped it and pulled herself up.

"So far, we have six dragon-infused Creeples, a massacred satanic cult, and a dean who somehow discovered dragon DNA. I'd say there's no turning back." They locked eyes for a few seconds, then nodded a silent acknowledgment that they were about to pass the point of no return.

"The professor gave us hope that the Creeples are alive— for now. So, that gives us a little time to check out some rare books."

"Let's go get Peabo." Spigs reached back and clutched T-Ray's hand.

The duo raced out and cut a hard, tight corner into the hall and—*WHAM*—ran smack into Chief McTaggart and Deputy Whipsnade.

S.H.A.D.O.W.

High Energy Laser Defense System

Exotic Technology Department
Washington, DC
Codename: PROJECT GOOZE

Name: Royal

Aliases: Purple Creeple

Identity: Twenty-inch-tall humanoid. Neon-purple hair. Prodigious ears. Oscillating mustard-yellow eyes. Click-clacking noise emanates from the skull region—a form of communication.

Creators: Three Aberdasher Academy of Science students.

Personal Abilities: Supreme leadership. Extreme intelligence.

Magical Powers: Draconic Kinetic Energy blasts from their eyes that super-charge inanimate objects into living, breathing entities.

Mystical Limitations: The metamorphosis can last up to twelve hours.

Potential Application: Particle-beam weaponry.

Comments: Cheez 'Em connoisseur. Arrogant/stubborn to a fault, yet quite endearing.

CHAPTER 24

Commissioner Gordon's Help

McTaggart, expanding his barrel chest, glared down at T-Ray and Spigs. "You two on janitorial duties tonight? Hmm?" He sneered. "I knew you'd eventually lead me to the scene of a crime." He pointed at the open private office with an eyebrow raised.

"Can I, boss?" Whipsnade rattled two pairs of handcuffs.

"Cuff 'em, Deputy. Homer 'Ace' McTaggart always gets his man—uh, and woman."

"Let's book 'em ... Murder One," Whipsnade spouted, his smile so wide his cheeks scrunched up his eyes.

"WHAT?" Both T-Ray and Spigs gasped.

"Slow down, Deputy. We'll detain them at headquarters until we learn what they're up to."

"Affirmative, Ace. I mean, Chief."

"So, he's 'Ace' and you're WhipSNERD?" Spigs flashed a sarcastic grin.

"That's Whipsnade, convict!" The scrawny but scrappy deputy

clamped on the cuffs, then led Spigs and T-Ray down the hall and out of the administration building. T-Ray mouthed to Spigs, "Where's Peabo?" They struggled to peer in all the rooms they passed on the way out. No Peabo.

The campus cops marched Spigs and T-Ray through the deserted, destroyed campus—as if it were a post-apocalyptic movie set. There was not a student in sight, since mandatory curfew was being enforced. They filed past fizzled-out vending machines, which had transformed back into coin-operated machines. There was heavy collateral damage from the cafeteria battle royale. The hoagie sandwich machine was on its side; tiny flames sputtered from within.

Whipsnade breathed down the teens' necks as they weaved through debris from smashed benches and picnic tables. T-Ray brushed her hand against Spigs's. He glanced at her, but she flicked her gaze upward. Spigs gulped as they passed below the looming Bell Tower—the clock hands displaying the time as 7:13 p.m.—imagining massacred bodies buried beneath it.

• • •

Inside an unadorned storage room beneath Bell Tower sat two distressed crates with faded stencil etchings that read *N.O.M.T., Ltd.* Frantic *CLICK-CLACKING* came from within. The agitated Creeples banged their heads against the sides, dispersing clouds of dust and soot from the crates.

A robed girl stuck her head in the door to investigate the strange noises, but the Creeples fell silent. At the sound of the door lock, a three-toed ashen-gray foot cracked through a crate panel. A second panel splintered enough for Skoota to poke out its blue-plumed head. *CRACK!* The broken panels flew out and smashed against the wall. Out leaped Skoota, followed by Coco and Beezer. Skoota waddled over to the other crate, *CLICK-CLACKING* and wiggling its ears. The superstrong Creeple kicked in the panels so Royal, Naz, and Tatz could waltz out to join them.

The Creeples had morphed back to their pre-catnip phase—back to their wacky oscillating mustard-yellow eyes. Presumably, their magical, mystery powers had diminished. They all waddled over to the door that kept them trapped inside the subterranean room. Tatz tried to sink its gnarly teeth into the wood, yet they were no longer razor sharp. The Creeples *CLICK-CLACKED* in frustration.

• • •

Chief McTaggart and Deputy Whipsnade paraded T-Ray and Spigs to the academy's Police & Safety Center on the far end of campus. Whipsnade removed the cuffs and locked the teens in a cramped fifteen-foot-square holding room that contained a table and four metal folding chairs.

T-Ray paced the confined room with her "serious thinking" face on: brows scrunched with a dimple between them. Spigs jiggled the knob, as if it might magically unlock. He peeked through the door's small window, spotting Whipsnade with legs propped up on his desk, thoroughly enjoying a Batman comic book.

"I can't believe those rent-a-cops took away our phones," Spigs groaned. "Isn't there a law against cruel and unusual punishment? What are we gonna do? Time's runnin' out."

"I know, I know!" T-Ray snapped back. "We have to figure out a way to reach Peabo." Back and forth she paced. "He knows all about biblical references. He went to Sunday school."

"Now how do ya know that?"

"Because I pay attention. Give it a try sometime," T-Ray snapped.

"What's *your* beef?"

"Sorry. Just frustrated. And scared." T-Ray stopped pacing.

"Now think! We're losin' critical time bein' in here."

T-Ray took a deep breath and walked over to the door. She looked through the little window and knocked, gesturing for the deputy to come over.

"Yes, Ms. Rogers?" Whipsnade peeked in through the cracked door.

"I know my legal rights," T-Ray said with authority.

"Your rights?" Whipsnade flouted. "What rights do you have while you're being incarcerated?"

"We're allowed one phone call each." T-Ray smiled.

"Who said?"

"Would they say it in every movie and TV show if it weren't true?" T-Ray placed her fists on her hips, voice brimming with confidence.

Whipsnade retreated into deep thought for a moment, which didn't come easy for him. "Come to think of it . . . WAIT, that's all made-up stuff. The chief stepped out, so when he gets back—"

"If we're not allowed to make a call within thirty minutes of being apprehended, we can technically sue the department. You want THAT on your record?" T-Ray said matter-of-factly.

Spigs mouthed, "We can?"

"You can?" Whipsnade asked.

T-Ray poked Spigs in the gut.

"OOOF! Yes, yes we can." Spigs straightened his hat.

"And you just have five minutes left to decide," T-Ray warned.

"Sorry, folks. You do the crime. You do the time," Whipsnade barked.

"Oh, Deputy. Commissioner Gordon always allowed for one phone call. And I wouldn't wanna be the one who breaks Gotham City PD's protocol. Just sayin'." Spigs laid it on thick as he glanced at the stack of Batman comics Whipsnade had on his desk.

Whipsnade's demeanor completely changed. Perspiration appeared on his forehead.

"You now have four minutes." T-Ray and Whipsnade locked eyes, each daring the other to look away. When tiny droplets of sweat dripped down into his eye, the contest was won.

"Well, Commissioner Gordon is—I mean, I do follow proper protocol," Whipsnade relented. "Okay, one phone call each, convicts! Then back in jail."

"Of course." T-Ray smiled. "You're the boss, Deputy Whipsnade."

"Yes, yes I am. And you two had better remember that." He blotted his soggy brows and led the teens into the outer office. Spigs followed him past the personal property bin on McTaggart's desk that held their confiscated cell phones. He stopped in front of a metal desk with a landline telephone—an archaic plastic push-button model.

"One call, jailbird." Whipsnade smirked at Spigs.

"OW! AH," T-Ray cried out from across the room.

"What? What is it?" Whipsnade rushed to T-Ray.

"I think I have something in my eye," T-Ray whined, rubbing it. "Can you please check?"

As Whipsnade focused on examining T-Ray's completely healthy eye, Spigs struggled to remember Peabo's number, but it was saved in his phone.

"So, have you wanted to be a deputy your entire life?" T-Ray asked innocently as she took off her glasses and opened her left eye as wide as she could. Behind Whipsnade's back, T-Ray gestured at something across the room. Spigs poked aimlessly at the push-button numbers: plastic squares lined up three rows across and four down. He was utterly befuddled. "DANG. What's up with this gadget? Straight out of the dark ages—like the 1990s. How long do ya hold down the button before you release it?"

"Well, I've always had a nose for sniffin' out crime, so it was a logical career choice." Whipsnade polished his shirt badge with his sleeve.

Spigs inched toward the bin holding the cell phones, but before he got there, Whipsnade started to look in his direction.

"BUT, Deputy! I have an important question." T-Ray grabbed Whipsnade's shoulders. "Can Batwoman and Batgirl coexist?"

Whipsnade pepped up, dropping his Deputy Diehard facade, and broke into a lengthy discussion of why the two superheroes should partner up to battle Red Claw. Spigs was at McTaggart's desk ready to snatch their cell phones, but he kneecapped an open desk drawer. Whipsnade spun his head and shoulder toward the noise. Spigs bent over to massage his throbbing patella.

T-Ray again reached for the deputy's shoulders and rotated him for a face-to-face. "You know, Deputy! YOU . . . bear a striking resemblance to Bruce Wayne," T-Ray voiced with authority, to regain the deputy's attention.

Whipsnade was pleasantly embarrassed. "I've always fancied myself a bit like him."

T-Ray hopped up on her toes to look over Whipsnade's shoulders. Spigs held up their cell phones and pointed to the clock on the wall.

"Deputy, I must say, it's been real and fun, but NOT real fun. Got to go now." With that, T-Ray choreographed a perfect low-spin leg whip that brought Whipsnade crashing facedown.

"Where'd THAT come from?" Spigs asked T-Ray in astonishment.

"There's a lot you don't know about *me*, Spignola."

The teens froze in place as they saw McTaggart fighting to open the front door with his foot as he held a tray of coffee cups and pastries. T-Ray grabbed Spigs's hand and rushed for the exit. They both shoved the front door open, which knocked McTaggart backward, splashing hot coffee all over his uniform.

Soaked in brown liquid, McTaggart danced around the room. "HOT! HOT! HOT!"

"AFTER 'EM!" bellowed the chief, and the two teens glanced back to see the campus cops climb on their Segways.

CHAPTER 25

Trapped and Caged

S mathers watched over his robed Disciples with narrowed eyes, ensuring they followed each of his instructions to the letter. They anxiously maneuvered through the Gothic-adorned chamber in a swift but orderly manner, setting up ceremonial candles and rearranging altars carved with ancient symbols. In Smathers's mind, these young students were his believers—Disciples. He had handpicked the select group for indoctrination in preparation for the ceremony.

Rachell Hobbs had proved to be one of Smathers's most faithful and dedicated converts. Only a few Disciples had full knowledge of the ritual's true objective, though he assured her she was one of the "chosen ones." He had judicially checked her background—mother divorced four times, a long line of stepfathers coming to fill the void—and knew she sought validation, making her easy to manipulate. So he acknowledged her often and stoked her ego, and she looked at him with absolute devotion.

Thanks to his own close observation and information gathered from Horace, Smathers also knew Spigs had a crush on Rachell. He had assigned her a special mission to extract any knowledge Spigs had about Professor Bodkins and her groundbreaking genetic research. Her data was a crucial piece to fulfill his sinister goal. Rachell was not able to fully deliver on the assignment, but she'd undertaken the next best thing: aiding in the kidnapping of Professor Bodkins. The professor was detained in a nearby subterranean room, being entirely uncooperative. No matter, Smathers would procure what he wanted from her soon enough.

CLICK-CLACKING and thumping noises echoed from the storage room. No doubt those nasty little beasties were causing the disturbance. Smathers frowned at the disruption, massaged his temples, and pointed to the storage room.

Horace directed a Disciple to investigate. He unlatched the three bolted locks to the storage room and cautiously cracked the door. *WHAM!* The door crashed open and slammed the Disciple against the wall. All six Creeples Aussie-splayed out and hurtled onto the closest unsuspecting Disciples. The Creeples tugged and twisted noses, ears, eyebrows, hair, and tongues. Horace and several other Disciples tried to intervene but retreated. The Creeples' victims screamed in a panicked frenzy, flailing around the main chamber and knocking over candlesticks and ritual regalia. In a flash, Skoota and Tatz hopped off and climbed to the top of an ornamental shelf. From there, the two snatched heavy ancient alchemy textbooks and hurled them at the robed figures.

"Get them! Or I'll stuff *you* inside those crates!" Smathers shouted at his flock.

Three Disciples ducked and dipped as they tried to fight back against the projectiles with their ceremonial staffs. Naz, Beezer, and Royal snuck under several Disciples' full-length robes. They tied their shoestrings together, sending them crashing to the cobblestones, and finished the task with their masterpiece—atomic wedgies, pulling the students' underwear up and over their heads.

With the abatement of their magical dragon powers, the Creeples' only weapons were their mischief-making chaos and madcap pranks. Coco kicked over an antique vase, flipped over a tray of incense, tossed a tray of amulets in the air, and trampled on a talisman.

As the pandemonium continued, Smathers thundered orders from his perch, but the scene was out of control. But an idea struck him. The reliquary! The Creeples had the Draconem blood flowing through their veins, so perhaps . . . Smathers hurried to a set of lavish maroon curtains. He pulled back the drapes to expose the hidden nook where the treasured reliquary was displayed. Royal *CLICK-CLACKED* and wiggled its ears at the gold-encrusted reliquary resting atop an elegantly carved stone pedestal.

Naz's six tentacles were drawn to the object, and it *CLICK-CLACKED* feverishly. The other four Creeples scampered toward Smathers and the reliquary. Smathers stepped aside, but two oblivious Disciples intervened, trying to stop them. Beezer and Tatz jumped on their backs and disabled them. All the Creeples cautiously inched closer toward the nook.

The captivated Creeples halted in front of the pedestal, hypnotized by the ruby-encrusted gold container. Trembling and buzzing, the reliquary's two metal fasteners flung open, and magenta energy discharged from its super bright core, illuminating the entire chamber.

Like children trying to catch fireflies, the Creeples scurried about, straining to capture the magical particles. But the magenta energy diverted and completely enshrouded the Creeples. They had succumbed to a zen-like state—a mystical trance. Smathers ordered Horace and four Disciples to recapture the powerless Creeples.

CHAPTER 26

Rare Books Collection

After escaping the campus cops, T-Ray and Spigs sneaked across the Quad, but they paused when they saw two students huddled at the base of Bell Tower. The tower's clock displayed 8:42 p.m., and they had expected the area to be void of students due to the curfew. Spigs recognized the two students as part of Horace's hooligans. T-Ray jerked Spigs down behind a dumpster when several more hooligans appeared on the Quad's perimeter, their heads swiveling up and down the street.

"Looks like Smathers called out his goon patrol."

"But why are they hanging around Bell Tower, and during the curfew?" T-Ray plucked two twigs from her auburn bun.

Spigs peeked over the dumpster. "It's like they're guarding it or somethin'."

T-Ray tugged on Spigs's shirt. "Get down!" He ducked just as McTaggart and Whipsnade cruised by on their Segways.

"See that? McTaggart just drove right past those students." Spigs looked at T-Ray. She shrugged. He leaned in close to her. "Listen, I'll divert these chumps while you find Peabo. Meet ya at the administration building."

"Spigs."

"Yeah?"

"Be safe." T-Ray pulled him in for a gentle embrace.

The red-faced Spigs spontaneously leaned in and pecked her on the cheek. He took a deep breath and jumped out from behind the dumpster. He strolled up to the surprised pair of hooligans. "Howdy, gents!"

"What are *you* doing out here?" said the first hooligan, a stocky senior. "No one's out past curfew."

"Yeah, weasel," his partner echoed.

"I got this, Nate," the first hooligan said.

"All yours, Luther."

Spigs raised his hands in surrender so the goons would turn their backs to T-Ray. "Guess I didn't get the memo. Studyin', ya know. Super big test in Molecular Transfusion class tomorrow."

Nate squawked, "Got the same test. Still confused about the syllabus."

"Dude! I've got this," Luther warned.

"Sorry, Luther. All yours." Nate stepped aside.

"Lost track of time, I guess." Spigs peered over the hooligans' shoulders. He saw T-Ray slip into the shadows.

"Study in your room," Luther demanded.

"Now why didn't I think of that? I'm goin' to head there now . . . if it's okay with you, Luther—or is it Nate?"

"Get on back to your dorm, and don't let me catch you out here again," Luther ordered.

Spigs jogged in the direction of his dorm, but a block away, he spied T-Ray cowering next to the administration building's entrance. He rushed over.

The two huddled close and tiptoed in to Professor Bodkins's office, their hands unintentionally brushing against each other.

"PEABO!" T-Ray cried out when they found him sprawled unconscious on the floor. Spigs shook Peabo's arms, and he groaned, eyelids fluttering open.

T-Ray moistened a towel and pressed it against Peabo's neck.

"Wha—what happened?" Peabo patted the back of his head and winced in pain.

"You tell us."

"Dude, ya okay?" Spigs strained to pull the groggy Peabo to his feet.

"Think so. I dunno what happened. I was downloading data from the professor's computer and then *WHAM* . . . nighty night." Peabo massaged his head. "Guess they came back for her computer."

The monitor was still atop the desk, but the main terminal was gone. T-Ray hurried over to the Einstein picture. The safe behind it was jimmied open and empty. "They came back for more than her computer. No question now. They've kidnapped Professor Bodkins."

"I'm calling it like I see it. The *they* is Smathers," Peabo affirmed, and dabbed the wet towel on the lump on his head.

Spigs clenched his fists in anger. Professor Bodkins was the only adult who had ever believed in him, and now she was in trouble. "Those lowlife scumbags! It's a definite act of desperation. So, our next move is to the library."

"You wanna check out books? NOW?" Peabo raised his arms and shoulders.

"In a way. C'mon, we'll fill ya in." Spigs helped Peabo to the hallway, and T-Ray took the lead.

"Wait! We have a problem." T-Ray gestured with her head to a wall-mounted security camera. Its red recording light flashed like a malignant eye.

"Dang, closed-circuit cameras are all over campus. They're so inconspicuous I forgot about 'em," Spigs whispered. "And I'm sure Smathers has access to them."

"He's got that one pointing directly at the professor's office." T-Ray groaned. "We have to shake him off, trick him into thinking we're going back to our dorms."

"How do we do that?" Peabo said.

"Follow my lead. Act dejected and defeated. Like we're giving up."

T-Ray faced the camera, slumped her shoulders, and frowned. The boys overly embellished her instructions by drooping their heads and walking with an exaggerated sway, like crestfallen souls.

"For the love of Pete. You're *not* going to a funeral." T-Ray shook her head at their overacting.

The teens made sure the cameras caught them heading toward the dorms. Peabo and Spigs followed T-Ray alongside the Metaphysics building, avoiding the cameras posted by the front and back entrances. They made a wide loop around the campus perimeter and finally made it to the library.

Wyvern Library was an impressive neo-Gothic stone-and-glass building near the entrance to campus. But more impressive than the spectacular architecture, and rather exceptional for an American high school, were the many historic and valuable British documents stored there—and envied by academics across the country. The library rose fifty feet, with an impressive square footage of stained glass. It was constructed with indigenous materials to fit its natural setting and had a native stone floor surrounded by rock walls, which gave the appearance the library was part of the Adirondack Mountains.

T-Ray held up a hand to make the boys stop and hid behind a tall Scotch pine.

"See any cameras?" she asked.

"One by the front door." Peabo pointed to the imposing double doors.

"Another by the fire escape." Spigs pointed to the blinking red light by the metal ladder bolted to the side of the building. He turned to T-Ray. "You're a library volunteer. Don't ya have a special key or somethin'?"

"No after-hours access," T-Ray said.

"Well, I'm *not* sneaking inside another hazardous-waste container," Peabo declared. "I swear I glow in the dark."

T-Ray studied the building as she led the boys closer, staying in the blind spot between the two CCTV cameras. She pointed to the corner window. "There, on the second floor, it's open. So, Spigs, you boost Peabo on your shoulders, and I'll climb over you two."

Spigs and Peabo removed their backpacks and stacked them against the building.

"Remember, I bruise easily," Spigs warned as Peabo climbed his shoulders and stepped directly on Spigs's hat. *CRUNCH!* "MY HAT!" He grabbed for it, making Peabo wobble and weave to control his balance.

"Forget the stupid hat. Now give me a lift." T-Ray smacked Spigs's arm. He whined but cupped his hands like a stirrup. T-Ray climbed over Spigs and onto Peabo's shoulders to get to the second-floor balcony.

"Peabo! Hold steady. If you get me killed, I'll kill you." T-Ray reached for the open window.

Peabo whimpered as T-Ray stepped on his head like a ladder rung.

"Don't be such a baby." She slipped through the window and popped her head back out. "Sit tight. Going to find the emergency ladder."

Peabo hopped off Spigs, and they both retrieved their backpacks. Spigs inspected his crumpled hat.

"My hat!" Spigs plopped down on the grass and tried to reshape it.

"Sorry, dude." Peabo patted Spigs on the head.

Moments later, T-Ray appeared and unfurled a rope ladder from the second-story window. Spigs slipped his damaged hat in his backpack, and the two both climbed up.

The library was quiet and dimly lit. A maze of shelves was packed with thousands of volumes. The teens took one step when . . . *SQUEAK! SQUEAK!* A high-pitched noise reverberated through the library. They dove behind a row of lounge chairs.

"What was THAT?" Peabo said.

"Make it stop." Spigs plugged his ears as the creaking got louder.

T-Ray peered around a leather lounge chair, then ducked back as the elderly Mrs. Buelwhacker wheeled by. The octogenarian librarian was pushing a book cart down the aisle.

"It's after nine o'clock. Why's she still here?" Spigs took his fingers out of his ears.

"She's re-racking returned books. A nice lady. Hard of hearing, though, but still keep it down. Follow me." T-Ray led them up a flight of stairs and to the back wall of the third floor, where a single door was marked "Rare Books Collection."

T-ray turned the doorknob. It was locked. "We just can't catch a break."

"Maybe this will work." Spigs held up the stolen key ring, which he'd managed to save from Whipsnade's earlier pat down by slipping the ring under his hat. He selected the one marked *S. A. S* and swiped it. The light flashed red.

"There's no other way in. I'm afraid it's a dead end!"

Spigs held out his hand and motioned with his index finger. "C'mon, Peabo. Cough it up. You know."

The sheepish Peabo sighed and pulled out a card from his wallet. T-Ray hid a grin when she noticed his *My Little Pony* plastic membership card. Spigs slid the card along the doorjamb and inserted it under the strike box, pressing the cylinder latch. He pushed open the door. "*Voilà!* After you, *mademoiselle*."

Creeples!

The small, cramped room was about forty feet by forty feet and pitch black. It had an intense aroma of grandma's attic: dust, mothballs, and oaky wood. T-Ray didn't want to turn on the overhead lights for fear of attracting Mrs. Buelwhacker. The teens clicked on their phones' flashlights. T-Ray located white cotton gloves to handle any delicate documents.

"Look for anything on cults or secret societies. And focus on manuscripts covered with calligraphy. Check the tables of contents for Magister Templi." T-Ray ran her gloved fingers over the book spines as she moved along the first shelf. The boys followed her lead. They judiciously but swiftly scanned up and down the aisles.

Once they'd given the shelves a thorough sweep, they checked the drawers for any unbound yellowish documents.

"More of those Christian pentagram symbols," Spigs said. "But not what we're lookin' for."

"I know it's in here." T-Ray kept flipping faded pages. "Now keep at it. Magister Templi."

"Let me get a look at that symbol you've been talking about." Peabo moved in close to Spigs. "YIKES! That's *not* a Christian pentagram. It's upside down! That's a demonic sign!" Peabo pulled back. "Listen, I've read enough to know we shouldn't be messing with the occult. *Mi madre* is going to kill me if she ever finds out." Peabo made the sign of the cross over his chest.

Spigs clutched Peabo's arms. "Peabo, we're *not* joinin' a cult. We're tryin' to stop one."

"Got one more place, but it may be tough getting in." T-Ray pointed to the back wall. "A walk-in closet. It houses priceless literary works. Not sure who has access, but if Smathers is hiding any info on his secret cult . . ."

"What're we waitin' for?" Spigs rushed over.

The nondescript metal door had a keyless pad mounted on the wall and no knob. It was a fingerprint-recognition system.

"Not sure your Little Ponies will be able to help us out this time, Peabo." T-Ray sounded deflated.

"Well . . . we tried!" Peabo turned back to leave. "I'm getting creeped out in here."

Spigs grabbed Peabo's collar as he attempted a quick escape. "Peabo, if I can open the keypad, ya think you could demonstrate your tech wizardry?"

"Uh, sure . . . I guess."

Spigs coolly unzipped his backpack, reached deep inside, rustled around, and removed his laser pointer. He twisted off its shirt clasp. "Easy peasy." He winked at T-Ray and beamed at his own cleverness as he used the clasp's flat end and carefully unscrewed the faceplate of the keypad. He popped it off, exposing the wires behind. Peabo dug through his backpack for his toolkit.

"You had a screwdriver this whole time?" Spigs said when Peabo set the tool aside and lifted a pair of pliers.

"Didn't want to interrupt your one-man performance. The way you flexed your muscles turning those tiny screws was priceless." Peabo grinned. Spigs felt his cheeks flush with embarrassment.

"Impressive. Now hurry up, you two!" T-Ray hissed.

Peabo stared at the circuitry panel for a few seconds. He delicately pointed to several colored wires, the electronic unit, and the memory cards. It was as if he was a surgeon planning to remove a vital organ. After a minute of twiddling and poking the wires, he simply shrugged and jammed the pliers into the panel—short-circuiting the keypad! With three beeps, the door slid open to reveal a room the size of an expansive walk-in closet. It was lined floor to ceiling with books.

T-Ray shoved them out of the way and rushed in.

"What precision." Spigs clapped Peabo on the back.

"Aha!" T-Ray lifted a heavy, frayed leather manuscript. She brought it over to a spacious table, where she delicately placed the artifact. It was locked by an antique latch. "*Not* another lock!" T-Ray groaned.

Spigs stepped up and unscrewed a ballpoint pen. "And now for my encore." With the needle tip of the ink cartridge, he easily jarred open the vintage latch.

"Once again, Ms. Rogers: *voilà!*"

"Very resourceful, Mr. Spignola." T-Ray nodded her approval and gingerly opened the manuscript. She arranged the loose sheets in a neat order.

"Impressive, now resourceful? At least I'm goin' in the right direction with her," Spigs muttered to Peabo.

"I'm going to gag." Peabo playfully stuck his finger in his mouth.

"It says that this is the manuscript for the 'New Order of Magister Templi,'" T-Ray said. All three crowded around the manuscript. Their individual flashlights skimmed over different detached pages.

"So, what's the deal exactly?" Peabo asked.

"Look." Spigs pointed a white-gloved finger. "Smathers's name is scrawled all in the margins."

"NO . . . WAY! It JUST can't be." T-Ray's eyes were fixed on a photo. Through a magnifying glass, she studied a black-and-white image of three men posing. She flipped it over. "*Cheshire, England: Lindow Moss Bog, 1938. The Wyvern Draconem Expedition.*"

Peabo moved in next to her. "So? It's an old photo of three dudes knee-deep in a swamp."

"It's an English bog, but look WHO'S knee-deep." T-Ray pointed at the man.

Peabo moved the magnifying glass in and out for focus and recognized the doughy man with the spectacles in the center. "Ah, it's only Smathers . . . SMATHERS!"

T-Ray elbowed Peabo in the ribs. "Keep it down."

Spigs seized the magnifying glass from Peabo. "1938! That's, like . . . aah, eighty-somethin' years ago. Heck, if it IS Smathers, he's either a time traveler or Freddy Krueger!"

"More like a bloodsucking parasite." T-Ray scoffed in disgust.

"He hasn't aged one day. Impossible!" Peabo closed his eyes tight, fingers rubbing his temples.

"What's he holding?" T-Ray pointed. "And is *that* the same gemstone ring on his finger?"

"Ya know who has aged?" Spigs's voice jumped three octaves. "That young dude next to Smathers holdin' a Colt revolver. THAT'S the Grim Keeper! He must now be over a hundred. And this mornin' he was about to fill me with hot lead from that same pistol."

"It just doesn't make any sense." Peabo's fingers continued massaging his temples.

"What's that oval object Smathers is holdin'? Kinda looks like a large—" Spigs gasped. "T-Ray, could it be . . . an EGG?"

T-Ray stared for a second at the wall, then recited in a hushed tone, "'At the precise time and place, the great Draconem Beast shall bestow omnipotent powers on a spellcaster who possesses its offspring, granting invincibility and eternal life.' So, if Draconem is a dragon, that means its offspring would be a—"

"DRAGON EGG!" Spigs lashed out, but rapidly cupped his mouth.

"And if this IS the Draconem Expedition and Smathers IS wearin' the Dragon Stone of Magic ring . . . he actually located a Wyvern dragon egg."

"I'm trying to follow along, but—" Peabo's eyes were still closed.

"The existence of real dragons is an awesome thought, but the idea Smathers has plans to gain immortality and almighty power from one is definitely NOT." Spigs flashed a frown at the realization.

"Dragon egg? Draconem Expedition? It's *sorta* coming together for me." Peabo was still concentrating but confused.

"And what's with the library's name being the same as the 1938 expedition?" Spigs asked.

T-Ray anxiously searched "Wyvern" on her phone.

"So Smathers must've acquired *some* powers of eternal life from that egg to have lived this long." Spigs shuddered. "He'd be pushin' a hundred and twenty."

Peabo finally had his thoughts together. "Okay, so assume the

Creeples' blood contains the dragon blood. Which came from Smathers's Draconem Serum, by way of the 1938 dig. Then Smathers must know the Creeples have the dragon blood and needs them to fulfill his evil plan."

"That's why Smathers wants the Creeples alive!" T-Ray nodded with glee. "So a Wyvern is a legendary demonic beast with a dragon's head and wings, a reptilian body, two legs, and a tail with a deadly barbed stinger at the tip."

"But what will Smathers do with the Creeples *after* he gets what he wants out of 'em?" Spigs brought up the question none of them wanted to even consider.

"And how does he plan to extract the dragon blood?" Peabo swallowed hard.

The trio knew the likely fate of their Creeples when Smathers was through with them.

Spigs and T-Ray flipped through more loose documents, trying to gather additional information. Peabo read a yellowish piece of notebook paper that had been preserved in the book. He let out tiny gasps.

T-Ray and Spigs looked at him. "What?"

"According to this, one hundred years ago, a rogue member poisoned all one hundred and thirty-two cult members during the sacred ceremony of the Dragon Realm."

"We know. And they're all buried under Bell Tower," Spigs added.

T-Ray stopped perusing her document and grabbed the two boys' arms. "Now it's all making sense. This rogue cult member took possession of their Magister Templi manuscript that has the secret codex with instructions on how to gain the powers of a Master Sorcerer."

Spigs tapped the corresponding line on the page he was reading. "Here's an interesting side note to the codex. Have you guys ever wondered where our school's kooky name came from?" T-Ray and Peabo shrugged. "In 1735, a British Egyptologist by the name of Sir Titus Aberdasher was the one person to have deciphered several of the divine master scripts from the Book of Thoth—penned in a language that was spoken in early Egypt for centuries. So his translations led to the creation of his codex. Thoth is the god of *knowledge* and *magic*, and its symbol is the All-Seeing Eye of Horus—the eye inside those pentagram symbols we keep seeing."

"So the Magister Templi cult was founded on Sir Aberdasher's codex. And the codex was based on his decryption of the magic Book of Thoth," T-Ray surmised.

Spigs continued. "As Peabo said, this rogue member killed all the other cult members a hundred years ago and pinched the Magister Templi manuscript and the Dragon Stone of Magic gemstone ring from the dead cult leader. Which all led to the discovery of the dragon egg in the Lindow Moss Bog in 1938."

"So this rogue member must be—"

"SMATHERS?" Peabo and Spigs squawked unanimously.

"There has to be something to that gemstone ring and Smathers living this long," T-Ray said.

"Let me sum it up for ya, Peabo. Whoever possesses the Wyvern dragon blood *and* the Dragon Stone of Magic ring on the date of this Dragon Realm will acquire eternal life and powers of a Master Sorcerer." Spigs scowled at the thought of Smathers's nefarious scheme.

"Revelation 11:7 . . . 'the beast that comes up from the Abyss will attack them, and overpower and kill them,'" Peabo quoted.

"So all along Smathers's wicked goal for the last one hundred years has been to become a Master Sorcerer." T-Ray cringed at the thought.

"With omnipotent powers, for *eternity* . . . YIKES!" Spigs squawked.

"But when? How? And what's with this Golden Dawn we keep hearing about?" T-Ray was desperate for more answers.

"This may help." Peabo waved a document. "'Cult members are to gather at the sacred site every hundredth year to resurrect the Dragon Realm.'"

"Smathers must've built Bell Tower on top of the sacred site to preserve it," T-Ray suspected.

"Or conceal it," Peabo added. "And Smathers knew he'd have to stay alive until the next hundredth anniversary, which is—"

"TOMORROW!" Spigs exclaimed.

"But WHEN tomorrow?" Peabo questioned.

T-Ray turned pale and shook her head in disbelief. "Smathers wants to create his own cult, the *New Order* of Magister Templi, and reign over his Disciples using ancient sorcery!"

"Don't sell Smathers short. He wants to reign over us. Most likely . . . all of *HUMANITY!*" Peabo declared.

Spigs scratched an itch on the back of his neck and looked up. "THAT'S IT! The Golden Dawn *is* the ceremony, the point in time when Smathers transforms into a MASTER SORCERER! And the letters N.O.M.T. are the initials of his despicable cult!"

"*Hush!* You two keep it down." T-Ray placed her finger to her mouth.

"But where does Professor Bodkins's research fit into all this?" Peabo asked.

"That has me baffled too. Anyway, we first have to stop that diabolical maniac from gaining unearthly powers," T-Ray insisted.

"But we have to save Professor Bodkins *and* our Creeples first," Spigs insisted.

All three looked at each other, processing the monumental undertaking ahead of them.

"Maybe it's time to call in reinforcements?" Peabo tossed out the idea. "I mean, like . . . *professional* reinforcements."

Spigs chewed the corner of his lip. "At this point, who could we trust? What adult would believe us?" he asked and received blank stares in response.

"They all could be under the influence of Smathers, at least the ones on campus," T-Ray suggested.

The boys nodded somberly.

"It's all on us!" Spigs gathered up the loose documents and reinserted them neatly into the manuscript.

T-Ray looked at her phone clock. "It's nine fifty-seven. It's time to take charge!"

CLASSIFIED

S.H.A.D.O.W.

High Energy Laser Defense System

Exotic Technology Department
Washington, DC
Codename: PROJECT GOOZE

Name: Tatz

Aliases: Yellow Creeple

Identity: Twenty-inch-tall humanoid. Neon-yellow hair. Prodigious ears. Oscillating mustard-yellow eyes. Click-clacking noise emanates from the skull region—a form of communication.

Creators: Three Aberdasher Academy of Science students.

Personal Abilities: Its electric cranium bolts can manipulate small molecular matter.

Magical Powers: Draconic Kinetic Energy blasts from their eyes that supercharge inanimate objects into living, breathing entities.

Mystical Limitations: The metamorphosis can last up to twelve hours.

Potential Application: Particle-beam weaponry.

Comments: Cheez 'Em connoisseur. A follower. Eager to please.

CHAPTER 27

The Devil's Disciples

Squatting down in the hallway outside the Rare Books Collection room, T-Ray, Spigs, and Peabo waited until the squeaks of Mrs. Buelwhacker's cart passed before they headed to the stairs. Spigs paused mid-step at the top of the final set of stairs and threw out his arms to stop his friends. He pointed to the beams of lights that flickered between the bookshelves on the second floor below.

"Could be McTaggart and Whipsnade," T-Ray whispered as she yanked on the boys' shirts.

"AGAIN with those clowns," Spigs complained as they crouched behind the balcony rail.

They were cornered. Mrs. Buelwhacker was now re-racking books on the third floor, and the campus cops were on the second floor.

"Can't just wait here; we're losing valuable time," Peabo said.

They peeked over the balcony and recoiled at the campus cops' powerful tactical flashlights advancing up the stairs.

"Time for a little diversion. Let's split up!" Spigs gripped T-Ray's arm. "Roomie, you're on your own." Peabo hopped up, and Spigs pointed him down the hallway to the left. "Meet back at the dorm."

T-Ray hugged Peabo.

"And if you're caught, there'll be a saw in your cake on visitin' day," Spigs chuckled.

Peabo tore down the hallway.

"Got these two, Deputy. You take the speedy one," McTaggart wheezed from climbing the stairs as he flashed his light on the two teens' faces. Spigs clutched T-Ray's hand, and they sprinted down the hall in the opposite direction of Peabo.

"Watch her legs, Ace. They're lethal!" Whipsnade yelled back, and then pursued Peabo.

The heavyset McTaggart lumbered as best he could after Spigs and T-Ray. They dashed into a spacious reading area with plush seating and private cubicles bound by rows of bookshelves.

"Game's over, kids. You've had your fun. Now show yourselves."

"Over here." T-Ray squeezed Spigs's hand and directed him behind the lofty Fantasy Readers' bookracks. It was tight quarters—their backs pressed to the drywall and their arms and legs crammed together.

• • •

Peabo's legs, which had helped him outrun school bullies successfully for years, seemed twenty pounds heavier as he sprinted down a long hallway. A glance over his shoulder revealed Whipsnade had gained on him.

"No way out, criminal." The deputy spoke through a crooked grin.

Peabo skidded to an abrupt halt and nearly slammed into a shelf of hefty medical journals. He was cornered by Whipsnade and three walls. Frantic, he swiveled his head left to right. A four-foot-square opening on one wall caught his eye. It was a dumbwaiter; a small freight elevator on a pulley system that moved bundled books between floors. Peabo knew desperate times called for desperate measures, and as Whipsnade struggled to unlock his handcuffs, Peabo called out, "Later, WhipSNERD!"

Peabo took a running start and dove headfirst through the opening. *CLANG!* His head banged into the metal lining. He tucked his knees to his chin, and the dumbwaiter gradually descended. Only trailing by a few seconds, Whipsnade dove on top, crushing the roof. The dumbwaiter's emergency system locked under the extra weight and stopped the descent. SNAP! The elevator's ropes broke under the strain, and the dumbwaiter plunged into darkness. Peabo pressed his hands to the sides to brace himself for the sudden impact as Whipsnade let out a high-pitched—*SCREECH!* The runaway dumbwaiter dropped four floors but stopped before it struck the basement floor. An air compressor decelerated the descent. Whipsnade and Peabo spilled out into a grungy storage space. The basement was filled with assorted machinery, shredders, and mounds of threadbare books stacked next to an old gas furnace, ready to be burned.

The two untangled their limbs, sat back, and massaged their

dizzy noggins. Both struggled to stand, unsteady, and inadvertently head-butted each other twice.

Peabo snapped out of it first and eyed a basement window that was ajar. He rushed over and leaped on a pyramid of loose books to reach the window. He struggled mightily as he kept slipping on the volumes of books. He made progress until Whipsnade seized one of his legs. Peabo thrashed about with all his might. To brace himself, he gripped a lever, which dumped a huge heap of furnace ash on top of Whipsnade's head. Peabo, freed of his grasp, slipped through the window.

"Mamma told me there'd be days like this. Just not this often." The crestfallen Whipsnade was covered head to toe in paper ash. "And that's ... WhipSNADE, BUB!"

• • •

T-Ray wriggled to release her pinned left arm. Spigs held his breath as McTaggart roamed the other side of their hiding space for the second time.

"Johnny Spignola!" McTaggart thundered between panting breaths. "Theresa Ray Rogers! Let me tell ya about someone who once made poor decisions."

SQUEAK! SQUEAK! SQUEAK! Mrs. Buelwhacker's cart drowned out his teaching moment.

The chief grumbled. "Grrrr! Mrs. Buelwhacker, could you please—?"

He was cut off by the yelp from his deputy in the distance.

"ACE! Red alert!" Whipsnade hollered in the distance.

"Hold on, Deputy! I'm coming!"

Spigs peeked to see McTaggart heave himself out of a lounge chair and waddle off in a panic. Spigs and T-Ray each glanced away, embarrassed by their face-to-face snug position. Several seconds of awkward silence passed before T-Ray mumbled, "Ah, I think it's safe now."

Spigs met her eyes. "Okay, um, let's, like, go find the Creeples and the professor," he stammered as he tried to squeeze out of their tight quarters. When he popped free, he reached back and grabbed T-Ray's hand.

The two teens slid down a banister for a quicker retreat to the first floor in time to see McTaggart yank open the basement door. When they rushed out of the building, their jaws dropped, eyes transfixed by the bewildering scene. Army reserve units were now patrolling the campus in a caravan of Jeeps and Humvees.

"We're now under, like, some kind of martial law," T-Ray speculated.

"Who called 'em in?" Spigs pointed at one of the Jeeps. "LOOK!"

The behemoth Hodag charged out of the darkness and pounced to a stop on its stout legs. It kicked back one rear leg and stampeded into a Jeep with its horned head. The force launched a soldier out of the side. The Hodag rammed its speared tail into the radiator grill, piercing the metal vents and leaving the engine billowing steam.

Two soldiers jumped into the bed of a Humvee, stationing themselves behind a rocket launcher mount. They positioned the mammoth Hodag in their crosshairs and fired, lighting the night sky with two fireballs. One missed, but the second exploded over the Hodag's head. The spooked beast retreated behind the Necrosis Physiology building.

"We could sure use their help!" Spigs motioned to the soldiers, who regrouped for another Hodag blitz. "We're running out of time."

T-Ray and Spigs raced after one of the Humvees. They waved their arms, trying to get the driver's attention. The Humvee stopped, and the annoyed commander hopped out of the passenger side. "All civilians need to be in their dorms! It's not safe."

"Tell us about it," Spigs scoffed.

"But . . . but you have no idea what's really happening around here," T-Ray said, catching her breath.

"I've got rampaging monsters running amok, and my orders are to eradicate them in the name of public safety." The commander's face was pockmarked and stern. "I repeat, return to your dorms."

"But these creatures aren't real, I mean . . ." Spigs glanced at his phone's clock. "Dean Smathers IS behind all this. He's wicked AND insane!"

"Son, most students think their headmaster is wicked. Now vacate or get locked up!"

The commander's wrinkled forehead and crossed muscular arms dared the teens to challenge him again. But before Spigs could come back with a wisecrack, the Mongolian Death Worm discharged a glob of acid that flew over the commander's head and splattered against the windshield of a Humvee. The soldiers inside screamed and leaped out as the windshield dissolved into a liquid mass. The Hodag roared from beside the ten-foot slithering

Death Worm and scuffed its clawed feet through the grass like a toro bull charging its matador.

CRRAAASH! The Hodag's stout horns flipped another Jeep onto its roof while the Mongolian Death Worm looped its gelatinous body around four soldiers, pinning their arms to their sides. Other soldiers rushed forward to help. They sliced the Death Worm's exoskeleton with bayonets and pulled their comrades free.

"Retreat! Retreat!" the commander screamed, his eyes bugging out of his head.

The soldiers loaded in the remaining Humvee and Jeeps and sped off, leaving T-Ray and Spigs facing down a snot-snorting, slavering Hodag and the acid-spitting Mongolian Death Worm.

T-Ray and Spigs backed away and turned to each other in disbelief. "RUN!"

They sprinted toward the boys' dormitory. Spigs heard the Hodag's thundering feet match theirs stride for stride, and he felt the hot, pungent breath from its bull nostrils on his neck. Spigs glanced to his right and saw the fear on T-Ray's face, though she didn't scream. Making a hasty decision, he slipped behind her to be an obstacle between her and the Hodag. With his hands on her shoulders, he propelled her forward and yelled, "Go, T-Ray, I'll distract it."

Her legs struggled to keep steady as he shoved her faster than she could normally run. "No, I'm not leaving—"

"Look out!" Spigs pushed her forward as the slithering Mongolian Death Worm slammed its slimy hindquarters between the two, which left Spigs trapped between two vicious crypto-creatures.

"SPIGS!" T-Ray shrieked from the other side of the Death Worm's gelatinous backside.

Spigs heard heavy, guttural breathing and spun around to face the Hodag. The enormous beast swayed side to side. With its bristly mane standing on end, it lowered its horned head with an angry snort. Two arms appeared from over the top of the slimy Death Worm and clutched Spigs's backpack, and a struggle ensued to tug him back over. T-Ray straddled the invertebrate and strained to lift Spigs off his feet. The Hodag charged! Spigs kicked frantically but slipped back down on the slimy skin. With one last attempt, T-Ray clutched the backpack with both hands and lunged over the worm's back, using her weight to heave Spigs up and over. *SQUISH!* The Hodag buried its horns in the side of the Death Worm—missing Spigs by a Hodag's hair.

Spigs and T-Ray raced through campus, not concerned with the CCTV cameras or the curfew. When they got to the dorm and raced to the boys' floor, Biscuit greeted them with a whine in the hallway.

"Now how did you get out?" Spigs picked up his fat feline.

T-Ray tested the knob; it was unlocked. She glanced at Spigs. He shrugged. She put her index finger to her lips and cracked the door. Spigs glanced over her shoulders, holding Biscuit up like a weapon, clawed paws first.

"*Rachel?*" he exclaimed in disbelief.

The pretty brunette was at Spigs's desk, her hand buried in the middle drawer. Startled, she popped up and displayed the dazzling smile that made Spigs's heart pitter-patter. She sashayed over to him and looped her arms around his neck.

"All this campus madness had me so worried about my Spigsy," Rachell purred.

T-Ray made gagging noises and rolled her eyes. Rachell ignored her.

"Wh ... what are ya doin' here?" Suspicion crept through Spigs's mind. "And how ... how did you get in here?"

"It was locked, Rachell." T-Ray gauged the sophomore with narrowed eyes.

Rachell let Spigs loose with a pout and shot a quick glare at T-Ray. "We need to talk, alone," she said.

Something shiny Rachell was wearing caught T-Ray's eyes. "Say, girl, where'd you get your charm bracelet? Witches 'R' Us?"

Spigs noticed the circular pendant dangling from Rachell's wrist. He saw the Eye of Horus, an inverted pentagram, and three sixes. He was confused.

"Stay out of this, DORK!" Rachell scowled at T-Ray.

"*Spigsy's* business IS my business," T-Ray shot back.

"Rachell, are you a ... ?"

"Disciple of the New Order of the Magister Templi? Yes!" She stuck her nose in the air, her face twisted into a nasty sneer. "And His Eminency has personally directed me to retrieve any genomic data from your work with Professor Bodkins. Now hand it over!"

"His Eminency? You mean Smathers." Peabo had appeared in the doorway. T-Ray and Spigs turned around and rushed over to hug him, but Rachell grabbed T-Ray's shoulder and spun her around.

"Hand it over!" Rachell held out her hand and wiggled her fingers. "That research is crucial to our cause. You infidels will soon be enlightened."

"Again with the infidels. I'm startin' to develop an inferiority complex," Peabo joked.

"Rachell, *now* ya've dun it." Spigs grinned. He knew what was coming.

T-Ray took a step back and dropped into a spinning crouch. Her swinging leg took Rachell's legs out from under her. She face-planted in Biscuit's cat litter box, knocking her out cold.

"Sure glad Wonder Woman's on MY team!" Peabo mimed a slam dunk. He kept his hand up for a high five, but T-Ray wasn't interested.

"How long were ya standin' out there, dude?" Spigs stepped in to high-five his roommate.

"Long enough."

T-Ray frowned at Rachell. "But we're still back where we started."

"Like, where's the professor? The Creeples? Smathers? We just don't have time to search the entire campus." Spigs paced the room.

"Got a wild idea." Peabo ventured over to his computer and typed frantically. "If I can hack into the academy's CCTV, I think I can follow Rachell's recent movements."

"It's worth a try." T-Ray draped a blanket completely over Rachell.

"She's NOT dead, T-Ray," Spigs said.

It took Peabo five minutes to hack into the closed-circuit

footage, and another few minutes for him to locate video of Rachell exiting her dormitory.

"Now, watch and wait." Peabo tracked Rachell on different security cameras as she headed to breakfast, to her classes, to lunch. Yet, when most of the other students retreated back to their dorms for the curfew, Rachell headed to Bell Tower. She hustled effortlessly through the tangled hedgerow to the back door.

"She had access to the tower the entire time?" Spigs shook his head. "No wonder she didn't club that robed dude. She was in on it the whole time. Whatta sap I am."

"I second that," T-Ray added.

"Look!" Peabo pointed to the image on the screen. "She's entering the tower from the rear."

"Jackpot!" Spigs said.

Peabo fast-forwarded the video to Horace, his hooligans, and a string of students streaming into Bell Tower. "This video takes place over the last hour. So, something's definitely brewing inside Bell Tower. Like, now!"

"Somethin' EVIL!" Spigs declared.

"Gathering of the devil's Disciples!" Peabo proclaimed.

"THAT has to be where Professor Bodkins and the Creeples are!" T-Ray was elated.

"Okay, so everything points to this Golden Dawn happening tomorrow—the hundredth anniversary of the cult massacre," Peabo said. "That gives us a little time."

Spigs glanced up at their Elvis Presley wall clock: 11:29 p.m. "WAIT! Just thought of somethin'. Technically one second past midnight will be tomorrow. So, what if—"

"The Golden Dawn ceremony starts at midnight. THAT'S IT! It's why they're all assembling tonight in Bell Tower. We've got to get in there and save the professor and the Creeples," T-Ray declared.

"And STOP Smathers's demonic transformation!" Spigs clutched T-Ray's arm.

"But the tower's guarded," Peabo warned.

T-Ray and Spigs paced the dorm room, thinking of how to secretly enter the tower.

"Spigs, you've become sort of an expert on these wild rumors about Bell Tower's infamous history. And you once mentioned rumors of cavernous passageways underneath the academy, right?" T-Ray talked with her hands as she paced.

"Yeah! And many of the rumors have been verified. So?"

"I know how to get inside." T-Ray stepped over Rachell. "At least, I think I do. When we were in Smathers's office, I remember seeing a small amount of caked dirt ground in the carpet. But none by the door. Now, wouldn't it make sense—?"

"Smathers has some secret passageway!" Spigs finished her thoughts.

"Now hear me out. You guys do your thing in Smathers's office. I'm gearing up." Peabo hurried to his trunk and pulled out the box of fireworks his brothers had slipped him. "I'll be the distraction. If you run into trouble below, like robed goonies, text me an SOS, and I'll fire off these bad boys right at the tower. They'll scatter out like cockroaches."

"What about her?" Spigs pointed to Rachell still sprawled out on the floor.

"Well, it works on TV shows." Peabo filled a jar with cold water and splashed it in her face. She flinched and let out a low groan.

"Follow me." T-Ray stepped over the groggy Rachell and dragged Spigs by his hand out of the dorm. "Let's go rescue our friends!"

CHAPTER 28

The Golden Dawn

Smathers scrutinized one of his Disciples who bent over to leer at Skoota. The Disciple exposed a *TCB* tattoo on the underside of his wrist as he skillfully inserted a catheter into one of the blue Creeple's pronounced veins on its arm. Skoota was strapped in place inside a hanging steel cage but squirmed fiercely—CLICK-CLACKING, baring its teeth, oscillating its mustard-yellow eyes wildly. Within seconds, the strongest Creeple had been pitifully anesthetized. It slumped in its cage. All the Creeples were caged, strapped down and now sedated.

The Disciple stepped back and bowed his head to Smathers, who was exceedingly pleased. He watched the iridescent blood steadily drip from the tubes attached to the Creeples' veins, collecting by way of gravity into bottles set below the hanging cages. He was fidgety with apprehension their magical dragon DNA may have been intermingled with other blood, preventing his malevolent scheme from succeeding. But right now, only Professor Bodkins's genetic research could tell him otherwise. Keeper was pouring over her data that very minute.

"Well done, Onslow. You may join the others." Smathers nodded as Onslow lined up next to Horace. They jockeyed for position next to their supreme leader, and Horace edged Onslow out with a shoulder.

"Let us begin." Smathers raised his hands over the reliquary.

• • •

"I've spent way too much time in this disgustin' place. I'm gettin' queasy," Spigs groaned as they broke into Smathers's office for the second time that day. "Ya sure there's an entrance to the underground?"

"Of course I'm sure . . . ish. Look for something out of place. Like you said, Smathers is a neat freak." T-Ray crept around the perimeter of the office, looking for any discrepancy.

"I see a tiny amount of dirt. I think." Spigs had bent down to observe a soiled spot.

T-Ray joined him by the grandfather clock. She pointed to a deep divot in the area rug next to the clock, as if it had been recently shifted.

Spigs knelt. "Specks of dirt here at the base."

T-Ray ran her hands up and down the antique clock's mahogany finish, opened the beveled glass cabinet to check the chimes, and then reached around the backside. "Aha, some sort of button," she said. "Here goes nothing." Both stepped back as the grandfather clock slid to the side with a mechanical whir.

Spigs pulled back the Persian rug to expose a floor hatch. "BINGO, T-Ray!" He struggled to lift the heavy wooden hatch to a circular metal shaft. His phone flashlight highlighted a ladder for the first two floors below, but the shaft turned dark and vacuous as it descended into the earth beneath the building.

"Ladies first." T-Ray climbed down the metal ladder without hesitation.

"Ya won't get an argument from me."

Spigs followed her and carefully descended the first two stories until his feet planted unsteadily on a crudely built wooden ladder that would take them deeper into the bowels under the academy. T-Ray was already five rungs down, and soft earth was their final landing spot.

"Kinda creepy down here." Spigs blinked repeatedly to adjust his eyes as his flashlight cut the dark. "Which way?"

"Bell Tower is due south from here." T-Ray opened the compass app on her cell phone. "So this way."

"Wouldn't be surprised if the tower was precisely one hundred and thirty-two steps from here." Spigs held onto T-Ray's shirt as she led the way through the dark void.

"Numbers do seem to have importance at this school."

They picked up their pace as they counted the steps toward the middle of campus. It took over one hundred and twenty steps for the teens' eyes to fully adjust to the darkness. Thirty more steps and they came to a wall in the side of the cave.

"Another dead end." T-Ray' shoulders slumped.

"Looks like this entire tunnel was excavated by hand." Spigs felt the dirt walls' choppy scars left by handheld shovels, and in doing so, he located a latch flush to a door.

Spigs and T-Ray strained to push open the heavy iron door,

and it finally swung free in a cloud of dust. The teens entered another subterranean passage and continued counting their steps down the corridor. These archaic tunnels reminded Spigs of the Hollow Earth conspiracy he'd read about while hiding in his bedroom from Aunt Gussy's indignation. It theorized there were inhabitants of inner Earth traversing by way of a subterranean world. At the teens' one hundred and thirty-second step, they came to a strikingly modern door. Spigs easily turned its brass knob and entered a small, dingy storage area.

Inside the mostly vacant room were two wooden crates, which T-Ray examined. The two timeworn crates were smashed and splintered on one side. Spigs crouched for a closer inspection. "It looks like the crates that were kicked out from the . . ." He plucked long strands of neon-green hair caught in the splintered panels.

"They're HERE!" T-Ray's eyes welled up.

Spigs used a ballpoint pen to scrape off caked grime, exposing the faded letters on the crates: *N.O.M.T., Ltd.* "More evidence of this New Order of Magister Templi."

"We should text Peabo and let him know we're in!" T-Ray worked her thumbs frenetically.

BONG!

The teens stood motionless, mouths agape.

"WHOA!"

T-Ray cupped Spigs's mouth to silence him.

BONG! BONG! BONG! BONG! BONG! BONG! BONG! BONG! BONG! BONG! BONG! BONG!

"Bell Tower's bells!"

"I know. They've *never ever* rung before," T-Ray whispered.

"I counted thirteen of 'em," Spigs said as the last bell's ring dissipated into the night air.

T-Ray clicked on her phone's clock. The bright screen showed *12:00*. "This is it—the Golden Dawn!" T-Ray squeezed Spigs's arm.

Spigs dashed to the opposite door in hopes it was an exit. He signaled for T-Ray to be quiet. As he turned the knob, faint reverberating sounds filled the room, growing louder and louder. Suddenly, the cobblestone ground started quaking and rumbling, kicking up years of dust that had accumulated in the stone's crevasses. Spigs and T-Ray were speechless and braced themselves against the wall, their teeth clacking together and knees jiggling.

Just beyond the storage room's three-foot-thick stone wall, Smathers disregarded the trembling and buckling on his side of the chamber floor. The Creeples' hanging metal cages swayed back and forth, clanking into each other. The Disciples recoiled in fear, hugging the walls. Smathers and Keeper stood motionless, eyes sparking with delight, gleefully watching bolts of magenta lightning blasting out from the Creeples' eyes into the cobblestone floor below them.

In the storage room, T-Ray and Spigs now clung to each other. "What's happening? Earthquake?" T-Ray screamed over the deafening noise of the earth's tremors.

"Stay with me!" Spigs shouted. He gripped T-Ray's hand and guided her along the wall to the door.

The thundering floor caused more dust clouds, and crumbling stone mortar cascaded off the interior walls and ceilings.

Spigs pulled T-Ray close and, with all his might, yanked open the cumbersome door, fighting to keep steady on the quaking floor. They emerged into a short hall and peered around a corner into Smathers's massive chamber.

"What the—?" T-Ray was lost for words. At the center of the extravagant chamber was an expansive, vacuous cavity in the floor, where a violent, rotating thermal spectrum of magenta energy swirled upward. "Smathers opened some kind of . . . black hole."

"Some sorta supernatural portal!" Spigs squawked over the thunderous noise.

"THE DRAGON REALM?" T-Ray cried out in fear.

At the opposite side of the chamber, near a stone doorway partially covered by ornate drapes, T-Ray caught a glimpse of a distressful scene: a dangling metal cage, with an ashen-gray arm that had blood trickling through a tube from its vein. "Over there! They're HERE!" she yelled, but neither of them moved. Their eyes locked on the turbulence of magenta energy blasting out from the portal down a hallway and corridor. The maelstrom's gravitational force was so strong it formed an undertow that sucked Spigs toward the abyss.

"Spigs!" T-Ray cried out.

"Run, T-Ray!" The vacuum force was too powerful and lifted Spigs's body.

"Grab my foot!" T-Ray extended one leg while she clutched a protruding stone in the wall.

Spigs latched on to her jeans with one hand and tried to crawl across the floor with his other arm. T-Ray's auburn hair ripped from its bun and whipped around her face as she struggled to brace herself against the wall.

Inexplicably, the magenta energy vortex vanished after it had streamed out and through the top of Bell Tower, yet the gaping, swirling supernatural portal remained active in the stone floor. The teens managed to regain their footing. They turned toward the chamber, ready to advance and rescue the Creeples, but stopped dead in their tracks.

Black ectoplasm WHOOSHED out from the vacuous portal and materialized into a gaggle of grotesque ghouls swathed in rotten flesh attached to partially exposed bones, and garbed in ceremonial robes. Blazing blood-red eyes gleamed from within their hoods. The malevolent spirits' unearthly wails and shrieks mixed with Spigs's and T-Ray's cries of terror as the teens ran down the hallway. With no doors to run through, they turned left down another corridor toward a set of stone steps.

Spigs felt something cold caress his neck, and the putrid scent of roadkill overwhelmed his nostrils. "Kick it into overdrive, T-Ray!" he screamed, too scared to look over his shoulder as the ghastly wails grew louder.

The two raced up the stone steps, two at a time, until Spigs bonked his head against something hard. He pushed on it to reveal a trapdoor. The ghastly ghouls vanished through the wall. Spigs and T-Ray made a mad dash through Bell Tower's main floor, flung open the front door, and rustled through the manicured bushes to find Peabo crouching beside his scooter.

"You'll NEVER believe—" Spigs tried to catch his breath.

"NO, *you'll* never believe!" Peabo interrupted and pointed

skyward. They all looked up at the vaporous magenta vortex arcing out of Bell Tower's belfry.

They watched in shock as the vortex's energy materialized into a mammoth scarlet dragon. It flapped its twenty-foot bat-like wings and landed atop the belfry on its two reptilian legs. It coiled its extensive scaly tail around its talons and lurched its massive horned beak skyward. Its eyes blazed red as it belched a torrent of fire from its mouth. It flapped its enormous wings and lifted off.

"Peabo, Smathers opened the Dragon Realm," T-Ray squawked.

"And released *that* thing." Peabo pointed to the dragon.

"LOOK OUT!" Spigs shouted, and dove to cover his friends. The scarlet dragon expanded its jaws and snapped down on a nearby lamppost, wrenching it free in a shower of sparks.

"Over there!" Peabo squirmed loose from Spigs. He leaped to his feet and motioned to the army reserve convoy rolling down the street in a three-by-three formation. "We're saved!"

"Uh . . . don't get your hopes up," Spigs said.

Gunfire echoed from down the street, and muzzle flashes lit the night, but the bullets were like bee stings to the dragon. It tossed its head in annoyance and flung the lamppost onto the hood of a Humvee. It dive-bombed the front line, snatched up a Jeep with its talons, and flipped it into the air. The crushed car landed near the front of the Cybernetics building.

"It's official, Peabo. The Golden Dawn has started," T-Ray affirmed.

"And we didn't get the Creeples. But we know their blood is

Smathers's connection to gaining the powers of a Master Sorcerer," Spigs expressed glumly.

"They're alive, but caged beneath Bell Tower!" T-Ray told Peabo with tears in her eyes.

The supernatural manifestation that opened the Dragon Realm had reactivated—REANIMATED—every one of the previous monstrosities and inanimate objects that the Creeples had zapped to LIFE!

All the shapeshifting Vending Machine Robots had groaned back to LIFE, transforming back into fierce, clashing marching machines. They trudged down the campus streets like marching metallic soldiers of the future, firing candy bars, soda cans, and hoagies that splatted against the army reservists' body armor.

The five Bog People once again staggered forth like possessed zombies, and now brandishing the feudal swords and spears. The army's bullets staggered them, but they just kept coming, as they were already dead!

The two gargoyle statues turned back into grotesque flying creatures. The fearsome figures swooped around Bell Tower, snapping their fierce jaws.

The Mongolian Death Worm and the Hodag stirred back to LIFE and stormed up the street.

A soldier cried out, "A six-headed beast! RETREAT!" He and two of his comrades scampered back to the Humvees but tripped over the venomous tail of the Ayia Napa sea monster.

The sea monster's six dog heads snarled and snapped. The soldiers shrieked and crawled under the nearest Humvee.

Creeples!

All the reanimated creatures had now painstakingly advanced across the Quad, drawn to the supernatural forces emanating from the Dragon Realm beneath Bell Tower. Spigs, T-Ray, and Peabo hid between dumpsters to avoid the onslaught of terror that was sure to come.

S.H.A.D.O.W.

High Energy Laser Defense System

Exotic Technology Department
Washington, DC
Codename: PROJECT GOOZE

Name: Beezer

Aliases: Orange Creeple

Identity: Twenty-inch-tall humanoid. Neon-orange hair. Prodigious ears. Oscillating mustard-yellow eyes. Click-clacking noise emanates from the skull region—a form of communication.

Creators: Three Aberdasher Academy of Science students.

Personal Abilities: No obvious abilities.

Magical Powers: Draconic Kinetic Energy blasts from their eyes that super-charge inanimate objects into living, breathing entities.

Mystical Limitations: The metamorphosis can last up to twelve hours.

Potential Application: Particle-beam weaponry.

Comments: Cheez 'Em connoisseur. Excessive intestinal vapors: flatulence. Extreme mischief-making behavior.

CHAPTER 29

Team Gooze versus the Red Dragon

The ferocious dragon's talons clutched Bell Tower's soaring spires. Its T-rex-sized head screeched and belched flames into the sky, lighting up the night.

"Yow! *Está en fuego!* That's one nasty *hombre*." Peabo stared in shock as Spigs and T-Ray gawked in astonishment from across the street.

"Straight out of Middle-earth!" Spigs squealed.

T-Ray tilted her head up and stared intently at the dragon atop the tower before typing something into her phone.

"Anyone have CliffsNotes on *Beowulf*?" Peabo asked, half joking.

"THAT'S the Wyvern red dragon," T-Ray exclaimed.

Peabo put his fingers to his temples and closed his eyes.

At the tower's base, several animated crypto-creatures had assembled.

"Satan IS referred to as the 'Red Dragon' in the Book of Revelation," Peabo piped up.

"And Smathers IS referred to as Satan in the Book of Spigs," Spigs asserted.

"This red dragon is obviously guarding Bell Tower," T-Ray stated. "And it's 12:09 a.m. Let's assume Smathers's transformation is underway, so we *have* to make our move, NOW!"

Peabo opened his eyes. "Hear me out. I'll distract the red dragon. You two bum-rush Bell Tower. Get in and save the professor and the Creeples. I'll be streaming all the action from outside." Peabo strapped on his helmet and turned on the attached GoPro camera.

"Just *what* do you have in mind to divert a dragon?" T-Ray's face was drawn with concern.

"Trust me!" Peabo placed a hand on T-Ray's shoulder.

"Once we locate the Creeples and the professor, we'll text ya," Spigs said.

"It's all on us, right?" Peabo flung his right arm skyward.

"RIGHT!" Spigs and T-Ray exclaimed.

Peabo hopped on his scooter, pressed the ignition switch, and goosed the motor. The smoking rear tire drew the attention of the red dragon.

"Wait, what's that fool doin'?" Spigs shook his head.

"GUYS! What's our rallyin' cry?" Peabo shouted over his revving engine.

"Teamwork—"T-Ray called back.

"Makes the dream work!" Spigs finished.

"It's all on US! *Carpe diem!* SEIZE THE DAY—TEAM GOOZE!" Peabo howled as he pulled his batch of firecrackers and a lighter from his bag. He torched two bottle rockets: *SWOOSH! SWOOSH! KABOOM-BOOM!* The mini-missiles detonated on both sides of the dragon's head.

"PEABO! Remember, it's a WYVERN dragon. Stay away from its deadly stinger—ON ITS TAIL!" T-Ray hollered. Peabo waved in acknowledgment.

The red dragon leaped off the top of Bell Tower, wings tucked, and dive-bombed Peabo, baring its razor-sharp fangs. A flame and a plume of smoke billowed from the dragon's mouth, ready to incinerate Peabo. He launched two more bottle rockets. *KABOOM-BOOM!* The dragon's own noxious fumes ignited in its mouth, rocking its head back. Its carcass flopped on the cement beside Peabo. The great beast shook its gargantuan head and lashed its venomous tail side to side.

"OOF!" The tail whipped the scooter sideways, knocking Peabo high off the back end. He crashed down atop the dragon's scaly appendage. "AARRGGH!" With a WHISK of its powerful tail, the disoriented winged leviathan flipped Peabo onto its ridged back. He shouted down to his friends, "I've got it from here . . . I think! You two—*vamoose!*" He used the scaly creases on the Wyvern's neck as handles and worked to carefully slip his backpack off one arm so he could retrieve some more fireworks. The red dragon thrashed about, and Peabo slid down its side. "Whooaaa, boy."

Spigs and T-Ray gasped below, but Peabo's sneakers found footholds on the dragon's scales, and he swung his right leg over the beast's back to regain his seat. Peabo WHOOPED as the dragon took to the sky, taking him for a terrifying ride.

T-Ray looked at Spigs. "We've got no choice. Let's go."

Spigs nodded, and they crept cautiously toward Bell Tower, avoiding the distracted Hodag, Mongolian Death Worm, Vending Machine Robots, and Bog People.

"Uum . . . a bit of a problem." Spigs pointed to the horde of ghastly ghouls that materialized out through the front door's keyhole. The grotesque phantoms rose up with mouths wide. They wailed in rage and seethed in agony as they swooped around the two teens.

"We thirst for vengeance!" they roared.

"It has to be the spirits of the massacred cult members."

"*Just great!* A fire-belchin' dragon wasn't enough; Smathers conjured up hundreds of century-old vindictive GHOULS!"

The ghouls were a mass of black and gray ectoplasmic particles, their oxblood eyes glowing and mouths dripping green goo. Spigs assumed a boxer's stance, glanced back at T-Ray, and shrugged, not sure he could actually punch an apparition. But he'd go down trying.

High-pitched whistles made T-Ray and Spigs duck and cover. *KABOOM! KABOOM!* A hail of Roman candles, courtesy of Peabo, set fire to the grass around the ghouls. They WAILED as flames engulfed their decayed flesh and robes. Spigs saluted Peabo. T-Ray yanked Spigs's shirt, and they raced past the scorched ghouls through Bell Tower's front door. The teens hustled down the hidden staircase and retraced their steps to the hall with the storage room, following the whooshing sound created by the Dragon Realm portal and the low, unmelodic chants of the Disciples in the chamber. They skidded to a stop at the sight of two Disciples flanking the doorway with arms crossed and eyes locked on the ceremony within.

"How do we get past 'em?" Spigs whispered.

"We don't. Not dressed like this. Follow my lead."

The two cautiously edged close against the wall, slinking down the hall and up behind the pair of robed students. T-Ray easily subdued her target by pinching a pressure point on his neck. The husky Disciple swooned, falling unconscious. Spigs had his Disciple in a headlock, neither side gaining ground. Spigs's bony arm kept the boy from yelling for help.

"Can I offer a finger?" T-Ray applied a pressure-point pinch, which made the boy crumple to the ground. They removed the Disciples' robes and slipped them on. The pair ducked into the ceremonial chamber.

They effortlessly blended into the crowd. Spigs and T-Ray settled in behind a row of Disciples seated on pews.

Spigs motioned to the supernatural portal in the middle of the cobblestone floor. It was the first time the teens had assessed the Dragon Realm up close. Magenta vapors spun like a maelstrom down into a hazy abyss.

At the front of the cavernous room was a raised altar. Egyptian symbols were carved into the stone walls. The aroma of sandalwood permeated the area surrounding the ritual candles that flickered shadows on the wall and cast an eerie glow over the Disciples, who chanted unnerving verses in methodical unison.

"This is just *so* gross. Like a pagan shrine for black magic," T-Ray whispered as she and Spigs jockeyed for a better vantage point behind the benches.

"Or a Dungeons and Dragons convention," Spigs muttered.

"Yeah, and here comes the Dungeon Master."

A white-robed figure ascended two steps from an elevated lectern to reach the altar's marble stand. The figure pulled back his white hood with pale hands to reveal—Dean Smathers. In front of him, placed on the altar, were bronze dragon talismans, a mortar and pestle, two silver chalices, and a tattered leather manuscript. Behind, garnet drapes hung from ornate runners that sagged under their weight.

"Behold! I am Yesterday, Today, and the Brother of Tomorrow! Better to reign in hell than to serve in heaven." Smathers raised his arms high and looked skyward.

"This is *soo* disgusting. Devil worshiping." Spigs cringed.

"Yeah, you think! And that must be your old friend, the Grim Keeper?" T-Ray pointed to a decrepit, hunched-over man whose belt holstered his rusty Colt Army revolver with a mother-of-pearl handle.

"Yup, that's ol' GK—straight out of *Tales from the Crypt*. And with a face that could cure hiccups." Spigs scanned the chamber for Rachell, worried she might recognize him, but another familiar face caught his attention. "Well, well, look who's standin' next to the GK."

"ONSL—!"

Spigs pressed his hand over T-Ray's mouth and grinned at the Disciple in front of them who had turned around. "Ah, she's, like, super excited about the Golden Dawn." The freckle-faced Disciple nodded with blank eyes and turned his attention back to Smathers.

"I convey the Sanctuary of Truth! A god sitteth upon my lips!" Smathers lowered his arms and voice. "My loyal and devoted Disciples . . ." He fashioned a stiff, menacing grin as he addressed his followers in monotone. "Science has exhorted us with delusions about our true nature as metaphysical beings. It will soon end." He thrust his hands skyward again, with all the gusto of a television evangelist.

All the Disciples appeared possessed, the life washed out of their eyes. They started to hum and chant in Latin verses while they swayed in unison.

"Take a closer look at 'em. They're *all* students . . . and, like, brainwashed! Our school's turnin' into the Occult Academy." Spigs skimmed the room of vaguely familiar faces. But he noticed T-Ray was still glaring at Onslow with a fixed frown. "T-Ray?" Spigs elbowed her to get her attention. "Ya still with me?" he asked gently.

"Huh? Ah, sure."

A livestreaming video alert from Peabo's YouTube channel vibrated Spigs's phone. With the Disciples chanting around them, he and T-Ray bowed their heads together over the muted video to watch the frantic action outside Bell Tower in total shock.

"It's DEFCON One out there!" Spigs screeched as T-Ray cupped her hand to his gaped mouth.

CHAPTER 30

In the Midnight Hour

Peabo shielded his eyes instinctively when an army reserve unit rolled in and blared spotlights into the sky from two trailers pulled by Humvees. His stomach lurched as the dragon dipped one wing into a roll. He regained his grip at the base of its neck but yelped as he flipped upside down and his feet momentarily left the dragon's back. His backpack tugged on his right arm as it flew out, threatening to loosen his grip. His sweaty fingers slid an inch down the scales, and he bit his lower lip, straining to hold on. He hugged his belly to the dragon's back, panting, and risked raising his head in time to see the dragon perch atop Bell Tower once more. Peabo's heart hammered so loud it drowned out the red dragon's roar, yet he forced himself into a sitting position. The soldiers below had leaped out of their vehicles. The dragon shifted beneath Peabo, spiny tail swishing through the lit night sky. Peabo knew the red dragon could incinerate the soldiers with a few deep breaths, and he had to stop it. So he swallowed hard and carefully shimmied up the dragon's expansive neck.

Creeples!

Peabo's presence was like an annoying horsefly to the red dragon. It shook its massive head and forced Peabo to cling like a baby monkey on its mother's back. When the movement stopped, he scooted up two more feet, keeping his backpack handy—pressed to his side. Frighteningly close to the red dragon's razor-sharp teeth, he reached back and dug two cherry bombs out of the backpack.

"How about some yummy jawbreakers, my scaly friend?" Peabo lit the two cherry bombs, and as the dragon turned its head in furious surprise, he hurled them deep down its throat.

The first firecrackers detonated with enough force to send flames spewing from the beast's nostrils. The red dragon leaped off the tower, trying to outrun the pain, but with a second *BANG!* its wings crumpled. Spinning uncontrollably, Peabo held on in a death grip as he and the beast plummeted toward the ground.

• • •

Spigs held back a cheer when he saw Peabo chuck the bombs into the dragon's mouth, but the live feed blurred in the crazy tailspin. He clicked off the video when T-Ray gasped in concern.

Spigs cleared his throat. "He's got the situation under control—sorta, I think. I *hope*." Spigs shoved the phone in his pocket. "C'mon, we have to find the professor and the Creeples or Peabo's epic diversions will be for naught."

Spigs perused the chamber again. However, this time he ignored the students and focused on the details of the room's makeup. He tried to remember where T-Ray had seen Royal earlier. His brows rose toward his hairline as he eyed a crack in the velvet curtains. A plume of Royal's purple hair peeked through. He motioned for T-Ray to follow him, and they shuffled along the outskirts of the busy room, heads down and chanting gibberish to blend in as they moved through the pews. They inched cautiously around the edge of the swirling supernatural portal—the Dragon Realm—passed a tabletop laden with alchemist's paraphernalia, and crept around ornate curtains to the Creeples.

The weakened Creeples were suspended in cramped cages hung from the ceiling with chains, trapped and immobilized. Intravenous catheters bulged beneath their ashen skin, leading to drip tubes that were gradually draining blood. The iridescent crimson liquid filled receptor bottles placed on the floor below.

T-Ray mouthed, "Follow me," to Spigs. She stepped confidently up to a husky Disciple on guard. Spigs retreated, as he recognized him as Luther, the lacrosse player whom he'd chatted with outside Bell Tower a few hours earlier. "Our esteemed leader has instructed you to inspect the outside perimeter," T-Ray ordered in a droning voice.

"Huh? Dean Smathers personally told me to stay at my post," Luther retorted.

"He's bestowing upon us the wisdom of the Magister Templi. Do you really think I should interrupt him?" T-Ray flicked her head in Smathers's direction, and Luther looked through the crack in the curtain. The dean was now on his knees chanting verses in Latin, and everyone followed his example. "Yes or no?" T-Ray stared at Luther through an impatient scowl.

"*You're* authorized to take over?" Luther wavered, looking nervously at the Creeples.

"He fears we may have had a security breach and wants you to investigate. Now, proceed!" T-Ray ordered. "And take these two Disciples with you to stand guard."

Luther hesitated. T-Ray looked him in the eye and dropped her voice an octave, making her sound authoritative. "Now, GO!"

Luther nodded, his eyes wide with anxiety, and waved the other two Disciples after him as he hurried out of the chamber and scrambled up the stairs.

"We have to move fast." Spigs tried to comfort the Creeples by poking his fingers through the cages to stroke their faces. "Sorry, little fellas, we'll get you out."

Using a wooden stool for a boost, T-Ray secured the vessels containing the Creeples' blood high above their heads. She toggled the switches back to reverse the blood flow. She looked at Spigs. "It's going to take a few minutes."

Spigs fed Skoota through the bars. "No worries," he whispered. He showed T-Ray the dried catnip he'd given the Creeple and sprinkled some in her hand. "Got a hunch ... Beastly Mode!" Spigs pressed his forefinger and thumb together to indicate "just a pinch."

As T-Ray sprinkled the last bit of dried catnip leaf into Naz's mouth, a frantic commotion ensued from the other side of the curtain.

"They're CHARGIN'!" shrieked a high-pitched voice Spigs vaguely recognized.

"Boss, it's 'em walkin' dead dudes," squawked a second deeper tone.

"Shut it! SHUT IT, ya numbskulls!" a man shouted back.

Spigs rushed over to see the Lyle brothers' backs pressed against the storage room door, straining to hold back the attacking Bog People. A leathery cadaver arm from a Bog Person poked through the doorway and was swinging a barbaric club with a chained spiked ball. *SNAP!* The door shut, and the arm plopped on the floor, still waving the weapon.

"Ya know . . . " Flitch briefly put on his carny hat. "We could pass 'em off as Egyptian mummies. But I'm still gonna lasso Godzilla out there! So, gird your loins, men, and ADVANCE!"

Flitch and his two flunkies charged into where Smathers had his spellbound Disciples chanting verses from parchment scrolls.

Flitch was puzzled by the bizarre formalities, but it was the caged Creeples barely visible through the cracked curtain that caught his attention. "What the HELL are ya doin' to MY cash cows?" Flitch shouted, disrupting the grandiose ritual.

Smathers barely batted an eye at Flitch and his flunkies. "Flitch, you have violated the sanctity of our sacraments."

"Simply hand 'em over, Dean, and maybe I'll only blast ya with one dose of my gas," Flitch warned.

A wicked grin curled Smathers's thin lips as he calmly faced the Lyle brothers, who stood in a ready stance with chemical tank nozzles aimed at him. "Enough! Apprehend the intruders," Smathers ordered.

Before the Lyle brothers could pull the triggers, several Disciples leaped on their backs and wrestled them to the ground.

Easily overpowered by the dozen Disciples, Flitch and the two Lyle brothers were gagged and bound to the pews with duct tape in the corner.

Hiding behind the curtains, Spigs pulled the drawstrings to his robe's hood down tight over his face. He elbowed T-Ray. "It's all on us. Game on!"

"A quick check on Peabo first." T-Ray motioned to Spigs to click on the livestreaming video. Peabo still rode atop the red dragon bareback, bombing the assemblage of reanimated monstrosities and crypto-creatures with firecrackers.

BOOM! The Globster sea slug and Fangtooth Fish thrashed and flailed at the explosion.

BOOM! The Vending Machine Robots were hit with firecrackers.

BOOM! The Mongolian Death Worm swallowed a bottle rocket that burned its translucent skin in an orange glow.

BOOM! The Bog People's leathery skin set ablaze.

Spigs turned to T-Ray. "He's okay—I think."

"Just a few more minutes for the Creeples. So, wait here. I have a score to settle." T-Ray crept over behind the gagged, pew-bound Gideon Flitch.

Spigs hustled after her. "T-Ray, are ya nuts?"

T-Ray leaned in to Flitch's ear. "If we get you out, you hand over all your animals to the local zoo." Flitch scowled. T-Ray started to retreat with a shrug, but he let out a muffled "yes" from his taped mouth. "Okay, you agree?" she said. He nodded eagerly.

Spigs thwacked the back of Flitch's head with his knuckles, making Flitch grunt. "And that's for mistreatin' our Creeples."

T-Ray's brow wrinkled. "Now, let's save *our* Creeples!"

Spigs rushed back behind the curtain and fiddled with the Creeples' straps and intravenous tubes, inspecting the levels of the reversed blood flow.

Smathers's booming voice filled the room. "Professor Bodkins. We've been expecting you."

T-Ray and Spigs froze, turned to each other, and scrambled back to the curtains. Their professor squirmed in the vise-like grips of two Disciples. They led her to the altar and forced her down to her knees. Onslow hovered behind them, supervising.

"You'll never get away with this, Smathers!" Professor Bodkins howled.

"But, my dear professor, I already have." Smathers flaunted a smarmy grin. "And your gene-splicing discovery has given me the means to further advance our noble cause."

"Sadistic cause," Professor Bodkins spat back.

"Now, don't be so harsh. Without your data, I wouldn't have had nearly enough of the Wyvern dragon's DNA to achieve my ... glorious conversion."

"So *that's* his endgame with the professor?" Spigs whispered. He and T-Ray observed the professor's demeanor change from fury to fear.

T-Ray smacked her forehead. "We should've figured that out. We learned DNA is a fragile molecule and decays over time, becoming less readable. The professor's research revealed for the first time genomic replication was possible, and so, with the school's advanced 3D bio-printer, Smathers could theoretically replicate his precious dragon DNA ... for eternity!"

"That's why Smathers closed the Genomic department. It stopped the peer review from being published, giving him owner-ship of her research for his diabolical scheme." Spigs clapped his hands together, then balled them into fists.

"Which means he doesn't care about keeping the Creeples alive once he extracts their dragon blood. Or the professor." T-Ray put her hand on his shoulder and squeezed.

"So, the Wyvern dragon's DNA gives Doctor Evil eternal life *and* soon the supernatural powers of a Master Sorcerer."

The two watched two Disciples aggressively push Professor Bodkins in front of the reliquary.

Smathers's tone turned stern as he instructed Professor Bodkins. "Now, place your hands inside the repository. Be enlightened. Purge your corrupted soul"—his mouth twisted in a sneer—"and your mind from the blinding darkness of science."

"He's gonna, like, wipe her mind. Gotta save the professor!" Spigs cried out, and stood up.

T-Ray tugged down on his shoulder. "Hold on. The blood reversal is almost complete." T-Ray bounced on the balls of her feet as she studied the dwindling blood levels in the receptors.

"Keeper," Smathers barked. "Collect those bestial mutants' blood and begin the replication process. Make sure we have enough to fill my chalice, or I'll fill a bucket with yours."

"Uh, T-Raaayyy . . . runnin' out of time here." Spigs watched Keeper hobble toward them, but at a snail's pace.

"Done!" T-Ray observed the final drip from the IV tubes.

The Creeples procured all their precious blood, and at that pre-cise moment, the magenta energy forces within the supernatural portal streamed back into the Creeples' eyes. Vapors swirled over and around Keeper. He froze with a look of panic, mouth gaping to expose his yellowed, decaying teeth. The Dragon Realm abyss was gradually collapsing.

"NO! The Dragon Realm! Keeper, what have you done?" Smathers thundered.

"It's disintegratin'. We did it! I mean . . . the Creeples did it!" Spigs whooped loudly.

"Intruders!" Keeper screamed, triggering a raspy coughing fit.

Professor Bodkins thrashed in Onslow's grip, fighting with every ounce of energy she had to keep him from forcing her hand into the reliquary.

"This will all be over soon, Professor," Onslow said through gritted teeth as he inched her hand closer. "Don't fight it."

"NOT—ON—YOUR—LIFE!" She tried to throw an elbow into his face, but he pushed her forward with his knee as the reliquary illuminated with a palpitating magenta radiance from within.

"GET THOSE TWO!" Smathers pointed to Spigs and T-Ray.

Spigs shoved T-Ray aside and flipped over three rows of pew benches.

Horace motioned for his hooligans to charge, but tripped over benches. Spigs and T-Ray ran back to the Creeples' cages, where the ashen-gray creatures had sprung back to life. They had snapped the metal chains and shredded the straps—traces of their magical powers returned thanks to the small amount of catnip they had consumed. But it was not a complete metamorphosis, as before; their eyes stayed yellow and their teeth were not razor sharp. Spigs's hunch was correct.

"Help us stop him!" T-Ray frantically unlatched the cages, and the Creeples leaped out, wiggling their ears and *CLICK-CLACKING* hysterically.

"NOOOOO!" Professor Bodkins howled. Her right hand hovered inches away from the reliquary. Her cry incited the Creeples, who all sprang from the shadows onto Smathers, Horace, Keeper, and Onslow in a flurry of *CLICK-CLACKING* chaos. The professor kicked the distracted Disciple in the knee and jerked back from the reliquary. But her hand struck the reliquary's lid, causing the opulent container to tumble off the altar, crashing to the floor—exposing a brightly glowing magenta orb the size of an ostrich egg.

"Seize them ALL!" Smathers howled, and his two dozen Disciples stormed after T-Ray, Spigs, and the Creeples. Spigs tussled with two attackers while T-Ray kicked and punched with perfect form, bloodying two noses and dropping one boy to the ground with his hands between his legs. A female Disciple latched onto Spigs's neck from behind. He shoved back against her, pinning her to the wall, but another Disciple struck Spigs across the face. His arms were now pinned behind him by a powerful grip while a muscled arm squeezed his windpipe.

The Creeples inexplicably stopped in their tracks, all mesmerized by the sparkling magenta radiance emanating from the super bright orb on the cobblestone floor. They waddled closer and started shaking intensely, seemingly enchanted by the mystical orb. The Creeples were quickly overpowered by the five Disciples.

"Told you I'd get you, nerd," Horace growled in Spigs's ear.

Spigs struggled all the way to the altar, where T-Ray had also been apprehended. Horace wrapped Spigs in a painful bear hug.

To T-Ray and Spigs's horror, they saw the Creeples were once again captured. Their eyes were hastily blindfolded with bandanas.

"So you two THINK you've severed my lifeline to mystical powers for eternity? I AM the divine one," Smathers gloated.

"Your Golden Dawn will *never* happen, Smathers!" T-Ray spat at him.

A crazed, psychotic smirk from a jutting chin twisted Smathers's doughy face. "Stopped me, did you?" he said in an odd whisper. He let out a low, wild giggle. "We'll see about that. I have your little beasts. But this time, we'll hasten their blood donation ... by way of their THROATS!" From behind the altar, Smathers picked up a black canvas sheath from which he pulled a double-edged sword the size of his forearm. He handed it to a Disciple.

"NOOO!" T-Ray and Spigs roared.

A sadistic leer spread across Smathers's face. "Oh, but I'll be merciful." From beneath the altar, he removed a small glass carafe of milky liquid with an eyedropper lid. "My newest Disciples, it's time to show your devotion by administering the rite of passage. First, those six fiends of nature, then our three menacing meddlers, and finally ... yourselves. Do it—NOW!"

He handed the carafe to Onslow, who inched up to the closest Creeple, Naz. Onslow stood over the blindfolded Creeple and prudently inserted the dropper into the liquid, pinching the rubber cap. He released it so the liquid filled the dropper. He held it with two fingers and with his other hand forced open Naz's mouth.

Professor Bodkins screamed, "It's the nectar from the oleander plant—from Smathers's office." She struggled against the two Disciples who held her wrists. "It's POISON!"

T-Ray and Spigs turned to each other in horror.

Spigs yelled, "Don't y'all see? It's a . . . suicide pact! Smathers has done it before!"

Onslow ignored him with a detached expression and focused on Naz. He dangled the dropper over the Creeple's elongated tongue.

T-Ray flailed and thrashed madly. "Onslow, please don't do it!" she pleaded, but he was determined to act out Smathers's command.

"Not on my watch!" Spigs muttered to himself. He squirmed enough in Horace's embrace to free his right hand and slid out his laser-pointer pen from his front pants pocket. With his arms immobile, Spigs used his thumb to click on the laser pointer and aimed it at Onslow's eyes.

"AAAH!" Onslow cried out as the tiny beam temporarily blinded him. Professor Bodkins saw her chance and dipped her shoulder into one of her captives, knocking him off balance, then yanked free from the second Disciple. The professor scrambled over to assist T-Ray with her captors.

T-Ray leaped to her feet and squared up to Horace, who had let Spigs loose to help Onslow. She dropped into her signature low-spinning leg whip and knocked Horace flat on his back.

"Stompin' out bullying, one at a time." Spigs beamed wide and raised his hand for a high five . . . and surprisingly, T-Ray returned the gesture with a hearty slap. She motioned toward Naz.

Onslow had wiped his watery eyes and resumed with Smathers's directive. The dropper appeared again over Naz's mouth, yet this time, he successfully SQUEEZED! Leaping over a pew bench with one arm outstretched like a ballplayer reaching for a foul in the grandstands, Spigs intercepted the deadly liquid with his palm. The toxic liquid sizzled and burned Spigs's skin. He fell to his knees in pain, shaking his hand to get the liquid off.

The Creeples all *CLICK-CLACKED* fervently, and Skoota and Royal shook free of their blindfolds. T-Ray instructed the Creeples to release Flitch. The dash of dried catnip had given them sufficient magical power to disintegrate the duct tape that had strapped down Flitch and the Lyle brothers. The carnival crew jumped into the action, helping the teens battle Smathers's cult of Disciples.

Big Lyle shielded Spigs and T-Ray, while Lil' Lyle stood beside Professor Bodkins. A blast from their chem-tanks unleashed a wall of fumes that forced several Disciples back and made a half-dozen others swoon to the floor. Flitch bore down on Smathers but backpedaled when Keeper upholstered his Colt six-shooter, cocked it, and . . . ! Flitch recoiled in anticipation of being shot, but the antique gun jammed.

Smathers leaped off the altar platform, seized a ceremonial staff shrouded in jewels, and scooped up the orb off the cobble-stones. He raced to the spiral staircase like a floating ghost in his white ceremonial robe, but he stopped three steps up to gaze back at the chaos. With a piercing, malevolent stare, he decreed, "Weak imbeciles. You have all failed me and denied yourselves enlightenment. You *will* experience my wrath. My New Order of Magister Templi has just begun."

Smathers bounded up the spiral staircase, using the staff like a cane. His Dragon Stone of Magic ring on his right pinkie and the orb pulsated in sync. Spigs rushed after him, but Onslow blocked his way, squaring up his shoulders. Spigs didn't slow and flung himself sideways into Onslow's chest, knocking him to the floor. He sat on Onslow's chest and pinned his arms down with his knees. Spigs noticed the familiar *TCB* tattoo on the underside of his wrist. Revenge fueled Spigs as his pale cheeks flushed with blood. He gripped the eyedropper full of the poisonous oleander plant and held it over Onslow's clenched mouth. Spigs grabbed his jaw to try and wrench open his mouth as Onslow had done with Naz.

"SPIGS! STOP!" T-Ray screamed as she rushed over. "That is NOT you. You're better than that."

Spigs was numb, raging inside. He stared daggers into Onslow's eyes. "*TCB*, T-Ray! Just—takin' care of business, that's all." Spigs held the dropper for a moment over the terrified teen's mouth and squeezed the rubber bulb, releasing a stream of poisonous droplets . . . that splattered on cobblestones next to Onslow's head. "Okay then, T-Ray. Here's another bully for ya." Spigs yanked Onslow's shoulders up and slammed him against the floor.

"Spigs, go after Smathers. I'm right behind you," T-Ray instructed.

Spigs raced up the spiral stairs.

Onslow managed to get up and brushed the dirt off his ceremonial robe. "I owe you one, T-Ray."

"No, I owe YOU one." She dropped down and spun low on one foot, whipped her other leg around, and knocked both of Onslow's feet off the ground. *WHAM!*

CHAPTER 31

Sorcerer's Den

All the while T-Ray and Spigs were saving the Creeples and Professor Bodkins deep in the bowels of Bell Tower, Peabo was once again airborne above ground, as the red dragon had recovered from Peabo's last detonation. He had one string of fireworks left and no escape plan. He maintained a white-knuckled grip on the red dragon's scaly neck and did his best to suppress squeals of fright as it dove down after army reservists and the crypto-creatures. The dragon had ignited a Jeep and effortlessly swatted the two soaring gargoyles out of the sky with its powerful tail.

Peabo's GoPro helmet livestreamed through the academy's CCTV monitors in the lounges and dorms across campus, with more tweets from Yapper:

**#GrotesqueGargoyles go mano-a-mano
with the Red Dragon!**

#TorresTheTerror saddles the Great Beast!

The crypto-creatures and Vending Machine Robots were lured to the supernatural forces emitting from Bell Tower, like moths drawn to a flame. The Mongolian Death Worm slithered its gelatinous body up the sides of Bell Tower, ascending like a boa constrictor in a jungle tree.

The red dragon didn't appreciate the invasion of its domain, and Peabo's gut jumped into his mouth at what was coming. The dragon launched outward and dive-bombed, but it pulled up at the last second, fanning its wings at the Death Worm. It chomped into the Death Worm's gelatin-like body with its fangs, and the worm tumbled off the tower.

#PeaboRocksNRolls the Red Dragon!

#MongoDeathWorm dangles from Bell Tower!

The red dragon wasn't done, and Peabo squeezed his knees tighter as it dove again toward the ground, seeking out another pound of flesh. Peabo slipped sideways onto the dragon's skeletal wing as the Hodag rammed its bullhorns into the dragon's side. Peabo screamed while the red dragon roared. It was *way* past time for Peabo's exit strategy, but his brief opening to slide down the wing closed as the wounded dragon circled for another attack.

The Hodag blew a triumphant snort through its bull nose. The dragon curled its barbed tail and whipped it out like a coiled spring, jamming its poisonous tip into the Hodag's scaly side. The shaggy red-haired beast crumpled to the ground. The dragon soared toward the tower's spire, and Peabo clamped on to its neck with both arms. But as the Dragon Realm portal gradually disintegrated beneath Bell Tower, it was depleting the red dragon's strength.

McTaggart raced up to a soldier manning a machine gun attached to a Humvee. The soldier had sighted the red dragon in his crosshairs.

"DON'T SHOOT!" McTaggart demanded. "There's a student on the back of that dinosaur."

"I have my orders." The scrawny reservist tried to push McTaggart out of the way, but McTaggart held his ground.

"From who?" McTaggart fumed.

A cigar-chomping reserve commander stepped out of the Humvee's front seat and waved his pistol at McTaggart. "Great Scott, man, there's a flame-spittin' Goliath up there. And it must be destroyed." The commander looked at the soldier. "Now execute my orders. Ready . . . aim—"

Whipsnade had sneaked up alongside the vehicle. He hurled his baton at the commander, swatting the pistol out of his hand.

"Didn't ya hear the chief? There's an Aberdasher student up there. So stand down, NOW!" Whipsnade picked up the pistol and handed it to McTaggart.

"Now, step back," McTaggart demanded. "We're the only authority around here. Excellent work, Deputy."

"Just doin' my duty to uphold law and order, Ace." Whipsnade gave a Royal Navy salute with his palm faced outward.

"Stand down, men," the reservist commander ordered.

The very second the three reservists exited their Humvee, the red dragon blasted two fireballs that reduced the empty vehicle to a mass of molten metal and rubber.

"Whipsnade, seize that Jeep! I know how we can get that student down." McTaggart pointed to the sprawling Pogopalooza

Tournament banner over the nearby gym. Whipsnade drove McTaggart alongside the building. McTaggart ordered the three reservists to climb on the hood and remove the banner. They were more than eager, as the campus cop had just saved their lives.

The red dragon and Peabo were perched on the side of Bell Tower. The dragon's strength was waning. Peabo frantically searched the ground for a friendly face among the pandemonium. He let out a happy *WHOOP* when he spotted McTaggart and Whipsnade gesturing to the stretched-out Pogopalooza banner held taut by the reservists. Peabo pulled out his last string of firecrackers, gave the dragon a hard kick in the shoulder, and tossed the firecrackers into its open mouth. "Super E-ticket ride, Smaug. But gettin' a bit chafed, so . . . *hasta luego, muchacho.*" Peabo swung his right leg over the dragon's back, lined himself up with the banner below, and leaped. *KABOOM!* The firecrackers exploded in the behemoth's gullet, expelling black smoke from its nostrils.

Peabo landed hard on the banner and bounced fifteen feet in the air, like a trampoline. He performed an unintentional double backflip. Dizzy, he lay back on the banner as the soldiers gently lowered him to the grass. Two soldiers helped Peabo to his feet.

"Look!" McTaggart motioned up to Bell Tower's belfry.

The red dragon hovered above the tower. Its mass was fading—dematerializing into a turbulent vaporous vortex. Seconds later, SWOOSH—it was sucked back through the tower's belfry, down into the collapsing supernatural portal of the Dragon Realm. And simultaneously, all the monstrosities—Bog People, Hodag, Vending Machine Robots, Ayia Napa sea monster, gargoyles, Globster sea slug, Fangtooth Fish,

Creeples!

Mongolian Death Worm—brought to LIFE by the Creeples' magic stopped in their tracks and reverted back to their original inanimate forms.

Raucous, thunderous cheers could be heard across campus.

Peabo nodded to the campus cops and saluted the army reservists. "Good get, guys. Loads of thanks! Love to rap, but gotta save mankind from an evildoer." He raced toward the tower's front entrance.

Meanwhile, in Bell Tower, Spigs trailed Smathers by a dozen steps up the tower's spiral stairs, but was gaining. Once Spigs reached the bell chamber at the belfry rooftop, he knelt to catch his breath but kept his eye on Smathers through the dozens of moonlit bells. Smathers stood tall and gazed through the stained-glass window at the campus grounds like a king on his imperial throne. He'd attached the pulsating orb to the crown of the bejeweled staff and held it like a royal scepter.

"It's the end, Smathers," Spigs called out. "There's nowhere to go."

"Once again, you're quite wrong, Mr. Spignola." Smathers lazily turned his head. "It's merely the beginning of my divine existence. The Golden Dawn *will* again reign over my New Order Magister Templi."

"Smathers, listen to me." Spigs inched closer, weaving and stooping under the numerous bells.

Smathers guffawed as magenta sparks of energy flickered out from the orb. Spigs watched in astonishment as dark, lightning-charged clouds appeared low in the sky just above the tower. Spigs took a deep breath and summoned his courage to step closer.

"I have to stop you. I WILL stop you," Spigs stated with bravado.

"Oh, really?" Smathers sneered. "And how will the likes of YOU stop *me*? Just what extraordinary power could you possibly possess?"

"The POWER of friendship! And with true friends, good *can* conquer evil," T-Ray declared as she, Peabo, and the Creeples stormed the rooftop. They all stood behind Spigs, who suddenly felt enormously empowered.

"It's over. Now give up!" Spigs took another step toward the dean.

"I am Lord of the Past and of the Future. Mine is the Unseen Forces. So, it's NEVER over. I don't die." Smathers's voice rose with each word. "I'm the Invincible One! The Wyvern is the source for my eternal existence and omnipotence."

"What's he mean, he doesn't die?" Peabo muttered to T-Ray. She shrugged.

"It means he's got the professor's research." Spigs's eyes widened in fright. "And he can replicate as much dragon DNA as he needs to stay alive, like, forever!"

T-Ray gasped. "LOOK! HE'S IN . . . TRANSITION!"

Smathers gave a mock chuckle as the orb atop his staff created a supernatural vortex of magenta energy that completely enshrouded him. The radiant orb once again entranced the Creeples. They wiggled their huge ears and anxiously *CLICK-CLACKED* as Smathers reached skyward with his staff, as though he was the Greek god Zeus. His oval magenta gemstone ring and the orb pulsated synchronously.

Creeples!

The swirling dark clouds a hundred feet above Bell Tower flashed with lightning and developed into the image of a grotesque goat-horned DEMON!

"That RING!" Spigs screamed. "Must be the source to all his evil powers."

"I WILL ENDURE," Smathers wailed above the rumbling, demonic clouds. "I will torment you all, until you roar with pain. Out of the chaos comes order!"

Smathers's eyes now blazed blood red. The flares of energy vapors swirled faster around him. He levitated three feet off the flagstone surface. His entire body composition began to pixilate, virtually translucent. He was dematerializing before their eyes!

"He's vanishing. We hafta stop him! He'll gain immortality!" Spigs yelped.

"We have to get that ring!" Peabo turned to the Creeples. "Skoota, Naz, Tatz, Royal, Coco, Beezer. Do your thing!"

The Creeples snapped out of their spell, nodded, and blasted their magenta lightning rays at the enshrouded Smathers. The manic dean simply snarled in their direction. The Creeples' magical powers were insufficient and crashed against the energy vortex that swathed Smathers.

Spigs took a deep breath, stepped back two feet, lowered his shoulders, and charged. He leaped through the supernatural cyclone.

"SPIGS!" T-Ray howled.

Spigs was adrift within the turbulent gravitational surge of the magenta vortex. His feet floated behind him, but he latched on to Smathers's robes.

Smathers buried his fingers in Spigs's thick hair, trying to yank him off. But Spigs gritted his teeth against the pain and moved his hands down Smathers's arm, searching for his hand and the ring. The thunderous clouds above Bell Tower crackled louder as the goat-horned DEMON image shrieked an ear-piercing sound.

Suddenly, something clutched Spigs's ankle. He struggled against the swirling gale to peer over his shoulder and through the haze of the vortex. Peabo gazed back at him on the periphery with one of his arms thrust through the spinning, vaporous force.

"I've GOTCHA!" Peabo yelled. "I think." He tugged on Spigs's leg, but the turbulence sucked Spigs back just as hard. Spigs refused to let go of Smathers.

"Peabo, let me go! I've gotta get that ring!"

"NOT letting him drag you to another dimension, dude! Besides, it's too late to break in a new roommate." Peabo's grip slipped, and he crashed back on his butt.

Spigs shrieked as he noticed *his* hands were pixelating. He was now face-to-face with Smathers. Both were translucent in appearance.

"I shall take you with me and torment your wretched soul for eternity!" Smathers smirked as he grasped Spigs's wrists.

"It's a death trap for Spigs. He's dematerializing into another dimension!" T-Ray cried out.

"SPIGS!" Peabo screamed. "GET OUT! FORGET THE RING!"

Spigs gritted his teeth and yanked one arm free of Smathers's grip, but Smathers held fast to the other. Spigs's free right hand inched toward the ring.

"Peabo, teamwork makes the dream work, right?" T-Ray circled around from behind him. She interlocked her forearm with Peabo's arm. "Hold tight, and when I say NOW, yank me out with all ya got."

"It's all on US! Take it, T-RAY!" Peabo clutched her forearm with both hands.

T-Ray took a deep breath, looked to see Peabo's reassuring nod, then turned and lunged half her body through the supernatural tempest. She flailed one arm in the swirling vortex, trying to locate any body part of Spigs. Finally, she had a slight grip on someone's dematerializing ankle—Spigs . . . or Smathers? She couldn't see clearly through the turbulence who it was, but T-Ray took a chance and yelled, "NOW!" over the roar of the energy force. She and Peabo simultaneously heaved with all of their might.

Out flopped Spigs onto the rooftop in a pool of sweat. T-Ray and Peabo picked themselves up and rushed over to help Spigs but nearly crushed him with a group hug.

Behind the teens, the supernatural vortex that had encased Spigs and Smathers now dissipated into a bright magenta mist. Smathers collapsed to the ground and gradually materialized back into human form. The goat-horned DEMON cloud mass above Bell Tower exploded into an atmospheric gas and disintegrated.

T-Ray turned her attention back to Spigs. "I was so worried. We just couldn't wait for you to get the ring," she said and pulled back from the hug, blushing.

"I'm okay, but am I all here?" Spigs held up his arms and kicked out his legs for a detailed inventory. Peabo and T-Ray began to pinch him all over his body. "OUCH! Okay, I'm all here!" Then Spigs flaunted a sly, beaming grin and held up the Dragon Stone of Magic ring with his thumb and index fingers.

The three turned to see Smathers cowering in the corner. The mystical orb detached from his ceremonial staff. He shrieked and lunged for the precious object, then drew back in alarm as Naz caught the rolling orb. Smathers gawked at the Creeples, who had surrounded him.

"Heathens!" Smathers cried out, recoiling at their existence. His arrogance had been replaced by fear. He kept inching back, away from the *CLICK-CLACKING* Creeples and out onto the cloister walkway. "Get away, you abominations." He spun around to flee but toppled over the edge of the belfry's parapet, screaming as he plummeted toward the ground.

Spigs, T-Ray, and Peabo rushed over. Inexplicably, a macabre screech made them cringe. Smathers reappeared, but in the sharp jaws of a possessed pterodactyl—Percy. Smathers's bloodcurdling screams echoed through campus as the two soared high into the crystal-clear night sky.

"Yo, Percy!" Peabo called out. "*Mi madre* always said to thoroughly chew your food!"

Percy flew higher, Smathers trapped in his jaws, until they were both out of sight. The swarm of howling ghastly ghouls followed them upward until they, too, vanished.

"The orb!" Spigs sat down next to Naz to study the now lifeless, dormant orb—its radiant glow dimmed and its pulsating energy extinguished. "But what is it? Or was it?"

"It's the nucleus of the Wyvern dragon's egg Smathers and his crew excavated in 1938," Professor Bodkins said, breathing heavily. She'd made it to the top of the stairs. "And part of the Creeples' DNA, and energy source." Beezer and Tatz sprang into Professor Bodkins's arms. "Well, hello. I've been eager to meet you."

They *CLICK-CLACKED* their introductions and snuggled deeper into her embrace. "Professor, it just occurred to me." T-Ray stood, holding Royal and Coco. "Smathers's demonic scheme to become this Master Sorcerer may have something to do with the academy's unique curriculum of alternative sciences."

"WEIRD sciences!" Spigs and Peabo announced with validation. Laughing, they high-fived each other.

"Now don't leave *me* hanging," T-Ray chirped. Spigs and Peabo turned to see her holding up her hand. They smiled and gave her an enthusiastic round of high fives.

"I completely agree with your assumption, T-Ray." Professor Bodkins stroked the two Creeples who gurgled happily in her arms. "Every department's research offered Smathers his chance to acquire and retain almighty powers once he located the ancient Wyvern dragon egg. Which is precisely why he spent the last ten years recruiting young science wunderkinds like yourselves."

"But what if Smathers DID gain some immortal powers of a sorcerer during his vanishing act?" Peabo worried as Skoota sat on his lap, licking Peabo's face.

"Well." Professor Bodkins sighed. "In mythological lore, he would need earthly help to maintain any powers that he'd acquired during his transformation."

Peabo expressed in a reflective tone, "'When justice is done, it is a joy to the righteous but terror to the evildoers.'" He looked

Sorcerer's Den

at everyone, including the Creeples, who stared blankly at him. "What? I did go to Sunday school, you know." Spigs, T-Ray, and the professor all cracked huge grins.

Spigs hugged Naz and helped Beezer climb up on his shoulder. "I'm just glad these little dudes are all right. They're basically the only real family I've got . . . seeing as how they share my DNA and all."

"Not so fast, Johnny," Professor Bodkins said. "Remember I told you when I ran your DNA, I found something interesting?"

"I'm all ears, Professor." Spigs could hear his heart pounding.

"I found a match in the ancestral database to an accomplished scientist at a major university. It seems you have relatives you didn't know about."

"In the field of science? I guess I come by it naturally. Hear that, fellas?" Spigs cuddled Naz and Beezer. "We've got new members on our team!"

Naz, Beezer, Coco, Royal, Skoota, and Tatz cocked their heads and *CLICK-CLACKED* at the teens. They twitched their prodigious ears forward, lapped out their elongated tongues, and bellowed—"TEAM GOOOOOZE!"

Spigs, T-Ray, Peabo, and Professor Bodkins were flabbergasted, slack-jawed. Did they just hear right? The Creeples actually . . . *spoke?* The Creeples sprang up on the belfry's ledge in a line and gazed out over the wrecked campus. Royal *CLICK-CLACKED*, and they each put one ashen-gray arm on the nearest shoulders.

After a moment of stunned silence, T-Ray cleared her throat.

321

"Guys, teamwork just saved our quirky little academy . . . and . . . possibly all of humanity."

"And I'd add . . . *true* friendship to that equation." Professor Bodkins beamed proudly at her Lab Rats as T-Ray linked her arms with the boys.

"Yeah, but somehow, I have a feeling it's the end of the Lab Rats," Peabo said solemnly.

Spigs was curiously quiet. A disconcerting gaze had washed over his face. He looked down and opened his gripped fist to reveal the Dragon Stone of Magic ring he'd just seized from Smathers's finger. HUH! The magenta gemstone was PULSATING in his palm. "Uuh, actually, y'all, I have a feelin' this is *just* the beginning!"

• • •

The campus Quad was back, and buzzing with activity, as some students congregated next to Bell Tower and others hustled to their classes. McTaggart and Whipsnade cruised the grounds on their Segways, once again, aiming to keep law and order. Whipsnade braked hard and hopped off. Believing he caught an offender in the act, he unclipped his measuring tape from his belt and held it up to a female student's stiletto heels to gauge their height. Two motorized skateboarders zipped by. One stuck out his opened hand and whacked Whipsnade hard on his butt. Whipsnade popped up and looked back at the teens with a leer, then glanced at his chief. McTaggart cracked a grin and motioned to Whipsnade to chuck the measuring tape in the trashcan.

• • •

Spigs, Peabo, and T-Ray lounged on the lower bleachers as the Aberdasher Academy basketball team warmed up on the court. Spigs and T-Ray sat together perusing the school's newspaper on an iPad.

"In addition to the successful crowdfunding campaign," T-Ray gleefully stated, "Aberdasher Academy graciously accepts a one-million-dollar grant from Mr. E. A. Crowley, CEO of the biotech firm Nomt Laboratories, Inc., to finance the Kelsey Rogers Gene Research wing of the Genomic department."

High fives slapped all around from the three ecstatic teens.

"And by unanimous decision and approved by Dean Sally Bodkins, Aberdasher Academy names the Creeples as the school's new . . . mascots!" Spigs exclaimed and pumped his fist.

"The Fightin' Creeples! That's episode fifteen." Peabo held up his laptop's screen.

"Who knew our own DNA would spawn six medical marvels and make us famous," T-Ray said.

Spigs stuffed the iPad in his backpack. "Ya know, we never did figure out the extent of their magical powers. Or the precise catnip dosage to keep 'em from morphin' back into their Beastly Mode."

"Speaking of beastly . . ." T-Ray acknowledged the approaching Rachell.

Rachell came up behind Spigs and weaved her fingers through his hair. "So how's my Spigsy?"

"Still breathin', no thanks to you."

"That whole thing with Smathers was *just* one big nightmare."

"Yeah. Nightmare!"

"And I've got another nightmare for you, Rachell." T-Ray stepped down from the bleachers and squared up to Rachell.

Rachell instinctively jumped back, anticipating one of T-Ray's vicious low-spin leg whips.

T-Ray leaned over to Spigs and kissed him on the cheek. He beamed and blushed.

Rachell turned, flipped her hair, and stormed off.

"Good riddance to the wicked wench." Peabo waved her off.

Courtside, the six Creeples each stood on the shoulders of six female cheerleaders. They WIGGLED their oversized ears, CLICK-CLACKED loudly, and shook pom-poms.

"They've definitely got their mojo back," T-Ray said through a wide grin.

"Look at 'em! They're ballin'," Spigs added.

The teens laughed and rose to their feet as the cheerleaders tried to work up the uninspired student crowd for the opening tip-off.

"Okay, gang. Let's leave 'em with one of our parents' cheers. Ready?" a cheerleader shouted through a megaphone.

"Rah! Rah! REE! Kick 'em in the KNEE! Rah! Rah! RASS! Kick 'em in the . . ."

Spigs thrust out his hands toward the Creeples. "NO! NO! Don't—"

The student section erupted in roars, cheers, and thundering stomps on the bleachers!

Epilogue

Alone man sat at a desk in the corner of the room, thumbing through a thick leather dossier. *Col. J. T. Carnacki* was embroidered above his white shirt pocket. He twirled one side of his thick, distinctive handlebar mustache that matched his finely cropped ginger hair, and his gaudy magenta gemstone pinkie ring sparkled from the fluorescent ceiling lights.

This remote underground warehouse facility had five thirty-two-inch wall-mounted flat screens that aired live CCTV scenes of Aberdasher Academy's campus. The black-and-white images flickered above olive-green file cabinets lined against the back wall of the sprawling, drab room.

Colonel Carnacki flipped through several folders within the dossier and stopped at a tab that read *Particle-Beam Weaponry Program*. He removed six documents, each with the same heading: *S.H.A.D.O.W. Report. Classified.* After reviewing each Creeple profile, he rubberstamped *AFFIRMATIVE* across the sheet of paper.

Creeples!

Colonel Carnacki closed the bulky dossier and secured the latch. He strolled over to the more than two dozen file cabinets. In the cabinet labeled *Classified: High Energy Laser Defense System*, he placed the dossier file in the top drawer. As he left the massive, dimly lit room, he crossed beneath a painted sign above the doorway:

SECRETLY **H**UNTING **A**LIENS AND **D**ASTARDLY **O**THER**W**ORLDS

Acknowledgments

As Spigs, T-Ray, Peabo, and the Creeples eventually learn on their mysterious, magical quest . . . "It's all on us, as teamwork makes the dream work!"

First and foremost, this book could not have come to life without the assistance of a couple of terrific editors, Colette Freedman and Hannah Sandoval, who both guided me, in different ways and stages, through the wonderful world of middle-grade fiction and helped to bring clarity, continuity, and flow to my writing. And who greatly assisted me in giving my mystical Creeples memorable personalities.

Also, many thanks to the tremendous team at Greenleaf Book Group Press for bringing my vision to the pages. Their input and professionalism were invaluable.

And lastly, I want to thank . . . ME!

So for those aspiring writers out there, I'm reminded of what is often said about perseverance: *The only way to fail at your dreams is to abandon them.*

Thanks, y'all!

About the Author

PATRICK D. PIDGEON works in TV, film, and theatrical production. *Creeples!* is his debut novel, but he has written two graphic novels and has also developed a mobile gaming app.

Patrick formed Pidgeon Entertainment, Inc., as a content development and production entity for global intellectual properties (IP). A collaboration and production outlet set up to align with strategic international media partners, it focuses on developing, building, and managing its portfolio in multiple genres and formats worldwide. One of his most iconic IP holdings is the wonderfully whimsical Worzel Gummidge, which he is producing as a TV series for the BBC.

Patrick has been mentioned in news articles about his work in *The Hollywood Reporter, Variety, The Times of London, The Guardian, Daily Mail,* and *India Times,* among others. A Memphis native, he studied at the University of Tennessee and earned a bachelor of arts degree. "As a political science major, my only logical move was to . . . Hollywood? Well, I guess politics will have to wait." He currently resides in Los Angeles.

Learn more at:

www.Creeples.com